THE BOY IN THE PAINTING

A WHY CHOOSE PORTAL FANTASY ROMANCE

MEADOWBROOK DUET
BOOK 1

G.B. BANCROFT

Copyright © 2026 by G.B. Bancroft.

All rights reserved.

No part of this publication may be reproduced, distributed, or transmitted in any form or by any means, including photocopying, recording, or other electronic or mechanical methods, without the prior written permission of the author/copyright holder.

For permission requests, contact authorgbbancroft@gmail.com.

The story, names, characters, and incidents portrayed in this publication are fictitious. No connection to actual persons (living or deceased), places, buildings, and products is intended or should be inferred.

No part of this book or illustrations were written, edited, or created with AI. No part of this publication may be fed into AI software, including, but not limited to, generative or assistive artificial intelligence training data sets.

Book Cover Design by Ash @wolfandbearr.

Developmental Editing by Maddi Leatherman, EJL Editing @ejlediting.

Copy Edits & Proofreading by K. Morton Editing Services L.L.C. @kmortonedits.

1st Edition March 19th, 2026

Paperback ISBN: 9798990175358

E-Book ISBN: 9798990175341

 Formatted with Vellum

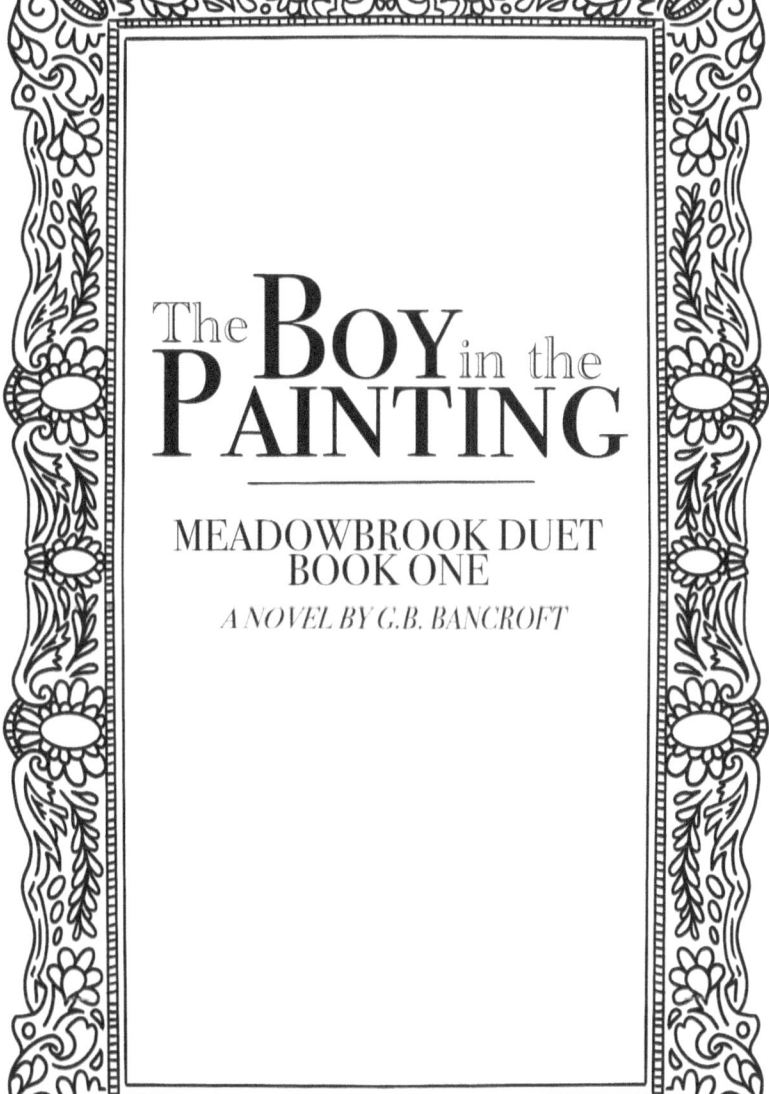

The Boy in the Painting

MEADOWBROOK DUET
BOOK ONE

A NOVEL BY G.B. BANCROFT

This book is for anyone who has ever had to be apart from their person and, irrationally or not, worried that they wouldn't come home.

I hope we never have to be whisked away to a magical world to escape grief.

CONTENTS

Content Warnings   9

1. Before   11
2. After   16
3. Nostalgia Eyes   24
4. Yes, No, Maybe   39
5. She's Back, Baby   47
6. Flirting Won't Kill You   53
7. Cinderella Needs A Dress   66
8. The Tailor   75
9. The Fated Champion   82
10. It's For A Good Cause, Right?   86
11. Magic Isn't Real...   97
12. ...But What If It Is?   104
13. Fuck Me. It Is   112
14. Explain   126
15. Can I Paint You?   135
16. Am I A French Girl Now?   142
17. What Else Do I Have To Lose?   158
18. Diners, Drive-Ins, And Dead Husbands   162
19. Dragon Breath   169
20. Memory Fishing   177
21. Crash Out   192
22. Dreamscape   199
23. Burning, Bagels   210
24. "Friends"   219
25. Flirting Might Actually Kill Me   225
26. How To Train Your Dragon... To Fight You   242
27. Fireworks   255
28. Numbers, Dates, And Other Filthy Things   262
29. Dreamscape, Part Two   269
30. Mornings After   276
31. These Tortured Sighs Of Mine   281

32. I Don't Need A Prize If I Have You	289
33. I Wish	295
34. Nearly There	300
35. Yeah, Sex Is Great, But Have You Tried Falling In Love?	310
36. Stabs And Scars	319
37. Evasive Maneuvers	327
38. Him	333
39. Moments In The Woods	342
40. I Remember	352
41. Giving Up Or Giving In	358
42. 100	361
43. Pre-Birthday Party	366
44. Pinky Promise	372
45. When Home Becomes A Person… Or Persons	383
Also By G.B. Bancroft	389
Acknowledgments	391
About the Author	393

CONTENT WARNINGS

Death of a spouse (off page, accidental, military aviation); exploration of depression, anxiety, and grief; discussion of suicidal thoughts (main character does not consider self-harm); artist block; minor acts of violence in a fantasy setting; drugs and alcohol; mentions of child abuse (to a side character in the past, off page); discussions of pregnancy and contraceptives (book contains no pregnancy); sex (including group scenes and light exploration of dominant/submissive dynamics and kink—breeding and primal).

1

BEFORE

ALICE

I've found that the best time to cut onions is when you're already crying.

My knife slides into the crisp white flesh as tears drip from my chin and splatter onto the cutting board. I've diced five onions already. *Five.* I don't *need* five onions, but why waste a good cry, right? If I'm going to get all puffy-eyed, then I might as well take advantage.

I suck in a disgusting sniffle as my blade reaches the root, the pungent aroma burning my sinuses. My head tucks to my shoulder, and I wipe my dripping nose with my sleeve.

Damn Costco and their industrial-sized bags of produce.

Strong arms wrap around my middle, tugging me flush to a warm body. Ryan's bony chin pokes the top of my head and my breath hitches; a new wave of sadness chokes me, tightening my throat until it's physically painful.

"I can hear your chopping all the way in the bedroom. What did those onions ever do to you?" Ryan asks, lips punctuating his question with a kiss to my crown.

"Nothing," I say. "They're just an easy outlet for all of *this*." My hands circle the air in front of my face—knife included. I huff a laugh, though it sounds pathetic, wet and broken between my sobs.

I grab another onion, but before my blade can pierce its layered skin, Ryan's hands wrap around mine, forcing the knife down. His sigh is a hot rush of air down the crook of my neck, and it pulls another swell of emotion to my throat. The counter goes blurry and I blink hard, trying to rid myself of the stinging tears.

"*Alice*," Ryan murmurs my name. It's not so much a scold of my neurotic tendency to find distraction in menial tasks as it is a reminder that I don't *actually* want to spend the last hours I have with him for the next nine months *cutting fucking onions*.

Calloused fingers dip under the hem of my shirt; they grip my waist with gentle reverence and urge me to turn around. Ryan's forehead meets mine, and I peer up at him through dampened lashes. Rich brown eyes stare back at me, shiny and red-rimmed.

He's been crying too.

I'm the crier in this family, not him, so the sight of his sadness so clearly etched across his face makes my soul keen. Deep within my chest I ache; it hurts me to see him hurting.

"What if I kidnap you?" I say, entering the bargaining stage of our goodbye. "If they call, I'll simply tell the Navy '*Sorry, Lt. Raine can't come to the boat right now, his wife is holding him hostage.*'"

The faint beginnings of crow's feet deepen into sharp crinkles around Ryan's eyes. "You can't do that."

"*But*, here me out, what if I *did*?" I try again, grasping onto any bit of humor I can so I don't sink to the kitchen tile under the weight of my worry. "Do they really need another helicopter pilot out in the middle of the ocean?"

I never intended to marry someone in the military. But

when one thing led to another in college... Let's just say I came to love Ryan more than I was inconvenienced by the Navy's need to steal him away. Except now, he's not jetting off to a school in bumblefuck Florida or a cushy detachment in Sigonella where I can visit. They're putting him on a boat. For *nine fucking months*.

Ryan's hand cradles my cheek, and the rough pad of his thumb catches an escaped tear. "Tell me what's wrong. Besides the obvious."

My hand comes up to rest over his. I lean into the warmth of his palm, cut through only by the cool platinum band on his ring finger.

"I'm scared," I admit.

"Scared of what?" he asks.

"Losing you," I choke out. "I know it's irrational, but this feels different than before. I won't get to call you. And I can't help but freak the fuck out every time I think about you being so far away for so long."

"Babe," Ryan sighs. "You can't think like that."

"I'm sorry. I don't mean to make this harder than it already is."

"You're not making it harder," he says, a sad smile toying at his full lips. "It's a shitty situation all around. *But*, think of all the painting you'll get done without me distracting you twenty-four seven."

I can't help but snort. "That's certainly one way to spin it."

Ryan hums, thumb mindlessly swiping over my cheek. "How about this? I help you finish dinner and then we play a board game before you drop me off."

"Okay." I take a deep, stuttering breath. "Okay, yeah. Let's do that."

I try to turn away, but Ryan clicks his tongue.

"Come here first," he murmurs.

His grip goes firm on my jaw before sliding around my nape

and pulling my face to his. My heart skips, and on instinct I melt into him. Any space between our bodies disappears, all my soft curves pressed against his hard edges. My feet arch to lift me higher and his head dips, our mouths meeting in the middle. They're too soft, his lips—and entirely at odds with the way he uses them.

I'm kissed breathless, and for a moment all my worry is forgotten.

Ryan pulls back, pecking my nose before his forehead finds mine again.

"I'll be fine," he promises. "And when I'm back, it'll be like I was never gone in the first place."

I reach up and hold onto Ryan's wrist like a lifeline, giving it three squeezes for three words, unspoken in this moment, but always known.

WOMEN IN THE CLOUDS

There are women who sleep in the clouds.

I think they do it because it is the only thing that resembles the airy touch of his calloused embrace.

I joined them not too long ago.

2

AFTER

ALICE

two years and eight months later

There's a certain kind of sadness that comes with the turning of each season.
    As fall shifts to winter, there's a subtle regret that permeates the dry, chilling air. It splits your lips, cracks them down the center with every taught holiday smile. It's a reminder that you haven't done enough. You haven't slathered on enough chapstick. You didn't go apple picking in September, even though you said you would. You couldn't get yourself out of bed on one too many Sundays.

Then winter wanes, and a deep-rooted sense of lost time breaks out of the frozen soil. Did you waste those months of hibernation? Did you cuddle your loved ones by the fire? Will you ever see those twinkling moments again—the ones tucked between garbage bags of ripped wrapping paper and red-cheeked champagne toasts?

These thoughts hurt so much more now than they did before. Back then, I could wave them away and laugh, pass them off as the musings of the tortured artist I liked to masquerade as.

Now, summer has come to visit, in all its humid glory, and it's brought a friend who reeks of roses. They're impossible to ignore, or dismiss with a half-hearted chuckle, that elusive pressure to *bloom*.

The hottest season might not have officially started yet, but I've battled that feeling for months. I've been stagnant, lost and longing. Two years stuck, my feet swallowed by wet sand at the edge of California beaches.

A third year standing there, waiting for someone who will never come home, would have seen me washed into the sea and swallowed whole. So, I packed up my bags. And now I'm here.

The unyielding weight of a new season turning—that prospect of productivity I haven't been able to embrace—plants a seed of doubt in my gut as my car pulls into the driveway. I may have moved, but I've only traded reminders of one death for another. This one should be easier to swallow, though.

The wheels crunch over gravel, and no later than thirty seconds after they do, my phone's ringtone blares through the car's speakers.

I jab the accept call button.

"You got there okay?" Steph, my agent and friend, says, forgoing a greeting.

"Yes," I drawl. "You didn't have to stalk my location. I would have called you once I got settled in."

"We both know that you'd forget," she says.

"You don't know if I had a reminder set."

"Do you?"

I chew the inside of my cheek. "No."

"Which is why we have location sharing on," Steph explains, slowly, in a tone you'd use to speak to a child.

She hasn't always been a mother hen. We've known each other for a decade and made it through art school together, so she knows I used to be much more self-sufficient. But our relationship shifted two years ago, just like *all* my relationships did.

It's not that I don't want to keep her in the loop, but time doesn't work the same anymore. It all blurs together; suddenly a week's gone by and I have fifteen missed calls and twice as many texts warning me that if I don't send proof of life then they're going to call my landlord for a wellness check.

Steph might have started as a friend, but she's more of a sister than anything else. Sophomore year, after staying with me while doing a summer internship in the city, she was 'adopted' by my parents.

Mom and Dad were always collecting strays like that, not that I minded. Everyone got something out of it: my parents had big hearts with lots of love to give, my friends got zany, surrogate parental figures that actually cared about them, and I didn't feel so lonely.

"Ali?" Steph asks, pulling my attention back to the phone, where the pink bubble around her initials lights up the screen. "Did you hear me?"

I wince. "Sorry."

"I asked if you're sure about this?" She pauses, but when I don't answer right away, she continues. "The guest room in our apartment is all yours. And if you don't want that, we have friends you can sublet from. If you were here we could go on all kinds of city adventures…"

I glance out the window, my gaze falling on the two-story Victorian of 874 Bayberry Drive. With its light-blue facade and large bay windows—ones that I used to curl up under with books from the library on summer days just like this—a sense of *rightness* creeps over me.

"I love you both, but I'm not moving in with you guys," I say.

"We'd all feel better if you weren't alone right now, babes."

My restless fingers find the three rings that hang from the chain around my neck, fiddling with the platinum bands.

"The answer is no, Steph," I say, firmer this time.

I love that I have friends who care about me. But it's getting tiring, having them breathe down my neck with concerned mutterings of how my mental health see-saws. As if I don't already know I'm three kinds of fucked up.

There's a bang of a door, and a soft voice filters through the speakers. "Is that Alice?"

"Yeah," Steph calls out, her voice further away, as if she's pulled the phone from her ear.

"Tell Erica I say hi," I say.

"Tell me yourself, you coward." My best friend since the second grade's voice blasts through the speaker. After I introduced them during the summer Steph stayed with my family, they quickly hit it off and never looked back. "I'm offended you don't want to live with us."

I sigh. "I don't want to get into this right now."

"Too bad, we're getting into it."

"What Erica means is that we care about you. And we hate the idea of you being cooped up alone in some house in the woods. At least in Cali you were in a city and around people—"

"Meadowbrook is a small beach town on the north shore, it's not the backwoods," I say, my fingers choking the steering wheel. I force my hands to release it, letting them fall to my thighs. "Look, I need this reset. I'll keep you posted if I need company. It's not like you're far away. You can come visit. Or I can take the train in and see you."

We're all quiet for a moment, and I find myself squirming on the leather seat in the silence. The timer of the phone call ticks higher, the seconds stretching out between us.

"You guys still there?" I ask.

"Sorry, I muted us so you didn't have to hear Erica's screeching," Steph says.

A soft snort escapes me.

"We hear you though, loud and clear," Steph adds. "And we'll be taking advantage of all those extra rooms you have once they're cleaned out."

"Did I mention it's unfair that you'll be ten minutes from the beach at any given moment?" Erica says. "I wish I had a rich grandma who left me her rickety-ass haunted house when she died."

"You're one to talk. Grammie-B lets you vacation at her time-share in Aruba every year. Why are you complaining?"

"Yeah, but it's not a *house out east*—"

"Okay, we get it," Steph interrupts her, and I can practically hear Erica's eye roll through the speakers. "Text us pictures later, okay?"

"I will," I promise.

"And you're still good to have that call with the gallery I set up for next week?" Steph asks. "There's a decent amount of prep to do, but they're excited to finally host originals from the elusive *Alice Raine*."

Dread fills my stomach, and my finger inches closer to the *end call* button. "Yes."

"I'll text you fifteen minutes before so you don't forget," Steph says.

"*Bye Steph*," I drawl.

"Bye babe," Steph says.

"Love you!" Erica screams.

The screen goes dark, and I lean back in my seat with a tired sigh. The engine rumbles, and I let it idle for longer than I should, staring out the front window with my foot pressed on the brake.

I could turn around right now; drive back the way I came and beg my landlord to lease me my old apartment. I could call Steph and Erica, hop on the next Penn Station-bound train, and crash at their place like they offered.

I do neither.

I'm already here. I've driven three-thousand miles for a fresh start and I can't back out now.

The sun lights up my white-knuckled fingers with gold; gripped around the emergency parking brake, I will them to pull the lever. They listen. The brake clicks into place.

I press the ignition and the growl of the car's engine stops.

There, I committed.

WHEN I HEAVE the last box over the house's threshold, I release a breath of relief. The hard part is done, at least the physically hard part is. Studying the packed foyer—where I've dumped all my boxes from the U-Haul—there are still weeks of work ahead of me to declutter and clean my grandma's things, and days more to unpack and organize my own.

However, I'm nothing if but a masochist these days, and all I've got is time.

The only deadline I'm beholden to looms at the end of summer, though I haven't been able to put brush to canvas once in preparation for the exhibit. I've already delayed my residency with them twice, and I'm thankful I have a team behind me who understands my situation, but the guilt of not producing any art is eating away at me.

Two years of drought has drained my creative well. And no matter how many times I pray to the muses for reprieve, they haven't yet blessed me with a rainstorm.

I'm hoping this move will change that.

I swat at the stray blonde curls that stick to my forehead. They've come loose from my hair tie, which desperately needs to be redone, but there's a kind of pleasure that comes from the tug of the fallen bun on my roots.

Like I said, masochist.

"Alright," I declare to the ghosts hiding in the floorboards. "Shower, then grocery store. I can't clean you up on an empty stomach."

The hardwood floor creaks its agreement as I trudge up to my room.

The house has lost its luster in the two decades since I last visited, the ornate runner on the stairs faded and the wallpaper peeling in the corners. School and sports got in the way at first, and then I was too old and too cool to spend my precious summers off at grandma's—and then I went to college. And *then* I was moving across the country with Ryan.

My fingertips run through the film of dust that's coated the furniture, stacked books, and her half-finished paintings that line the hall. I wipe the grime on my leggings, and the slash of gray stands out against the black polyester.

It's clear Nana embraced clutter towards the end. Maybe it gave her comfort, to be surrounded by all these things. There's a method to the madness, a safety in the ability to get lost in your own home, all with the knowledge that with a few steps you can find your way back to the warmth of your bed.

It already makes *me* feel less alone.

I only wish that he was here too, tucked beneath the covers when I crawl into bed tonight.

Falling

There comes a point where
you just close your eyes—

let go, and fall.

Not in a bad way.

But hopefully into
something good.

3

NOSTALGIA EYES

ALICE

The metal handles of the grocery basket dig into my forearm as I stare at the different types of pasta on the shelf. I've been frozen, deciding between pastina and macaroni for five minutes—which isn't a long time, but is forever when you're grocery-store-perusing.

The former has that childhood nostalgia that I've been huffing since I opened the front door of 874, but the latter is more versatile.

Fuck it, I'll buy both.

I toss them into my cart, the dried pasta rattling in their blue cardboard homes, and check out. With my canvas totes thrown over my shoulders, and my hands busy forcing my wallet into my purse strapped across my chest, I push open the front door with my hip.

My eyes squint at the bright flare of the sun, temporarily blinded as it begins its dip beneath the marina's horizon. Main Street runs perpendicular to the small bay, an arrow shooting all the passersby directly to the bobbing sailboats and ferry dock.

Soft swaths of pink and orange streak through the western half of the sky, melting into the darker blues of encroaching night to the east. My cheek twitches, as if it wants to break into a grin. One of the perks of this town being nestled on Long Island's north shore is that you get both sunsets *and* sunrises over the water.

A couple sits at one of the benches lining the dock, sharing a melting ice cream cone. The salty breeze carries their giggles over to me and the light douses their hair in brilliant gold.

They seem at peace. Happy.

Maybe I should try to paint here.

I could bring my travel watercolor set, which I'll have to dig for, since I don't know when the last time was that I actually used it. But it should be tucked in the box that has all of—

My thoughts are cut off as a solid body collides into me, and I go tumbling onto the sidewalk. I wince a curse as my palms scrape against the pavement, bracing my fall.

"Fuck, I'm so sorry. I wasn't looking." A shadow descends as the person who barreled into me kneels at my side. His voice is smooth and soft. Kind. "Are you okay?"

Sucking in a breath between my teeth, I lift my stinging hands. The scuffed skin is red and indented with bits of rock and sand, but I'm not bleeding.

"Yeah," I huff, detangling my arms from the straps of my bags. I quickly shove the few fallen groceries back into their totes, groaning at the wet spot blooming on my carton of eggs. "I can't say the same for my eggs though."

I ready myself for the feat that will be going back inside to ask for an exchange but freeze when lithe hands ornamented with a leather watch pull the damaged carton from my grip.

"Shit. I'm running late for something but—here, let me give you some cash to buy new ones."

I look up and am frozen again, lips parted at the most unique looking man I've ever seen. His hair is pure white, strands sticking up at weird angles as if he's run his hands through it all day. A smattering of freckles, much like mine, line the bridge of his nose, sitting under circular glasses. And beyond those panes of glass are brown eyes that err on the side of red. Wide, wise, and weathered, they bore into me.

They are nostalgia incarnate, those irises.

The soft glow around a cherrywood fireplace on a stormy evening. The rusted chain of a bike that should have given out years ago but holds firm and carries you home. The sparkle of amber seashells over molten sand, the ones that prick the soles of your feet when you run home at sunset.

"Here," he repeats, breaking our gaze and holding out a twenty.

"That's too much," I say, shaking my head.

"No, it's not," he says. Then, one eye squints as he winces a nervous smile. "It's also the only cash I have. Please take it."

When I don't immediately take the bill, my brain taking too long to process the interaction, the man grabs my wrist. I choke on a shocked squeak as his soft hands press it into my palm and guide my fingers to curl around it.

"There," he says.

His hands linger on mine for a second longer than is appropriate for two strangers. But his white brows knit together, a small crease forming between them as he stares at the place our flesh connects—as if he, too, is confused as to why he hasn't let go.

He clears his throat. "Sorry again."

A nervous tick twitches his expression as he drops my hand, stands, and pockets his wallet before scurrying away. I watch as he jogs towards the water, his brown dress shoes smacking against the pavement. He makes an abrupt turn west down Maple Drive and disappears with the dying sun. A second later, the streetlamps flicker on above me, the clicking of their timers making me flinch.

I grunt as I stand, the twenty-dollar bill crumpling in my fist.

"Strange," I say, turning back to the market, but the word is swallowed by the wind.

Along with a fresh carton of eggs, I treat myself to a pint of chocolate fudge brownie ice cream, courtesy of the kind stranger.

I DON'T GO to the marina the next day, or the day after that. I'd like to say I tried, but that would be a lie.

No, for a whole week I stay cooped up in the house, a bandanna knotted around my crown to hold back my curls, as I dust every baseboard, wipe off every shelf, and break down every moving box I unpack.

Cleaning is the greatest form of procrastination. You have so much to show for it, yet none of it is what you need.

I'm throwing the last of the cardboard carcasses into the garage on the seventh day of my purge when my phone buzzes against my thigh. I sigh, a familiar thread of dread weaving between my ribs as I pull it from the pocket of my leggings. It's been a quiet week, and they've let me unpack in peace, so a check in was bound to happen at some point.

> Proof of life?
> STEPH

With my lips mashed together in an unamused expression, I snap a picture of myself from way too high of an angle.

> Thank you. I hope cleaning and unpacking is going okay.
> STEPH
>
> But more importantly... proof of art?
> STEPH

I groan, scrubbing a hand over my face.

What I *also* haven't done this week is work on any of my pieces for the exhibit. Sure, I have plenty of half-started projects shoved into the drawers of my grandma's studio, but they're all pieces from *before*. I couldn't unpack them without getting blurry-eyed. How was I supposed to stare at them for hours on my easel?

Tears don't mix well with oil paint.

I respond to Steph with the emoji of the little French painter—at least, I assume he's French, given the beret on his head.

> That's not a real answer.
> STEPH
>
> You said you had stuff you were working on in April??
> STEPH

"Goddamn it," I grumble, my head falling back.

I did try to paint in April. But all I did was glare at the blank canvas for two hours, a brush grasped in my hand so tight I thought it would snap. My knuckles became so stiff that I had to run them under hot water afterwards.

> Alice... I can't push this commitment back again. It'll look bad.
> STEPH

> You still haven't turned off read receipts, so I know you're seeing this. I don't understand how you're so bad with technology.
>
> STEPH

I pinch the bridge of my nose and type out a reply that will satisfy her.

Probably.

Hopefully.

For now.

> I scrapped those.
>
> I'm doing research on something new. I have a library trip planned for inspiration.
>
> Will report back later.

> Fine.
>
> STEPH
>
> BUT I need pics of sketches or notes on your ideas by this time Tuesday.
>
> STEPH
>
> And that's not up for debate. So don't even try. I will not see you blacklisted!!!
>
> STEPH
>
> Also, Erica says you should FaceTime her and show her all your grandma's vintage clothes so she can pilfer some when we visit.
>
> STEPH

I like her messages rather than responding, my shoulders sagging with a relieved sigh.

I just bought myself forty-eight hours.

IN COLLEGE, students often referred to the library as *the stacks*. It was a self-explanatory nickname, though I was partial to calling it *the maze*. Despite the neat, gridded rows of shelves, stacked five floors high, you could absolutely get lost in it. There were many nooks you could tuck yourself into: the stray desks left in the awkward three feet of space between the wall and the edge of a shelf, the random armchair pushed against the window next to the reference book section, or the study room no one wanted to climb up four flights of stairs to get to.

But more than that, you could disappear. There were never eyes on you in *the stacks*.

There are eyes on me here.

The pinpricks of his gaze tickled my neck thirty minutes after I sat down with my pile of art history books.

When I was in school, I adopted the habit of flicking through these kinds of books in search of inspiration. I'd pull tiny pieces from them: a color that struck familiar, a particularly haunted expression in a portrait, or a motif that twisted my gut.

In art, half the battle is harnessing inspiration when it strikes. The other half is developing the dedication to see that inspiration to fruition. I'm able to do neither, as of late. And nothing pops out at me as I flick through the last pages of a book on Rococo art and architecture.

The heat crawling up my spine doesn't help either. This library is too small, and there's nowhere to hide.

There's only one study area: a few wooden tables that sit in the open space between rows of books in the main room. I had no choice but to sit here, where all the eyes can see me. Or really, the *kind stranger's* eyes.

Turns out, he's one of Meadowbrook's librarians.

My suspicious gaze slides from my book to the man. He casually strides between the shelves, ID badge and keys jingling from where they're clipped to his belt loop, re-stocking books from a wheeled cart.

Full pink lips move as if he's muttering the alphabet, searching for the home that matches the author's name. His free hand runs through his curious white locks—and it's no wonder his hair was perfectly disheveled the other day, because his fingers grip the strands of hair like a crimper as he scans the bookcase. When he finds the spot he's looking for, he reaches up, forearm flexing as he tucks the book into place on the top shelf.

It's then that his eyes dart over to me, peeking over the pushed-up sleeve of his brown cardigan. They widen when he realizes *I'm* watching *him*.

He quickly averts his gaze and has the audacity to pretend he wasn't sneaking glances.

I huff, crossing my arms as I lean back in the old chair without care of how it squeaks under my shifting weight. He was nice enough the other night, but my *stranger danger* sense is tingling, and if I want to keep this library in my rotation of places to visit, then I need to nip this in the bud.

I clear my throat—the sound loud in the quiet study room. We're the only two here, so I don't feel bad about making noise.

"Do you need something?" I ask.

The man freezes, one hand poised on a book half pushed onto the shelf. His eyes squeeze shut with a wince. Two *long* seconds pass. Then, those red-brown irises find the crystal blue skies in mine.

His shoulders hitch with a deep breath, as if he's readying himself for confrontation, before he scoots his cart out of the way and strides to my table. His steps falter halfway as he considers where to stop, attention bouncing between the empty seat next to me and the empty seats across.

He chooses an undisclosed third option, taking a perch on

the side of the rectangular table with no chairs. Not too close to make me uncomfortable but not looming so far above me to intimidate.

I hadn't noticed it outside the market, hunched over my broken eggs, but he's quite tall. The classic long-limbed and wiry stature you associate with academic boys.

Nervousness is written all over his pinched features as he awkwardly scratches the back of his neck.

"You're the girl from the grocery store," he says.

"*Yes*," I draw out, cautious, but also curious. "What about it?"

His face twitches, as if he wants to smile at my slight hostility.

"I'm sorry," he says. "I was rushing home and wasn't paying attention." His voice has the same soft timbre that it did before, and the calming lilt relaxes my tense shoulders. "Did you go in and buy replacement eggs? Or did you pocket the money for next time?"

"Um, technically both?" My tongue runs over my teeth, and I glance around the room, needing a break from his intense gaze. I get skittish when I'm being perceived too thoroughly, and he's got a stare that makes my skin feel like glass. "They let me exchange the eggs, so I went ahead and stocked my freezer with double the Ben and Jerry's. Thanks for enabling my chocolate addiction."

He huffs a laugh. "Happy to be of service."

An awkward silence stretches between us, and the white-haired man's brows knit in confusion as he continues to stare at me.

"Well, if that's all..." I start.

"You look so familiar. Are you a student at MBU?" he asks, abruptly.

Meadowbrook University is the local state university in the

area. Campus is about twenty-five minutes south of town, but I remember my grandma complaining about how students would rent houses around here.

"Do I *look* like a student?" I ask, one brow quirked.

"I sense that may be a trick question." Twin spots of embarrassment pink bloom on the apples of his cheeks. "I only ask because I feel like I've seen you before. Well, before the other night, I mean. And a ton of students stay in town for summer sessions so…"

"I'm pushing thirty, so no, not a student," I say. "Though I'm somewhat flattered that my baby face lets me pass as a bachelor's student."

"I could have been talking about grad school," he volleys back, a tentative smile dancing on his lips. "I'm twenty-nine, too. We're not *that* old."

"Eh." I scrunch my nose. "Debatable."

We aren't old, not by a long shot. But there's a part of me that rebels at the notion, one that screams *I'm falling behind*. That I'm wasting what few years left I have in my prime. That I'm going to enter a new decade at the end of August, and I haven't done what I wanted to by now. That I don't have what I *should* have by now.

Birthdays are another stark reminder of what was stolen from me.

My fingers find the chain at my neck, pulling the rings free of the confines of my shirt; they twiddle with the bands of their own accord as the taste of my mouth sours on my tongue.

"If you're not a *grad* student," the man drawls, eyes twinkling behind his round glasses. "Are you new in town?"

He shifts, palm bracing against the table as he leans closer. My gaze traces over the vein that stands out on the back of his hand, pops across the moles dotting his forearm, and lands on the name tag pinned to his cardigan.

Harley.

Haven't heard that one before.

"Kind of," I answer.

"That sounds like there's a story there," Harley says.

"Yeah…" I sigh, shooting him a tight-lipped smile. I'd rather not dig into the details with a stranger. It never goes over the way I want it too and always ends in one form of pity or another. And I hate being pitied. "My grandma used to live here, but she died and left me the house. Now I'm setting up shop."

Harley rears back. "Oh, I'm sorry to hear that."

Again, that awkward silence descends. Like an afternoon deluge, it pours over us, soaking the oakwood tables and the fibers of his cashmere sweater. He tugs at it, adjusting where the sleeves bunch around his elbow. He's got good hands—long nimble fingers that I imagine have flicked through many books in this library.

"Well, I'm gonna get back to my stuff if that's okay?" I ask, not knowing where to go from here.

"Sorry. Honestly don't know why I'm so chatty today." Harley hops off his perch and walks backwards. He jabs one thumb towards the cart he left marooned in the aisle and palms the back of his neck with his other hand. "I'll be over there restocking the shelves if you need anything."

"Will do, thanks," I say.

But just as he's about to turn around, my stomach betrays me. A loud gurgle cuts through the air, and I wince, instantly remembering that I didn't eat breakfast.

"Ignore her," I say, pointing at my stomach in a feeble attempt to distract from my own mortification. I don't think there's anything worse than bodily noises ripping through a quiet room.

Instead, Harley stops, smiles, and asks, "Do you have a library card?"

My brows furrow. "Um..."

"Because then you can take those guys home." He points to the books stacked on the table. "You know, so you can go eat. I love going to the café down the street, Mad Mug. You should stop by. They have the best coffee and sandwiches." Then, he blanches, as if embarrassed by his rambling. "Or you can ignore me and stay. Studying *is* what a library is for."

I purse my lips to hide my amusement, though the action doesn't stop a subtle tease from rolling off my tongue. "Are you trying to get rid of me?"

Harley surprises me by not responding right away. He sucks his bottom lip between his teeth, chewing on it as he settles on an answer. "Would it be inappropriate to say you have been a distraction the past two hours?"

A cute scrunch in the straight bridge of his nose lifts his glasses, and my heart flutters in response. It's a tiny thing, fleeting too, the way it patters around in my chest like a kid chasing after a butterfly. But then, my stomach dips, low and nauseating, because it hits me that this man is flirting with me. And I... want to flirt back?

Panic bubbles in my throat, and I'm overcome with the need to leave.

"Yes, it probably would be inappropriate," I whisper, and clear my throat as I gather my things. "But I might take you up on the coffee rec. Do they also have pastries?"

Harley nods.

"Great." I stand, throw my bag over my shoulder, and stack all the books I want to take with me into a neat pile. "I'm pretty sure I have a card from when I was younger but I'm sure it expired. Can you look me up in the system or sign me up for a new one?"

Harley nods again, and I follow as he silently heads to the front desk. Swiveling in his chair, he methodically scans my books and clicks a few buttons, then pauses, fingers hovering over the keyboard. A soft laugh escapes him.

"I'm so rude. I can't believe I haven't asked for your name," he says, peering up at me through his white lashes.

"Alice Raine—" My throat catches on itself. I clear it. "Um, it's probably listed under Alice Quinn."

His fingers tap out the letters of my name on autopilot, but they stall mid-way through.

"*Alice*," he draws my name out as a whispered prayer. His eyes flash with something vast and unnamable, but it disappears with a small shake of his head. The keyboard clacks with his resumed typing and with a final click of the mouse he leans back.

"There you are. Last check out was…" Harley scrolls with the roller on his mouse, and a warm smile, the kind that infects everyone who encounters it, cuts across his cheeks. "Twenty-one years ago. I'm amazed we have records for this far back." He shakes his head again, as if in disbelief, mumbling, "I should have thought of that."

"Thought of that for what?" I ask, canting my head.

"Just research on someone who used to live here." Harley waves a nervous hand in the air. "Anyway, you should be good. Memberships need to be renewed every five years, but it looks like maybe your grandma kept renewing yours. It still has time on it. I can print you a new card if you want, or if you can't be bothered to carry it around, I can search you up every time."

"I'll take you up on that offer. I'm sure I'd forget it at home even if you printed me a new one," I say, grabbing the pile of books off the desk and turning to the door. "I appreciate the help."

"My name's Harley, by the way," he calls out as the automatic doors squeak open.

"I know. You have a name tag on," I say over my shoulder.

He frantically looks down at his chest and curses, and the

cuteness of it all makes me snort. And as I hurry down Main Street with my boon of art history books, my tongue traces over my curved lip, and I realize that I've caught his infectious smile.

All too quickly it fades, when a similar grin—that of a memory rerun so many times it's gotten fuzzy at the edges—flashes in my mind.

They have the same one.

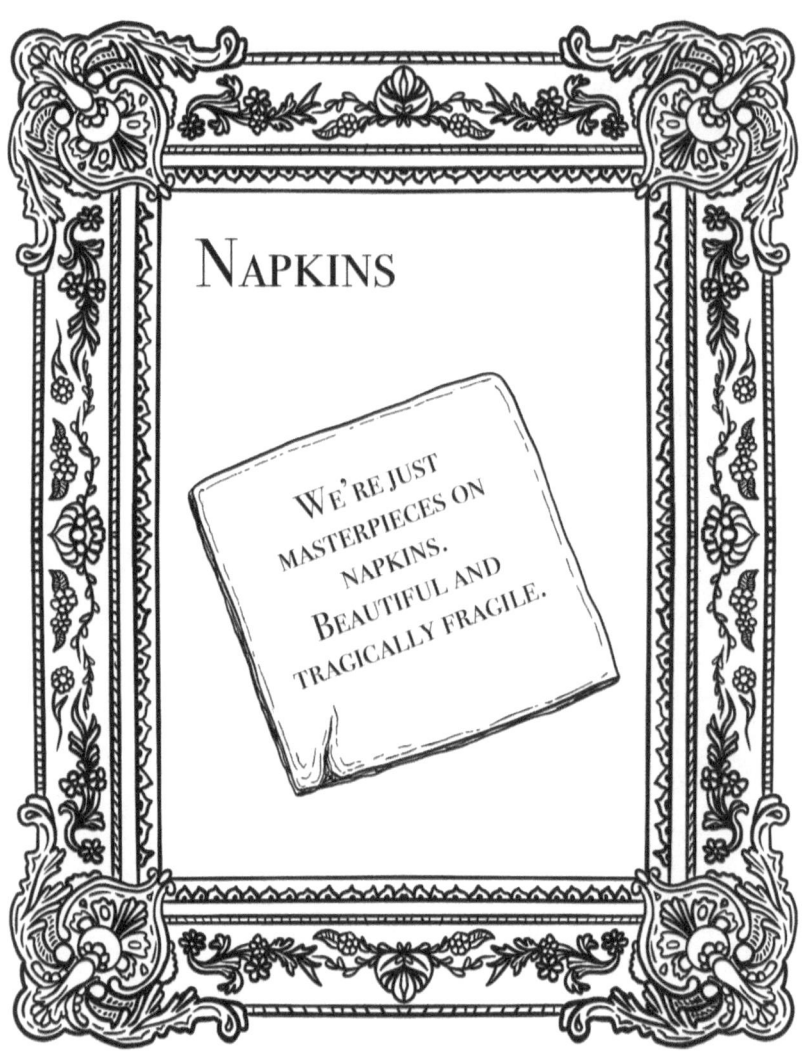

4

YES, NO, MAYBE

ALICE

The walk to Mad Mug is short, but the brutal beginnings of summer heat cause sweat to bead on my forehead by the time I push into the café. A bell rings above me, and air-conditioning blasts my damp skin, sending relieved shivers down my spine.

It's busy, though the crowd is deceiving; a line extends to the door, but there's a few tables empty. There's one in particular, tucked in the corner where the two windows meet, that strikes my fancy. I beeline for it, laying claim by dropping my books onto the tabletop, then grab my wallet and join the end of the line.

A restlessness overtakes me as I wait, as if all the forward motion in my flight from the library was the only thing keeping my mind occupied. Now that I'm stopped and still, a familiar spark of intrigue invades my brain. Compositions flash in the frames of gray as I blink.

Soft and messy strands of hair, an odd color that would be a challenge to mix. The gentle curve of glasses against a sharp cheek, a perfect juxtaposition. The constellations that could be drawn between freckles...

My fingers flip the thin wallet over and over; I pull my card out, then push it back in, repeating the action every time I get to step closer to the cashier. It does little to distract me from the sudden *need* skittering through me.

It's a specific kind of twitch in my fingers, the relentless presence of a new muse making itself known.

"What can I get you?" the cashier asks as I step forward, my time in line lost to my thoughts.

"Some sanity and a sense of direction in life would be great, please," I mutter, not missing a beat, and instantly regretting it. My face scrunches into a wince. "Sorry," I add, attention flicking to the menu board. "I meant one of the chocolate croissants and an iced mocha."

But the cashier only laughs, rich and full.

"*That* is the best thing I've heard all day," she says. Her voice is as smooth and luscious as her laugh, and I'm unsurprised the darkly feminine energy extends to her visage too. A long swath of shiny black hair descends from her ponytail, but the raven locks are intertwined with two other colors—one platinum-blonde patch cutting through half her bangs, and one copper-red section where an undercut would be.

A glance down for a nametag leaves me without answers, the space where it should be pinned to her black tank top blank.

I re-focus my attention on the growing curve of her rose-tinted lips as she adds, "Unfortunately, I don't have any sanity to spare."

My cheeks heat with embarrassment; I'm in rare fucking form today. Though, it's nice that she's humoring me rather than casting me a weird look.

"Just the croissant and an iced mocha then," I say, awkwardly tapping my wallet on my palm.

"You got it." A wink of an amber iris punctuates her drawl as she types my order into her tablet. "For here?"

"Yep."

"*Perfect*," she purrs the word. "That'll be seven even."

My brows furrow at the screen where my card is poised to tap. Eyes flicking back to the chalkboard menu on the wall, I do the mental math.

"Um, I think you forgot to charge me for the croissant?" I ask.

"Nope, I'm giving it to you on the house," she chirps.

"Oh," I say, tapping my card to the reader. *What's up with this town and kind, uniquely beautiful strangers?* "Thanks."

"You're cute." She shrugs, as if it's reason enough to comp someone part of their order.

My airway constricts as I blink my surprise. Her sharp black eyeliner becomes jagged with the crinkling edge of her amused eyes, then she hands me a metal stand with a number for my table.

"Your stuff will be right out," she adds.

"Thanks," I repeat, turning on my heel and escaping to my table.

For the second time today, I feel the pinpricks of someone's gaze on my neck. They don't leave me as I sit down, or when my coffee and pastry come—delivered by a different barista. Nor do they leave when I succumb to the restless nagging of my fingers, digging into my bag for my sketchbook.

It's not there, and I silently accost myself. I have three different pens in this tote, but no paper. What kind of artist leaves the house without a sketchbook?

One who lost her spark.

The ominous words float from my brain, loop around my neck like a noose, and tighten. With an ego death impending, my attention snags on the napkin holder.

I rip a whole stack from the plastic box and click open my pen.

THE INK-FILLED nib scratches across the brown napkin, catching on the coarse texture in a delicious way, until—of course—it doesn't. I huff my frustration as the sheet rips under the pressure of my pen, the black ink having soaked the paper through to the point of frailty.

I ball it up and toss it into the pile of crumbled rejects, which sits a mess next to a smaller stack of proper sketches.

A pronounced Adam's apple. The crisp cut of a shirt collar against a neck, fading into no head. A soft smile peaking below the stretch of an arm. The folds of a cashmere cardigan at an elbow.

They're incomplete ideas, a whispered promise of *more to come*, and I'm frantically grasping at them. There's something *right there* that keeps slipping between my fingers—something about *him*. The longer I scrawl his portrait onto napkins, the more insistent my pen becomes, a sense of déjà vu guiding my hand. I'm lost to my fervor, chasing after the elusive and desperate to capture it.

"You're going to run me out of napkins."

My body jolts at the sudden intrusion in my space, and a woman's amused, breathy laugh follows my surprise. I pull my makeshift canvas close and place my pen across the top to block the drawing from view as the nameless cashier drops into the empty seat across from me. She brandishes a goading smirk, jabbing a finger at the pile of discarded doodles.

"Whatcha drawing?" she asks.

I purse my lips, sucking the flesh of my cheeks between my teeth, and her gaze flicks over the action. A spark of heat flashes in her eyes, orange flecks set in an unnaturally bright shade of yellow. Late night campfires come to mind, the ones that blaze hot enough to melt the sneakers you insist on perching against the stone pit. Embers of tension float in the air between us, singeing my skin like the pinpricks of eyes did earlier. Her eyes, I assume.

Her attention has the same intensity as Harley's did, but hers is unwavering—*unnerving*—in the way that a cat's is in the moment its pupils dilate, and you question whether it will pounce.

"Doodles," I say with a shrug.

Her smirk grows into a charming grin as she leans forward, propping her elbow onto the table and resting her chin on her palm.

"You're new," she says.

"New?"

"In town."

"That's the second time someone's asked me that today," I mutter. She lifts a brow as if to ask me to explain, and for a reason beyond me, I do. Though I keep it short. "Dead grandma. I got the house."

The woman's dark brows knit together in confusion, then rise with sudden recognition, hiding behind her bangs. "Are you Lacie's granddaughter?"

"Uh, yeah..." I say, stunned. "Did you know her?"

"It's been a while, but she's hard to forget. And word spreads fast around here when houses suddenly have u-hauls in front of them. I was wondering who moved in," she says. "She would come in every Wednesday morning. Sit right where you are for three hours people watching with those funky green glasses."

She hums, deep in thought, eyes narrowing on some invisible thing outside the window.

"Three shots of espresso, in separate mugs, one for each hour she'd sit here," she says, knocking her knuckles on the table. "And she'd bring a bagel with lox cream cheese from

Strathmore down the street. I always told her we had bagels here too, but she'd shake her head and tell me they didn't taste right." The woman huffs and rolls her eyes. "As if I don't get my bagels delivered from Strathmore every morning. They were the same damn egg-everythings."

Any tension my shoulders had gathered from the woman's presence lessens at her fond ramble about my grandmother. Nana always was a bit *particular*. I think that's why we got along when I was a kid; I hadn't learned to hide all my little quirks yet, and she didn't mind since she had some of her own.

A snort escapes me.

The woman leans back, adopting a posture that screams of smug success at having pulled a positive sound from me.

"Thank you for that," I say, cautiously. "It's nice to hear her talked about. I don't have many people left who knew her."

No one left, actually. Steph and Erica only met her at my wedding.

The woman nods, as if she understands. "Yeah, well, now I know the reason why I like you already. Lacie also had that air of mischief around her."

"I may have a few marbles missing but I definitely don't give off an *air of mischief*," I say. "I'm very well-behaved."

Her tongue pokes her cheek. "I'm sure you are, Trouble."

The air shifts from a softening awkwardness to something I can't quite name as I swallow the thickening spit in my mouth. My blood pumps faster, throbbing at the juncture of my neck. How is it that one word—one casually drawled nickname—can have such an effect?

"My name's Alice," I whisper the correction.

"Jessa," she says, extending a hand my way. She's not as pale white as me, her skin glowing with a subtle sun-kissed warmth, and her nails are painted with shiny black lacquer. "And I'm the owner of this fine establishment, if you were wondering."

"Alice," I mutter, shaking her hand.

"You said that already," Jessa teases.

"And I said had a few screws loose, didn't I?" I huff, stray nerves skittering along my skin as I slip my hand from hers. My pulse grows louder, beating at my wrists. I turn away, collecting my napkin sketches and carefully tucking them into one of my library books.

"Can I be forward with you?" Jessa asks.

I peer at her through my lashes, but don't stop my tidying up. "Sure..."

"Do you want to go out sometime?"

My hands freeze, one gripping the rough canvas edge of my tote, and the other white-knuckled around a book on Monet.

"Like... a date?" I squeak out.

Jessa shrugs. "Your words not mine."

My mouth parts, the starting stutters of a response snapping between my teeth.

The rings hanging down my chest, hidden beneath my shirt, begin to burn against my skin as I panic. Jessa must see my brain working double time to reply, because she leans forward with a soft laugh and outstretched palms.

"I'm sorry, I'm just a no-beating-around-the-bush type of person. *And* I'm a habitual flirt. You can ignore it, or flirt back, I won't complain either way." Her silky tenor wraps around me, oddly adept at settling my nerves. "But I would be lying if I didn't say I'd love another friend in town who isn't retired or in college. And that I think you're gorgeous."

"How do you know I'm not retired? I could be a Benjamin Button," I say, unable to hold back the quip, despite my body's blaring alarm to *abort mission*. It's the same anxiety induced urge to flee as in the library, spurred on by the sudden realization that I'm experiencing an emotion that I haven't in years.

Attraction. Or something akin to it.

I don't *notice* people like that anymore. Yet somehow, it's happened twice in one day, and I'm completely caught off guard by my body's intense reaction. Harley intrigued my muse, and Jessa is making my heart race as if I've ran a marathon.

It's not that I'm not tempted to say yes, but it's all feeling like *too much*. I've always been attracted to women, but I never got around to dating them. Getting together with Ryan at seventeen meant that I never needed to date around at all. I was one of the *lucky ones*. One and done.

Except now…

"I'm pretty confident that reversed aging isn't a kind of magic found in this world," Jessa riffs on my joke. "You a realm-walker, Alice?"

"No," I say, chewing on my lip as I finish putting away my sketches.

"So, what do you think?" Jessa asks.

It's been years, I remind myself. *It's okay to say yes.*

"Sure," I say, bravely, and despite the sticky film of guilt that wraps around me. "I wouldn't mind a beach-buddy? I haven't been in a while."

"Totally," Jessa says, smiling brightly. "Give me your number. I'll text you."

5

SHE'S BACK, BABY

JESSA

The bells I installed above Mad Mug's door ring out like a death knell as Alice leaves, because dead is what I'll be once Ori finds out that she's back and that I didn't tell him right away.

Or maybe I'll be spared from his wrath when he sees her—cute button nose smattered with freckles, full cheeks, and ink-smudged fingers—and the past twenty years of shit he's ignored comes crashing through his window.

He'll understand. Eventually.

My phone buzzes, and Harley's name pops up on my screen.

> She came by???
>
> HARLEY
>
> Did she remember you? I don't think she remembered me.
>
> HARLEY

> Stop by after closing. I don't want all this in texts in case Ori snoops. You know how he is when you act weird.

UGH
HARLEY

I'm not going to act weird.
HARLEY

> Babe…

I SWEAR I WON'T
HARLEY

> Uhuh.

Also. Funny story. I'm behind because I was distracted by her before and put a bunch of sci-fi in the autobiography section and now I have to go back and fix it.
HARLEY

So idk when I'll be done for the day.
HARLEY

> Then stop texting me and hurry the fuck up?

Yes, ma'am.
HARLEY

A smile curves my lips; it doesn't matter that Alice was a distraction for him today, the man is chronically late every day of his life. Even when we were kids, we'd have to tell him something started fifteen minutes earlier than it did so he'd be on time.

So, I'm not surprised that when he pushes through the door, it's no less than forty-five minutes after we close.

"Hey, I'm sorry I'm—" Harley stops short at my raised palm.

"No apologies," I chide. There's a firmness to my tone, one

that sends a visible shiver through his body. My pointer finger curls, beckoning him over. "Drop the bag. Come here."

The café is dark—only the service lights above us are on and humming, and they paint us in soft ochre hues. Harley's pale white skin glows where he's spotlighted, and the expanse of his long neck bobs at my commands.

The strap of his leather messenger bag slides from his shoulder, and the tote *thunks* heavily on the tile floor, undoubtedly full of books. Ever since we came to Meadowbrook, he's been hungry for every scrap of information on humans and their world's history. I've always wondered if it's an obsession born of his own curiosity, or a way to prepare for what lies ahead if we ever get to go back home for good.

Harley slots perfectly between my legs, and my thighs squeeze his slender hips. He's taller than me, but if anyone in this small town peeped though the glass windows there would be no mistaking who held the power here. His hands find purchase on the counter on either side of me, and his forehead falls to my shoulder, body melting into mine.

This close, the scent of him is strong. Paper musk, cinnamon, and a hint of soft linen. It soothes the beast that prowls inside of me, unable to be released in this realm.

The tip of Harley's nose nuzzles my pulse-point as he scents me back.

"Hey," I whisper, my arms snaking around his body.

One hand anchors at Harley's nape, my thumb brushing against the soft crop of his hair. The other runs a line up and down his back, and he shudders under my subtle ministrations. But when his hips push forward—whether intentional or not—my grip on his neck becomes firm, and I pull his head from its burrow at my collarbone.

"*Babe.*" I tsk.

A pained expression tightens Harley's features, and a sound akin to a whine escapes him. "Please? I've been hard all day."

I snort and make no move to address the growing pressure of his hips on my core. "Didn't you want to discuss the extremely convenient return of our blonde friend first?"

Harley's head falls back with a groan, highlighting how quickly his pulse thumps beneath his skin. "That's why I'm hard. She smells like fresh sugar cookies, and I couldn't keep my eyes off her. I was so confused. And when I realized who she was—"

"I asked her out."

"What?" Harley squeaks, head snapping forward.

"I asked her out," I say, slower this time, annunciating every word while my nails trace patterns over his throat. "She said yes."

"She did?"

"Well, sort of." I lick my lips, choosing my words carefully. "It's the friendly kind of hang out. A *get to know you* type of thing."

Harley's eyes narrow on me, suspicion tucked between his lashes. "I take it that means she doesn't remember you either? Not at all?"

"No," I say. A smirk curls my lips, my devious nature blooming in full force. "But you're right that she does smell good. I know she's *technically* Ori's fated, but she smells like ours. I want her."

"*Jessa,*" Harley grinds out, rubbing his hands over his face. His glasses tilt, skewed above his knuckles as he digs into the pressure points at the corner of his eyes. "That's not why I sent her to Mad Mug. She was *hungry*. I wanted her to get *food*, not to be hit on."

"I assured her it didn't need to be romantic," I say, pulling at the crook of his elbows to free his face from his hands. "At least not at first. There's no way she won't fall for us. I'm incredibly charming."

"You're incredibly demanding is what you are," Harley

huffs, letting his hands fall. They land on my thighs and squeeze, all his nervous hope apparent in the pressure of his fingers on my flesh. Quietly, he asks, "Are you sure about this?"

I nod. "This is our chance to have it all, Harley. Heart *and* home. I got over my anger a long time ago. I know you did too. So, why not try?"

His jaw works back and forth as he thinks. "Ori hasn't gotten over it, and she's his Champion. How are we going to tell him?"

"We're not," I say with a shrug. "At least, not yet."

"That feels like a huge overstep."

It takes all my willpower, but I manage to hold back my eyeroll. Ori may be my best friend, but he's had enough time to get his shit together. If he won't lead us, then I will.

"He'll realize he can't outrun Fate when he meets her," I say, fully believing it. "And by then, it'll be too late." I run a thumb over Harley's jaw, tenderly stroking back and forth. "Hopefully it'll push him to talk to you, too. He can't keep ignoring you."

A moment of intense stillness passes between us, one where the weight of the past two decades of searching—of *waiting*—lifts, ever-slightly.

Finding Alice changes everything.

"So… what next?" Harley asks, softly.

"As much as we don't want to rush things, time isn't on our side." He nods his understanding; there are larger forces at work here, and we only have a few months left to reclaim our home. "We need to be careful though… She's got this haunted look in her eyes."

"I noticed that too."

I grab his head, my thumbs resting on each of his high cheekbones, and pull our foreheads together.

"We'll figure it out," I say. "You trust me, right?"

"With my whole heart." His minty breath puffs over my lips, as if he had chewed gum before coming over.

"Good," I say. "Then let me take care of it."

I press a single, chaste kiss to his cheek, then slant a second heated one over his soft and pillowy lips. I hum at how easily he yields to me, and my tongue laps up the groan that slips between the seam of his parted mouth. Harley's hands slide up my thighs and wrap around my hips, tugging me forward so our bodies are molded together. He grinds his hard length against me.

Breaking our kiss, I *tsk*. "You know the rules."

"*Jessa*," Harley whispers my name. It's not a plea for his release—no, the man loves to be edged within an inch of his life, and he's desperate to please.

To please *and* be praised for it.

I curl my fingers through his soft, white locks, tugging on the strands the way he likes as I push his head lower.

"On your knees."

6

FLIRTING WON'T KILL YOU

ALICE

A hazy cloud of creation settles over 874 like a thick fog. I embrace it, get lost in it, and the world is forgotten. My body thrums, elated. I survive off a rotation of spoonfuls of peanut butter straight from the jar, air-fryer dinosaur chicken nuggets, and flat Diet Coke.

Best of all, I barely sleep. I don't have time for it, and no time for sleep means no time for nightmares that like to cosplay as dreams.

Detailed ink and charcoal sketches of Harley are strewn across my studio, explorations of the doodles I'd scrawled onto napkins a week ago. I've even attempted a few of Jessa, too. And even though none have made it past the sketch phase—and an empty canvas sits on my easel—I'm more fulfilled than I have been in months.

These ideas aren't contenders for the exhibition; my gut unfortunately knows that with certainty. But they're a start—a sign of blooming after a long winter.

It's progress. It's *something*. And something is far better than nothing.

I'm rolling my kneaded eraser between my fingers, playing with the tacky rubber, when my phone's alarm blares. I scramble in pursuit of it, rummaging through the mess of shit on my worktable, finding it under a pile of charcoal-stained paper towels and crumpled throw-away sketches.

The bright screen flashes with a reminder: *Beach Day*.

"*Fuck*," I mutter as I hit the snooze button and swipe through my missed notifications.

Emails I ignore. Erica and Steph's messages get noncommittal likes so they know that I'm alive. But I pause on the four unread messages from Jessa.

"*Double fuck*," I groan, clicking open our thread.

> Did you want to meet at the beach or want me to pick you up?
>
> JESSA

> I'm guessing no response means you're either busy or too scared to make a choice. No worries. Why don't you meet me in the parking lot at Avalon Cove and then we go from there?
>
> JESSA

> I've got beach chairs and an umbrella covered—they live in my trunk. And I have all the fixings. So don't bring anything but yourself and your bathing suit.
>
> JESSA

> BTW my housemate might come too since he's off work today. But let me know if that makes you uncomfortable and I'll tell him to fuck off.
>
> JESSA

My thumbs hover over the keyboard as I consider what to

respond with. Would a '*Sorry! I forget that time and my phone exist sometimes. See you in a few hours!*' work?

She seems like the type who'd get it, based on our interaction at Mad Mug. And we've been texting on and off the past week, participating in an unofficial game of twenty questions.

Jessa lives with two others in a house on Cedar Lane. She's worked at Mad Mug for almost a decade but has owned it for five, having taken over for the previous owner when they retired. She has an insatiable sweet tooth. She listens to punk rock music and while she wants a tattoo, she's scared of needles. And even though all those facts sound like a checklist of things you ask someone to get to know them, the back and forth hasn't felt forced.

Except now I've gone and ignored her in the two days leading up to the plans we made.

As if Jessa can sense my discomfort from across town, a new message from her pops up.

> Text me back, Trouble. You're making me worried.
>
> JESSA

> Sorry! Was in an art fog all weekend. I can explain later?
>
> Also, I'm notoriously bad at texting.
>
> I'm looking forward to later. It'll be good to get out of the house.

> We'll work on the texting bit.
>
> JESSA
>
> Don't forget to put on sunscreen. I have a feeling you burn easy.
>
> JESSA

My cheeks heat and I quickly like her last message before locking my phone.

It could be a byproduct of finally creating again, but I feel lighter, more open than I did last week, and bubbles of nervous excitement pop in my stomach.

Later, after I've rinsed off in the shower and slathered myself in sunscreen, guilt stalls my feet at the threshold of the house. The door is open, my fingers wrapped around the brass handle, but the four inch step onto the porch feels like jumping off a cliff.

A demonic voice whispers in my ear, urging me to go back inside. *Shut the door. Stay.* It gets crueler the longer I stand there. *Why are you excited? How can you possibly enjoy anything when Ryan isn't here to? He would have gone to the beach with you. He loved the beach. Why are you trying to replace him? Shut the door. Cancel the plans. Stay.*

There's safety here, in the house. To be tucked away in my studio, just me and my memories and my attempts at art. I hurt here, but not any more or less than I have over the past two years.

Sea salt air blows through the open doorway; it smells a lot like hope.

I close my eyes. Hold the breeze in my lungs.

Hope promises connection and assures loss. Hope guarantees an incredible high and teases more weekends in the studio with my muse. Hope is excellent at convincing me the inevitable crash out at the end of this will be worth it.

Hope is dangerous for a woman like me.

If life's going to hurt regardless, I might as well get something out of it. And I'm desperate to paint again.

I step onto the porch and pull the door shut behind me.

∼

JESSA'S WAITING, perched on the back rim of her vintage pickup truck, when I pull into the parking lot. She's the only person lingering among the few cars and many empty spots; Memorial Day is a week out, so the summer crowds haven't hit in full yet.

Black bikini straps poke out from the neckline of her tank top, and long, muscular legs stick out from cutoff denim shorts. Her hair is pulled back in a high ponytail like it was at Mad Mug, but her split-dyed bangs brush over a large pair of cat-eye sunglasses.

A wide smile that shows off pointy canines spreads across her face when I hop out of my car. "I told you not to bring anything."

I shrug, my tote bag shifting on my shoulder. "It's only my essentials, don't worry."

"I'll worry as much as I want." She huffs, but her tone is playful. "I need to know if you'll follow directions. Seems like that's a big N-O." Jessa grabs the folded beach chair and bag of towels sitting at her feet. "C'mon, I already sent my housemate ahead of us with the other stuff."

"I was wondering why you only had one chair with you," I say. "I forgot you said they were coming."

Jessa taps the side of her sunglasses as we wind down the small path to the beach. "I'm always thinking ahead."

"Or you're a control freak?" I ask, fighting a smile.

"I prefer a less controversial title," Jessa says. "But yes, I prefer to be the one calling the shots. You should get used to that quick or we'll have issues."

Dirt and gravel turn to sand, and the hot grains slide between my toes and my sandals; this is the worst part of going to the beach, the walk between the parking lot and the water.

"I don't necessarily mind that," I say, slowly. A cloying wisp of sadness crawls up my neck, making me shiver even though the sun beats down on us in full force. "I've made enough decisions for a lifetime."

"Easy," Jessa says, not skipping a beat. Is she ignoring my sudden melancholy, or does she not recognize it? "I've got you covered, babe. Consider me your official decider of things. I already do it for my housemates, what's one more in the pack?"

I bark a laugh. "Okay."

Jessa studies me for a long beat, glossed lips pursed. She hums thoughtfully, then turns her attention back to the water.

"What?" I drawl.

"Nothing."

"Why did you make that noise?"

That devilish smirk climbs up her sharp cheeks. "No reason."

"You made a judgy noise."

"It was no such thing."

"Then what was it?" I press. There are fewer things I hate more in the world than unexplained thoughts.

Jessa spins, long swath of hair whipping through the air, and walks backwards as she talks to me. "I was only thinking that maybe you aren't a brat after all."

My eyebrows hit my hairline. "Where did you get that idea?"

Jessa clicks her tongue. "Don't play dumb, it doesn't suit you, Alice." She spins again, returning to my side. She leans in close to fake whisper in my ear. "You're still trouble though."

Gooseflesh rushes over my chest as I inch away from Jessa and peer down the beach. A smattering of umbrellas line the curved stretch of sand.

"Which one is yours?" I ask.

"The red one," she says, pointing. It's the last and farthest down the strip of beach, near the curve of tall grass that marks the start of the nature preserve.

Many of the beaches on the north shore of Long Island are rocky, especially compared to the south shore. Up here, on the edge of the Sound, it's more common to go boating, paddleboarding, or kayaking. But there are still gems like Avalon Cove, where the sand is granular and warm. I shuck off my sandals and let my feet sink into it fully. It burns, but I know it'll feel amazing when I hit the cooler grains by the water, and that only pushes me to walk faster.

When I get to the red umbrella, I falter.

Lounging in the shade on a striped towel, with aviators perched on his nose and donning a pair of bright red boardshorts that show off way too much thigh, is the librarian I've been drawing by memory for the past week.

"It's *you*," I say.

Harley sits up on his elbows, lifting his sunglasses and tucking them into his white hair.

"Hey, Alice." His eyes squint with his smile, and their red tint glows in the natural light. "How are you?"

I train my gaze on Jessa. "Meadowbrook's librarian is one of your housemates?"

"Yeah," Jessa says, confused, dropping her bag under the umbrella. "Why, is that a problem?"

"He's the one who recommended I stop by Mad Mug," I snark, though there isn't much heat backing the words as I toss my bag down in the shade next to hers. I'm not angry, more shocked, and slightly embarrassed as I try—and fail—to avoid looking at his lean chest. "Now I know why. Nepotism."

Jessa playfully pokes Harley's ribs with her foot. "He's a loyal grassroots marketer."

"Stop that." Harley squirms, smacking Jessa's foot away. He glances my way, and I can't tell if the pink on his cheeks is the start of a sunburn or a self-conscious flush. "Sorry. Did she not mention me coming today? I can leave if you want."

"No, it's fine. She mentioned it," I say, albeit a little awkwardly. "It's a small town. I don't know why I'm surprised."

I shift on my feet, waiting as Jessa unfolds the chair she brought and sets it in line with the two others in the sun.

Jessa strips out of her clothes, tossing them over Harley and onto her tote in a wrinkled ball. She drops into the middle of the three chairs, patting the empty seat to her left. "Your throne awaits, mi'lady."

"Funny," I snort. I shuck off my T-shirt and drape it over the back of the chair, then do the same with my shorts. "Did you guys meet here or did you know each other from before Meadowbrook? I think you mentioned moving here after high school?"

I look up when neither of my beach companions answer, catching both staring at me. The ocean whooshes in my ears, crashing waves filling the void of silence. Jessa's head tilts, the action decidedly predatory as she sweeps her gaze over my exposed body. My muscles tense under her attention, but it's not in fear.

I'm exhilarated by it, and I think that's scarier.

"I know. I'm fluorescent," I joke. "I practically reflect the sunlight."

"You're *hot*, Alice," Jessa says plainly, settling back in her chair. "That's why we're staring."

"Um..." My tight smile twitches. "Thanks?"

"You're welcome," Jessa says smugly.

I glance at Harley, and he looks like a deer frozen in headlights.

"I'm sorry about her." He winces. He flicks his sunglasses back down over his eyes and lays back, hands clasped on his stomach.

"Why are you apologizing for me? I didn't say anything wrong," Jessa says. She raises a brow at me. "Right? Friends can compliment each other."

"That wasn't a compliment, Jessa," Harley mumbles. "That was blatant perusal."

"So, you *don't* think she looks good in that blue bikini?"

"I didn't say *that*."

I bite my lip, holding back a laugh as I take my seat in the lounger. It's familiar, the way they tease and bicker. Playful, with ease, as if they've spoken a variation of their back and forth a thousand times before. It gives me pause. The tension undercutting the banter sounds an awful lot like foreplay.

"Then what's the problem?" Jessa drawls.

"You're making her uncomfortable—"

"Hey, it's fine," I say, interrupting them. I might not have the muscle I used to, my middle and thighs squishier than they were when I fenced in high school, but I'm not ashamed of my body. I'm confident, and I know I'm attractive. Ryan always made it a point to remind me of that until it stuck in my head. "I'm not used to the attention, that's all. I don't get out much."

Their heads whip to me.

"Why not?" Jessa asks.

I burrow my feet into the sand, tunneling until my toes wriggle against the cooler, damp layers.

"Not my cup of tea, bars and clubs. Or really, anywhere that's too public," I say.

I leave out the *anymore*—that I used to be a daring adventurer. At least, when I had my partner in crime to do it with, one who would push me towards things I would never have done by myself.

"I get that," Harley says, shifting his arms behind his head.

I allow my gaze to wander over his chest, appreciating the faint trail of white hair down his navel. I had thought his hair was bleached, but maybe he has a type of vitiligo, if it's naturally that light.

Harley continues, "I'm a bookworm, my default is no sun and no loud spaces. It's nice on occasion, but not all the time. Jessa helps pull me out of my shell when it's been too long since I've seen the outside world."

"Hell yeah, I do, babe. I'm the extravert to your introvert."

I relax in my chair. The breeze and the serene crash of

waves are a perfect backing soundtrack to our conversation, and I close my eyes, basking in it.

"I'm a painter. My default is similar to yours, Harley," I say.

"Ah," he drawls. "That's why you checked out all those art books. What do you paint?"

You.

"People," I say. "Portraits, mainly, but with a twist. Depends on what I'm trying to say with it."

The project that propelled me into notoriety was a series I did on vulnerability. I opened a form online where people could submit their most intimate secrets and fears and turned each into something dark and beautiful. It went viral online and the rest was history. I ended up crafting a hundred portraits from strangers' pain.

Well, almost a hundred. I sold number 99 in my last exhibit and had big plans for a larger gallery around number 100. But then Ryan died, and I never finished it.

Wasn't able to.

Can't.

"That's cool," Harley says.

"Some think so."

"Can we see one of your pieces?" Jessa asks.

Absolutely not.

"Uh, maybe later. I can pull up my website. My phone is in my bag, and I don't want to get up," I say with a nervous laugh.

"Fair," Jessa says. "Paradise makes me lazy too, and once my butt is in this Tommy Bahama lounger, I'm not moving until I'm dizzy with heatstroke."

"You won't even get up for some water?" I tease, thankful for a change in subject. Talking about my art feels too intimate for this setting. I point at the blue and white cooler on wheels sitting under the umbrella. "You brought a whole fridge with you."

"That, my darling, is what Harley's for." Jessa holds out her hand above him expectantly.

Harley huffs, but he gets up and rummages in the cooler, pulling out a water bottle. "I'm not your errand boy."

"*No*," Jessa draws out the word with evil intent. Harley cracks open the cap and hands the bottle dripping with condensation over. "But you are my good boy."

Oh?

"Gods above, Jessa. Not *now*," Harley mutters under his breath.

He glares at her, and she stares goadingly up at him as she sips. They seem to have a full conversation by the time she's done drinking, in that way that two partners who've been together for years can. He snatches the bottle from her hand, re-caps it, and tosses it into the cooler.

"I'm going to the water to cool off," he mumbles, trudging off to the shore.

"I don't know why he's embarrassed," Jessa says once his feet hit the water, lips curling up. "He likes being bossed around."

"Okay..." I say, biting my lip to hold back my questions.

Jessa pulls her glasses down to narrow her eyes at me. "What's wrong?"

My attention is drawn to the shore, where Harley paces back and forth in the shallows. His hands are perched on narrow hips, and the bright red of his shorts stands out against deep ocean blue. My fingers twitch with the urge to paint the scene—to paint *him*—but Harley isn't in harmony with his surroundings. The red of his shorts too warm, the ocean and sky too cool. I would have to marry the two halves of the color wheel to make him belong.

"Um... are you two not just housemates?" I ask, though I have a feeling I already know the answer.

"We're best friends who fuck," Jessa clarifies. She flicks her black and red ponytail over the back of her chair as she settles into the seat. "We also love each other."

"I feel like that's something you should have mentioned earlier," I mutter.

"Why does it matter? I thought this wasn't a date, *beach-buddy*?" Jessa teases.

"It's not," I say, frowning. "But if I had said yes at the coffee shop, wouldn't that have been cheating?"

"Not if we're both okay with it."

"So, you're in an open relationship?"

"No," Jessa says with finality. "Well." Jessa tilts her head back and forth. "No. It's more that we're open to the right people."

"I'm confused."

Jessa stretches out with a sigh, sun-kissed arms reaching up to the sky, glistening with a thin sheen of sweat. My own thighs stick together as I shift in my seat, the sunscreen I'd slathered on already melting.

"I knew the second I saw you that you would fit with us. And chatting with you over the last week has only solidified that belief. But I don't want to lay it on too strong and scare you away," she says. "Harley won't admit it as easily, but he's smitten too."

"You're so fucking forward," I huff. "You guys just met me."

"Eh, it's part of my charm. Is it working?" Jessa asks with smirk like sin.

A traitorous spark of arousal fills me at the sureness in her tone.

"Maybe," I admit.

I can't lie—have always had a hard time doing it. They're both wildly attractive, and conversation comes easy with them. Plus, my mind is already mixing the colors of the ocean for a painting of Harley wading in the water. When was the last time I even *had* the urge to crack open my tube of Phthalo Blue?

I'd be silly to not follow this inspiration, to snub it out before I see it to fruition.

Desire blooms in my chest. There's a healthy amount of fear too, and the same, pervasive guilt I've carried with me ever since Ryan died.

Am I *allowed* to find someone attractive again?

Scratch that. *Two* someones.

"Good," Jessa says, pulling me back from my thoughts. "I'll continue to lay it on this thick so you don't misread my interest. You ever been with a woman like me before, Trouble?"

"I haven't been with a woman ever," I blurt out.

"That's okay. I'm happy to be your first," she says, and I'm thankful she doesn't make it a big deal. "The thing you've got to know about me is that I don't play games. I say what I want, and I expect my partner—or *partners*—to do the same. This isn't a date? One hundred percent, it isn't. You'd know if I took you on a date. You want me to stop flirting? Tell me. You only want to fuck Harley? I know he'd be delighted. I'd respect your choice, but I'd also ask to watch."

Heat, not from the sun, but from the visuals her words conjure, crawls up my neck.

How strange it is, to be so openly desired again. Even stranger, to desire again.

"You understand?" Jessa asks.

"Heard, loud and clear," I whisper.

Jessa's smirk only grows. "Good."

She studies me, as if waiting for me to bolt—as if she *wants* me to run so she can give chase. But I'm trapped, my thighs glued to the canvas seat with sweat, sunscreen, and want. There's no instance where I get up of my own accord. Jessa's nostrils flare, and she hums, pleased, before lowering her chairback so she can lay flat.

"Why don't you go to the water with Harley?" she suggests. "You look a little flushed."

7

CINDERELLA NEEDS A DRESS

ALICE

"It's my lunch break. Wanna grab a coffee?" Harley asks.

I stop tapping my pen on my sketchbook. There are fifty little splats of ink on the page from my mindless patter, and I quietly curse as I click it closed and look up. Harley's got this smushed grin on his face, the kind that says he's amused and trying to hide it.

"Sure," I say, shoving my chair back and gathering my things. His question isn't a surprise; we've developed a mutual routine in the near two weeks since our beach day.

I'll come to the library in search of inspiration—though it's mostly a farce. I just want to get out of the house, and the views are nice here. *The views* being quick glances of Harley's white hair between bookshelves, and the infuriating wrinkles on his cardigan sleeves that he pushes up and pulls down as the bone-chilling AC ebbs and flows.

I'll take some notes, space out, and sketch my sub-par ideas for the gallery until his lunch break, at which point he'll ask me to grab a coffee. Then we'll walk to Mad Mug in comfortable silence.

He never tries to fill the space with small talk. It's delightful.

Even now, as his shoulder bumps into mine—since I can never manage to walk in a straight line—Harley sighs contently, gaze far off.

And when we get to Mad Mug, Jessa will comp our drinks, beaming every time we walk through the door, and chat with us between our bites of pastries and sips of coffee.

It's been pleasant, to exist with people who aren't aware of my past. There's a freedom to our interactions. I don't have to tiptoe around them—they don't know me well enough to recognize the grief that undercuts the laughter they pull from my lungs.

Still, I relish my newfound energy. Every text, every surprised smile, every blush that rushes to my cheeks from their playful banter, makes me feel alive.

For so long, all I've done is survive. This is a new kind of progress for me.

I wanted to tell Steph and Erica all the details, but when they called to check in the day after the beach, I couldn't get the words out. I'd only mentioned that I'd *met some nice neighbors.*

What if they take this progress and run with it? What if they expect me to jump into a serious relationship? What if their eyes light up with hope, and I disappoint them when I can't reach the arbitrary milestones of 'healing' they think I should be hitting by now?

They don't get it. This kind of grief isn't something you get over in a year, or two, or ten. It's something that lives with you forever.

I've come to realize that healing is more a matter of figuring out how to survive, then re-learning how to live, and then re-discovering how to love. I think I've got step one down. I'm currently working on the second. Don't know if the third is in the cards for me.

We stop at Mad Mug's door, and Harley pulls it open for me. He sweeps his hand forward with a slight bow and a dramatic flourish, to which I roll my eyes and step into the café.

"Thanks," I say, joining the end of the queue. Harley follows, nestling into me, chest brushing against my shoulder. His head lowers, lips so close to my ear that his breath is a warm puff on my skin.

"You always do that," Harley says.

"Do what?" I ask, side-eyeing him.

"Roll your eyes when I hold the door open for you."

"I say thank you."

"Sure, but you also roll your eyes. Why is that?"

I shift to face him fully with a quirked brow—does he really not know?

"I roll my eyes because you do it the same way every time, like you're some gallant knight sweeping your arm out for a lady," I explain, stepping forward with the line. "It's funny."

"But you roll your eyes..." His brows knit together as he steps forward to match me, slowly piecing his thoughts together. "...and that's how you show your amusement?"

I knock my knuckle into his chest twice. "You're learning."

Harley holds my gaze, and I shift away—though I'm too slow, and my knuckles drag down his shirt and snag on the buttons as they return to my side.

The damage is done. It's not much. Not anything, really. It's only the first time I've initiated any sort of touch with him outside a quick hug hello or goodbye. What's a playful graze of a knuckle over cotton in the grand scheme?

But sometimes, small moments are big ones. Time slows, tension grows—and connection isn't one of those things you can take back.

JESSA HUFFS as she takes the empty seat next to Harley, dropping his sandwich on the table. "Here. A new combo. If you give it your stamp of approval, I'll put it on the menu."

Harley quickly drops his book and picks up the thick toasted bread, marked with the dark lines of a panini press.

"*Fuck, that's hot,*" he curses after taking a bite, holding his mouth open to cool down the food.

"Yeah, no shit," Jessa says, shooting me a look that screams *men are stupid.*

I snort and tear off a piece of my croissant to pop in my mouth. Buttery, flaky goodness explodes on my tongue.

"I've been meaning to ask... are you ever going to let us sneak a peek at that sketchbook of yours?" Jessa asks, plopping her chin on her hand. Her bright amber eyes dart to my bag, where my sketchbook pokes out over the edge of the canvas. "You said you do portraits, but you never showed us any." She leans forward, whispering, "Are they risqué or something?"

"What?" I choke on my croissant, coughing and slamming my fist against my chest to clear it. "No. Nothing like that." I dust my fingers off on my shorts. "I just get weird about my sketchbook."

I don't let *anyone* see the raw ideas I throw around for my pieces. But there's something missing from my most recent sketches that I can't name. Like memories that don't get all the details right. They're exploratory, and while the emotions they evoke within me are *correct*, they feel more like the path to something than the *final something*.

It'd be embarrassing to show them an unfinished thought. And I don't want them seeing my stalker-level renditions of them.

"I can show you some of my old stuff," I offer, grabbing my phone. I open my saved album and pass it off. "Here."

Jessa lays the phone flat on the table and her and Harley's heads knock together as they look.

"These are beautiful," Jessa says.

"Thanks," I say, quietly.

Harley eats while Jessa swipes through the photos, and I let my gaze drift off through the window while I wait for them to finish.

My oversized croissant is gone by the time my phone rings, cutting through the silence at the table.

"Steph is calling," Jessa says, holding out the phone to me.

"Shit, I should take that." I snatch it and swipe over the accept button. I tuck the phone to my ear. "Hey, I'm out. Everything okay?"

"Yeah, no emergency—wait, you're out?" Steph asks, and I wince, curling towards the window for a false sense of privacy.

"I'm at a café," I whisper.

"Oh. Okay. Well, I need a favor," Step says. "You know the Carlton's Young Artists Gala?"

"Yeah..."

"Well, there was a snafu with our Aruba flights and now we can't go."

"To Aruba or to the gala?" I ask. "Is your regular sitter not available for Tito? I can come get him and watch him at my—"

"No, no, the cat is fine," she says. "I need you to go to the gala in my place."

"*I'm sorry?*" I whisper-yell, tucking even closer to the window. I can feel Jessa and Harley's attention on me like spotlights. "*What do you mean go in your place?*"

"I don't have anyone else to give my tickets to and I can't ruin these relationships by no-showing. You know this world and how to schmooze. All you have to do is show face, make a little donation, and talk me up to whoever says hello. *And* it's for a good cause!"

"I don't have a dress," I mutter.

I do have a few formal gowns at the back of my closet from Navy Balls, but I can't bear to put them on again. Or donate them.

"Then go to the mall? I'm sure there's something discounted from prom season."

"*Steph.*"

"Alice."

We pause, and I know if we were in person we'd be having a staring standoff. As much as I want to stick my feet in the dirt and continue to say no, I know I'll be the one forfeiting this match. They've helped me so much the last few years. I *can't* say no the one time they ask me for a favor.

"Fine," I groan. I quickly dig into my bag for a pen and grab a napkin from the dispenser. "What are the details?"

"Next Thursday, 7:00 p.m., Gotham Hall. I'll forward you the email. Oh, and you can bring a plus one!"

"Got it," I mutter, pen scratching over the brown napkin. "I'll make it work."

"Thank you for this," Steph says, a hint of somberness filling her tone.

My pen swirls between my fingers, and a doodled flower starts to grow from the napkin's edge. "Of course, I'm always here for you guys when you need me."

"And we're always here for you," she says. "Cool?"

"Yeah. I've got to get back to my coffee," I say.

"God-forbid your latte runs cold."

"It's a cappuccino today."

Steph chuckles over the phone. "Bye Ali."

"Bye Steph."

I hang up and slowly turn back to Jessa and Harley. Harley seems concerned, while Jessa has mischief lighting up her expression.

"Who's Steph?" she asks, with a sly smile.

"My agent," I say, tucking my phone in my bag. "And one of my best friends."

"What did she want?"

"To ruin my week." I tongue my cheek. "I'm now attending a gala next Thursday in the city, but I don't have a dress." I scoot my chair closer to the table, muttering under my breath, "Nor do I have anyone to go with."

"A gala? I didn't know you ran in such fancy circles," Jessa drawls. "You can borrow a dress from me."

"It's okay. I'll try to find one at the mall…" I grimace, knowing the nearest mall with suitable options is a forty-minute drive away.

"Nonsense," Jessa says. "That shit's expensive and I have the perfect one that I haven't worn yet."

"But you're so much taller than me."

"Easy fix." Jessa waves a hand in the air. "Ori can hem it."

"Is that the best idea?" Harley whispers, eyes going wide behind his glasses.

"It's time," Jessa says, patting his shoulder. At my confused expression, she clarifies, "Ori's our third housemate. He's also the proud owner of Curious Suits & Curiouser Tailoring. We'll pull a favor to get it altered for free."

"Oh," I say, grabbing my coffee and taking a sip. The milk has cooled to room temperature. *Bleh.* "You haven't mentioned him a lot."

Harley cringes. "He's sort of a recluse."

"More than me?" I joke.

"Putting it lightly." Harley matches my awkward smile.

"Is he also…" I waggle a finger between the two of them. "You know?"

Harley's cheeks tint—he flushes so easily, it's crazy. And it's such a pretty peach. He quickly diverts his attention to his sandwich.

"No..." Jessa says, though the word comes out more disappointed than firm.

It doesn't take a rocket scientist to catch that there's unsaid history to unpack, but I don't pry, giving them the same courtesy they have given me.

"Anyway, you'll take me up on my offer?" Jessa asks.

"Um, sure."

"And I assume your agent gave you two tickets?"

"Yeah..."

Jessa smacks Harley on the shoulder. "He'll take you."

"What?" Harley squeaks around a bite of his sandwich.

"Oh no, it's fine," I rush. "I can go alone."

"Alice, I've known you for what, three weeks, now?" Jessa says, hands pressed flat on the table. "That's enough time to for me to know you're fully capable of soloing it. But just because you *can* doesn't mean you should *have to*."

The words strike something deep in me, and I meet Harley's eyes over the rim of my room-temperature cappuccino. The red-brown color of comfort glows in the afternoon light, and they crinkle in that way eyes do when you smile only with them. A secret conversation floats between our gazes, it's a reassurance on his part, that if I said no again he'd back me up. At the same time, a laughable camaraderie forms as we weigh the trouble of disobeying Jessa's demand against the trouble of breaking free of our comfort zone.

"It could be fun?" Harley whispers.

It's the tentative hope lifting the end of his sentence that pushes me to say, "Okay."

8

THE TAILOR

ALICE

"His name is Ori?" I ask. The name rolls off my tongue, sweet in its shortness.

"It's short for Orazio," Harley says.

His shoulder bumps into mine as we walk down the street. He's got the garment bag holding my dress slung over his shoulder, and the plastic crunches with his every stride.

I wring my hands together at my waist. I don't know why I'm nervous to meet this mystery housemate of theirs, but my skin crawls every time I think about him.

"You all have very unique names," I say.

"As do you."

I puff air between my lips. "No, I do not. I'm a regurgitation of my mom and grandma."

"How so?"

We reach a strip of sidewalk that desperately needs a makeover, and I hop over the cracks in the stone, careful not to step on one. It's a strange dance, avoiding the idea of bad luck.

But I've grown superstitious in peculiar ways, and I don't take chances anymore.

Whenever I think of a car crash while driving, I tap the door three times, kiss my knuckle and lift it to the air, like some kind of prayer to a god I don't worship. When I see a coin on the ground, I always pick it up, because to walk away from fortune is ill-advised, but I put them in a jar that I never pull from, because what's good luck to me was someone else's bad luck first. And I always end conversations with a variation of my love, even if it's only a heart.

I know that when I stop doing these things, that's when shit will fall apart.

The *one day* I fell asleep on the couch and didn't send my daily '*Sweet dreams. I love you. I miss you.*' text, was the last day *I* got a text back.

So, I avoid the cracks in the pavement as if my sanity depends on it.

"Alice?"

"Huh?" I glance up from the concrete. "Sorry, I spaced out."

"You're good." Harley laughs. "You were saying something about your name?"

"Oh, right," I say as we turn onto Arbor Ave and its smooth sidewalk. "Nana's name was Lacie. Mom's was Celia. Mine is Alice. Can you spot the trend?"

Harley hums, adjusting his glasses on the bridge of his nose.

"Think butterfly and flutter-by. Listen and silent?" I say, trying to guide him to the right answer.

It must click, because his expression lights up. "They're anagrams."

"Yep."

"I think that's cool. You don't?"

I shrug. "I go through phases. It's much better than being a junior, but it would be nice to have a name fully my own. I don't know, most people don't get it, or say I'm being overdramatic when I try to explain."

"I don't think that's being dramatic," Harley says, adjusting his hold on the garment bag. "Carving out your identity is hard enough as it is. I can imagine it added a layer of complexity to growing up that most wouldn't be able to relate to." He pauses, then adds, with a thoughtful smile, "Especially if they're deep thinkers and feelers like us."

I huff a laugh. "You know, only a few others have said as much. And all of them have become my best friends."

"Well, that's something to look forward to." Harley seems to grow inches as we come to a stop at Curious Suits & Curiouser Tailoring. He pulls open the door for me, though unable to wave his hand forward as he usually does. "Here we are. Ladies first."

In good humor, I roll my eyes, which makes his grin widen. "Why thank you, kind sir."

Stepping into the shop, I'm hit with the warm scents of fabric and leather. Sample suits, ties, and the works hang from dark brown shelves along one wall. Along the other, a large three-paned mirror stands around a circular alteration's platform. Next to that is a door to what I assume is a dressing room, and at the back of the shop, behind a large desk with a register on one end, is a standing screen made from the same dark wood as the shelves but inlaid with an intricate gold pattern.

"Ori!" Harley shouts. "We're here!"

There's a loud sigh, then a soft rustle of fabric. The scrape of a chair pushing back noisily against the hardwood follows. Strong footsteps echo behind the standing screen, approaching at a steady pace; only seconds pass, but it feels like hours before the man who makes them appears.

Gooseflesh rises on my arms, and I inch closer to Harley. There's a thickness forming in the air, an invisible fog of fear rolling over us.

Why am I *afraid*?

Nervous, I get, but *afraid*?

My throat bobs around nothing as a mountain of a man is revealed; black hair, expertly styled and long enough to softly curl around his ears, sits above somber navy-blue eyes. Strong features carve out a pale face like marble. His nose is set slightly to the left, a bump clear on the bridge, as if he's broken it before, and his jaw is lined with dark, neatly groomed stubble. He's in a simple shirt—a black short-sleeve that shows off thick, muscled arms. The material has a luxury sheen to it, as not to take away from the formality of the navy slacks it's tucked into. A silver-buckled black belt shines at his waist, and a matching watch glints at his wrist.

A dark, foreboding aura emanates from him as he stalks to us, dress shoes clicking with each step.

Without a doubt, this man is a predator.

Not in the will-murder-and-kidnap-you kind of way, but in the will-ruin-your-life-if-you-let-him-in kind of way.

"This is the friend you've been telling me about?"

I blink out of my daze, and the blood drains from my cheeks as I realize Ori's scrutinizing gaze is set on me. My head tilts back to meet his eye. He's massive, inches taller than Harley—he's got to be at least six-four.

Harley's hand falls on my shoulder and squeezes. "Yes, this is Alice."

Ori's expression darkens. "*Alice*."

His voice has a deep timbre, gravelly yet rich. It's the kind of voice you want to hear when you fall asleep, to wrap around you as a lullaby. But the way my name flicks off his tongue... it's rough, as if it tastes like ash to him, bitter and unpleasant.

Ori's intensity slides to Harley.

"Alice?" he repeats, my name a cursed question.

"As we have established." Harley huffs an awkward laugh and pushes me towards the door next to the mirrors. "We don't want to waste your time. We know you're very busy. So, let's get her into the dress so you can work your magic and then we'll be out of your hair!"

It happens fast; Harley flicks on the light in the dressing room, shoves the garment bag into my hands, and closes the door in my face, leaving me to stare at the woodgrain in confused stupor.

"Well, that was fucking awkward," I mutter.

I notch the garment bag's hanger on the hook sticking out of the wall, unzip the bag, and reveal the dress Jessa's lending me. Though, it's more like she's gifting it to me, since we're altering it to suit my smaller frame. It's a beautiful dark blue gown, with butterfly sleeves, a deep v neckline, and a full silk skirt. I can see why she hasn't worn it yet, it doesn't seem her style. Far too soft for all her sharp edges.

Harsh but muffled conversation filters between the angled slats in the door. I try to eavesdrop as I pull the dress on and step into my heels, but it's too hard to make out the words.

The hinges squeak when I exit, and I wince, hating how loud they ring out, cutting off Harley and Ori's conversation. I shoot them both a tight-lipped smile, bunch the dress's skirt in my fists, lifting the hem well-clear from my unbuckled heels, and shuffle over to the mirrors.

Harley's beaming expression appears over my shoulder as I step onto the alteration's platform—his pure awe reflected in the pane causes my smile to turn shy.

Ori joins him, though his countenance is much harsher. He's assessing in his perusal of my form in the mirror, with his arms crossed over his chest.

"Are your heels broken?" he asks.

My fingers clutch the dress tighter. "Um, no?"

"Then you need to buckle the straps," Ori says, circling me. He yanks open a drawer in the small dresser set next to the mirror, pulls out a magnetic tray of pins, and kneels before me.

"Don't be stupid and cause yourself to trip. You'll break an ankle."

"*Ori*," Harley scolds.

The tailor tucks a few pins between his lips and reaches for my dress. He tugs it from my clenched fingers, muttering, "I can't mark the new hem if you don't let go."

"Shit. Sorry," I say, dropping the fabric.

The dress billows to the floor, a web of wrinkles fanning out from where I fisted the fabric. Ori glares at the creases, and a long sigh releases from his nose—it strikes me as the kind of drawn out sound a brooding dragon would make.

"I'll have it steamed before you pick it up," he grumbles, then ducks his head to pin the hem to its new length.

"Thanks," I say.

I find Harley in the mirror and give him a *look*—the pinched-faced side-eye that screams *what the hell, dude?*

Harley mouths out *sorry*. Then, adds out loud, "It looks great on you, Alice."

"Thanks, Harley," I say, forcing a chipper tone despite the tension in the room. Harley's a sweet guy, but the man slowly marking his way around my ankles has me on edge.

"I don't think we need to do anything to the waist. No wonder Jessa never wore it. This definitely wouldn't have fit her right." Harley fills the space with his nervous chatter. "What do you think, Ori, doesn't it fit Alice perfect?"

Ori peers up at me through thick black lashes. It's a slow glide—up my thighs, to the dip of my waist, and through the center of my chest, where it stops. It lingers there, over my heart, where my rings lay perfectly in the V of the bodice. The lighting in the room doesn't change, but shadows overtake his expression.

My pulse thunders in my ears, erratic as I wait for him to ask about them.

He doesn't.

His perusal continues. Up my neck and over my chin, my lips, my nose—I watch him catalog each of my features with terrifying precision.

Then his gaze meets mine, and it's as if he sees right through me. My skin is window glass, transparent, and it chills, frosting over in the shadow of his midnight blues.

"Sure," Ori finally says.

It takes me a second to process the single syllable. But by the time I open my mouth to snark a reply, Ori's head is ducked and refocused on his job.

Sure. I scoff internally.

Sure. I roll the word, unspoken between my tongue and cheek, as he refuses to meet my eye for the rest of the appointment.

What an asshole. Can he not manage to be cordial to a customer? I mean, I'm not paying, according to Harley. But still. I don't even *know* him.

Sure. The word repeats, ringing in my ears. It's the most half-assed of yeses; the response you give when you don't give a crap but don't want to cause a stir.

Why does that one word feel like a rejection?

And more confusingly, why the fuck do I care?

9

THE FATED CHAMPION

ORAZIO

She's beautiful.

That's the first thing I thought when I laid my eyes on her again.

Why's Harley looking at her like that? was second. His dopey smile and too-honest eyes betraying his infatuation with the new 'friend' he made at the library.

This must be a dream was third, right as her name rolled off my tongue.

Alice.

Five letters that haunt me.

I'd recognize her anywhere, the broken beast inside of me screaming out at the whiff of her sugary sweetness that I catch in the air.

She's different than the last time I saw her, but only in the way age changes a person. Platinum bleached and toned hair has darkened to a natural, light sand, and soft curves have filled out her short frame.

If I were ten years younger I'd be happy. *Ecstatic*. Relieved to see her again, no matter the circumstances. But now?

Why the fuck is she in Meadowbrook?

Our brief exchange passes in a blur. Harley hurriedly pushes Alice into the dressing room, and I find myself clenching my jaw so tight that my molars might crack. My whole body, in fact, is wrought with tension. Every muscle is flexed. My knees are locked. The vein on my forehead throbs.

Years ago, I'd learned to accept things as they were.

No Alice. No Champion. No tourney. No crown.

I didn't like it. But I'd accepted it. There wasn't another option, at the time.

No Alice meant no future. Not at home, at least.

"Will you let me explain before you freak out?" Harley asks, suddenly in front of me. His wide brown eyes plead his case.

"Absolutely fucking not," I snarl. I already know what he's going to say, and I already know Jessa's the mastermind behind this bomb being delivered to my shop. She knows I have a soft spot for Harley, and she also knows I never would have agreed to meet with Alice if they'd told me she was back. I've made it clear that we were to move on from our delusional dreams of reclaiming Arcadia. "Why would you bring her to me?"

"I thought maybe you'd be happy," Harley whisper-yells. "Or at least feel the same excitement we did when we realized who she was. Jessa thinks that if we gain Alice's trust, then she'll be open to the idea of—"

"We have three months until our birthday," I snap. "And it's clear she doesn't remember us. You cannot possibly expect her to help if she can't even remember who we are."

"I know you asked us to stop looking for her years ago, but this is *home* we're talking about," Harley pleads. Lithe hands grip my biceps, giving me a gentle shake. "Arcadia needs you. It needs her. And she's *your Champion*, Ori. You're meant to be."

"No." My head shakes, and cruel, silent laughter huffs from my nose as I break his hold. "No, she's not."

"*Stop lying*," Harley says. A deep-rooted frustration cracks his voice. "I understand not wanting me, but how could you forsake your bond?"

A tiny traitorous needle of hope pokes between my ribs, threading through my heart.

"Harley." I sigh. My fingers itch to cradle his cheek, instead, I force my palm to rub over my own stubbled jaw. "That's not why you and I—"

The dressing room door creaks open, and the woman I once dreamed of knowing steps out. Harley immediately turns his attention on her, wiping away all his pain and worry in favor of a cheery smile.

More words are exchanged between the three of us, but it's a blur as I move on autopilot, marking Alice's hem at Harley's request.

But when my gaze wanders, stalling over her chest where three rings lay, the few stitches hoping to mend my broken heart rip open.

I've seen those rings before, on fingers laced together. My inner beast howls at the memory, and the wound in my chest bleeds as fresh as it did seven years ago on the subway, when I saw her with *him* and she didn't remember me.

No. Alice isn't *mine*.

Not my Champion. Not a future I can count on. Not *anything* to me.

I still alter her dress.

I don't want to. And at the same time, I do. My beast is desperate, and it will take whatever scrap of a claiming it can—to make something for her, and for her to wear it.

My fingers snap together, and my shears slice through silk.

I cut. I pin. I sew. I steam the wrinkles out and iron the seams between steps. I get lost in the monotony of stitches; it calms my beast some, just as my mother said it would when she first taught me. I check the length on a mannequin, and then I stare at it until my eyes burn.

I picture her in it, and I hate myself for it.

As I pull the dress off the form, I catch a whiff of her scent—vanilla and sugar—and nearly choke on it.

I stuff the dress in its garment bag, and in the throes of my roiling anger, I make Harley a matching tie with the scraps.

If they want to entertain the notion that she'll stay—that she'll remember who she is and suddenly accept a fate she clearly never wanted—then they can go at it. She's a waste of their time, and I will have nothing to do with it.

10

IT'S FOR A GOOD CAUSE, RIGHT?

HARLEY

We step into the venue, and I realize my tie is too tight. At least, I think it might be. Not earlier. Earlier it was perfect. But now? It's a noose around my neck. Or maybe the air is different in here than it was on the train?

I don't think that's right.

I'm flushed and fidgety, have been since I picked Alice up to head to the station, and I tug at the luxe fabric that Ori forced on me before I left. The tie matches her dress perfectly, and I'm 100 percent positive he crafted it from the scraps he cut off in alterations.

His curt demand to change had rung loud in the kitchen as I grabbed my keys and wallet.

You have to match, he'd grumbled as he rounded the island, tugged my old, green tie off, and replaced it with the new one.

Ori's hands are large, but his fingers are surprisingly nimble, and I had held my breath as they tied the knot around my neck.

There, he'd said as he expertly adjusted the fabric, thumb brushing over my chest. It had made me shiver; his voice always does. It's deep and rumbly and—

"Do you need some water?" Alice asks, tugging me out of my thoughts and to the side of the ballroom. She chuckles, glancing out at the overwhelming space. "Or is it the opposite problem and you need a drink?"

It's dimly lit, with pops of amber beaming up along the walls and washing over the vaulted ceiling. The charity's logo, made of crisp light, spins above the stage, and music drifts between the buzzing guests who are looking for their number in a sea of identical round tabletops.

"Because I think I need a drink, stat. Or should we find our table first? I hate feeling directionless in a sea of people," Alice adds on a murmur, pressing close to my side.

"Same," I say. "Let's do that."

"Which one?" Alice's eyes crinkle with humor.

I quickly scan the room and catch a line forming at a high-top bar on the other end. I point to it. "Bar first. We can scope out how the tables are numbered on the way."

Alice spins towards the bar, her dress fluttering with the sharp action. "Smart. No wonder Jessa volunteered you."

She grabs my hand, pancaking our palms together, and tugs, whisking me across the fancy carpet. My breath stalls in my lungs, as it does every time she touches me.

A man in all black, clearly staff, rushes past us at a brisk pace, harshly whispering into a headset. "What do you mean you *lost* Dr. Steier? She's ninety years old and uses a cane. She can't possibly have disappeared that quickly."

"That doesn't sound good," I murmur, and Alice snorts.

"She's hard to keep in one place for long." She wiggles her fingers at her temple. "Artist brain."

"You know who he was talking about?" I ask as we reach the bar, leaning in close so she can hear me over the music and chatter. While the height difference between us is offset by her heels, I'm still taller than her. "She sounds important."

"Yeah, Dr. Steier's one of the co-founders of the charity. Always makes a big speech to kick things off."

My face pinches in confusion. "I didn't realize you'd been to this before. I thought we were here in place of your agent?"

Alice's hand tightens around mine; I don't know if she realizes she hasn't let go yet, but I leave it be. I enjoy the easy lacing of our fingers.

"Yeah, I stopped coming a couple of years ago," Alice says, clearing her throat. "It was an excuse to travel home and see everyone, you know? But then I missed one because of a move, and after that I never made it back."

"Wait, you used to live here?" I ask.

Her hand, manicured for the first time since she moved here, scratches at her neck. Alice's curls are pinned in a messy chignon at the base of her skull, and it leaves the pale expanse exposed. Red lines of irritation form in the wake of her nails.

"Yep, I grew up in the city," she says.

"You were that close?" I whisper.

"Sorry?"

"To your grandma, I mean," I stumble. "Only a train ride away from Meadowbrook?"

Was she truly only a two-hour train ride away this whole time?

"Oh. Yeah. I used to spend summers out in Meadowbrook, but that stopped in middle school. I was too ambitious in my extra-curricular activities and got busy—dual art and sports hobbies did not make for a lot of free time," Alice says with an awkward chuckle. "I actually benefitted from one of the community programs this charity started. Dr. Steier is part of why I went to college where I did. She taught there. Got her hands in everything, that woman..."

Her voice trails off as we make it to the front of the line and place our orders with the bartender. Her hand finally releases mine, and my palm mourns the loss of her heat.

As much as I'd like to *think* we know Alice, the truth is that there's two thirds of her life we know nothing about. A few weeks of fast friendship and tentative flirtation, however pleasant, is nothing in comparison to nearly twenty years of absence.

The watch on my wrist ticks, and while it shouldn't be possible, I feel each click of the second hand in my bones. Time isn't on our side. We only have until August...

Alice gets some mixed drink off the specialty menu listed on an acrylic stand and I opt for a rum and coke. We clink our glasses and take a sip of our respective drinks—our lips both twisting at the strength.

"Okay. I see how it is. Get the guests drunk so their wallets get loose," I tease, shaking off the burn of liquor in my throat.

"Shhh, don't reveal their secrets. It's for a good cause," Alice snickers. The lights dim and brighten three times in quick succession, a signal to get to our table. "Let's find our seats. It's so awkward walking between the tables once speeches start."

Alice grabs my hand again, and my heartbeat thunders in my chest. We weave between the other scrambling patrons until we find our table, which is already full, save for two empty seats meant for us.

I place my drink on the table before I pull out Alice's chair for her. Her lips twist, and now I recognize the pucker for the hidden smile it is. Her eyes roll, but she accepts, and takes her seat gracefully.

"Alice? That you?" A man across the table laughs, an obnoxiously haughty *ha-ha,* as he leans forward to dramatically squint at her.

He stands, rounding the table to lean in and kiss Alice on her cheeks the way fancy people do in movies. A frown pulls at my lips as his hand falls to the top of Alice's chair and he hunches to chat, crowding her in. I'm not usually the territorial type, that's more Ori or Jessa's thing, but this man's proximity to my... *date*... has my hackles rising.

"I was expecting Steph and Erica to roll in fashionably late," the man says.

Alice smiles up at him, but the polite dimple in her cheek divulges her discomfort. I've seen her real smiles. This isn't one of them.

"Flight issues with their vacation, so she called in the cavalry. How have you been, Chad?" Alice asks.

Chad. If the man hadn't already set my jaw to grind mode, his name would. Chad sounds like a player. And based on how *his* date is sourly staring at Alice from across the table, I'd be correct.

"Oh, you know, the usual," he says, slimy businessman gaze sliding to me. "You finally ditch the guard dog from college?"

Alice stiffens, leaning away from him. "I'm sorry?"

Chad's head jerks at me. "He seems much more your type."

There's a singular beat of silence. I can't see Alice's face, but I don't need to. At her edges, the air vibrates with anger. Sometimes, emotions are so strong they can saturate the world around a person.

"Actually, my *husband* is deployed right now, so my friend kindly offered to accompany me," Alice says.

At the same time Chad's expression drops, my gut sinks.

Husband?

In an act of godly timing, the conversation is cut off by the lights dimming completely and a video rolling on the projectors next to the stage. Chad quickly ducks low and slinks to his seat.

"Asshole," Alice mutters under her breath.

She slides her chair closer to the table and grabs her drink, downing it one go. She casts me a nervous glance, and I try to act natural in return.

Calm. Cool. Collected.

Not totally freaking out.

Pretending that what she just said isn't sending me into a spiral of epic proportions—pretending as if I didn't hear it at all.

Alice's attention shifts to the stage, where an ancient woman—Dr. Steier I presume—drones on thanking tonight's sponsors.

I sneak glimpses of Alice throughout the fanfare; I analyze the tight set of her jaw, her fingers tapping at her glass and the lack of a ring on the fourth finger of her left hand.

There are no rings at all, not on her fingers. But there are around her neck.

A single chain, from which three rings dangle. Two simple platinum bands of different sizes, and one with three tiny diamonds embedded in it.

She wears them all the time—never hiding them—though they often go unseen past the neckline of her shirts. I'd assumed they were her parents' rings, or her Nana's, or simply an artistic fashion choice. Artists are eclectic like that, *right*?

How stupid was I, to not consider the obvious?

The thoughts are a storm rattling my brain as Dr. Steier finishes her speech.

Is she still married? If so, where is he? Is he military and deployed, like she said? Or it is that she's divorced and doesn't want to admit it?

No. You don't wear three rings around your neck if you're divorced.

Fuck.

I think I've figured out what's haunting our Champion.

I grab my rum and coke and drink deep.

WE'VE HAD TOO much to drink.

We stumble down the stairs of Track Fifteen in Penn Station and jump through the first train door we see. Alice limps towards the center of the car, where she falls into the four seats that face each other. We're on one of the last trains home, and this line isn't as popular as others, so we're in the clear to commandeer all four.

"God, my feet are killing me," Alice groans, throwing her feet onto the green and blue plastic cushion across from her. She tosses her purse onto the seat and throws her forearm over her eyes in dramatic fashion. "I definitely have popped blisters on my ankles, but I don't want to look at the carnage."

Chuckling, I brace a hand against the shelf that runs along the top of the car and step over Alice's extended legs. I rid myself of my suit jacket, tossing it onto her purse, and quickly loosen my tie, adding that to the pile too. My fingers stop after two buttons of my shirt pop open. *There.* Now my flushed skin can breathe.

"Never again," Alice mutters. "Next time I need to go somewhere fancy, I'm wearing flats. Or I'll bring emergency socks in my purse like we're at a middle school dance. I don't care how stupid it looks."

I worry my lip, holding back my amusement as I dig in my pocket. Tucked where my cash used to live in my wallet are a few bandages.

"Here," I say, plopping onto the seat across from her. I grab one of her feet and pull it into my lap. Alice squeaks, hands bracing against the cushion as if she's been knocked off kilter. "I have bandages. *And* they're the hydrocolloid ones."

"Oh?" Alice says, eyes wide and cheeks flush. "So swanky."

"More like prepared. Though, I must give credit where it's due—Jessa slipped me these before I left."

"*Ah.* That tracks."

"Yeah?"

"She needs to be in control even when she's not here," Alice snickers.

I huff a silent laugh through my nose, shaking my head. She's not wrong.

I push Alice's dress past her ankle, my finger brushing over the smooth skin of her calf. She flinches, pulling back.

"I can take them off—"

"Nope." My fingers wrap around her ankle firmly. "Let me help you." I peer at her over the rim of my glasses. "I want to help you."

The icy blue shock in her irises melts into vibrant glacial waters. She relaxes, and her foot settles in my lap.

"Okay," she whispers.

"This is the eleven-eleven train to Meadowbrook, stopping at Woodside, Jamaica, New Hyde Park, Mineola..."

The conductor drones on in their heavy accent, and I resume my work, deftly unbuckling the strap of Alice's heel and sliding it off her foot. It gets tossed onto my suit jacket, the pile of our belongings slowly growing.

My fingers caress the top of her arch and trail up to the harsh, red indents around her ankle. I rub them away. Slowly. Methodically. And when my hand naturally slips higher, thumb massaging into her calf, her sharp intake of breath has my lips twitching.

"Are you ticklish?" I ask.

"Not particularly," Alice rasps.

Her skin is smooth and warm, and I'm tempted to reach higher. I would give her whole body a rub down if she asked—but she didn't, so I make my descent back to her wounded heel.

"Please stand clear of the closing doors."

The train beeps three times and its doors slide closed. The car jerks into motion as I rip open the bandage. I twist her foot to reveal the broken blister, and gently place the bandage over the exposed, raw skin.

I take my time repeating my actions on her other foot, and once I'm done, I pull her dress skirt back into place and pat her shins.

"There," I say.

"Thank you," she says, softly.

The train rumbles, and we stare at each other, lingering in the intimate moment. A melancholic longing shines in her expression, and I wish to wipe my thumb over the glistening tear track that cuts through her blush. It's a devastating sight—raw in its realness.

When did she start to cry, and why is it that something as simple as me placing bandages on her wounds pulls such emotion from her?

What has happened to this woman, that she carries such a heavy weight?

Alice's tongue darts out to trace along her bottom lip. She looks as if she wants to say more, brows pinched, but the loud squeak and slam of the train car door interrupts her. One of the conductors clamors down the aisle, keys jangling from his belt.

"Tickets please," he says.

Alice pulls her feet from my lap and shows him our tickets on her phone. He clicks his hole-punch on a strip of paper and notches it at the top of our seats, judging us with a deadpan stare. He tongues his cheek but doesn't say anything more as he turns to leave. The metallic slam of the train door closing behind him sounds like punctuation, ending the quiet moment he walked in on.

My buzz makes me brave, and I decide that now is a better time than any to ask the question that's been on my tongue since we sat down at the gala.

"Alice?"

"Yeah?"

"Why do you wear those rings as a necklace?"

Alice sighs, head falling forward. It hangs low as she stares at her lap, and her fingers lace together. Her thumbs circle each other, as if she's soothing herself.

"About that," she says, voice attempting to be light and airy, but coming out rasped. "I didn't move to Meadowbrook because my grandma died. At least, not completely." Alice lifts her head, but her attention strays out the window, and her reflection overlays the blurred backdrop of sleeping neighborhoods. "I was married—am married? I don't know. Becoming a widow at twenty-seven was confusing. The government considers me single during tax season now but it's not like I chose to be apart from him."

"I'm sorry," I say. I don't know what else to say in response to this information.

Jessa is going to freak. Ori... I don't want to be near Ori when he finds out. We care for her, but their bond is different, and now it's infinitely more complicated.

I just won't say anything. It isn't my secret to tell.

There, problem solved.

"It's okay," Alice says, as if it's instinct to placate others of her pain. "Well, it's not, but you know what I mean. Saying thank you to pity never sits right."

"I don't pity you, Alice. But I do feel like an asshole for coming onto you like we have."

She releases the window from her somber gaze and turns to me with a quirked brow, studying me like she does the art books she flicks through at the library.

"Flirting won't kill me," she deadpans. "Nor will it summon Ryan's ghost, if you're worried about being haunted."

I blink at her, and it takes me a second to realize she's trying to crack a joke.

"Are you joking with me right now?" I ask, needing to be sure.

"Half joking and half serious," she says, a sad smirk tilting her lips. Alice moves, switching from sitting across from me to next to me. Her hip bumps into mine, our thighs flush. Her head brazenly drops onto my shoulder, and my body stiffens. "If I wasn't okay with it, I'd say so."

"Why didn't you say something before?" I whisper into her crown.

"Why didn't Jessa say you two were together before asking me to the beach?" she volleys back. "Some things you just need to work up to." Her shoulder rubs against mine as she shrugs. "People get weird about grief. Then they get tired of it. I liked that you didn't know," she whispers. "Promise me you won't get weird?"

"I promise," I say without hesitation. I would certainly try my best.

A beat passes between us, and we make it through two stops before Alice breaks the silence.

"You're not going to ask how he died?"

"No, you don't have to tell me," I say. "I rush a lot of things in life, Alice, but I want to take my time getting to know you."

"That's not the response I expected. Others ask." Alice yawns, and her feet brace against the seat across from us as she curls into my body heat.

"We don't have to keep talking," I say. "About that or in general. You can close your eyes if you're tired. I'll wake you when we have to switch trains."

Alice yawns again, this one more drawn out.

"Thanks, Harley," she says, and the somber tone doesn't make it sound like she's thanking me for being her personal pillow or alarm clock. It sounds like she's thanking me for not prying.

It's confusing, because everyone deserves patience and understanding. Especially when it comes to death.

I can only hope she'll give us the same when it's time.

My lips find her crown, and I gently place a chaste kiss atop it. "Not something you need to thank me for, Alice."

11

MAGIC ISN'T REAL...

ALICE

Harley walks me to my door. He doesn't have to, but I've learned that's simply who he is: a gentleman. He chooses to do the little things for those around him, not out of obligation or for optics, but because he wants to.

He's entirely too considerate for his own good.

Our shoulders brush as our feet crunch over the gravel driveway. Well, his dress shoes crunch over the gravel—my bare feet make no noise as they tenderly pad over the rocks. If you go slow, it's not *terribly* painful.

That piece of wisdom can be applied to other situations as well.

A moth flutters around the porchlight, unfazed as we stomp up the old wooden steps. My toes curl over the coarse fibers of the welcome mat as I unlock my deadbolt; I'm slow to fit the key in the lock, hesitant to twist the knob and push open the door. If I do, then I lose this warmth at my back.

Maybe the alcohol hasn't left my system—despite the two hours that have passed since my last sip—because as I turn and lean back against chipped paint, a dangerous thought passes through my head.

What a terrible shame it would be, to have gotten all dolled up, and not end the night with a kiss.

Who am I and where has the half-sane Alice gone? Didn't you tell this man about your dead husband an hour ago? Why would he try to kiss you after that?

"Thanks again," I say, forcing a chipper smile on my cheeks. "I had fun, blips aside."

"Blips?" Harley's head cants to the side. His white-blonde hair, which was tamed for the event, now sits in messy waves under the amber glow of the porchlight. "*Oh. Those,*" he says, in casual realization. He closes the distance between us, and I tilt my head back to keep holding his gaze. "You're good, Alice. As I said before you took your nap, you don't have to thank me for being a decent person."

My lips twist. "Except for when you hold a door open for me, or pull out my chair, or put bandages on my blisters. Or when you walk me to my front door after a date."

"Of course. Except for then." A genuine grin shows off a row of straight teeth—his canines aren't as pointy as Jessa's—but it only lasts a second before it falls. His expression pinches as he asks, "Was this a date?"

My neck heats. "I'm not entirely opposed to the idea of it being one."

Harley's Adam's apple bobs, and I hold my breath as I home in on those pillowy lips of his. There's a sketch of them on my desk upstairs, but I can't remember if I captured the precise angle of his cupid's bow. Would it be considered research to request a first-hand account of their curve?

"Will you dance with me?" I ask, suddenly. His brow furrows. "These charity galas never have a dance floor, and I think that's a shame, because I like to dance, and we're all dressed up," I add. "It seems like a waste."

Harley considers me for a moment before his expression breaks back into a grin; it's so easy for him, as if a smile is the natural resting place of his lips.

"We don't have any music," he says.

I shrug. "We have the katydids and the crickets. Can't you hear them crooning for us?"

He hums, a matching sound to the buzzing as he gazes out at the night-shrouded trees that line my property. "They are fairly loud tonight."

Harley bows slightly and offers me a lithe hand, the action in line with the strange formality he often embodies. Our palms slide together as he pulls me flush against his chest. His other hand glides over my waist, and mine goes to his shoulder, fingers curling into his cotton button-down. We sway, and after some time, Harley begins to hum. It's a languid melody, nothing like I've ever heard before, but reminds me of a Celtic lullaby. With the backing of nature, his intonation creates a relaxing harmony.

I melt in his arms, lay my cheek on his chest, and fall into the sensation of his heartbeat thumping against my skin.

Too quickly, his humming stops.

"I really like you, Alice," he whispers. "I don't want to mess this up for us."

I tilt my head to peer up at him. "You won't."

There's a cosmic force at work here, pulling me to this man. He's impossible to resist. It's as if I'm a fish who was tempted by too-good-to-be-true bait and caught on a hook. Now, I'm being reeled in, whether I want to be or not.

To fight it would be to hurt myself, but to accept it would mean my end. It's a lose-lose situation. And I have very little fight left in me, anyway.

The meager distance between us closes, and I swear time stops. The second it takes for his head to dip stretches out and my soul disconnects from my body, watching as his lips descend... and hit my cheek.

His lips are soft, if my freckles are to be believed.

"Sweet dreams, Alice," Harley murmurs, his cheek nuzzling against mine.

I'm stunned still, but I can't even be mad, because the respectful action is so fucking cute that my throat swells with emotion.

"Night," I squeak out, gaze falling to my feet as I blindly grab for the doorknob. "I'll see you at the library soon. I'll text you."

I twist the brass, push open the door, and take a single step over the threshold. Except my foot doesn't hit hardwood—I fall into open space. My arms windmill, trying to catch my balance, but there's nothing to catch onto.

I scream.

There's a frantic shout of my name, though it warps in the air before reaching my ears, both far away and close as I plummet through a disorienting version of darkness.

I land softly in a patch of grass, somehow cushioned by the air. I blink up at the night sky; except it's not *Meadowbrook's* night sky. This one is decidedly vibrant, unmarred by a single cloud, and full of too many twinkling stars.

Am I hallucinating right now?

I roll over with a groan, and *nope*—my fingers dig into the signature texture of dirt and weeds. I'm in some kind of field, but I'm supposed to be in my house. My chest goes tight, my breaths not filling my lungs. Sitting back on my heels, I wipe my hands off on my dress and attempt to stop hyperventilating. But then the smell hits me—sickeningly sweet florals that make my head spin and vision blur.

"What the hell?" I mutter.

A thump sounds next to me, and Harley's body pops into

existence. He's quicker than me to roll over, scrambling to his knees and crawling to me.

"Shit, Alice, you landed in the poppies. Are you okay?" he asks. His head frantically swivels left and right, then locks onto something in the distance. His nostrils flare, and his skin adopts a terrifying pallor. "We need to leave."

Harley's hand wraps around my wrist to pull me up, but I rip it out of his grasp.

"Where the *fuck* are we?" I demand.

I scramble to standing, and the world tilts on its axis. Harley's lean yet strong arms are there to steady me, though I push him away.

"I can explain as soon as we get—"

"No. Don't touch me," I snap. "Did you drug me or something?"

Oh my gosh, is that her?

No, it couldn't possibly be.

It's too dark to be sure. But it could be.

The high-pitched voices rush my head all at once. Vertigo tilts the world, and I stumble again. Harley catches me, and this time I let him.

So few humans fall into Arcadia. Why wouldn't it be the prince's Champion? Don't be stupid.

I'm not stupid.

But you are doubting that it's her.

I squint against the dizzy sensation, head panning to find those behind the incessant gossip ringing in my ear. But through slitted lids, I note that there's only me and the man scooping me into his arms bridal-style present.

And flowers. A whole meadow bursting with them.

Who is that with her? The prince's friend?

Surely not.

When's the last time you saw him?

Usually, it's only the prince that comes to visit.

Or the damned cat.

"Will you all shut up?" Harley growls at the flowers, tucking me tightly to his chest. "You're overwhelming her."

A deep and dreaded sense of déjà vu washes over me. As if I've been here, and have heard these voices before. But that's not possible.

For one, flowers can't *talk.*

And yet...

So, it is her.

See I told you.

This is terribly pleasant news!

The queen won't be happy.

She may rule, but she isn't the queen until she's crowned. And there's still time yet until the tourney.

That's true. Do you think she plans to fight?

"Be quiet, or I will come back and prune all of you," Harley snaps, and he picks up his pace, re-adjusting his hold as he carries me *somewhere.*

I don't know where we're going—I have no clue where the hell we even are.

One moment, we were on my front porch, and now, we're in some kind of dream. Or a hallucination. Except his chest feels awfully *real* against my cheek.

A snort escapes me.

I'm going insane. Yep. This is it. The big one. The capital B-I-G breakdown. The one I don't come back from.

I've gone completely mental.

My body starts to shake, not from the cold of midnight, or from fear, but from laughter. Cruel, exasperated laughter. Because I'm not scared—I'm fucking pissed.

This is what I get for trying to kiss a boy when I'm still in love with the last one.

"We're almost there," Harley says. "Don't worry. Once we're back in Meadowbrook I'll explain everything—"

"It's fine," I mutter. Fatigue washes over me; it's as if I've run a marathon. Even though I haven't taken one step, my limbs ache. "You don't have to explain."

"What?" Harley's steps falter, but when they resume, it's gravel crunching under his shoes, not grass. I blink up at Harley, taking in his wild and panicked expression. "Do you remember now?"

"Huh?"

"Do you remember us? From before?"

"I don't understand." The words slur together, and Harley's face blurs, crestfallen. We ascend stairs, his footsteps creaking over carpeted wood now. I think it's my house, but I can't be sure. My lids are too heavy, and darkness closes in. "Remember who?"

Harley curses, but it's far away as sleep pulls me under. "I'll explain everything when you wake up. Just trust me, okay? Please trust me when you wake up."

12

...BUT WHAT IF IT IS?

ALICE

My subconscious has always erred on the vivid side. It's a blessing when I'm dreaming and a curse when nightmares creep in. Tonight, I'm somewhere in the middle, stuck in a purgatory of twisted recollection—lost in that in-between state of waking. My heart is fierce in my chest, pumping my blood with a panic.

I know something is *off*, but I can't place *what*.

I reach out. My palm slides over the foggy mirror of memories and comes away wet. It's me in the reflection, but not.

It's a cloudy day and children scream on a playground.

Someone dumped fresh wood chips beneath the swings and monkey-bars, and my nose greedily sucks up the scent.

There's grass between my toes, and they curl, digging into the dirt like roots at the edge of the action. I'm trapped, halfway between the kickball field and the jungle gym, unsure of where to go next.

Turn back? Go home?

It's getting late—the sun is at an angle in the sky instead of straight up—and I have to cover my eyes and peek between my fingers to get a good look at it. Nana would want me to go home. She's cooking spaghetti tonight and doesn't like when I'm late for dinner. But I don't want to go inside yet.

Going inside means that I have to go to bed, and that means Mom and Dad come tomorrow, which means it's my birthday. It being my birthday means that summer's almost over, and that means school is starting soon, and the kids at school are mean...

If I just stay here, then tomorrow won't come.

I wander across the field to where the nature preserve starts, plopping myself under the big tree—the one that's marked all over with carved hearts and initials. It's nice and cool here in the shade, and it gives my sweaty skin a chance to dry. The leaves are a pretty canopy, and they allow me to stare straight into the beams of sunlight without my eyes going splotchy.

A little longer outside will be fine. Nana won't mind. We live down the street anyway.

I close my eyes, and wish. Wish and wish and wish.

Can the sun slow down so today doesn't have to end? I like it here: where there are views other than skyscrapers; being close to the beach and the salty air that makes my nose tickle; with paint stuck under my fingernails from when Nana decided it was time for me to try out acrylics in her studio.

Can time just stop. Please?

"Who are you?"

My eyes snap open, but it's hard to make out the silhouette of the boy standing in front of me. He shuffles nervously from foot to foot at the edge of the shade, like he's got too much energy to spare and doesn't know what to do with it.

"Who are you?" I huff. "I'm trying to relax here."

"I-I'm sorry," the boy stutters, stepping back. He's flooded with sunlight, revealing his own perplexed expression. "I didn't mean to bother you."

My head tilts to the side, curiosity getting the better of me. "I'm Alice."

"My name's Harley," he says, pushing a set of thin wire glasses up the bridge of his nose. "I've never seen you around here before."

I shrug. "My Nana usually takes me to the beach, but I wanted to go to the park today."

"Oh," he says, face scrunching into deeper confusion. "But we're in the Meadow?"

He turns sideways to unveil a large field of flowers. They grow wild and tall, and I get the sudden urge to run through them.

"Whoa..." My mouth gapes open, and I scramble forward; my fingers dig into the grass and my knees scrape over the tree's exposed roots. I squint and shake my head, because surely, I must be dreaming. There's no more park. Just the flowers. They span the entire rainbow in color, and their shades are so uniquely bright that they're hard to look at. "That's weird."

A giggle escapes my growing grin. I've never been awake in a dream before.

"Anyway, can I sit with you?" the boy—Harley—asks. "My friends said they'd be back soon, but I hate being alone and the flowers are mean to me when they're not around."

"The flowers are mean?" I ask.

"Yeah," he sighs.

"Like cause of the pollen? And you have allergies that give you the sniffles?"

"No." His lips contort like he's trying to find a better way to explain. "You're not from Arcadia are you?"

"Clearly not." I shift into crisscross-applesauce, patting the ground next to me. "Might as well tell me about it while we wait for your friends."

He plops down, also barefoot. His soles are just as dirty and grass stained as mine.

"Well, I'm trying to memorize the paths, but the Wandering Woods make it hard. The trees like to play tricks and want you to get lost. But right now, we're in the Meadow, and if you go that way"—Harley points in one direction—"then you should get back to town. And if you go that way"—he points in another—"then you can go to the Lake in the Sky. It's kind of a pain, climbing up the ladder, but it's fun once you get up there."

Harley continues to tell me about a Dark Forest that's shrouded in night twenty-four seven, and the ladies who sleep in the clouds. Apparently, they're the ones who make it rain by crying. He explains all sorts of magical things, plucked straight from my storybooks at home, that I start to question whether it's a dream at all.

"Can you pinch me?" I ask, cutting Harley off.

He casts me a strange glance. "Why?"

"Just do it," I say, grabbing his hand and positioning his fingers on the flesh of my forearm. "Pinch me."

"Okay..."

His nails dig into my skin, and I squeal at the pain.

Harley yelps in turn, screeching out a horrified, "I'm sorry!"

"It's okay," I eek out between uncontrollable fits of laughter. "This is freaking awesome!"

He looks at me like I'm crazy but doesn't comment on it. At my insistence, he explains more about Arcadia—the realm I've somehow fallen into. We stay, tucked under the tree for another thirty minutes, until two other kids dash into the meadow.

And when he stands to meet them, offering his hand for me to join in their next adventure, I take it.

I THROW AWAY ALL my drawings of Harley. I rip the pages from their sketchbooks, ball up the loose ones, and chuck them all in a big black garbage bag. Said garbage bag gets tossed in the bin and set out on the curb on Monday morning, and I watch as the green truck gobbles it up at the ass-crack of dawn.

Ridding myself of the reminders of him hasn't stopped the

spiral of memories flashing behind my lids like I thought it would. They're pervasive, and they dominate my dreams, taking over the few hours of sleep that I manage to sneak in between re-runs of my comfort movies.

Memories of that meadow.

Memories of strange creatures.

Memories of *them*.

Except it wasn't them *now*, it was eight-year-old versions of them. Of us. Together. But that can't possibly be real. Because I remember what happened that summer. I *remember* that day.

I fell asleep under the tree in the park. I was *super* late for dinner. Nana freaked out. And she was about to call the neighborhood watch to start up a search party when I stomped up the porch stairs.

My phone buzzes for the hundredth time from its spot on the coffee table.

I sit up on the couch and swipe open my messages, teeth grinding at the unanswered string of texts from both Harley and Jessa.

See, the thing is, I could logic this all away easily, had I woke up the morning after the gala with two things: a glass of water on the nightstand and a bottle of Advil.

I could say what happened was a way-too-vivid hangover dream.

There. Easy. Done. No more mental breakdown over *talking flowers* and *other realms*.

But Harley acknowledged it. The text I woke up to from him dragged me to the cliffside, and as a result, I'm teetering on the edge of disassociation.

I *can't* fall again.

I re-read our exchange from Friday morning.

Hey, I'm sorry about how last night ended. I would have stayed until you woke up, but that felt like a breach of privacy at best and a creeper move at worst. Can I come over later to explain? I imagine falling into Arcadia freaked you out. It's a lot to take in, but it will make more sense if you hear the backstory.

HARLEY

> Did you drug me last night?

I had to ask, because it's the only explanation... except I know that it isn't. I've done my share of drugs in college, and not one has done *that* to me. Whatever *that* was.

And Harley was there with me. He... saved me?

The truth is there's no logical explanation.

No!!!

HARLEY

No, Alice. I would never do that.

HARLEY

Please, can I come over to explain? Or call? It's easier said out loud...

HARLEY

> I don't think that's a good idea.

Okay. I can try in text...

HARLEY

> Don't bother. I need some space.

Oh. Okay.

HARLEY

Are you sure?

HARLEY

I ignore him after that. Ignore everyone, actually, except for a proof of life text I sent to Steph. I think her and Erica can sense I'm not okay, though. But I don't want to bother them—and I don't even know how to explain what's bothering me.

The world is simply tilted off its axis.

I scroll through the unread messages that have come in over the past few days.

> I know you said you need some space, but I wanted to make sure you're okay?
> HARLEY
>
> Jessa brought home leftover pastries... Do you want me to drop some off?
> HARLEY
>
> The books at the library miss you. The art section is feeling a little unloved.
> HARLEY
>
> How are you feeling? Do you need anything?
> HARLEY
>
> Can you text one of us back so we know you're alive, please?
> JESSA
>
> I'm not joking around, Alice. Don't ghost us.
> JESSA
>
> Hey, I need to get the canvas specs finalized soon. Any updates on the big ones? Less concerned about the small boys. Also dying to see some progress pics...
> STEPH

Unfortunately, there are no *progress pics* to be shared. I no longer possess the sketches of my ideas to fake them. And I don't know what the fuck I'm going to do.

I toss my phone onto the couch and jab my fingers into my

temples. I need to get out of the house. My head is full of static and my thinking muddled. I need fresh air. And I need clarity.

My feet bring me to the park.

13

FUCK ME. IT IS

ALICE

Alone swing sways in the wind, the hinges squeaking like a metronome, and the yellow plastic slide of the jungle gym has lost its luster, streaked with black from too many sneakers scraping over it. No children hang from the monkey bars, nor are there any kicking up dirt on the baseball diamond.

Meadowbrook has aged, and everyone who would use this place with any sincerity has grown up.

Or left. Like I did.

The big tree is still here though, calling to me from across the field. With its wide trunk marred with lovers' carvings, it bumps against the nature preserve's thick brush, where weeds thrive and the tall, tick-filled grass grows.

I remember one summer we were obsessed with playing witches, and we'd pour potions at its base, convinced we could make the tree bloom roses despite the fact that it's a red oak. We'd pluck dandelion wishes from the baseball outfield and steal petals from the hydrangea bushes—but only the pink ones, *not* the blue ones—to mull with parking lot rocks and a splash of water from the drinking fountain. Our tiny hands would smear the paste on the roots like a salve, staining our palms in the process. The sprinklers would wash it away daily, a clean slate for the magic of tomorrow.

Sitting underneath the canopy of leaves, I rest my head against the rough trunk. I kick off my shoes and let the blades of grass tickle my toes.

Maybe it was happenstance that we chose *this* specific tree to anoint with our wonder. Or maybe we had conjured an enchantment with our concoctions.

I close my eyes and breathe in the morning dew. Could it be so easy as simply *wishing* to go there and—

Oh! She's back!

Is she sleeping?

I think so?

My eyes pop open, but I'm no longer in the park. A sprawling field of flowers extends around me.

I'm definitely not drugged or in an alcohol-induced hallucination this time. Which means I either fell asleep real fucking fast or this is *real*.

I pinch my forearm. Pain blooms between my nails. I wince, watching the blood rush back into to the two crescent indents in my flesh.

"*Fuck me.*"

My gaze scans over the Meadow—it's the same as in my dream, lush and full. The strong aroma makes my head spin, but not nearly as bad as it did last time.

"Okay. This is real. That's *totally fine*."

Why is she talking to herself?

Is she okay?

She's been gone so long. Maybe she went cuckoo like the queen.

Oh, I should hope not.

My head whips from side to side, scanning for the source of

the feminine voices. I scramble up to standing, brushing dirt off my ass.

"Hello?" I call out.

Is she talking to us?

Last time she didn't do that.

Just ignore her. If the queen finds out, we could get weeded.

Everyone threatens us with that.

But unlike the rabbit, the queen will do it!

I step forward, but suck in a pained breath as a rock stabs my sole. My shoes are nowhere in sight though, so barefoot it is.

Leaving the safety of the shade, I wander into the Meadow. The sun brushes my skin in warm waves as I stroll between patches of flowers, studying them with scrutiny. They don't look any different than regular flowers. Unnaturally vibrant, sure, and some of their petal patterns are ones I've never seen before, but it's not as if they have *mouths*.

I lean forward and whisper at a particularly garish bundle of coneflowers, "Can you hear me?"

What's she doing?

We're over here, dummy.

Shhhh. If we're quiet, she'll leave.

I pivot towards a patch of creeping phlox, aster, and milkweed. The wildflowers bristle when my attention sets on them, as if rustling in the wind—except there isn't any breeze to be found.

"How are you talking if you don't have mouths," I whisper at the blooms, but I get no response. "Hello?"

A bee buzzes, landing on one of the flowers.

"Can *you* tell me about this place?" I stare at the bee, who rubs his hands together on the petal's edge. When he flies away, I frown. "It's rude to ignore people, you know."

I straighten, crossing my arms over my chest and puffing out a sigh.

"It also makes me sound fucking crazy, scolding telepathic flowers and bystanding pollinators," I mutter, turning in a circle to study the tree line.

There are four paths that cut holes in the thicket, splitting the field into equal quadrants, as if the field is the center of a compass and the trails each mark a cardinal direction.

I should run home. It would be the sensible thing to do. But my curious muse screams over my survival instinct.

My fingers twitch with familiar need. Intrigued. *Inspired.*

How can I *not* explore a world made of magic?

I PICK THE WRONG PATH.

Technically, I can't be wrong, since I'd be lost either way, but fifteen minutes in and there hasn't been an interesting sight yet. There's only one line of winding dirt, about two persons wide, that stretches between the trees and wild brush.

It isn't until I consider turning back that the scent of smoke hits my nose. Not quite campfire, something earthier. It quickens my pace, and the first fork in the trail comes into sight.

I stop, pulling off the hair band that lives on my wrist, and twist it around one of the branches next to my current path; that way I'll know my way back to the Meadow.

It's only another minute of walking before the trail breaks, opening to a small garden. At its edge, on a wrought-iron bench, a gray-haired woman smokes. The joint is tucked between bony, arthritic knuckles, and she suckles it with practiced ease. Loose gardening clothes hang off her frame; dirty-kneed cargo pants are tucked into work boots and a weathered T-shirt shows off tanned arms dotted with age-spots.

"Hello?" I ask, peering around the trees.

The woman doesn't jolt in surprise. She simply turns her

wrinkled face my way, thin lips set in a neutral line, and cocks a single brow. "About time you wandered back."

My head tilts. "I'm sorry?"

She tsks, as if I've offended her. She takes a slow drag of her joint, and smoke puffs out her nose before she speaks.

"Would you like a hit?" she offers.

"Um, what is it?" I ask, taking a measured step closer.

She scoots to the far side of the bench, patting the empty space next to her. "It's got a little bit of this and a little bit of that."

"Ah, I see," I say. "No thank you."

"You sure? Helps to loosen the joints."

"I'm okay, thank you, though."

A beat passes between us, one where I shift awkwardly in place and she stares at me with narrowed lids over navy-blue irises. She also doesn't blink.

Creepy.

I inch backwards. Maybe it wasn't such a good idea to explore.

"You look older," she says.

I pause. "You know who I am?"

"'Course. Everyone around here knows about the infamous *Alice*," she snickers, taking another drag.

"Do they, now?" I deadpan.

"My grandson made sure of that. Bit obsessive, that one."

"Okay..." I drawl, not quite following. "And where is *here*, exactly? I seem to have forgotten why I'm so well known in..."

"Arcadia?" The woman's brows hit her hairline. A rough laugh floats in the space between us as she shakes her head. "Of course you wouldn't remember, that's what happens when you're gone too long." She flicks ash off her joint and brings it back to her lips. "Human minds are so fragile," she mutters. Smoke unfurls around her in unnatural ways, curling down her frame rather than dissipating.

"And you aren't? Human, that is."

"No. Can't you tell I'm a shifter?"

"You look human. It's confusing."

"Less confusing than hopping between worlds?" she snickers. "I've been hiding out here, waiting for you to show up instead of passing on. You're late, like usual. Now, come sit."

My hands find my hips, and I chew on my lip. This woman is talking in circles. I'm tempted to turn around and abandon my adventure, but what keeps my feet rooted is the thought that this could be my chance to get some real answers.

This woman is the only person I've seen in this strange place, and she's got loose lips, *and* she knows who I am. That must mean something.

"Do you—can you tell me more about that? About Arcadia, and why I'm here?" I ask.

"I could. But I don't think the current *queen* would want that. She'd much rather keep you in the dark. Or better yet, away from here entirely," the woman mutters. A cruel smirk curls her lips. "Good thing I don't give a flying fuck about what she thinks."

"Who's the queen?" I ask. The woman snorts, and her throat must catch on itself because she starts hacking up a lung. I rush towards her to help, but she waves me away. "I'm sorry. I'm trying to understand. But I know absolutely *nothing* about this place outside of gossiping flowers and the fact that a man I went on a date with might be from here. I just want answers."

I groan, sitting down on the bench and dropping my forehead into my hands. A swell of emotion rises in me, irrational and overwhelming.

A comforting hand lands on my back, and my muscles tense. It rubs slow circles until I calm down.

"You can call me Memaw, dearie. It's what my grandkids call

me," the woman says. "Why haven't you asked that prince of yours for answers, if you're so in the dark?"

I peek at her from between my fingers, mutter an exasperated, "Who?"

"The man you're dating. Are you not with my grandson?" It's her turn to cast me a confused glance. "How long has it been since you were here last?"

"Um... from what I can gather, twentyish years or so?"

Memaw sucks in a concerned breath. Her hand leaves my back, and she settles against the iron bench.

"You're cutting it down to the wire then, aren't you?" she murmurs.

"I don't understand."

"To the tourney," she clarifies. "Arcadia is sustained on the magic born between an Heir of the kingdom and their human Champion when they compete in the tourney." She pokes a bony finger into my chest. "You're a Champion, Alice. This land calls to your heart. And you need to decide whether you're going to fight for it."

Memaw drops her joint onto the dirt, mushing it into the ground with the heel of her work-boot. I stare at her, slack jawed as she rambles on.

"There are always two Heirs. Two Champions. Usually, you come here when you're young to prepare. And when you're in your prime, the tourney occurs to choose who wears the crown," she explains. "But you changed things when you left. Your counterpart broke tradition, taking the crown before she was meant to. Now, the land is suffering. Arcadia is angry, and its magic is as volatile as its interim ruler."

"You must know that sounds insane. I'm not some kind of knight or hero," I rush. "I can't *save a kingdom*."

Memaw studies me with tender affection. "Can't you?"

The question is ominous in its simplicity.

"I don't know," I whisper. A shiver runs down my spine. I

have the awful feeling that there's so much more that I don't know—that I *want* to know. "I have more questions."

Memaw hums, but we're interrupted by a terrifying roar. It echoes through the air, and the woods rustle in response, despite the lack of wind. It's a whooshing hush, like the leaves are terrified of what the monstrous sound means.

I balk at the clear sky.

"They're fighting again," she grumbles with a scowl. "Idiots, the both of them." She pats my knee twice. "I think it's about time you get going, dearie. Ask that boy for your answers. I've got things to prepare for here. Seems we're having a tourney after all."

She stands, and waddles towards the cottage faster than I can blink.

"Wait—" I call out.

"Don't be a stranger!" she calls back, dismissing me with a hand over her shoulder. "Get going before they find you!"

Two blood-curdling roars rip through the air, and I stumble backwards before rushing down the path. There are monsters in the woods, and I'm not about to stick around and become an afternoon snack.

But when I reach the fork in the road, it's not the same as before. Where three paths once converged, there are now four.

Panic sizzles through me as I search for the hairband I tied around one of the branches, coming up empty.

I know, for a fact, that I tied it next to the path I came from, because I'm not wearing it. And when I'm not wearing it, it's in my hair. And it's not in my hair.

I press my hands to my curls, scrunching to confirm as much. More evidence resides on my wrist: the indent still fresh from where it once pressed into my skin.

Murmured curses fall from my lips as I fail to find my marker, again and again, until I've made three turns around the intersection.

This is fine. *Completely. Totally. Fine.*

"Left. I veered left when I went down the old woman's path," I whisper to myself. "That means I came from there..." I point at the trail. It's no different from the others, a dirt path two-persons wide and lined with weeds. "This has got to be it."

I walk. And walk. And walk, until I start to wonder if I chose wrong again. But it's like the woods read my mind, and the trees shift, the footpath opening up to a meadow.

Except it's not *my* meadow.

I freeze, one foot on the dirt trail and one foot in the grass, because I'm not alone. My instincts tell me to run, but my limbs refuse to comply. I'm rooted to the earth, locked where I stand.

The beast is massive.

Its white scales ripple as it curls in a protective ball in the grass, and the sunlight bounces blue iridescence off the natural armor. Wings bristle at its back, fanning out to span what must be forty feet before tucking tightly to its serpentine body. It huffs, and it sounds more annoyed than in pain as it licks at a wound on its wing.

There's a loud thump—I would flinch if my muscles would let me—as a mace-like tail flicks through the air and pounds on the earth. Cat-like, the tail seems connected to the beast's mood. It thumps again, the monster's frustration palpable, and the pointed barbs slice into the ground, pluming blades of grass and dirt.

A minute passes where I simply watch the beast. It doesn't notice me, and I'm sure it's because I don't breathe for those sixty seconds.

When oxygen becomes paramount, and my lungs suck in a single greedy breath, that changes.

The beast tenses; its head whips around, and all I catch before I cower behind the safety of raised palms and closed lids are a pair of furious navy-blue eyes. There's a roar, a rumble of the earth as it rushes me, and a gust of unnatural, blistering hot air.

I think it sniffs me.

My body trembles as its burning breath crawls over my skin. One—two—three counts pass, and the scorching presence disappears.

"What the hell are you doing here?" a deep, rasping voice growls.

My eyes snap open as a large hand wraps around my wrist, right over where my hair tie should be. The mountain of a man drags me into the field, and I stumble after his large strides.

"Ori?" I manage to choke out. I've only seen him once before, but I'd recognize his stature and dark tresses anywhere.

"I asked you a question. Answer it," he barks, head snapping to glare at me over his shoulder.

My shock at how this man can turn into a beast fades, quickly overshadowed by anger. "Excuse me?"

"How did you get to Arcadia? Did you follow me?" he asks.

"I didn't know what Arcadia was until ten minutes ago!" I dig my heels into the dirt, but Ori continues to drag me through the field. "Will you stop manhandling me?"

"No. You shouldn't be here. You need to leave."

"I want to leave, but I got lost." My hysteria grows, and I smack his veined forearm. "But I'm not going to let you drag me to god-knows where so you can fry me up with your dragon breath and eat me!"

Ori growls—but thankfully lets me go instead of continuing his game of tug of war with my arm.

"You shouldn't be here," he repeats.

"You said that already," I huff as I rub around my wrist.

"Because it bears repeating. And you don't listen."

Ori's seething, it's clear in the way his fists clench at his sides. Each breath he takes is labored, heavy, and full of rage. But *why* is he angry? And why is he angry at *me*?

Something primal bursts in my chest.

"You don't know me," I grind out between clenched teeth.

"I know you enough," Ori sneers. He storms away, hands flying to the heavens as he leaves me in the center of the clearing. "You can stay lost if you're so set on it. I don't care."

"Why are you such a dick?" I yell, running after him. "You were standoffish at your shop too. Terrible customer service. I should have left a bad review on Yelp." Ori casts me a glare over his shoulder. "Are you like this with everyone you meet? Or is it only me that's won the honor of your ire? Is it because Harley asked you to alter my dress for free? I said I would pay you."

"You didn't answer my question," he says, ignoring mine.

"Which question?" I loose a frustrated cry as I try to catch up to him. It's hard to keep his brisk pace; his strides are twice the size of mine.

"How. Did. You. Get. Here?"

"The first time or the second time?"

Ori halts at the edge of the clearing, right before a new path leads into the woods. He turns, slowly, nostrils flaring as he stares down his nose at me. "All of them. *Explain.*"

"Well, the first I fell, I guess? It was after the gala, and Harley had walked me to my door, and I must have tripped over the threshold or something because all of a sudden I was in a patch of fucking poppies—"

"How did you get back to Meadowbrook?" he interrupts.

"I don't know. Harley was with me, and I woke up in my bed as if nothing ever happened." I close my eyes and rub my hands over my face. "I feel like I'm going crazy here. Truly. I must be having a mental break."

"Unfortunately, you're not," Ori mutters, that deep voice of his rumbling through his chest. "And the other time?"

"That's this time." My hands find purchase on my hips. "I was at the tree in the park—"

Ori grunts, as if to tell me to hurry up.

My tongue violently pokes my cheek. "I closed my eyes and when I opened them I was here again. Same place, with the stupid talking flowers..." Ori's unwavering, impatient stare warns me off from rambling. "And then I got lost trying to get back and somehow found you. And now we're here."

Ori sighs. His gaze darts to the woods behind him, dark and menacing.

"Arcadia's calling to you," he says. The same haunting words the old woman murmured.

"Yeah, I'm going to need a little more detail than that, Beast."

His attention whips to me, and it lashes my nerves. "*Beast*?"

"Isn't that what you are? All growly and brooding and asshole-ish?" I ask, crossing my arms. We have a standoff of sorts, glowering at each other. I'm the one to break. "Do you even know how to get me back to Meadowbrook?"

"Of course. The Wandering Woods are dangerous, and their paths change every day, but it likes me, and I've memorized the combinations."

"Amazing," I say, with all the sarcasm I can cram into three syllables. I wave my hand at the path behind him. "Can I trust you to lead me out of here, then?"

There's one hesitant second of consideration on his part.

"You can trust that I don't want you here," Ori says, pivoting on his heel and storming down the trail.

"That's clear," I mutter under my breath.

We travel in tense silence, my focus entirely on not tripping over a stray root or puncturing my sole on a sharp rock. Somehow, in a short five minutes, we're back in the meadow I recognize.

The red oak, identical to the one in Meadowbrook Park, looms at the center. Is it the tree itself that is a gateway, or is a stranger magic at work?

When the quiet becomes unbearable, and we're ten feet

from the tree, I speak. "Are you going to explain any of this to me or no?"

"No."

"Why not?"

"Because I don't want to." Ori takes a deep breath. "Don't come back here."

My teeth grind. "Who put that stick up your—"

Ori doesn't let me finish my sentence. His large hand lands on my lower back, pressing forward with unnatural strength. I trip over one of the tree's gnarled roots and fall.

Like the night of the gala, I don't land where I think I will. The world shifts as I blink, and my ass hits the dirt of Meadowbrook Park.

14

EXPLAIN

ALICE

Waves crash into my shins. Foamy white bubbles pop against my skin and spray salty droplets up my thighs.

The ocean has always been a place of solace for me in the same way art has. It quiets my mind until there's no anxiety left—until only the whooshing tide of emotion rolling in and out remains.

Sea grass sways in the breeze behind me; the rustling blades are a comforting whisper. I follow suit, gently rocking. An inch to the left. An inch to the right. Like the wind. Like the tide. It lulls me into tranquility.

I gaze out into the deep blue until my toes are pruned—long enough that the quicksand has swallowed me to my calves, anchoring me to the earth.

Seagulls' shadows glide across the water as they circle overhead. Their piercing caw breaks me from my trance.

Is there one specific way that you're supposed to react to

learning of magic? Of another world? Of a man who can shift into a beast?

How am I supposed to move on from this, now that I know? Am I wrong to be angry at the lack of information, rather than terrified of what little I do have implies?

I'm always so *angry*, underneath. I can only ever admit that to myself. It's stuck beneath layers of sinew and flesh, fortifying my bones, flowing through my veins. It poisons my breath, tightens my throat.

You'd think anger would make you hot. Ill-tempered. Brash. But it just makes me numb. The riptide of my bitter rage hides beneath a sparkling surface, and it lies in wait to drown me.

I've swam against the current for two years, and now I'm seriously questioning if *this* is what will finally pull me under.

Arcadia. Magic. Shifters. An old woman with ominous words, proclaiming I'm some destined hero for her kingdom. A man with white hair who makes me want to paint again. A woman who pulls a flush to my cheeks. A beast who boils my blood.

I cannot deny the fact that I *feel* around them.

I've given myself twenty-four hours to process my visit to Arcadia, but processing isn't helpful when you don't have all the information.

I drag myself from the water, dig myself out of the sand.

My journal lies open on my towel, today's page bearing a single line scribbled above a simple rendition of a wave in black ink. I close it and toss it into my bag. The pen follows, as does my hand, diving into the tote. The latter emerges with my phone.

My fingers are quick to type out my message. They hit send, pause, and add another.

> Can I swing by after closing? I want an explanation.

> Also, can it be just us? I don't want to see Harley yet.

It only takes Jessa a few seconds to reply.

> Door's always open for you, Trouble.
> JESSA

JESSA'S BEHIND THE COUNTER, a dishwasher crate balanced between one arm and her hip, as she places mugs onto the backbar. The bell above the door has her split-dyed ponytail whipping through the air, her gaze finding mine. I shouldn't be able to see her golden eyes from this far away, but they glint in the low light.

"Hey," she says with a soft smile.

"Hi," I whisper, lingering in the doorway.

She jerks her head towards my regular table. "Go sit. I'll be done in a second."

Jessa takes her time finishing her task, pouring us twin cappuccinos in the process. The air grows thick in the café as I wait, though it doesn't make me tense. Her lack of panic at my presence disarms me; her casual confidence piques my curiosity.

Does she not feel any shame for holding so many secrets?

The mugs clink on their saucers as she places them on the table.

"That was more than a second," I say.

She barks a laugh, flopping down into the seat across from me. "Fuck, Alice. You and Harley really do have the same sense of humor."

"I couldn't not take the opportunity."

"I know. I should know better." Jessa grabs my coffee and

takes a sip. An imprint of her lips, mauve pink, remains on the white ceramic. Her expression twitches with teasing mirth as she puts it down, then takes a sip of her own, making a matching set. "In case you think I drugged it."

Annoyance tickles the back of my neck. "I think that was a fair thing for me to assume given the circumstances."

"I'm not judging you," Jessa says, and it sounds genuine. She cups her mug with both hands and relaxes in her seat. "You have questions. I've got answers. Throw 'em at me."

My lips purse, and I stare down at my fingers, woven tightly on the table. There are a thousand ways I can start this conversation, but there's one question that's bugged me the most.

"Harley asked if I remembered him." I swallow the forming lump in my throat. "Have I met you guys before I moved here?"

Jessa adopts a strained smile. "Right to the killer ones, huh?"

"I wouldn't know," I say.

"True." Her feline eyes flick over me, assessing. "We've met before."

"When we were kids?"

"Yes."

"But it wasn't... here."

"No."

"It was in Arcadia," I say. A statement, not a question. "Which is another... realm?"

"Yes."

I nod, and my fingers unlace. I hook the saucer between my pointer and thumb and drag it closer. "Why don't I remember?"

Jessa's jaw ticks. "I don't know."

"The old woman I met said it's because I was away too long?" I half ask, half state.

Her entire body tenses as she leans forward. "What do you mean, old woman?"

I divert my gaze, following the curved edge of the pastry

display case. My stomach churns, a mixture of dread, confusion, and frustration curdling. All the events I swallowed at the beach come up, word vomit spewing between us.

"I had a dream about it, but maybe it was a memory? I don't know. I went to the park to clear my head and then I was in Arcadia again, in the same spot I was with Harley after the gala. I wandered for a while, and then I smelt smoke. There was this old woman and she offered me drugs—which I didn't take—and she said some weird fucking shit that only confused me more. I mean, it was crazy talk of princes and tourneys, Jessa. And who the hell is this queen everyone is scared of? Is she evil?" I suck in a breath, desperate for air. "And then I stumbled upon a fucking *dragon*. Did you know that Ori's a dragon? Is that why he's such an ass? Are there more of them? Are they all that growly?"

Jessa blinks, mouth parted in shock. I wait for her to respond, but it seems I've broken her.

Then, a conniving smile cuts her cheek as she lifts her coffee to her lips and mutters, "No wonder he's been in such a foul mood."

"Jessa, I need you to explain. *Now*."

"Sorry," she says, placing her mug down and scrubbing a hand over her cheek. "Let me start at the beginning." I lean forward, hanging on every word. "Arcadia's a realm where magic is real but doesn't always make sense. The flora and fauna are wild and wonderful, as are the people who reside there. And those people..." Her attention drifts off as she describes her home; awe and sadness buff the bronze of her irises. "We're all shifters, Alice. Everyone in Arcadia—at least, the folks who are born there—has a second form."

I nod, slowly letting her confession settle in my brain. "So, Ori *is* a dragon."

Jessa huffs. "Yeah. But that's not why he can be a dick. His parents were actually super sweet people. His Memaw too.

That's who you must have met—old bat has camped out in the Woods ever since her Champion passed."

I almost miss her use of past tense for Ori's parents, and I tuck away the nugget for later.

"What are you, then?" I ask.

"A cat," she says.

"A cat?" I repeat.

Jessa smirks. "Yeah, but a *big* cat."

"So, a tiger?"

"Of sorts. Our beasts don't always align with creatures from your world." She shrugs and takes another sip of her coffee. "We can't shift here, which is a bummer. Otherwise, I'd show you."

"That's okay," I say, unsure if I want to see her other form. Ori's dragon was unnerving enough. "What about Harley?"

"He's a white rabbit."

I snort, and her smile only grows.

"Fitting for him, right?" she asks.

"Yeah," I say.

We fall into a passive silence, and I take the opportunity to sip my drink. Jessa watches, gaze darkening as I latch my mouth over her lipstick stain. The bold espresso hits my tongue, and I swallow it back, letting it warm my throat.

Jessa continues her explanation, "Humans will occasionally fall into Arcadia. Sometimes they spend an hour there, sometimes a week. Sometimes they come back and only a minute has passed. Time doesn't always transfer over the same. Usually, it's no big deal."

"Okay..." Another gulp of coffee slides down my throat.

"You were with us for months, Alice."

I choke, coughing. My mug clanks as I set it down. "I'm sorry, I thought I heard you say *months*."

"Arcadia calls to some more than others, wants them to stay.

We call those people Champions," she presses on. "You are one of those people."

"No, that's impossible," I argue. "I would have known if I was gone for months. Especially as a *child*."

"I just told you the magic we're dealing with here doesn't make sense. Are you telling me there was never a day when you spaced out in a daydream and time seemed to stop? Or a day your parents swore you weren't in your room, but suddenly you were there, sitting in the middle of the carpet as if they weren't just screaming for you in a panic?" Jessa asks, her voice taking on a note of frustration.

I shake my head, but I immediately think of my dream. Of that summer day I fell asleep under the big tree...

"You're shaking your head, but you still believe me," Jessa says.

I stare into the foamy cap of my coffee. "I can't *not* believe you."

"I hate double negatives. They make my head spin."

"Sometimes they're more accurate," I say. "I can't believe you so easily. But I also can't deny the truths that are staring me in the face."

An ominous beat passes between us.

"You said I'm a Champion," I whisper. "The old woman said that too."

Jessa nods. "Arcadia has royalty. But the way they transfer power is different than a simple, *'hey kid, you're next in line, here you go'*. The family *always* has twins. And when those twins turn thirty, they fight for the crown in a tourney."

"Like to the *death*?" I balk.

"No, no. Not normally," she says, though the consolation doesn't quell my panic. "Heirs don't fight alone."

"Okay."

"They have Champions that are chosen by the realm to help them in the tourney."

"Jessa, I thought you weren't the type to play games. Stop drawing this out as if it's a CW drama," I say, though I've consumed enough fantasy media to see where this is going. "Are you telling me that I'm *the chosen one*?"

Jessa's darkly feminine laugh fills the room. "Yeah, Trouble, that's exactly what I'm saying."

"But how do you *know*?" I ask.

"Because you fell into Arcadia. And you stayed for a long time. And you and Ori have the same birthday. Champions always do. It's a marker of your bond."

"And how do you know *that*?" I ask, exasperated.

"Because you told us. And we had a party the second day you were with us. August twenty-seventh," Jessa says, lips curving around the rim of her mug.

"I don't remember doing that."

"As we have established."

I close my eyes, pressing my fingers into the pressure points under my brow. "So, Ori is... the prince. Of Arcadia."

"One of them, yes."

I suck in a stuttered breath, hold it for a second, and then let it whoosh out of me. "I'm going to leave this conversation with more questions than I came in with, aren't I?"

Jessa's expression softens with patience. "It's a lot to take in. That's why Harley wanted to talk in person. We're upending your life with this information."

"You're only upending my life if you're asking me to help." I swallow around the rising panic in my throat. "I assume that you want me to participate in this tourney? Was this all a ruse to get me to trust you all so I'd say yes?"

"I'd be lying if I said no," Jessa says, cautiously. "But I don't think it's productive to slam you with anything more than this right now. Take a few days. Let it soak in. Text me more questions as they pop into your head."

I down the rest of my drink. It's lukewarm now, the worst

temperature. Coffee only tastes good hot or cold, not in the in-between. The mug *clinks* as I place it back on its saucer, and the sound strikes fear into me. My teeth bite into my lower lip, chewing on the skin until metal blooms on my tongue.

"I think what I'm the most upset about is how you—" I cut myself off with a sigh. My voice lowers to a whisper. "I thought you both genuinely liked me."

Jessa's hand slides over mine. Her palm is rougher than it should be, small callouses dotting the flesh beneath her fingers. One firm squeeze makes my heart skip a beat.

"We do," she says. "Wanting you to help and wanting *you* are not mutually exclusive desires."

Oddly enough, I believe her.

15

CAN I PAINT YOU?

ALICE

Three whole days of nothing pass.
    I have things to do. A whole list of them that I re-scribble on a notepad each morning, as if doing so will trick my brain into finally ticking one box off. The issue is that they all require me to leave the house. But my mind and 874's walls are eerily proficient at convincing me that if I stay, then I can pretend anything on the other side of them doesn't exist.
    But that's not true.
    They exist. *Magic* exists. And the sadness that squeezes my heart when I think of running away from it all—as confusing as it is—is very much real.
    Harley and Jessa have become more to me than strangers, more than acquaintances, and I'm embarrassed with how I treated Harley while coming to terms with this new reality. Confronting Jessa was easy—her candor allows me to push my fear aside and match her frankness. But with Harley, it's different.

We're too similar. And like Harley had whispered to me on my front porch, I don't want to mess this up between us.

It's that sentiment that pushes me to talk to him, but I still struggle with the act of *doing*.

It takes me an hour to muster the courage to wrap my hand around the doorknob. It takes another to twist when my fingers meet the tarnished metal. And another after that to step outside.

But once my body makes it over the threshold? I'm free from the shackles of my anxiety.

Funny, how it's always like that.

The mountain of such a simple task can be torturous to climb. Insurmountable, as you gaze up at its peak. You chip away at it slowly, hour by hour, day after day, making vertical progress until you glance back at the slope and think: *fuck, I might not make it today, but turning around would be as terrible as continuing.*

So, you trudge on. Blisters on your feet. Sweat-dampened shirt sticking to you like a second skin. Sunburn tickling your nose.

Then you reach the top, and you think: *fuck, that was stupid of me. That wasn't that bad at all. Look at the view from up here.*

You smack yourself over the head as you sit, basking in the cool breeze of your accomplishment. And after you pick the flowers that only bloom up on the peak, you start the climb down. The journey is quicker on this side of the slope. It's easier too, but bittersweet—you skip down the cliffside with the understanding that the next time you need flowers, you'll have to repeat that whole process.

Again. And again. And again. And again.

Turns out, it's every day that you climb the mountain.

For getting out of bed. For walking down the stairs. For putting your hand on the doorknob, and again for twisting. For stepping outside, even when you know you'll feel better if you *just fucking do it.*

For the simple things that are now hard.

For the hard things that were always hard.

I stare up at the library's entrance, the proverbial tip of today's mountain, smacking myself over the head for waiting as long as I did to come here.

Time to pick my flowers.

Harley isn't at the front desk when I walk in, nor is he stocking the shelves of the main room when I drop my tote on the table I favor. I sit and wait him out; I know he's here. Jessa told me as much via text this morning.

I open my Renoir reference book and his trilogy of dancers stares back at me; in the city, in the country, at Bougival. It struck me last night, after I fudged another update for Steph. I'd torn apart my bookshelf in search of *anything* to give her, when I found *it.*

This was how I wanted to paint us: with me, slow-dancing on my blistered heels under porchlight. The memory of his hand on my waist is raw and speaks more of my vulnerability than of his. The picture is vivid in my mind, clearer than crystal.

My pen scratches along the paper, the fourth iteration of us in this notebook taking form with each hatched ink line. I'm consumed by the act of creation. The person typing at the computers to my left fades away and the air conditioning becomes a droning whir in the background. All my focus is on us. I smudge a blotch of ink with my thumb, casting shadows on the bottom of my dress.

"Alice?"

My thumb lifts from the page as my head lifts from its hunch.

"Hey," I say, a whisper of a smile in my tone. "Took you long enough to notice I was here."

Harley's pink lips part in shock at my snark before mashing together. Anxiety fills his expression. "Can I sit?"

"I came to visit you, Harley. Of course you can sit," I say, and he pulls out the seat across from me.

He plays with the rolled sleeve of his cardigan, thumbing the fold like he's unsure if he should cuff it once more or leave it be. "Jessa mentioned you might come by."

I nod. "I had a very candid conversation with her the other day about everything."

Harley's throat bobs. My gaze follows the pronounced tendons in his neck to the collar of his shirt; back up it roams, to his sharp jaw and around the curve of his ear, until it lands on his messy white hair.

He's so much prettier in person than in my head.

I'm still contemplating what undertones I should tint the shadows of his locks. Should they match the rusted-red in his eyes or lean earthy-brown, like the freckles that dot the straight slope of his nose, darker now than at the start of summer?

"And?" he asks.

"And I think I'm tired," I say. "And that I enjoy your company. And that I need to paint something for my exhibition."

His brows pinch, and I slide my sketchbook across the table. The clock ticks high on the wall, and I realize an entire hour has passed since I arrived; the air conditioning is on its break and the person who was clacking away on the computer has left. An intimate quiet blankets us.

"Is this us?" Harley asks, the knot of his brows tightening as he studies the sketch.

"Yeah. There are more in there, too. You can flip through, I don't mind," I say.

He licks the pad of his pointer finger before turning the page. His eyes flick over the sketches, and slowly, the crease marring his forehead flattens. Expression slack, Harley reaches the last one, and his finger traces over the dried splotches of ink.

It's reverent, the nimble caress, and I can only imagine how the paper feels, to be grazed in such a way. Cherished is a special kind of touch.

"You drew *us*?" Harley asks again, with different words, as if he can't trust his own eyes.

"I drew *you*," I clarify. "There are more. At home."

"Really?" It's an innocent, hopeful gaze that asks the question.

"Mhm."

Harley's attention falls on the sketchbook at my hum, and he smiles. A small one. Miniscule. The secret kind. The dainty stretch of lips over teeth you can't stop because it is pure, unadulterated joy.

I shift in my seat, apprehension climbing up my back. My fingers twitch towards the sketchbook, my nails hooking into the elastic band that wraps around the cover when it's closed. "Can I paint you, Harley?"

Shock is usually a gray pallor on skin, but on him it's two dots of peachy pink on his cheeks.

"Why?" he asks.

"Because I want to."

"Oh."

"And because I can't seem to draw anything besides you lately. And Jessa, a bit," I admit. "It's... been an issue since Ryan died."

Harley's teeth chew on his bottom lip. "Artist's block?"

I snort, but it's humorless. "Something like that."

"I mean, I'm honored, Alice. But this is not what I was expecting you to come here to talk about," he titters.

"I definitely want to talk about the other stuff too, *Mr.*

Rabbit," I lightly tease, and he cringes. "No? Not a good nickname? I'll work on something else then." I close my sketchbook and wrap the elastic around the cover. "Everything about you makes a lot more sense now. But I figure it's a deep dive best done in private. And I wanted to chat with you face to face first, to apologize for ignoring you."

"It's okay."

"Things between us feel... bigger, if that makes sense?" I ask. "I like Jessa, but it's easier to separate my feelings from the facts with her. With you—" I cut myself off with a sigh. "With you it's all meshed together."

"Alice—"

"I'm not doing a very good job of communicating right now," I huff, my hand coming over my mouth to hide my grimace. "I'm sorry."

"It's okay," Harley repeats, firmly but kindly. He leans forward, teeth nibbling once again on his plump bottom lip. "Does this mean we can't take you out on any more dates?"

My lips twist with amusement. "I don't think the answer to that question is no."

"I'll take a not no over a full no any day," Harley says, and I laugh, happy he understands what I mean.

It's a yes, but...

It's a door cracked open.

It's a let's take it day by day.

Harley tries to contain a beaming, hopeful smile, but it doesn't work, and all his exuberant light shines on me.

"How about we start with you coming over after work?" I offer.

"Like a hang-out on the couch date?"

I shake my head and stand, packing up my stuff. "More like an I'll paint you like one of my French girls date. With a side of twenty-questions."

"What?" His face pales, and his glasses slip down his nose.

"I don't usually paint with a live reference but since you're here..." I shrug and sling my tote over my shoulder. "Wear your suit if you can."

16

AM I A FRENCH GIRL NOW?

HARLEY

My suit is heavy in its garment bag, hanging over my arm as I press a finger to Alice's doorbell. The modern ding is sharp, cutting through the air with a no-nonsense attitude, which seems at odds with the house. The old Victorian, with its ornate white trim and eggshell blue exterior, would be better suited for something much less sensical.

The door swings open, and Alice's blonde curls fill the threshold. They're pulled away from her face, tied off with a blue bandana that matches her tank top. She prefers that color: blue. She's always wearing it, though the shade differs day to day. Sometimes it's light, matching her eyes, or dark, like midnight, but it always makes her skin glow.

"Welcome to my humble abode." Alice mocks a curtsy, waving her arm out for me to enter. "Or rather, my grandmother's. I haven't quite made it mine yet."

I'm hit with the musk of old house as I step over the

welcome mat. It's that heady mix of sun-bleached paper, damp wood, and potpourri.

Alice shuts the door behind me, and the click of her turning the deadbolt raises the hair on my neck. I shift from foot to foot, waiting for her to lead me through the house.

"Everything okay?" she asks, peering up at me. Suddenly, Alice looks so tiny. It can't possibly be more than an inch or two difference without her shoes, but something about her being barefoot has me feeling like a giant looming over her.

To be fair, I am eight inches taller.

"Yeah," I say, my voice cracking. I clear my throat and try again. "Yep. All good here. Do you want me to take my shoes off?"

A twinkle of mischief sparkles in her crystalline eyes; they always glisten when she's about to tease me, and I hold my breath with anticipation.

Banter is my favorite kind of foreplay; the tension of words volleying back and forth, the subtle power play. It makes my blood pump something fierce. But Alice's is different than Jessa's. Where Jessa is ruthless and sharp in her ministrations, Alice is playful, tentative, and exploratory. She doesn't dominate our interactions, she guides them. It's new, but pleasant, territory.

"I don't have a preference," Alice replies. I toe off my oxfords and kick them underneath the empty coat rack as Alice hops up the staircase. "C'mon. We're going to be up in my studio."

"Studio sounds fancy," I say, following. The stairs creak under my weight.

"I say studio as a loose term, even though this is the closest I've gotten to a real one," Alice explains. I run my fingers over the floral wallpaper as we climb. "Since we used to move to a new duty station every two years, I'd end up taking over the second bedroom in whatever apartment we'd rent. It was pretty bare bones. But Nana lived here a long time, and was an art hobbyist, so she left me an awesome set up."

"Is she why you got into painting?" I ask as we crest the landing and head down the hall.

"She taught me when I would come to visit. But I didn't consider doing it as a career until I was in high school." Alice pushes open a wooden door, hinges squeaking. "Here we are."

"Wow," I say, slack jawed as I take in the room. "Definitely worthy of the studio label."

"Right?" Alice's twinkling laugh rings out.

She passes me, stopping at a large sewing table in the center of the room to fiddle with a sketch pad. The table is similar to the ones in the back of Ori's shop, topped with pattern lines and ruler markings that make no sense to me. The base holds a series of thin drawers with labels scrawled in cursive, and beyond that is a smaller desk with a sewing machine pushed against the wall. A rack of thread is mounted above it, and stacks of drawers line the empty space on either side.

"Do you also know how to sew?" I ask.

"If I did, don't you think I'd have done my own alterations for the gala?" Alice teases.

"Oh, yeah. Oops."

"Unfortunately, that part of crafting did not come naturally to me, even with my grandma's guidance," Alice grumbles, mechanically ripping pages from the sketchbook. The rhythmic tear of the paper from the spiral coil pings though the air. "Would have saved me the annoyance of interacting with that asshole of a roommate you guys have. You sure he's a prince? I thought they were supposed to be cordial."

"Yeah..." I sigh, scratching at my neck. Ori is... complicated. And even I can't predict when his moods will shift from caring to coarse, or vice versa.

I meander deeper into the room. All alone, set before open windows, is an easel with a large, blank canvas sitting on it. A glass palette sits on a table along with jars of brushes and different liquids, a faint chemical pine smell wafting from them. There are studio lights too, plugged into the wall, but they're tucked in the corner.

"This is bigger than I thought it would be," I say, eyeing the canvas. "You're really going to paint me on this?"

"Yep," she chirps, though it's muffled around a piece of paper she's tucked between her lips.

I swallow the giddy lump that forms in my throat. When I said I was honored she wanted to paint me—*us*—I meant it.

I've always been a wallflower, looked over in favor of others. I'm not like Ori, whose masculinity seeps into his every breath. He's a warrior and a prince, and even when he's only this town's tailor, he breaks perception.

Nor am I as enticingly beautiful as Jessa. She's a siren, luring people into her vicinity with a few words and a ringing laugh. Back in Arcadia, she was on the path to becoming a beloved and charming knight for the royal family.

But I am... me. Awkward. Nervous. Always stuck in a book. Useful for strategy, not execution. Not a warrior. Not a shifter with a formidable beast. Not a predator.

Prey.

Only Ori and Jessa have seen me as worthy of something more.

But Alice thinks I'm worthy of being *painted*? Of being gazed upon with the intention of reverence and provocation? Of being turned into *art*?

She's gifting me the veneration of a lover—and she doesn't even love me.

I think I fell in love with her a long time ago. When I saw her sleeping under that tree in the Meadow, my eight-year-old self said *yep, you have a crush*.

I was devastated when we lost her. We all were.

And when I saw her again—when I scented the vanilla

sugar sweetness wafting from her pulse point and heard her name fall from those plump pink lips—those feelings came crashing back with unnatural force. They've only grown in the weeks since, as we've gotten to know who she's become.

"Most people are surprised by how big original pieces are compared to the prints we sell online. But scaling up is how we can pack in more detail," Alice continues, pulling me from my thoughts. She floats by me to tape two sketches to the bottom of the easel, then grabs tubes of paint from a drawer underneath her palette.

"I need you in your suit," she adds as she fiddles with her paints, blobbing colors onto the glass. I lay my garment bag over the table and start undressing. "Then I'll position you and set the lights," she continues. "The bathroom is down the hall—oh jeez!"

Alice drops the tube of paint she's holding, and I freeze with my pants around my ankles.

"What?" I ask.

She quickly bends to pick up the tube and promptly turns around, waving a hand over her shoulder. "Nothing! I wasn't expecting you to strip in here. Proceed."

My lips pinch together at her modesty, and I continue swapping out my regular work slacks for my suit pants.

"You've seen me in a bathing suit. What's the difference between that and boxers?" I ask.

"Other than the fact that your boxers are green plaid and the bathing suit you wear the most often is the brightest fucking fire-truck red?" Alice mutters. She mindlessly plays with her jar of brushes; her fingers twitch over the bristles in a repetitive motion, as if the action calms her. "I guess nothing."

My stomach flips at the prospect that I might make her as nervous as she makes me.

I finish buttoning my suit and snag the tie from its garment bag pocket, then approach Alice.

"Can you help with the tie?" I ask. "I suck at it."

"Hm?" Alice hums, glancing up from her brushes. "Oh, sure."

She rounds the easel, and I hand her the fabric. She has to reach up on her tiptoes to hook the tie around my neck, and it brings her body near flush with mine.

"How many pieces do you need to make?" I ask, distractedly, as she deftly knots the fabric around my collar. Tingles erupt on my skin at the occasional brush of her fingers on my chest.

"It's my choice. Usually, I have anywhere from ten to twenty," she answers. "But I imagine I'll be rushing to get ten done before my deadline in August."

"Will they all be of me?" I tease.

"Maybe."

"Wait, really?" I blanch.

Alice shrugs, tightening the knot around my neck with finality.

"It's entirely possible I paint you ten times and call it a day," Alice says, so casually. Does she not realize how that sends me into a tailspin of awe? She pats my chest twice, right over my heart. "All set. Now hold still. I'm going to pose you like my own personal mannequin."

She pushes me back a step, delicate hands wrapped around my shoulders, until I'm centered in the empty space beyond her easel. I bite my lip to hold back my laughter as Alice hops away, stares at me with her tongue poking her cheek, head tilted, and then hops back, adjusting me again. My arms are lifted into a traditional dance stance. My feet are scooted apart, then back together, then apart again. I'm angled towards the widow, and then away from it.

It's cute, watching her figure it out. I wonder what she sees when she looks at me—why does an inch to the right or left makes a difference to her brain?

She sets up the studio lights next, and I'm momentarily blinded by the pop of the bare bulb. A sheer fabric is draped over it, diffusing the light to her satisfaction and casting me in amber shadows.

Last, she sets up her phone on a tripod, facing us, and taps on her camera. The little red recording light blinks. And then she's slipping into my arms.

Her fingers fall on my outstretched palm.

Her chest brushes against mine.

Her waist settles into the crook of my other hand, and my fingers instinctively curl into the fabric of her tank top.

Her thighs bracket one of mine, and if either of us pressed forward...

"Harley?"

"Yeah?" My gaze is pulled from our intertwined legs to her face, and I'm lost in the smatter of freckles on her nose.

"Keep your head up like this, okay?" Alice asks, and I nod. She tilts her head to the camera, and hums at whatever she sees. "Don't move."

"Yes, ma'am," I whisper.

The muscles at her waist contract with a small gasp, as if I've shocked her with the honorific. Then her body turns to liquid, and she slips out of my hold.

Alice takes a measured step away, tilts her head again, and nods to herself. "Perfect."

Perfect.

Does she realize I would do anything she asked of me if she keeps purring praise?

She plucks her phone from the tripod and connects it to a speaker on the table.

"Is it okay if I put on music?" she asks. "It'll be low enough for us to talk, but it helps me focus."

"Of course," I mumble, trying to speak through as closed lips as possible.

Alice laughs, and scrolls through her music app. "You can talk normally. I only need your head angled the same way for the lighting."

"Ah." My jaw relaxes. "Can you tell I've never modeled before?"

"No, you're a natural."

"Lies."

"It's not a very hard thing to do," she says, pressing play. A soft guitar plucks a somber tune, and a feminine voice croons a few beats later. "You've been modeling for me for weeks without knowing it."

My tie is suddenly too tight around my neck as it blooms with heat. "You know if I was someone different, I might consider that stalker behavior. Always lurking in the library, watching me, pen scratching my visage onto paper..."

Alice hides behind the easel. "Sorry."

"Don't say sorry. I enjoy it, the attention," I admit. "More than you probably realize."

A knitted brow and two narrowed eyes peek around the canvas. "Yeah?"

"Mhm."

She disappears again. Her shadow stretches along the hardwood, and I watch it religiously as she pours a viscous liquid on the palette, mixes paint with it, and strokes her brush over the canvas.

"I don't know why I'm surprised you and Jessa are kinky," Alice says.

"I didn't mean it like *that*."

"Didn't you?"

I definitely did. "No."

"So, you're *not* turned on by the idea of Jessa watching us fuck?"

I choke on air, tears welling in my eyes as I sputter and cough while trying not to shift my pose. "Jesus Christ, Alice."

Tinkling laughter fills the room. "I'm only pushing your buttons. You're cute when you blush." Alice peers around the canvas again and winks. "And I need the color for reference. You have warm toned skin. Your cheeks get peachier than mine."

"Oh," I whisper.

Alice goes back to painting; one song ends and another begins, a deep masculine voice singing out this time, accompanied by piano.

"Are you guys Christian?" she suddenly asks.

"No." My brow twitches. "Why do you ask?"

"Well, you used Jesus Christ as a curse."

"Oh. That's just something I picked up here," I say. "Arcadia doesn't have religion the same way humans do. We believe in gods, but they're more a powerful species who wander between realms and wreak havoc than all-knowing creators. They're to be feared, for sure, but are not necessarily worshiped."

She dunks her brush into a jar of water, and the water clouds as she swishes it around. "That's comforting."

"Is it?" I ask, genuinely curious. "Most humans seem drawn to the idea of a god being their salvation. At least, from what I've read on the topic."

"I've never believed in any of it," Alice admits. And though her voice is soft, there's a bitterness clinging to her words. "There's too much horrible shit in the world for it to be true. Either there is no god—as in, no one omnipotent being that controls the universe—or they're a sadistic narcissist who takes pleasure in torturing their creations."

Her candidness is a cold and violent wind blowing through the room. "I haven't heard an opinion like that before."

"People tried using religion as a means to comfort me when Ryan died. It always left a sour taste in my mouth." Alice's shadow stills. "It was hard to hear people say he was in a better place, you know? Kind of like a big *fuck you*. It's not as if he was sick for years and suffering. Why would heaven be a better place than by the side of the person he chose forever with?"

Her brush strokes resume with increased intensity, and the song on the speaker changes to something upbeat and contradictory to the somber mood.

My lips part, but nothing comes out. What's there to say? Nothing I can muster could hold a candle to the weariness in her voice.

Alice breaks the silence with the clearing of her throat. "Why are you guys here, anyway?"

"In Meadowbrook?" I clarify.

"In this realm in general," she says.

I chew on my cheek, considering the right way to phrase it. Alice waits, patiently, and another brush *plunks* into her water jar.

"To find you, originally," I say. "Some stuff went down with Ori's brother and his Champion. After a while, we figured we might as well start building lives that we'd enjoy."

Alice pops around the easel with one hand braced on her hip; she waggles a brush at me with the other. "Are you going to elaborate on the whole 'stuff-that-went-down' bit?"

"Um, yeah, I can." I hesitate. "It's kind of a long story."

"Well, you're stuck here for another twenty minutes minimum," she says, a small lopsided smirk cutting her cheek. "No moving until I say so."

"Are you sure this isn't some new kind of interrogation-torture technique? My arms hurt already."

"Just think of it as payback for keeping secrets," Alice says, returning to her canvas.

A seriousness drapes itself over me. "I'm sorry about that, by the way."

"Apologize by explaining."

"Okay." I take a deep breath. "I don't know how much Jessa told you, but if you have a question—"

"I'll butt in and ask, don't worry."

My tongue turns to cotton in my mouth.

"We were eighteen when everything fell apart," I start, slowly. The memories flash behind my lids as I blink, sending shivers down my spine. "Most Champions are called to Arcadia when they're young. And then they end up living with the royals until the tourney that decides who rules. Not to be morbid, but the Champions are usually orphans or come from a bad home situation. So, it's not necessarily a bad thing when they just... stay."

"I wasn't an orphan," Alice states.

"No, and I'm glad for that. Being an orphan sucks," I say, knowing from experience. "But that isn't the norm. Ori's twin, Enzo, found his Champion, Maven, at six, which was also abnormal. She didn't have many memories from this realm, and from what I can gather the ones she did have were not pleasant. That's part of why things fell apart. She got it in her head that Arcadia was her home, which it *was*, but she developed a kind of... ownership over the realm." I sigh. "Enzo fell for her when we were teenagers. *Hard*. But that's often what happens with Champions and Heirs. You share a special bond."

I pause, waiting for Alice to react to that information, curious to see if she picks up on the mention of their bond. But she stays quiet behind her easel, so I continue.

"Enzo was always like a puppy, following her around. But as we got older, he changed. Maven was controlling. And she convinced him that they didn't have to wait until the tourney to take over the kingdom."

"So, she staged a coup?" Alice asks, catching on.

"Essentially."

"Did you fight back?"

I wince. "That's the catch. Special magic binds the realm to certain rules." My tongue swipes over my teeth. "We *can* fight, but dragons are powerful. With their human counterpart, they're even more so. Their scales are impenetrable to the average person—only Champions and other dragons possess enough inherent magic to pierce their armor."

A chilling breeze wafts through the open window.

"She killed his parents?" Alice whispers.

"Yeah, Alice. They killed Ori's parents." I close my eyes, trying to banish the scenes of carnage that ensued while we fled the castle. "Maven is a brutal warrior, and with no Champion at his side, Ori was at a disadvantage. Not only in the battle after the coup, but he cannot compete for the crown alone." I shake my head. "Ori nearly got killed trying to protect us. Jessa and I grabbed him and fled into the Wandering Woods to save his life. It kept us safe, guiding us to the Meadow."

I grind my jaw on the swell of emotion gathering there. "We hadn't been to the Meadow in years. We thought the portal had closed. But there it was, open and beckoning us to this realm. At first we viewed it as a blessing. We hoped we would find you before it was too late. But years passed with no luck. Jessa and I have kept hope, but Ori gave up a long time ago."

Alice sets her brush down on the palette, rounding the canvas to stand before me with her hands on her hips. She takes a deep breath and pushes it out slowly, puffing out her cheeks. "Okay, so what I've gathered is that this Maven chick is a raging bitch."

I snort, even though it's not funny. "She is."

"And Enzo sounds just as terrible, if not worse." Her gaze hits the floor with a sigh, and a million questions flash across her conflicted expression. "I don't remember much from when we were kids, Harley."

"Do you want me to tell you?" I ask, tentatively.

"Maybe. But not all at once. And not today," she says, looking back up at me, with a small, sad smile. "Are you and Jessa *sure* that I'm Ori's Champion? He and I have gotten off on the wrong foot and you make it sound like we're prophesized to fall in love or something."

"While it's common for Heirs to form romantic connections with their fated, it's not *mandatory*. Many simply have strong friendships, like a platonic soul-mate," I say, quoting a book I once read in the castle library on the topic. When we lost Alice, research on the Champions was all I could do to help. "Though it's his loss if he can't see how amazing you are."

Alice quirks a skeptical brow. "And *that* makes is sound like you want to add him to this polycule situation you and Jessa are pursuing with me."

"Well, yeah," I admit. Her brows hit her hairline in shock and my cheeks heat. "I've always had feelings for him. In an ideal world…"

My words trail off, embarrassment stalling my tongue. I pray my eyes communicate my meaning, and that she understands.

Ori and I have a complicated relationship; for most of my life I thought my feelings were one-sided. But a few years ago, Ori came home from his apprenticeship upset and drank himself silly. I joined in. One thing led to another, and he kissed me.

He told me he wanted me.

He also told me he thinks he's broken.

Then he passed out. And when he woke up the next morning, curled around me on the couch, he freaked out, pulled away, and refused to speak of what happened ever again.

For a long time, I took it personally; my longing for him often warred with a bitterness at his refusal to acknowledge us, though it never wavered in its intensity. It took a while, but between many thoughtful gestures on his part that showed he cared, and much deep reflection on mine, I came to realize that Ori was simply missing a part of himself.

Alice doesn't remember, but we were best friends as children. Pack. Family. Even after she disappeared, I think we all moved through life assuming she would come back and slide into our dynamic as if no time had passed. She *fits*—a missing puzzle piece that connects us all together.

Even if Ori can't see it yet, I'm sure she's the key to opening his heart.

It's a selfish thought, but in this, I find myself greedy. Why can't I have it all? Jessa, Alice, *and* Ori.

Alice sighs, closing her eyes and rubbing her temples.

"I'm going to need five business days to process all of this," she mutters, and I take that as the end to our conversation about Arcadia. She walks to her canvas, scrutinizing it once more. "You can drop the pose now. I'm done for the day."

"Thank goodness." My arms sag with relief, and I shake them out. "Will you need me to do this again?"

"Not necessarily. Maybe when I get to the details. The video I took should be good enough in the meantime," she says as she starts to clean up her workstation.

"Oh," I say, unable to hide my disappointment.

"Why? Did you want to model for me more?" she teases.

I give her a shy shrug as I inch closer to the easel. "Maybe."

"Noted," Alice says, chewing on her lip. "Well, even if you're not modeling for me, you can still come over and just... hang out or read or whatever while I paint. I'll need to beat the dust out of it, but there's an old bean bag chair in the attic I can drag in here for you to use."

"Yeah?" I say.

"Mhm," she hums.

"That sounds delightful, Alice."

I round the easel as she clears the area, dropping supplies on the main table. My brows knit together at the amorphous blobs of paint marking the canvas. It *generally* resembles two people dancing.

At the risk of offending her, I tentatively ask, "That's supposed to be us?"

She snorts a laugh and comes back to my side.

"It's an underpainting. I lay out shadows and highlights and undertones, and *then* I go back in and carve the rest of it out," Alice explains. Her shoulder knocks into mine as she stares at the fresh painting. "Trust the process."

My gaze slides from the canvas to her freckled nose.

"Only if you do the same with us," I whisper.

It's a request twofold; to trust us enough to fight and win back Arcadia together, and to trust us with her heart. Both are at stake here.

17

WHAT ELSE DO I HAVE TO LOSE?

ALICE

Sometimes sketching in ink and pen is too permanent. Right now, my fingers are hesitant to commit to anything that could leave an echo of a shadow behind to haunt me. Even pencil churns my gut, because despite owning three different types of erasers, there's no way to expunge the textured indents that linger when the graphite is gone.

But an Expo marker and a plane of pristine whiteboard? Now, that's a blank slate every time you swipe a Windexed paper towel over it.

Contemplating the future demands a certain level of impermanence. Anything more is a promise I'm not willing to make.

I pop the cap off my marker and sniff. Pungent chemical blueberry fills my nose.

These markers may be old, but they still pack a punch. Ryan bought them for us, overly excited that he found the same brand from when we were in elementary school, to make discussing our duty station options less stressful.

It had worked. Our pros and cons list were both colorful and fun-smelling. Although, his favorite color-slash-scent was black licorice, the menace that he was.

It seems fitting to use them now, as I figure out where I want my life to go.

Blueberry for the facts. Licorice for pros. Cherry for cons.

The marker squeaks as I drag it across the whiteboard. *Do I help them save Arcadia?*

THE FACTS:

1. Magic is real (cool)
2. Another realm does exist (also cool)
3. My new friends can shift into beasts (scary?)
4. I'm a chosen one(?) (still skeptical)
5. I have developed ~~a crush~~ two crushes
6. Need to finish gallery pieces before August 20th

PROS:

1. Could learn how to swordfight and become a badass
2. Could save a whole-ass kingdom from an evil queen (become a hero of myth and legend?)
3. Magic???

CONS:

1. I've only known them a few weeks (it feels like longer)

2. Grumpy asshole dragon teammate
3. I could die

I stare at that last one for so long my back aches, hunched over the whiteboard lain out on my coffee table. They've parsed around the details of how dangerous this tourney I'm supposed to fight in could be, but I can read between the lines.

Dragons and swords and evil queens who have murdered their predecessors all point to elevated risk.

Oddly enough, the idea of *me* dying doesn't fill me with fear. Despite what I've told my therapist, I've often thought about it. Not in a suicidal way—but in a series of *what ifs*.

Would it be peaceful, when I'm ninety years old and go softly in my sleep after I've lived a fulfilling life? Or would it be tragic—a car accident from a drunk driver, a slip down the stairs and a crack of my noggin on the floor, a cancer diagnosis down the line from years of drinking unfiltered tap water?

And then there's the *after*. Would there *be* anything of me to leave behind? When I'm just a tiny dot on the family tree of my children's children's children's homework assignment, and my body turns to dust in my grave, will someone *know* me? Will someone parse my personality from my brushstrokes and call me a friend? Will they accept my ghostly hug of comfort as they stare at varnished oil?

I think every artist creates with the hope that a piece of them survives long past their inevitable demise.

I haven't been creating, though. Not like I once did.

Sardonic laughter bubbles in my chest.

Is that not already death for someone like me?

I haven't been living at all, these past two years. Not really. Only surviving. I've been alone, even with Steph and Erica supporting me from the sidelines. But they can only do so much.

If I died tomorrow, they'd mourn me, sure, but they'd have

their own lives to go back to after the fanfare. They'd push forward, continue planning their forever, and move on. They'd have each other.

I don't have anyone.

Except, that isn't exactly true anymore.

Harley and Jessa have offered me... more. Companionship. Inspiration. Harley's blush alone promises my muse a resurrection. They're offering me the potential of a future.

I pluck the black marker from the table and find myself scrawling additions under the list of pros.

4. My muse likes them
5. Belonging (they make me feel again)

The word strikes me fiercely. It speaks to the ease in which I've fallen into friendship with them and the strange prickle of awareness I get when they're around. My hand finds my chest, rubbing at the sudden ache there. It also speaks to the pull I feel towards them, the desire cloying at my ribs that's grown impossible to ignore.

They mentioned fate quite a few times in their explanations of Arcadia and why I'm the one they need. But if fate has the final say, why do I have the chance to walk away?

From one perspective, this list makes it look like there's nothing else left to lose but myself. A sane person wouldn't take the risk.

If you glance at it another way, turn it around, upside-down, it looks like I have everything to gain. I only have to choose it.

I grab my phone and open up my thread with Jessa.

> Tell me more about the tourney.

18

DINERS, DRIVE-INS, AND DEAD HUSBANDS

ALICE

Jessa picks me up in her beat-up truck, sans Harley, and drives us to a diner a town away. It's one of those places with chrome outfitting and a neon sign that's open twenty-four seven.

The red pleather cushions stick to my thighs as I slide into the booth across from Jessa, picking up the menu that the waitress dropped on the table. There are too many choices packed onto the laminated cardstock—do I go classic burger and shake, or do I get breakfast because diner home fries can't be beat? Soon enough my knee starts bouncing with my indecision.

"I'm glad you texted," Jessa says.

I glance up from my menu. Jessa's staring at me, her own menu discarded by the salt and pepper shakers. Freshly showered, she lacks the sharp makeup she normally paints onto her eyes and lips. It softens her disposition, though her angled cheeks could still cut diamonds.

"Yeah?" I ask.

"Mhm," Jessa hums, tucking her damp hair behind her ears. "I mean I figured you'd ask me out eventually…" The teasing lift of her brows pulls silent laughter from my chest. "What more do you want to know, Trouble?" she presses, gently tugging the menu from my hands. "Lay it on me."

"I want to help. But I need to understand how dangerous it's going to be to go against Maven." I tuck my hands under my thighs, knee still bouncing. "Harley said she killed Ori's parents."

Jessa sucks in a deep breath and releases it slow. "More than I'd like it to be. Under any other circumstance I wouldn't ask someone with little to no training to participate in this, but magic binds the participants. Only you and Ori can compete in the tourney." I nod, and she continues. "No matter which trials occur in the tourney, I expect Maven to attempt sabotage or try to harm you. But I'll protect you outside the arena, and Ori will protect you inside of it. That's his job. It's what he's made for."

Implied obligation drips from her words. But it's hard to fully believe that the Ori I've interacted with has some kind of natural instinct to care for me buried in his chest.

"Why hasn't he asked me to help himself?" I ask. "He shouldn't make you two do everything. Isn't he the one who's going to rule if this works out in your favor?"

Jessa grimaces. "He's been… busy."

It's a cop-out answer, but the waitress conveniently takes that moment to drop off water and ask us for our order. My knee stills, and I panic, not having decided on which milkshake flavor I want, let alone what food.

"We'll have two of the cheeseburgers, no tomato. A strawberry milkshake and a chocolate one. Oh, and waffle fries instead of regular," Jessa says.

I gape, and Jessa shrugs as the waitress jots everything down.

"How did you know what I'd end up ordering?" I ask once the waitress is out of earshot.

"You always ask for no tomato anytime you get a panini at Mad Mug," Jessa says, lifting her water to her lips. Condensation drips off the plastic cup, forming a puddle on the table. "And you have a thing for chocolate. Mochas when you don't order a cappuccino. Chocolate croissants over the almond ones."

My pulse hammers in my neck as I grab a napkin from the dispenser and swipe the pooled water away. I'm not entirely surprised she noticed all that from the few times I'd patroned her café; Jessa is clearly the attentive type. It's only the confidence in which she states these facts about me that sends me reeling.

I fold the napkin and motion for Jessa to use it as a coaster. Her lips twitch, amused, as I nervously do the same to my water.

"Speaking of Ori," I say, deciding now's as good a time as any to ask my burning question. "Does it bother you that Harley wants a relationship with him?"

"Do you think it bothers me that Harley wants one with you?" she counters.

My brows furrow as I lean forward, my voice dropping low. "You've made it clear it's the exact opposite."

"Then why should it bother me that Harley wants him too?"

"Because... I don't know."

"Here's the thing, Alice. You don't remember what they were like as kids. And you don't know what they were like as teens or even what they were like five years ago. Those two have been a long time coming. All Ori's got to do is pull his head out of his ass." Jessa steeples her fingers together and rests her chin atop them. "Dynamics like this aren't uncommon in Arcadia. Shifters are more open than humans with their sexuality and don't shy away from pack life. We do what works for us. And it doesn't bother me to share you or him, as long as I trust the person I'm sharing you with."

"So, you don't care if Harley's with Ori. But *you* don't want to be with Ori?" I clarify, trying to wrap my head around the relationship.

She makes a gagging noise. "Absolutely not. Love him like a brother though."

I fall back against the booth, and all the air deflates from my lungs. It was one thing to consider dating two people who liked each other and who both liked me. But could I handle adding another person in the mix—one who actively makes my blood boil whenever I'm in their presence?

My tongue goes dry, and I grab my water.

"You're asking a lot about our dear Heir," Jessa leads, tongue running along her teeth with devious intent. "You develop a crush after Ori helped you out of the woods, Trouble? Big strong prince, swooping in to save the day."

My gasp sucks liquid down the wrong pipe, and I choke, falling into a coughing fit at the suggestion.

"Oh, goodness, are you okay?" The waitress appears with a platter of our food.

I shoot her a thumbs up, covering my mouth with my other hand as I continue to cough. My face is surely red, but thankfully the tickling sensation at the back of my throat clears by the time she finishes depositing our burgers, shakes, and fries on the table.

"Anything else I can get you two?" she asks.

"Nope, we're all good," Jessa chirps, and the waitress disappears through the two-way doors of the kitchen. Then to me, she asks, "Are you sure you're good?"

"I'm fine." I clear my throat. "Also, for the record, it didn't go down like that. I would have found my way back to the Meadow eventually." I take a sip of water—*not* choking this time. "And I have not developed feelings for a man who I've only met twice.

I only have crushes on you and Harley and that's more than enough for me."

Fuck. That was corny.

Jessa grins wide, canines poking into her lower lip. She spares me from more teasing, pushing the basket of fries towards me. "Eat, Alice. Before they get cold."

I grab one and shove it in my mouth. Crispy and salty and warm, I hum, grabbing another. "Fuck, these are delicious."

"Best in the area," Jessa says. "Dip it in your shake."

I do, and I moan a curse at how perfect the combination is. Jessa laughs, and we fall into easy conversation as we dig into our burgers.

It takes a special kind of person to not get whiplash from the way I popcorn between topics, so I'm thankful that Jessa follows my lead. From magic to relationships to summer beach plans to crazy tourists at her shop, it flows without interruption.

At some point, though, as I dunk the last fry in the squirt of ketchup we've been sharing, laughing at one of Jessa's jokes, guilt slithers between my ribs.

Nothing in particular triggers it; it simply appears.

Grief is a notorious assassin; it comes in for the kill without a whisper of notice.

I pull my phone out of my back pocket and type out a quick message to Harley. Luckily, he's quick to respond.

> You've told Jessa about Ryan, right?

What? No.
HARLEY

No, I wouldn't tell her about that.
HARLEY

My thumbs freeze midair. He... didn't tell her?

"Who's texting?" Jessa asks. "Everything okay?"

"Yeah, it's just Harley," I mutter, gaze trained on my phone.

"He was upset he couldn't come tonight. He's covering for one of the other librarians who had a family emergency," she says, but I'm focused on typing out a response.

> I assumed you told each other everything.

We do.
HARLEY

But I figured you'd want to tell her in your own time... was I wrong? Do you want me to talk to her about it for you?
HARLEY

"You need to know something," I blurt out, slamming my phone on the table. I'm overwhelmed with the need to rip this bandage off quick. "I was married. His name was Ryan. And he died, two years ago. And that's the real reason why I moved out here. I needed a fresh start."

I grab my milkshake, the cold glass freezing my palm, and take a few brain-splitting gulps. The roof of my mouth freezes, and I squeeze my eyes shut at the pain.

When they open, and Jessa comes back into focus, I note the shock paling her features. A fry dangles from her mouth, pinched between her perfectly white teeth.

We stare at each other, and I hold my breath as I wait for her response. The diner bustles around us: glasses clink, forks and knives scrape along ceramic plates, teenagers howl laughter from the corner booth. Jessa's attention slowly dips to my chest, understanding flaring as she takes in my necklace.

The platinum bands are cold against my flushed skin.

Jessa pops the rest of the fry between her lips, licks the salt from her fingers, and wipes them on a napkin.

"I..." she starts, stops, and sighs. She stares at the crumbled napkin in her hand for a moment, then lifts her head. "Are you okay?"

Breath finally fills my lungs. There isn't pity in her gaze, only concern. It pulls her usually smirking lips down, swipes a line between her brows. My head bobbles with the swell of emotion that hits me.

"Not really. But I haven't been okay in a long time," I admit. "I've been lonely." My voice cracks, and I grab my shake again, sucking until the straw only pulls chocolate-flavored air to my tongue. Jessa's quiet, allowing me the space to continue. "I don't want to be alone anymore, Jessa. And I want to help you."

Hope sparks in her golden irises, even as the rest of her face shows her solemn understanding.

"Are you sure?" she asks. It's not just a question about the tourney, but if I'm sure about *them* too.

"You guys are the first people I've felt comfortable with since he died."

Jessa nods to herself, as if she's jotting down a to-do list in her head. "Then we need to start training as soon as possible. The tourney is on your birthday." A hint of a smile crinkles the edges of her eyes. "Fair warning, I've been told I'm a bit of a drill sergeant."

19

DRAGON BREATH

JESSA

"Hey, Dickwad!" I yell across the moonlit field. "We need to talk. Shift."

Ori's pearlescent white dragon swings its massive head my way. The dragon chuffs, uncomfortably hot breath washing over me.

Oh, he's *not* about to give me a fucking attitude.

My hands find purchase on my hips, and my boot heel beats down on the grass repeatedly. "*Shift*, Ori. I'm not going to say it again."

Magic skitters over his scales, and the taloned beast turns into the gruff prince I grew up with.

"What?" he says in lieu of hello. His nostrils flare. "Why do you smell like her?"

"Alice and I had a lovely date at the diner, during which she agreed to help us. I'm going to start training her tomorrow," I say, cutting right to the chase. "I figured you should know in case you wanted to help. You know, since it's your crown we're trying to win."

If Ori had showed his face at home, he would have been up to speed on the situation with Alice. But *no*. After he found her here, he'd freaked out and went full beast mode—slapped a sign on his shop that it was closed for the week and fucked off into Arcadia to throw a tantrum.

Normally, I'm fine with him disappearing here to blow off steam in dragon form. Even I need to shift every once in a while to appease my beast, but it's dangerous for him to stay here too long. Even if the Wandering Woods have shielded us from Maven's wrath before, the longer he's here, the more likely Enzo is to pick up his scent and trail it to the Meadow.

Glacial navy eyes stare at me unbelievingly. "No."

"Ori—"

"I said no, Jessa," Ori snaps, surging forward. "You're not seeing the whole picture and are meddling in business you shouldn't."

I don't flinch as he stops short of my face, his growl vibrating the inch of air between our noses. This stupid dragon is going to be the death of me. He cannot see past his own snout; *he* cannot see the whole picture.

"We cannot give up this chance to save our home," I seethe between clenched teeth. "We have a chance to all be happy. *Together*. Here, where we belong." My nail jabs into Ori's pectoral. "If you want her, you need to grow the balls and tell her. Same with Harley for that matter."

"I *don't* want her."

"Bullshit. She's your fated. Of course you want her."

"She *left me*," he roars. "She left all of us."

"We were eight fucking years old. Get over it!" I throw my hands out to my side. "We all lost something when Alice left. But it's a gift that she found her way back to us. Accept it."

"You don't understand," Ori insists.

"Of course I don't understand. Because you won't talk to

us!" My shout echoes in the field. The trees surrounding us bristle; the leaves whisper their judgment.

"I don't have anything else left to say," he says, hand rubbing at his chest.

I shake my head; clearly, I wasn't going to get anywhere arguing with him. He always does this—retreats when it gets hard. It's why I have to push him. I'm the only one with the balls to do it.

"She met Memaw, by the way, right before you found her," I add. "Alice might not remember, but she *knows*, Ori. I've told her as much as I can about Arcadia and she still wants to help. I'm not going to let your stubborn attitude fuck this up for us." At his shocked expression, I dig the knife in his gut with my words and twist. "We have everything to gain and nothing to lose, except her. Again." I turn my back on my prince. "She'll be by the house at ten tomorrow to train. Come. Or don't."

He doesn't call out to me as I shift. The comforting magic blankets me, and I shake out my fur as I dash between the trees back to the Meadow.

Trouble walks through the gate to our backyard a sensible three minutes before ten. She's dressed in workout attire like I asked, but maybe I should have thought through that request before giving it. Her bike shorts hug her ass like a second skin and her baggy T-shirt catches on the curve of her hips, draping low and hiding that tiny waist I want to wrap my arms around.

"Hey," she calls out, walking past the fire pit and hammock to the large swath of grass to where I'm standing. "I hadn't realized your place butts up against the park."

"Yep," I say, glancing back at the chain-link fence. Beyond the silver cross-hatching is the end of the park's baseball field. "Makes it real convenient when we need to get to the portal."

I splay my arms out wide, inviting Alice in for a hug. She takes the bait. We wrap ourselves around each other, and I relish the tight press of our bodies.

"Is that what it's called?" Alice huffs, her chin notched on my shoulder. She pulls away from me, taking a step back with her nose all scrunched up. "A portal sounds science-fiction-y."

"We could call it a rift, or a thinning of the veil between realms, or something else entirely. But portal is the most straight forward," I say, shrugging. "Not that it's mattered much before, when it was only us three managing it."

Alice nods, attention drifting around the backyard. The red oaks and maples are tall here, and their widespread branches provide us with a wealth of shade in summer.

The scratch of the screen door sliding open and closed rips though the air, and Ori stomps out of the house in his own version of training gear. It's what we use in Arcadia—traditional fighting leathers—and he looks sorely out of place with both Alice and I in modern spandex.

At least he showed.

He stops five feet away, with his whole body angled towards me, as if he can't stomach even looking at Alice. Alice is his mirror, shoulders stiff and arms crossed defensively.

"Why are you in gym clothes?" he rasps. "I thought we were training."

"Well hello to you too," Alice mutters under her breath.

"We are," I drawl, tossing a hand at the cones I've set up in the backyard. They're bright orange dots in the green. "But we can't jump in with swordplay in leathers on day one. I need to assess her fitness level first. Then we'll work on some calisthenics and cardio."

Ori's a rock, his expression unreadable. "Then why am I here?"

Alice scoffs. It's a soft sound that escapes her throat, with her head turned the opposite direction of Ori. But she doesn't know we have heightened hearing, and Ori's jaw ticks in response. His fingers dig bruises into his biceps.

"For team bonding," I drawl. "I know there was a rocky start between you both, but you have to play nice if you actually want to win. There are three events in the tourney. One for the Champions. One for the Heirs. And one for the both of you. *Together*. Can you both handle that?"

Ori grunts, which is better than him storming away. It means he's taking this seriously.

"Alice?" I ask.

"Yeah, I can manage that." She finally glances at my growly prince. There's confusion mixed with melancholy in the gentle dip of her frown as she studies him. "Though it would be nice to get a thank you, *Beast*."

It's the first time I've seen them interact face-to-face and the tension between them is much worse than I thought. It's clear they're drawn to each other—why else would they be so affected by each other's presence? But Harley was overselling it when he told me things were awkward.

"I'm not going to thank you for solving the problem you caused in the first place," Ori grumbles, and I cringe at how it causes Alice's jaw to grind.

I'm going to have to find a way to get Ori to show he cares, fast. Otherwise, he's going to push her away, and lose all of us in the process.

ALICE GROANS, an arm slung over her eyes as she lays in the grass. Her chests expands in quick succession with her breath, and a flush blooms beneath her sports bra, crawling up her neck. She ditched her baggy T-shirt a while ago, exposing her sweat-slicked midsection in an attempt to beat the oppressive heat.

Maybe I should have us train at the gym next time. The gym has air conditioning. But out here, we can mimic Arcadia's outdoor arena... and we get privacy.

"Get up, we're not done," Ori says. He glares down at her and makes no offer of a hand to help her up. I don't know if she's noticed that he's actively avoiding touching her. "If that's the best you can do, we might as well not even try to enter the tourney."

"Oh, fuck *off*, dude," Alice says. Her forearm slides off her eyes, over her forehead, and pushes into her loosened ponytail. "I used to be fit. I was a damn good fencer in high school. But I haven't worked out in a couple of years... cut me some slack." She groans as she pushes to sitting. "And I'm not a quitter."

"It's no biggie, Trouble, give it a few weeks for muscle memory to kick in," I say, attempting to diffuse the mounting tension. I offer her my hand and heft her up. "I didn't know you already knew how to wield a sword. That'll make things easier later."

"I have a feeling that what I know won't be the same kind of swordplay you're used to. But hopefully my experience will ensure I'm not incompetent." Alice dusts grass and dirt off her ass. Out of the corner of my eye, Ori huffs, pacing away to go run another agility drill between the cones. "I don't need him to like me or anything," Alice adds, leaning in close. "But he's infuriating."

"I'll speak to him about his behavior." *Again*. "But in the meantime, Harley and I will make it up to you. Show you how grateful we are, ya' know?"

My coy lilt draws a spark of a smile from her.

"Yeah? How do you intend to do that? Outside of Harley being my model of course," Alice volleys back.

"I could always fill in for him from time to time," I tease. "I'm partial to the nude version though."

"Maybe after a few drinks." Alice laughs, that twinkling

sound filling our yard. Wind-chimes. Sunlight. Sweet tea sliding down your throat.

At the sound, Ori trips over air—or maybe it was the last rung of the drill ladder—and falls on his back. It's a big commotion, and we gape at him as his hands swipe over his face. A pained groan rumbles in his chest.

"You okay over there?" I call out.

Ori stills, his chest expanding with a deep inhale and collapsing with a release. Then, he pushes off the ground with unnatural speed, making a break for the house. "I'm getting some water."

It's almost comical, the way he storms across the grass. The screen door to the house sticks a quarter of the way open, and he fights with it, practically ripping it off its track to make enough room for his broad shoulders to slide through.

Scratch that. It's *absolutely* comical, watching him try to fight his attraction to Alice.

Thing is, you can't fight fate. Not when it comes to love.

He'll give in eventually.

20

MEMORY FISHING

ALICE

My brush swipes over the amber-white highlights I've mixed on my palette. My wrist flicks, dotting the points in Harley's hair that glint under porchlight. It's a halo that casts his frame in an angelic glow.

I step back a few paces, as if I were someone staring at the canvas on a wall at the gallery. My head tilts. My brows pinch and lips purse.

It's nearly there.

My gaze trails down my painted figure; contrasted to his in cool shadows, my skirt drapes off my frame and is swallowed by darkness in the corner. It's my favorite part of the piece. It makes me ask *why*.

Are those shadows representing ghosts that drag me down? Or is the white-haired angel lifting me up? Can it be both at the same time—being torn in two?

That's the core of it. The midnight silken guilt. The warm amber hope. The ghosts of the past, always dancing in step with me; the visions of a future, loosely wrapped in the palm of my hand.

His palm, my hand.

Ryan's ghost, Harley's breath.

Contrasts in spades, pulling me apart.

It's *nearly* there.

Every time I step back from the piece, my eyes stray back to Harley's face. The way he *looks* at me. It's distracting.

I drop my brush on my palette, dust my hand off on a spare rag, and then do something crazy. Well, not *crazy* crazy, but something my college professors who fell in love with my semi-realistic style would probably cringe at.

I smear Harley's otherworldly face. My fingers play with the tacky paint; the pale tones spread out, a blur in the night scene. You can still see his features, but they're hazy, as if in motion.

Snagging my paint rag, I step back again. The stained washcloth fibers scrape across my fingerprints and under my nails.

Now, when I look at the painting, my eyes go to the center first: my face.

I follow the line created by painting-me's gaze, tilted away from Harley's as if looking into his eyes was too much to bear. It marks a diagonal across the canvas, along the vibrant blue of my skirt swishing between Harley's legs. I swoop along the hem to the bottom left, into the darkness—the shadows, the guilt cloying at my edges.

Up I'm lead, along the curve of my body, to his hand which grips my waist. I hook around, back through the center of the painting, now focused on Harley's blurred visage.

I trail around his halo of light—the hope, the maybe, the what if—the curve near the top of the canvas—and then I slide down his other arm, where our palms connect. So sweet. So gentle. So hesitant. And yet, the way our fingers lace together—my pinky hooking around his pointer—betrays a longing to fully weave together. It's a small detail; one I hope an attentive eye finds.

And then I'm back to me.

A perfect loop: my mind; my thoughts; my feelings. My averted gaze. My temptation. My avoidance. My inability to fully detach. My yearning.

Circular.

Yeah, this one is done.

I'll touch up some of the details after the paint settles, but it's good to go onto the drying rack for now.

The *fwick* of Harley turning a book page beyond my easel pulls me back to reality.

I toss my paint rag on the worktable and join him in his lounging. This part of my studio has become a nest of sorts, with two beanbag chairs and a pile of blankets and throw pillows amassed in the corner for him to use whenever he wants.

Harley reads. I paint. It's nice, existing with someone.

No pressure to be anything. No need to fill the air with mindless words. If we chat, we chat. If we don't, we don't. I used to do the same thing with Ryan, except he was a video game fanatic, and instead of the steady sound of pages turning, I would listen to the sporadic clack of his custom keyboard.

Fuck. I'm going to have to paint this too, aren't I?

The through line of this collection becomes clearer every day. I don't want to say it out loud, though. Just in case I jinx it.

Harley snaps his book shut and curls towards me, cheek smushed against the bean bag chair. "You done for the day?"

"Yeah," I say, then shift so I can stare at the ceiling. The mounted fan whirs, blades moving so fast they almost look motionless. I have a question for Harley, but I don't know how he's going to react. "Ori's helping me train with Jessa."

"I heard. I also heard you're a little prodigy with a wooden sword."

"Ugh, stop schmoozing me," I scoff, but it has no bite to it. I smack his chest, and his resulting smile is bright titanium white. Pure and genuine, there's no trickery in the split of his lips. "Jessa has rose tinted glasses. It's only been four days." I drag my hand to my belly and play with the ties of my shorts. "Anyway, things are awkward. I can gather it has something to do with us as kids and me leaving Arcadia. But I don't remember that, and you and Jessa have kept your mouths annoyingly shut about it."

Harley's smile fades, and he almost looks... sad. "That's because we don't know the whole story."

"What do you mean by that?"

Harley sits up, bracing his forearm on the mushy nest of pillows and blankets. "Alice, when we say you left, what we mean is you disappeared. One moment, we were all running around in the woods, and the next you were gone. Ori followed you. He came back alone, promising you'd be back soon—that we should wait for you in the Meadow. But the portal he said you guys found was closed by the time we made it there. We never saw you again."

I suck my bottom lip into my mouth and tug at the skin with my teeth, considering my next words carefully as I curl towards him.

"I want to remember," I say.

"Okay."

"But I haven't remembered anything else since I was last in Arcadia," I continue.

"Okay..." Harley's face twitches, and he adjusts his glasses with his middle finger.

"Do you think we could go? Visit, that is?" I ask. "Maybe it will help me remember. The magic or whatever."

A tepid grimace crawls across his face. "I don't know if that's a great idea."

My fingers find his hand, and I hook my pointer around his pinky, linking us together. "Please, Harley?"

He sucks in a stuttered breath, as if he's shocked to hear his name whispered so sweetly.

"Okay," he rasps.

"Okay?"

"Okay." Harley nods like a bobble head. "Yeah, we can go. I have tomorrow afternoon off. There are a few places I can take you that should be safe."

"That was far too easy. I only said please once. You didn't even try to negotiate terms of a trade," I say.

He shrugs one shoulder. "I'm not a hard person to convince."

"Clearly."

"Especially when it comes to pleasing the women in my life."

A beat passes between us; it's palpable, thick.

"Thank you," I whisper.

"You're welcome, Alice," he says without skipping a beat. He groans as he rolls out of the nest and hops up on two feet. "Now, can I get an early peek at the finished product?"

THIS TIME, I walk through the tree in the park as if it's air.

I glare at the flowers in the Meadow, which are annoyingly quiet as Harley pulls me towards a path across the field.

"Why do they ignore me?" I ask, dragging my feet. "I'm not insane, right? They did talk before?"

"Yeah, they talk alright," Harley grumbles. His hand clenches mine, and my stomach does a little flip. "But they probably won't gossip around you anymore."

"Because?"

"They know who you are now. And anyone not explicitly

fighting against Maven and Enzo's occupation won't want to be associated with you."

I shake my head. "I'm not even going to pretend to understand the politics that keep flowers from gossiping."

Harley's laugh is a colorful sound, as if canary yellow and tangerine swirled together. It has me picking up my pace to walk side-by-side with him rather than a step behind, and I keep my hand curled in his, allowing myself to lean into his arm.

"I don't blame you," he says, and I catch him smiling down at me from my periphery. "It does sound ridiculous when you put it like that."

A sneak glance away from the root-speared path reveals Harley's tinting cheeks. It's all nervous wonder shining in his expression, as if he's embarrassed by his delight or worried I'll judge him.

As if I could be anything other than excited by his attention.

I huff it in brief moments between brushstrokes and inkblots. Before sips of coffee and while books are shelved. I hoard it like inspiration, covet it like summer sun.

Before I know it, we're stopped at the dead end of a winding path. Tied around two pegs staked in the dirt is a rope ladder that extends up. And up. And *up*. It breaks through the canopy of trees and disappears into a thick layer of clouds.

"Alright, you first," he says, letting go of my hand.

"What?" I squeak.

His lips quirk in a subdued smirk. He adjusts his backpack and grabs onto the ladder with one hand. Motioning with the other, he says, "Up you go."

My gaze flicks from him to the ladder to the cloud it leads into. "Where does that go?"

"Somewhere awesome," he says, cryptically. "You first, and then I'll follow."

"How high does it go? Is it some kind of treehouse?"

"Alice, you won't believe it until you see it. Trust me. Climb the ladder."

"I'm not afraid of heights or anything," I say, slowly shuffling towards the frayed rope and wooden slats that look like they could easily snap under my weight. "But this doesn't seem particularly safe. Considering there's no end in sight."

"You won't fall if that's what you're worried about."

"No," I drawl. "No, I wouldn't be afraid of falling."

"Uhuh." Harley's tongue pokes his cheek. "Well, you can't fall, even if you wanted to. It's spelled to make you have three points of contact once you're past the first rung."

"That's awfully convenient." I go to climb, but stop, my hands wrapped tightly around the scratchy rope. I speak over my shoulder at Harley. "What if someone is missing an arm or a leg. Would they not be able to climb? Or would their prosthetic count? Or would they be able to have two points of contact?"

Harley pauses, but not because my question caught him off guard, but because he's actually giving the answer real thought. "I can't say I've been here with an amputee to know the answer to that question."

"Fair enough," I say, and start to climb in earnest.

The ladder sways when Harley hops on behind me and starts climbing, but my hands and feet stay secured to the rope and rungs with ease. There's a tingle on my palms, a faint brush of static, and I wonder if it's magic that I'm feeling.

When we crest the top of the trees, my eyes go wide at the view: miles of foliage stretch out, cast in splotches of cloudy shadows and midday sunlight.

"Just wait until we get to the top!" Harley calls out.

"Where's the top, again?" I toss down to him, a feeble second attempt to wring an answer from him.

His boisterous laugh careens on the wind, brushing my

cheek with a cool kiss. "Impatience will get you nowhere, Alice."

My grumble is muted by my smile as I continue to climb. We reach ridiculous heights, the once towering trees shrinking. Clouds circle us, and I pause to wave one hand through the airy wisps.

Soon enough, we break through the fog, and again, my eyes go wide.

"*What the hell?*" I whisper as I crawl through a hatch in a wooden landing.

Harley follows, promptly covering the hole we emerged from with a hinged metal door.

"Yeah, it's pretty right?" he says, perching his hands on his hips and gazing out.

It's more than pretty. It's *impossibly wondrous.*

The clouds are a dense, opaque white that flattens out like a plain, stretching for miles in every direction. Wooden planks create walkways around the expanse, leading towards a stone tower. Impossible, for such a heavy thing to stand atop nothing but vapor.

Boulders surround its base, imbedded in the clouds. It's reminiscent of a castle on a cliff, the clouds mimicking foamy white waves, an occasional wisp curling around the stones. Roots of oversized air plants wrap around the rocks too. Their fanned leaves form shaded areas mimicking palm trees on a beach. The whole things is beach-like, especially with the body of water ahead of us.

Again, impossible.

The light blue water, the same color as the sky surrounding us, laps against the cloudy shore. Water meets the horizon, the lake extending far beyond my line of sight.

"You had the same look of awe the first time you came here," Harley says. It's so soft, almost wistful, that I don't think I was meant to hear him.

"I was here before?"

Harley nods. "We came here a lot. We don't have any oceans in Arcadia, the land stretches on and on… This is the closest you're able to get to a beach."

To that, I have no words. "A lake in the clouds."

"Technically we call it the Lake in the Sky."

"Same difference," I mutter. I go to step off the wooden landing but pause. "Is it safe to walk on this? Won't I fall right through?"

"Nope," Harley says, pushing past me and walking right off the ledge.

A worried breath fills my throat in the second it takes for his foot to touch the clouds, but I'm immediately relieved when he finds solid purchase. Harley jumps up and down, and while the substance underneath his sneakers makes no sound, it kicks up around him, sticking to the bottom of his soles.

"See? Completely solid. The paths are only there to keep from dragging cloud dust inside," he says, offering me a hand. "C'mon. I have more to show you."

I gently rest my hand in his, and he lets my favorite pink-cheeked smile of his loose before pulling me across the cloud.

I'm walking on a *fucking cloud*.

I wish Ryan could see this.

The sudden thought doesn't sour my mood so much as sobers it. If I were to make a list of all the parts of life I wish he could see, it would go on forever.

"The water is also safe to swim in. That's why I had you bring your bathing suit," Harley says, gifting me the option to focus on his voice rather than my grief. "There's a small shower area around this corner that you can change in."

We stop next to one of the shaded rocks, where a pink and white striped sheet spreads out. On it are two neatly rolled towels and a wicker picnic basket.

I raise a brow at Harley, and he scratches the back of his neck.

"I figured I'd come early rather than having us both lug a million things up the ladder at once. I got us bagels and snacks and some lemonade... nothing too fancy," he says.

I suck my bottom lip between my teeth. "You turned this into a picnic date?"

"What? No. I mean, yes?" Harley rambles nervously. "Is that okay?"

I nod. "It's sweet. And thoughtful. I just wasn't expecting it, though I wasn't expecting all that either." I swipe my hand out at the water.

"But is it *okay*?" Harley repeats.

It's obvious what he's worried about—overstepping, going too far, going too fast. But I'm acutely aware that there's no right or wrong here, only the strange middle ground of my mind that we have to navigate.

Though, I might not be communicating that middle ground clearly enough for him. The overwhelming urge to calm and reassure fills me, so I do that the best way I know how. I give him a hug.

My cheek smushes against his chest, his heartbeat thumping in my ear, and my hands fist the back of his soft T-shirt. He tenses in my embrace but quickly melts into it, arms wrapping over my shoulders and smushing me closer.

"It's more than okay," I say. Then add, on a whisper, "You know I like you, right?"

"It's nice to hear you say it out loud," he admits.

I pull my head back; my chin finds his chest as I meet his pretty eyes. The rusty shade is darker than usual, swirling with something I can't place.

"You need things to be stated explicitly?" I ask.

"I definitely enjoy that, yes," Harley says. His gaze darts

away as if he's recalling a memory, and his cheeks pinken. "Do you?"

I nod. "It removes any guess work when someone says what they mean versus me trying to figure it out in body language."

Harley's glasses have slipped down the bridge of his nose, and I squeeze one arm between us to adjust them. My finger trails down the freckles dotting the straight slope, then *boops* the tip.

"I'm going to go change now," I whisper.

He visibly gulps. "Okay."

"You going to let go of me so I can?"

"Oh." His arms release me quickly and he steps back. His hand finds his neck again, the skin there likely to become raw if he keeps rubbing at it—or if I keep making him nervous.

I should stop doing that. But I *like* making him nervous. I *like* teasing and flirting. I *like* pulling that blush to his cheeks and making his nostalgic eyes darken.

I've become obsessed with all his colors.

WHEN I COME out of the little beach shower stall, shoes off and bathing suit tied tightly around my hips and neck, I squirm at the first touch of my toes to the clouds.

"Oh, I hate this," I call out, feet wriggling in the unfamiliar texture as I approach our set up and toss my clothes into my bag.

Harley laughs from where he's lounging out, shirt off. "You'll get used to it." He stands, tosses his glasses onto the sheet, and grabs my hand. "C'mon, the water will make you feel better."

We splash through the shallows, and the cool water shocks my nerves. I yelp and jump onto his back, my body latching onto the only other source of warmth here.

"Fuck, that's freezing! Why's it so cold? It's closer to the sun than the ocean!" I screech.

"I don't know, I never asked that question before." Harley's rumble of amusement joins in as he drags me deeper into the blue. "You're full of curiosities, aren't you?"

The waves lap lazily around us; it's the calmest body of water I've ever swam in outside a pool.

"Sorry about that," I mutter as my body slowly adjusts to the temperature.

Harley lets go of my hand. "Why are you apologizing?"

I shrug, dipping my body below the surface until the water hits my lips. Not everyone I've met has tolerated my random questions—many find them annoying, and others find them confusing. Only a few people have found enjoyment in questioning the world as I do. I quickly learned to stifle the urge or apologize for it when the wonderings slip through my filter.

But Harley—and Jessa too—don't seem bothered by it.

I blow bubbles as I tread, gazing around the deserted lake. The water is salty, like the ocean, which is backwards to what it should be.

Harley floats on his back, basking in the sun with his eyes closed. He sighs, and it's as content a sound as any I've heard.

"How does it feel?" he asks.

My mouth pops above the water's surface. "How does what feel?"

"The water. I read somewhere that being immersed in it can help stimulate your brain. Figured being in Arcadian water might help spur your memory."

"Um..." I hum as I join him, floating on my back and staring up at the *cloudless sky*. The blue blends in with the water, and it's like we're floating in a vast nothingness. "Not feeling any particular way yet."

Harley's face turns to me, water cutting a line through his

cheek, and cracks one eye open. It glows red in the direct sun. "Maybe if you relax."

"Not a terrible idea."

I close my eyes and let myself slip deeper in the water. My ears dip under, and the unique and garbled whooshing of the lake yells over any thoughts chattering in my head. At some point, Harley's fingers skim the surface of the water, brushing mine, and I link our pinkies so we don't drift apart.

And then I relax.

Hours later, after we swim and snack, Harley doses off in the shade, and I open my sketchbook.

I doodle little scenes, scratchy black lines filling the moleskin pages like a patchwork tattoo. The lake. The tower behind us, floating on a cloud. Imaginary fish swimming in the vapor and air-plants reaching towards the sun.

And of course, I draw Harley.

The trail of white hair below his navel. The bright red swim shorts that he favors. The lazy drape of his arm over his eyes. The peek of his front teeth that his parted lips gift me, peaceful sighs rolling off his tongue as he sleeps.

I'm lost in trying to replicate the reflection in his glasses that sit on the sheet when Harley wakes. There's a rustling, and his shadow falls over my sketchbook. His bare chest hovers an inch away from my back—the magnetism between our skin spreading gooseflesh up my arms.

"Have I told you how much it means to me that you draw me?" he whispers in an awed, sleep-rumpled rasp. The puff of his breath spreads deliciously over my neck.

"I think you've mentioned it a few times," I say, turning my head. Our noses nearly bump as our eyes meet.

Time slows, *inches forward*, as Harley licks his lips. My gaze falls, locking onto them. He's *so close*. All he has to do is lean in and—

"Have you had any luck remembering?" Harley asks.

My lashes flutter, and I refocus on the hopeful pinch of his brows. It's such a genuine expression, his entire focus set on the reason why we came here in the first place. Meanwhile I'm lusting after him.

"No," I whisper. I honestly haven't thought about the past at all since we floated in the water. I've been inextricably focused on *him*.

I need to get my head out of the gutter.

"That's okay," Harley reassures me. "We can try again another day."

Innocence

Remember when we went to your apartment—
you forgot your wallet—
and when we turned to leave, you pulled me
aside and said:

"Wait, I've never kissed you during the day."
Or maybe you said, "in the light."
(I loathe to admit I can't remember which)

And then you lifted my chin and kissed me.
There was no lust in that kiss. Only innocence.
Full of air and light and blushing cheeks.
I miss that.

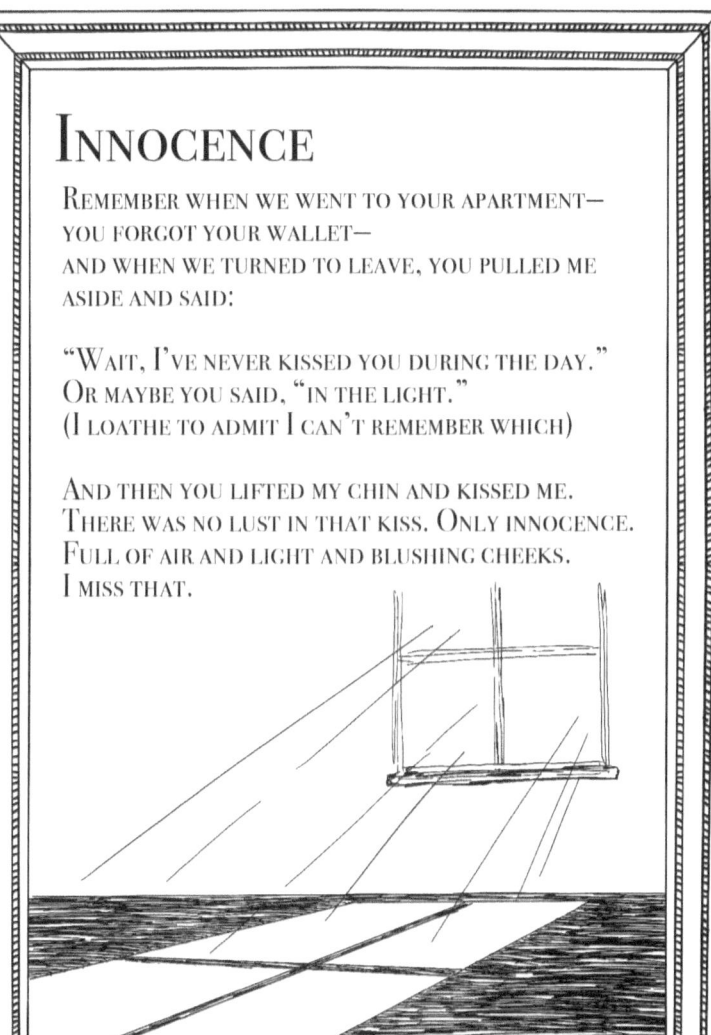

21

CRASH OUT

ALICE

Just when you think you're getting somewhere, you crash out.
It happens quick and unexpected, a light bulb popping; one minute you can see, and the next you're in the dark. The filament gets too hot, the light's been on too long. It dies.

You die too, a little bit, every time it happens.

9:03

The time stares back at me. Above it, the date. Sunday, June twenty-second.

9:04

The clock changes shape on the screen. Another minute gone. Four in total have passed since the notification popped up with a bright *ding*. Why hadn't I turned off the yearly reminder?

Oh right, I'm a masochist now.

Other notifications light up my phone—junk emails and spam texts—but I swipe them away, my eyes burning as I stare at the calendar icon on my lock screen.

Today: ANNIVERSARY!!!!

Four exclamation points. I was *that happy* when I typed it into my phone. I didn't need the reminder back then—how could I ever forget—but the dot it put on my calendar gave me joy. I relished the countdown leading up to it, and to our subsequent celebrations.

Now, the date takes me by surprise.

How did the first third of summer go by in such a blur? Is it the salty air that dulled my senses? Did Meadowbrook ruin me with that mystifying sensation of being on vacation, the one that makes you wake from a coma every morning, not knowing if it's a weekend or a weekday, but it doesn't actually matter because you're *away*?

Or is it the company I've been keeping, who have distracted me better than any piece of media can?

How could I *forget*?

I haven't prepared as I have the last two years. I didn't crack open our fifty dates book and scratch one off, so I'd know what we'd do today. I didn't make a reservation at a new restaurant. I didn't buy a lemon-raspberry cake to split with my favorite ghost.

10:32

The clock shapeshifts again, this time accompanied by a

buzzing. Steph calls. Then Erica. But they know I don't want to talk today. I hit end on their calls without picking up.

Texts follow. Concern. Reminders that they're there if I want to chat. *Sending love.* I swipe those away too.

11:04

Two hours. I'm still in bed.

Time is weird like that. It moves quick as lightning and then not at all.

Thoughts rush but don't stick; emotions lurk in the corner, threatening my numbed defenses.

I turn over. Fresh cold pillow hits my cheek. Sheets get caught and twisted in my legs. I kick at them to no avail, then give up, accepting my fabric shackles.

Jessa's messages come next. I glance away from the calendar reminder to read their previews.

Concern. Questions. *Am I not coming to train today?* More concern.

I don't swipe them away, but I don't open them yet. I can't.

I can't get up yet.

Today: ANNIVERSARY!!!!

11:35

Jessa's picture pops up with the rhythmic vibration of her call. She set that up in her contact for me—a selfie of us and Harley at the beach. It almost makes me smile. We look happy.

I let it run through without picking up, but feel bad about it, so I gather the courage to open up my messages.

I click on Harley's name and type quickly.

> It's my anniversary. I should have known I wouldn't be able to get out of bed today. Can you tell Jessa and let her know I'm sorry for missing training without warning?

Alice :(

HARLEY

> What do you need? Do you want to be alone? Do you want to paint?

HARLEY

Do I want him here, he means. His presence, in whatever way I need—existing together, no pressure. My thumbs pause, thinking. Finally, they speak, much more concisely than my tongue could right now.

> Can you both come over?
>
> Bring your choice of takeout. Something new.
>
> And lemon cake.
>
> Please.
>
> And thank you.

You got it. Give me an hour.

HARLEY

An hour.

I sigh, exiting my messages and staring at the lock screen.

Today: ANNIVERSARY!!!!

I will give myself one more hour.

I'M WAITING by the window when they roll up in Jessa's truck. They each carry two plastic bags as they rush up the gravel driveway, rocks crunching under their sneakers. I catch a glimpse of a yellow smiley face on one of Harley's bags—there's nothing like crying over a pint of pork fried rice.

When their boots hit the porch, I swing open the door. The violent screech of ungreased hinges catches them off guard; both jolt to a stop halfway up the steps.

Jessa has the same soft smile on that she gave me the day I asked her to explain Arcadia. I hadn't clocked it then, but it's a tentative tilt of her lips, the kind of cautious tenderness you reserve for a wounded animal. As if it will bolt if you move too fast. As if it will break if you handle it too rough.

"Hey," Jessa says, and the velvety rasp stabs my chest.

Their faces go blurry.

"I miss him so much," I whine as the first tear falls.

Jessa's bags of takeout hit the porch, and she rushes forward. I stumble as her body collides with mine; I'm encircled in her warmth, steadied by her strong arms. She tucks my head into the crook of her neck, squeezing me tight.

"Oh, Trouble..." she whispers into my crown.

For some reason, that's what wrecks me. Those three syllables burst open the damn, smash it all to pieces; the waters begin to flow in sincerity as I heave.

I hate it—the way my eyes burn. The way I can't catch a breath. The way my heart keens, wails, throws a tantrum and bruises my ribs with well-placed kicks. The way my tears soak Jessa's shirt and the way the fabric sticks to my cheek.

"I'm sorry," I choke out.

Another presence curls around us, Harley joining in on the group hug. His chest presses into my back, strong and soothing. They wrap me in safety.

"We've got you, Alice," he mutters. "We've got you."

"Why the lemon cake?" Jessa asks, sucking icing off her fork. "I thought you were partial to chocolate."

We've made a pillow fort in the living room. Oddly enough, this was one of the dates in the book I have tucked in the drawer of the TV stand. Ryan and I did it on our second anniversary.

It's a nice tribute.

"You know how people get the same cake every year to celebrate?" I say, picking at my cuticles.

"Ah," she croons in somber understanding. "Should have connected those dots."

"Ryan loved lemon," I say. It's weird speaking about him like this. But also, kind of nice. They didn't know him, so it's as if they're meeting him for the first time with every new piece of information. I've found I can't talk about this stuff with Steph or Erica; their memories are also tainted by grief. It always ends in a sob-fest with them. "He was a fiend for anything sour. But lemon was his favorite."

"He had good taste," Jessa says. She lifts the plate and her tongue darts out, licking a long stripe through the icing stuck to the ceramic.

"Did you seriously just lick the plate?" Harley asks with disgust.

I snort. I'd do the same if I had more of an appetite. My half-eaten piece is sitting on the coffee table next to Harley's empty plate.

"Hey. It's a no judgment zone. That means Alice can snot all over my shirt and I can lick icing off the plate," Jessa says.

"What do I get to do then?" Harley asks.

"Lie there and look pretty."

"But I do that all the time. What's something equally as gross that I can do?"

I shake my head at their heatless bickering. "Can we watch another movie?" I ask, interrupting.

Jessa discards her plate and crawls onto our makeshift mattress of couch cushions. "We can do anything you want. We don't have any plans except for you today."

Harley rolls closer and tugs me to his side. It's as if he can read my mind—or maybe he simply noticed I needed grounding. I can't linger in one thing too long when I'm like this, otherwise I space out. And when I space out, large chunks of time escape me.

He physically pulls me away from the cloying, itchy sadness.

"No plans except for *cuddling* you," Harley corrects. "Because you cannot have a pillow fort without cuddles. That's a rule. I read it somewhere."

"You say that about everything. Now stop hogging her." Jessa smacks him with a throw pillow, but since I'm tucked under his arm, she also hits me. "Sorry, Trouble, you're necessary collateral for his punishment."

I shake my head again, but this time I actually smile with silent laughter. "You can both cuddle me. I'll lay in the middle."

After a one-sided pillow fight, and Harley's valiant effort to fight back one-handed, Jessa puts on a movie and curls up on my other side. They make comments about what happens on the screen, but I don't pay attention.

Even if I wanted to, I couldn't. Not when I'm stuck in my head. Certainly not with Harley's heartbeat under my ear. And definitely not with Jessa's hand twining with mine over my stomach.

Bracketed by these two, I manage to fall asleep.

22

DREAMSCAPE

ALICE

I'm flying.

    The air is brisk on my cheeks, and I sniffle to keep the snot from dripping out of my nose. They all convinced me I'd be able to handle it. They said it'd be worth it, even if I look like Rudolf when I come back down to earth.

    It's worth it. Definitely worth it.

    I eek and yelp and scream and laugh as we soar through the clouds. I don't dare lift my hands from Ori's scaled back—I don't want to fall—but I'm tempted.

    I technically can't fall, since I'm strapped into a harness made for this kind of stuff. Ori said it might be uncomfortable to wear, but it's better to be safe. I don't disagree with him. The harness digs tightly into my thighs and around my stomach, but it keeps me securely fastened between his mighty wings.

    Ori roars.

    The vibration shakes me, pulling a crazed giggle from my throat. It's like a roller coaster ride, the cart rumbling as it rolls over the tracks. The peaks and valleys are the same, but the view is better.

Woods stretch on for miles below us, fall foliage in full bloom. I've been in Arcadia for over a month now, and the crisp air is refreshing after getting so many extra summer days after my birthday.

My stomach swoops as Ori carries us high, lets gravity plummet us through the air, then spreads his wings to glide low above the flora.

When the rush wears off, a calm washes over me. I hug Ori's neck tightly and rest my cheek on his scales. They're smooth, and warm, like the heater pad my mom runs in the microwave and puts on her back when she's sick. Sometimes she lets me use it on my neck, but only after it's cooled off. Ori's dragon has that same temperature, and it makes me want to nap.

He must sense my lethargy, because we break through the lowest layer of clouds and circle over a clearing.

His dragon huffs a warning, and I hang on impossibly tighter as we drop, his wings fanning out to stop our momentum. His taloned feet hit the grass, singing the green with his unnatural heat.

I unclip the harness like Ori showed me and slide down his scales. When my shoes hit the ground, I stumble on wobbly legs, but a pair of strong arms catch me.

Jessa's got the strongest muscles of all of us—I know because we had a flexing competition the other day and the bump on her arm was the biggest. Harley and I were the same, and Ori was somewhere in between. He was bummed out afterward and challenged Jessa to see who could climb a tree the fastest.

Ori's kind of a sore loser, but he won their race and that brightened his mood. Jessa doesn't care about winning so much as having fun.

"Did you like it?" she asks.

"It was crazy," I croon, and laughter leaks out of her wide smile. "Why aren't you guys making him take you up there all the time?"

"Because it's technically breaking the rules," Harley says, sidling next to me. His freckled nose scrunches, causing his round glasses to hitch. "And the one time I did go, I dropped my glasses. I had to lie to Jessa's parents about how I lost them in the woods. I was terrified."

"You technically weren't lying," Ori says, having shifted back into his human form. "You did lose them in the Wandering Woods."

Jessa snorts. "Yeah, while he was a hundred feet above them, hurtling through the sky."

Ori untangles himself from his harness—the leather drapes over his human frame in oversized loops, but it fits his massive dragon perfectly. Before we got in the air, he said that as he gets older and taller his dragon will grow too. That was crazy to hear, because he's already way bigger than a moose. And those things are big.

"Wait, why is it breaking the rules for you guys to fly with him?" I ask, my brain catching up with Harley's words as Ori joins our huddle.

"Only fated Champions are supposed to fly on dragon-back," Harley answers.

"It's a pride thing," Ori says, shrugging. "But I don't really care. If I like you well enough, you can join me in the air. I'm cool like that."

"Stick it to our parents and their stupid rules," Jessa calls out, lifting her fist to the sky. Her dad is the head of Ori's parents' guard. One day, she'll be a knight too. "But before we do that, let's go get lunch. I'm starving. Do you think the bakery will have croissants?"

She throws an arm around Harley's shoulders and holds her other one out for me. I tuck myself into the fold, and she starts leading us back to the footpath. But when I glance back at Ori, expecting him to be on our heels, he's still in the clearing, watching us with a tilted head and a frown.

I keep my hold around Jessa's waist as I dig my heels in the grass, bringing us to a stop.

"C'mon, Ori," I call out, holding out my free hand for him. "What are you waiting for?"

His frown quickly morphs into a defensive scowl. "Nothing."

He stomps forward but doesn't join our embrace.

I roll my eyes and grab his billowy white shirt, forcing him to my side. He yelps his surprise, and his eyebrows jump into the mop of black waves that hang on his forehead. My hand settles on his waist, a match to my other on Jessa's.

"There. Now we're all the same," I preen with a smug smile.

Ori's cheeks pinken. They've been doing that a lot this week. It makes him look silly.

I'VE NEVER MET anyone with my birthday before. In Arcadia, lots of people have the same birthday. Ori's parents do. And so do we—all four of us. Ori, me, Ori's twin brother, and Maven. Maven's a human girl too, but she's been here a lot longer.

Apparently, when humans come here, it means we're special.

Ori's parents explained it as being kind of like one of my storybooks, or a movie. Arcadia chose us because we have magic inside, and when we grow up we'll be Champions of the realm.

I'm still confused as to how that works, but I'm trying not to think about it too hard. Yesterday was really long, and today's our birthday. I don't want to ruin it by asking too many questions.

"I want to have a tea party with the flowers," Maven says, tucking a piece of her dark red hair behind her ear.

"Then go do that," Ori says. "Enzo will go with you, won't you, Enz?"

"Of course," Ori's twin brother says with enthusiasm. Enzo's got the same hair as Ori, black and wavy, but different eyes. His are a yellowy hazel where Ori's are deep blue. "I love tea. And the flowers aren't too mean when you're around, Mave."

Maven stomps her foot with a frustrated growl. I only met her this morning while we all ate breakfast, but I can already tell she acts like the mean kids at school.

Enzo's super sweet. He showed me around the castle last night. Ori's a little scarier, but it reminds me of how my friend Erica's older brother acts when I go over to hang out. He puffs out his chest and explains to us the rules of games we already know how to play.

Bossy—that's the word.

Maven is bossy too, but in a different way.

"It's supposed to be a birthday party. You can't have a party with only two people," she says.

Enzo's smile falters, and he glances around at the rest of us for help. Harley, the boy with white hair, looks slightly terrified. Jessa seems more concerned with picking the dirt out from underneath her fingernails; she said she was up early training with her dad.

I stay quiet; I'm the new kid, I don't think I get a say.

"It's all our birthdays. We all get an equal say," Ori says, as if he can read my mind. "If you want it to be a group event, then let's vote. I want to go to the Lake. What about you, Alice?"

"What? Me?" I squeak.

"Yes, you."

Ori stares at me expectantly, black brows raised high above his navy eyes. They're really pretty eyes.

"What do you want to do today?" the prince presses.

"Um... I don't know, I haven't been to the Lake yet," I say, tentatively. "It could be fun. But I'll do whatever. I don't really care."

Ori turns back to Maven with his arms crossed over his chest. "See? Two votes for the Lake. Enzo, what do you want to do?"

Enzo's hand scratches his neck, and he looks even more uncomfortable than before. In a quiet, timid voice he says, "I kind of wanted to swim today."

Maven throws her hands up in the air with another growl of annoyance. "Fine. We'll go to the freaking Lake."

"Can't we combine it all?" I ask. It doesn't seem fair to make her unhappy on her birthday. "Have some tea and swim?"

"It'll be a hassle," Ori says. "But if you're offering to carry the kettle and cups up the ladder, then sure."

"Why do you need a ladder to get to the Lake?" I ask.

"It's the one in the sky," Harley chirps.

"Oh, you did mention that yesterday," I say, nodding.

My head is starting to spin. There are too many new things to keep track of, and everything is strange—but only strange enough that it still makes sense when you think about it.

"It's not the same," Maven pouts. Then she twirls around, flicking her long red hair over her shoulder. "Whatever. We'll do what the new girl wants."

~

"Alice, dear!"

Ori's mom's twinkling voice halts my skipping. I spin, searching for her in the busy cobblestone square.

There. Sitting at the edge of the fountain is the queen. She's in a casual frock today, similar to my own cotton dress, which is suited for the surprise heat wave. Harley explained to me that the seasons here work how they do back home, so we're through the worst of it since we're deep into September.

"Come here, I have someone I want you to meet," the queen calls across the square. No one pays her any mind, the townsfolk hustling on with their day. I pad over, my dirtied shoes squeaking over the worn stones.

"Hi," I say, suddenly shy.

She's so pretty, it's intimidating. Her hair is long and curly like mine, but black in color like Ori's. It's shiny and flows freely down her back, making her look like a princess. Which I guess she is, except more important, because a queen is more important than a princess.

Her smile is kind as she pats the space between her and an older woman on the fountain's edge. The stone is damp from fountain splatter, and I hesitate to sit.

"I don't want to get a wet spot on my butt," I say.

The queen and her friend laugh, and I cringe, but they don't push me to join them.

The woman next to the queen is old, like Nana. She's got wrinkles around her eyes and mouth, and they deepen when she purses her lips to look me over. A weird scent hits my nose, and I realize she's got a cigarette pinched between her fingers. But the smoke wafting off it doesn't smell bitter; this is sweeter.

The queen's friend takes a slow drag. Smoke puffs out her nose before she speaks with a smirk. "Want some, dearie?"

"No?" I say, more a question than an answer. My wide eyes flick to the queen, who laughs again.

"You can't offer the child a joint," the queen scolds in that kind, smooth voice. It's like a lullaby. "Alice, this is the twins' Memaw."

"You're Ori's grandma?" I ask, tilting my head at the old woman. I glance between the two women who don't look alike at all. Where the queen's features are soft, Ori's grandma is sharp.

"Sure am," she says, lifting the smoking stick to her lips. "And you're Ori's Champion? 'Bout time you wandered in here. Was getting sick of the other one."

The queen sighs, and her dainty fingers pinch the bridge of her nose.

"You mean Maven?" I ask.

Ori's grandmother grunts.

"What my mother-in-law means is that she's excited to meet you. She doesn't spend a lot of time in the castle or town anymore, but she'll make more appearances now that both you and Maven are here," the queen explains. "She's going to start mentoring you both on what it means to be a Champion."

"Why don't you live in the castle anymore?" I ask.

"Unfortunately, their Pop passed on a few years ago, so I moved out to a cabin in the woods for some peace and quiet," Ori's grandmother says. She waits a beat, sucking on the cigarette again. "You know, four out of six things you've said have been questions. Curiosity like that once killed a cat."

"My Nana says my curiosity is what makes me creative."

"Sounds like a smart lady."

"She is," I say. "My mom's smart too. She's a scientist, so she's curious but in a different way."

The queen and Ori's grandmother share a look, and it makes me scuff my toe on the cobblestone.

"Alice, dear," Ori's mother says, softly. "Do you miss your family?"

My brows knit. "That's a silly question."

Ori's grandmother snorts, and smoke comes out her nose.

"Of course, I miss them," I continue. "They're my family."

Sadness darkens the queen's eyes; they churn like storm clouds. "And they treat you well?"

"Yeah," I say, confused.

"They never hurt you?"

"No, they're my parents," I say, getting frustrated. "Why would they hurt me?"

"Sometimes family doesn't act as family should," the queen says, again with that smooth voice. "I only wanted to make sure. Maven's family wasn't kind to her."

"Well, mine don't do that," I huff, crossing my arms.

"I believe you," the queen says.

"You enjoy it here, Alice?" Ori's grandmother asks sharply, and I shrink back. "Does Arcadia make you curious enough to want to stay? If you never found that portal home, do you think your new friends could become your new family?"

WAKING from my dreams of Arcadia is soft. Not a jolt, not a gasp, not a snap of my lids, but a slow flutter of my lashes. They tickle my cheeks as I rouse to a dark living room, lit only by the movie's selection screen previews rolling on repeat. The DVD player whirs. It's likely overheated, but it serves as a calming underscore to Jessa and Harley's deep-sleep breathing.

We're a tangle of limbs, blankets, and pillows, and even with the air conditioning making the house crisp, I'm on the verge of too hot.

My shoulder is notched in Harley's armpit, my cheek pressed to his rising and falling chest. We haven't moved much in our nap. Jessa's the only one who's shifted in slumber; her head has claimed my stomach as a pillow, and her arm is woven between my thighs, hand reaching across my body to wrap around Harley's calf.

A smile sneaks onto my lips.

I take my time soaking in how peaceful they look. Gratitude slides between my ribs and wraps around my heart as I gently brush a strand of Jessa's bleached bangs off her forehead. The longer I stare—the longer I linger in this content their presence brings—the louder Memaw's voice is in my head.

Do you think your new friends could become your new family?

The answer is annoyingly clear: they could. If I let them.

It's that nasty second bit that has my fingers pausing their trail down Jessa's cheek.

Ryan became my family. I put him before everyone, sometimes before myself. But that's relationships, right? You take turns putting each other first. It all evens out if you stay together long enough.

These two are clearly willing to do that for me. They show up when I ask them to. They don't push or pry in ways that make me uncomfortable. They made space for Ryan's ghost at our coffee-table dinner.

When everyone talks about my life to me—my therapist, my friends—they always use words like *moving on* or *pushing through*. I know they don't mean to have this effect, but those terms make me burrow into my bitterness.

Sure, I don't want to feel this terrible, but I also don't want to *move on* or *push through*. That feels like a disservice to my love. That feels like I'm trying to find a replacement. But there could *never be* a replacement. That's what's so fucked about it all.

But maybe, there could be a table of four with three seats filled instead of one. Not a replacement—an addition.

The urge to capture this moment seizes me. It feels monumental. Singular. An earthquake; a shift of the tectonic plates under my feet. My free arm somehow contorts enough to snag my dying phone from the couch behind us. I open my camera and set it to video, then I swivel it around us at different angles, capturing how our bodies mingle.

This is my next piece.

My fingers itch as I lock my phone and toss it back onto the couch.

I hold my breath as I detangle myself from Jessa, lifting her head off my lap and laying it onto the blankets beneath us. She doesn't stir, completely knocked out. I slide away from Harley, and he sucks in a quick yawn, sleepily curling into the empty space I leave.

I pause, kneeling next to both of them, and again, gratitude strangles my heart. I don't want to wake them, but I need to thank them.

I bend and press a gentle kiss on Jessa's forehead. I twist the opposite way, lips pressing an equally soft kiss to Harley's. But unlike Jessa, when I pull back, Harley's eyes are open and gazing up at me.

"What are you doing up?" he asks in a deep, slumber-laden rasp.

He's a vision—sleepy smile and dimpled cheeks spotted with freckles, thick white lashes hanging low over glittering irises, and long fingers combing through messy locks.

"I'm going to go paint," I whisper. "It's the middle of the night. Go back to sleep."

Harley blinks, slowly, and then squints—he doesn't have his glasses on, so I'm sure I'm blurry this close.

"Can I come?" he asks in that same, sleepy rasp.

I tilt my head, emotion swelling in my throat. "Why?"

"I like watching you when you're at peace," he says, as if it's the most obvious explanation in the world.

23

BURNING, BAGELS

ORAZIO

She's everywhere and I hate it.

In my backyard, sprouting like a dandelion weed that I once wished on. She shows up with this big smile for Jessa, roaring and ready to go with whatever stupid exercise the knight has planned for us. I keep picking at her, spraying poison with my words. But it's as if someone blew her seeds all over the yard and she's rooted herself for good.

In my shop, although she was only here once. Every time I bend over to cuff a trouser leg or pin a skirt hem, I see her, standing there, looking at me in the mirror with a confused expression. Because she didn't remember me. Didn't *see* me.

In the library, where she trades sneaking glances with Harley. She's going to ruin him, if she keeps stringing him along. His soft heart never hardened like mine with age. It will break, and I won't be able to comfort him, because I'll be muttering *I told you so*.

In Mad Mug, where she eats lunch with my friends on the days we don't train. She laughs, and covers the twinkling sound with her hand, as if she feels the need to hide her joy. It infuriates me. I can't even get a mid-day coffee in peace anymore.

Even in Arcadia, I scent her on the wind. Cloying vanilla and teasing sugar. It's impossible, my imagination playing tricks on me. It's either that or the Woods are mocking me with the taste of her in the air. She hasn't been here since I found her wandering.

Worst of all, she's in my dreams. Her younger self taunts me with the last good memories of my childhood. Her older self does the same, reminding me of the last time hope pumped through my veins. It's a secret memory I'd rather forget, of her sneaking glances at me across a rumbling subway car.

It was an accident, running into her. I would have called it fate, had it ended in a different outcome. I'd rushed to catch the 1 after my apprenticeship ended for the day, needing to make it to Penn Station as soon as possible, and slipped in just as the doors were closing. I'd flopped into the lone empty seat at the center of the car, and when I finally lifted my head, my heart stalled in my chest. She was older, but I knew she was mine.

That's where the dream usually starts.

There's suspicious recognition in her eyes, but she doesn't say anything as her ear-muffed head falls on the shoulder of the man next to her. He presses a kiss to her forehead, and the first fissure spreads through my soul. Her ungloved hands cross on her lap; two rings glint, stacked together on her left ring finger.

Married.

Not mine.

His.

A second fissure cracks. My inner beast roars, pounding at my chest.

They get up two stops later. It's not the one I need, but I follow anyway. I call her name, and she pauses, glancing back, perplexed. Her golden brows knit and her pink lips part, and I think she's going to say something—hope for her to acknowledge my presence. But her husband slings a protective arm over her shoulder, ushering her towards the stairs to the street. I call her name again, but she ignores me.

Another train arrives, and the crowd swallows them in the rush to exit. Someone knocks into me, and in the moment it takes for me to right myself, I lose track of her.

Panic.

There are too many people—too many scents in the sea of black parkas for me to know which way she went. With a racing heart, I stumble up the stairs.

I burst through the exit turnstile and lope up to the street corner. Taxi's honk and the steam from a halal cart hits my face as I spin in place, trying to catch a whiff of her to follow. But it's too late. Harsh winter air hits my cheeks, and I'm left, a bolt of fabric tucked under my arm, as the masses swirl around me.

How could her soul not recognize mine?

I blink hard, trying to refocus my exhaustion-blurred eyes on the needle I need to thread. The fiber bounces off the eye for the thirtieth time and I growl, tossing both onto my worktable.

I can't focus because I haven't gotten any sleep. And I haven't gotten any sleep because I'm plagued by *her*.

The clock on the wall shows it's only 10:02 a.m., too close to my noon appointment to escape to Arcadia and shift to blow off steam. But I could flip the break sign on the door and grab a coffee.

At the bagel shop, of course, because I can't go to Mad Mug anymore without catching Jessa's evil eye or a glimpse of blonde curls.

My hands dig into the pockets of my slacks and play with the loose change jingling there as I walk. It takes four minutes and thirty-two seconds to get to the run-down mom-and-pop shop. The store has seen better days—the butcher-block cutting boards behind the register have a dip in them from years of wear—but you can't get a better bacon, egg, and cheese on an everything bagel anywhere else in town. Or a cheaper drip coffee.

The bitter smell mixed with the overwhelming stench of yeast hits my nose the second I walk in. It's the end of morning rush, so there's fifteen people mulling about in front of the display cases, waiting for their orders. A few tourists muse over the specialty cream cheeses, one of their noses scrunching at the lox spread. They turn to the person in line behind them to ask a question and—

My dress shoes make an obnoxious squeak against the tile as I come to an abrupt stop. Half the heads in the shop turn; human gazes bounce over me, and upon realizing I'm nothing special, hop back to watching the sixteen-year-olds behind the counter throw bagels into brown paper bags.

"Orazio!" Marie, the old shop owner, calls out. Her voice has the raspy edge you get from smoking for forty years, along with the overly enunciated and elongated vowels of her heavy Long Island accent. She hobbles out from behind the baskets of bagels, arms outstretched. "I stopped by to show you the pictures of my granddaughter's wedding the other day, but the shop was closed. Stay here, I'll grab my phone from the back."

She talks as if I have a choice to turn around and leave, but I can't, especially with the pair of crystal blue eyes shooting daggers at me. Marie's a quirky human, her and her husband both are, but they're nice enough, and welcomed me and Jessa with open arms when we both opened our shops in town. She, however, cannot read the room to save her life.

The woman rushes towards the office at the back of the store as I step into line, right behind my blonde plague.

She's a tiny thing, barely reaching my shoulder.

I watch her through my periphery, never giving her direct eye-contact. A fact that clearly bothers her, given the miffed huff she expels through her nose. She probably expects me to initiate a conversation.

That's not going to happen. I don't want to talk to her any more than I have to.

I'm only entertaining this farce for Jessa and Harely. There's no way she can be ready before August, and I fully expect whatever plans they have to fall apart by the time our birthday comes around.

A phone is shoved into my line of sight, and a too-bright picture of Marie's husband in his custom suit I made for his granddaughter's wedding shines up at me. The man is beaming in the forest green three-piece tux.

"He looks hot, right?" Marie snickers. She flicks her finger over the screen, rolling through some more pictures of the wedding party. "You dressed him good. I wasn't sold on the green at first, thought it'd be too flashy. But with Millie's husband wearing his white uniform and their bridesmaids wearing the green too, it worked great."

"I did match the screenshot you gave me," I mumble.

"Oh yeah. You know, I forgot I gave you that," Marie says, swiping again. "Look at this one. Her husband's a sweet guy, smart too—he's an officer in the Navy. But he's not a real looker, huh? It's a shame you set up shop after she met him. I wish I had another grandkid to set you up with. You'd make me some cute great-grand babies."

I stiffen at the mention of children, meanwhile Alice shifts uncomfortably next to us, clearly eavesdropping. She's trying to get a better angle to see the pictures Marie's waving around. But when she finally sneaks a glance though lowered lashes, her whole body goes rigid.

"Hey, Marie?" someone calls from the back of the shop. "Can you come back here? The mixer's acting up again."

Marie clicks her tongue and rolls her eyes. She shoves her phone into her back pocket as she shuffles away. "I'll show you the rest the next time you come in."

"That's not necessary," I say, but Marie waves me off over her shoulder.

"Give this one a large even if he asks for a small, got it kid?" she yells, pointing at the teen working the register before disappearing through the swinging kitchen door.

The teen gives her a thumbs up before motioning for Alice to order. I follow, stepping up behind her to keep the line moving.

"Um, can I get an egg-everything with veggie cream cheese, a sesame with regular cream cheese, and a poppyseed, toasted, with butter? To go, please."

A frown deepens the corners of my lips as I recognize Jessa and Harley's orders. I've picked them up on many Sunday mornings before.

"You know the butter will melt, right?" the teen at the register asks. Their grimace speaks to having been yelled at one too many times by people who get unnecessarily angry about what happens when cold butter meets hot bread.

Alice's head tilts, as if it never crossed her mind to get frustrated with someone over the outcome of her own choices.

"Yes…" she drawls out slowly.

"Then that'll be $10.25."

"Damn, I was close. Thought it'd be an even ten." She slaps a ten down on the pink countertop and then digs around her purse for a quarter. This place prefers cash. Did she know that, or is she just the type to carry it around?

"The specialty cream cheese is an extra twenty-five cents now," the teen says.

"Sorry, I know there's a quarter in here somewhere," Alice says, chuckling awkwardly as her arm rummages around in the large tote she's always carrying around. The teen stares at her blankly and the line behind me grows.

My fist curls around the quarter in my pocket. Impatience

gets the better of me when that nervous laugh hits my ears again, and I toss the coin onto the counter.

"Here," I say. "Stop wasting everyone's time."

Alice freezes, arm swallowed past her elbow by her canvas tote. Her head lifts and turns, and our gazes clash for the first time since I walked in the shop. Her brows knit. The divot that forms between them is no longer than a standard top-stitch, the early days of a future wrinkle.

There's a slow blink of confusion as she takes me in. And then something *shifts*.

No, I don't like that look at all.

There's a soft sadness there. A deep melancholy.

My insides churn.

Why is she looking at me like that?

Meanwhile, the cashier swipes the cash off the counter and the register dings as they access the drawer. The old machine spits out a receipt.

Alice breaks our stare.

"Thank you," she mutters as the cashier rips the paper and hands it to her. It's unclear if the thank you was directed at me or the teen, but it's likely the latter.

"We'll call out when it's ready," the teen says, and Alice walks into the mulling crowd. "What can I get for you?"

"A small coffee. Black," I say, handing over four singles. The coffee is three. The kid will keep one. "Ignore Marie."

My tone is curt, purposefully so. I want to get the hell out of here. My neck is overheating with annoyance from being in the vicinity of *her*. The teen's swallow is audible as they nod.

I scratch at the overgrown beard lining my jaw as I wait for the kid to pour my coffee. The coffee I don't even want anymore.

When they slide the Styrofoam cup over the counter, I grab it and take off. I ignore the two pinpricks of hatred searing the back of my head and shove open the door with my free hand. I move so fast that the glass barrier nearly slams shut to block out Alice's call.

But it doesn't. And her twinkling timbre calls out my name.

"Ori—"

I keep walking, pushing myself down Main Street. Her quick steps follow; there's three of hers to every one of mine.

"Ori, stop," Alice huffs. "I have something to ask you."

"I have no answers to give you."

"It's important."

I ignore her.

"God, you're such an ass." I catch her frustrated mutter before her hand snatches the sleeve of my rolled-up button down. My pivot is lightning fast, yanking my arm free of her grasp. She flinches, stepping backwards.

"What?" I growl.

Her expression flips through several maddening emotions before settling. It's quick, but I catch them all. Shock. Fear. Anger. Determination. It always lands on that last one. Her lips set in a fierce line. Her jaw ticks. She grows inches in aura, even though she stands at a meager five-four. Her feet shift into a wider stance, like she's bracing for a fight.

She also looks tired. There are bags under her eyes, and they're bloodshot, as if she spent all night crying.

I hate it. I hate the way it's on the tip of my tongue to ask what's wrong. But I can't—I refuse to open myself to her.

"I need to know what happened the day I left Arcadia. I've got some of my memories back, but not that one," she says. "It feels important."

I step forward, leaning in so close that I'm sure she can feel the heat of my breath on her nose.

"You broke a promise," I say. *And then years later, you broke me.*

Jessa was wrong when she yelled at me to get my shit

together. To join them in this pursuit of a woman who will ruin us.

I don't want *Alice*. I don't want the person who rejected me in the worst way possible: by choosing someone else.

I want my fucking life back.

I walk away. Alice doesn't follow.

Of course she doesn't fucking follow; I was always the one following her.

I toss the full to-go cup into the first trash bin I pass.

24

"FRIENDS"

ALICE

"He's such a freaking jerk," I practically growl into the phone. "He practically threw a quarter at me yesterday, and then, in the most asshole-ish manner possible, told me to get out of his sight."

I slam my front door shut with my foot and stomp across the creaky floors to the kitchen, heavy tote slung over my shoulder. My best friend sighs on the other end of the phone.

"Wait, is this the same guy that tackled you like a linebacker at the grocery store?" Steph asks.

"What? No, that's Harley. Harley's my friend." My lips mash together at the not-totally-a-lie-but-kind-of-a-lie statement. I switch from headphones to speaker, throwing my phone onto the counter so I can start putting away groceries. "And he didn't tackle me. We ran into each other. Also, that happened over a month ago."

"Sorry, I'm all over the place. I'll get everyone straight once I put faces to names when we visit this weekend," she says. "You know what would help, though? You actually taking a picture of yourself and the new friends you're replacing us with."

"*Steph.*"

"Yeah, that was out of pocket. I know we're irreplaceable." She chuckles. "But back to your impassioned recount of events. Please continue."

"This guy is the tailor who hemmed my dress for the gala..." I huff and lean on the counter, my elbows digging into the black marble. Again, it's a small fib. A peek at the truth, but not the full thing. I need to ease Steph and Erica into this craziness. My palms squish my cheeks as I mutter, "Sometimes I see him around town. It's a small town."

"Do we know this hot tailor's name?"

My hands fall from my face and slap onto the counter. "I didn't say he was hot."

"You didn't have to. You never tell us anything about anyone anymore. Either he's a 'first prize smoked brisket at the county fair' piece of meat hot and you feel weird about finding someone attractive again, or he's the literal devil incarnate," Steph says.

"Yeah, your analogies still don't land the way you want them to," I mutter, suddenly feeling a little too exposed. The annoying truth of the matter is that Ori is both of those things. And it's unbelievably frustrating.

"Whatever," Steph chides with affection. "I have to admit, it's nice to hear you so lively. There's a lightness to your voice that I haven't heard in a while. Even if you're raging about some guy—who *isn't* attractive—you sound happier."

She pauses, and I want to open my mouth to speak, but I can't get my lips to part, so she continues.

"I guess I was wrong. Moving to Meadowbrook *was* the thing to get you out of your funk and bring back the old Alice."

Wrong. I think, immediately. It's not the town that has let this tiny stream of light into my dark mind; it's the people within it.

And then resentment slaps me across the face.

Is that how they really see this phase of my life? A *funk*?

I've taken a daily cocktail of anti-depressants for over a year. It's not a *funk*.

My husband died. And every day since, it's become clearer that it will never be a *funk*. There's no *going back* to the old me.

I clear my throat. "I finished another piece for the gallery."

"Oil or acrylic?" Steph asks, easily switching to business mode.

"I have been doing most of them in acrylic since we don't have enough time to properly dry and varnish oils," I say.

"True. But I'd make it work. People don't need to get so close to the paintings that their nose comes away stained." I can hear her eye roll. "I'm excited to see them."

"Hopefully they don't disappoint."

"Alice, you couldn't disappoint me," Steph says.

"Sure," I say, though I know it's not true. "I'm going to put away groceries and clean the house now. I have company coming and I need to sweep the cobwebs off the molding in the guest room."

Steph snorts. "We'll text you the train times."

"YOU SNEAKY BITCH!" Erica screams from down the hall, except it's that squeal-scream you make when you're outraged in the best way.

Steph's black brows rise to her hairline as she and I each hook a corner of the fitted sheet over their bed.

"You didn't say you were painting yourself!" Erica continues, though now she's huffing at us from the doorway of the guest room. "This is an extremely important development.

Who are the people you painted yourself with? I need answers, Alice. A.S.A.P."

My left eye twitches as I run my hand along the sheet's edge to the next corner. "Can we not talk in all-caps, please?"

"Sorry," Erica whispers dramatically. "But you literally never paint yourself or people you know. That's part of the whole schtick you went viral for. People are going to *flip* when they find out."

The fitted sheet snaps into place as we hook the other two corners into place.

"People aren't going to flip because these are only for the gallery. I'm not making prints of these," I say.

"You're not?" Steph says, reaching up to adjust her long brown ponytail. "That's news to me."

I shrug, avoiding their prying expressions by grabbing the top sheet. I flick it out of its fold, and the fabric puffs out over the bed, slowly descending in a bubble.

"This collection's personal," I murmur. "I'm calling it '100'."

There's a quiet beat as they process the meaning behind the name—they know it's importance.

It took me a while to commit to it, but after Harley and Jessa slept over the night of my anniversary, I couldn't deny it anymore.

My previous collections were all ten to twenty pieces inspired by internet strangers' bearing their hearts to me in an anonymous submission form. Their most vulnerable secrets, fears, and stories were cherry-picked by me and turned into something beautifully cathartic.

Each exhibition was labeled by the number lot featured: *1-20, 21-40, 41-55, 56-70, 71-80, 81-90, 91-99*. Seven collections with ninety-nine portraits of strangers' pain, and now, an eighth solely dedicated to portraits of my own.

I'm number 100.

Steph helps me fold over the top sheet at the head of the bed, and we repeat the process for a thin quilt over that.

"Steph, come see. They're amazing," Eric says, much less dramatically, once we're done.

"Okay." Steph sighs. "Alice?"

"I'll be right there," I say, tossing a freshly covered pillow onto the bed as they patter down the hall.

Once they're out of earshot, I fall onto the bed. My lids fall too, right to my cheeks, blanketing my irises in darkness. I hold them there—*one, two, three seconds*—before snapping them open and forcing myself to my studio.

Steph is staring at the latest piece I've finished, still perched on the easel, when I walk in. It's of Harley, Jessa, and me wrapped together in our pillow fort cuddle pile. Lemon cake is half eaten in the corner, where the coffee table cuts into view. I'm at the center, of course, serene and tortured. The pinch in my brow could be taken either way. Am I lost in a dream or caught in a nightmare?

Can it be both?

"Who are they?" Steph asks. Her arms cross over her chest as she turns to face me. "They're in all the others on the drying rack too."

I run my tongue over my teeth before answering. "My new friends."

"Friends. *Right.*"

My phone decides to buzz at that exact moment, three rapid notifications in my back pocket.

> Want to come over tomorrow night? The heatwave is supposed to break.
>
> HARLEY
>
> And I want to cuddle you around a fire.
>
> HARLEY

> Jessa says we can make s'mores.
> HARLEY

>> My friends are visiting this weekend.

> What??? Why didn't you tell us?
> HARLEY

>> I thought I did the other day. Maybe you were too distracted by your book.

> Hmm. Very possible.
> HARLEY
> Bring them over. I want to meet them.
> HARLEY
> We can make an afternoon of it.
> HARLEY
> Jessa says she'll fire up the grill. She's a pro.
> HARLEY

>> What about Ori? You guys can come here instead, so we don't get in his way.

> He... went home this weekend.
> HARLEY
> Bring them over. It'll be fun.
> HARLEY

"*Earth to Alice,*" Erica croons. Her short, bleached-blonde hair fills my periphery as she leans over my shoulder. "Who ya' texting? *Ooo*, it's one of the *friends*."

"You want to meet them?" I ask. "They invited us over for a barbecue and s'mores."

They both stare at me as if I'm stupid for asking.

25

FLIRTING MIGHT ACTUALLY KILL ME

ALICE

The thing about not having a sex drive for two years is that when it finally comes back, it hits you like a semi-truck that's lost control on the freeway.

The seconds leading up to the collision make you jittery: when you know you're in the truck's blind spot and you have no time to decide what to do.

You see it coming. You can't stop it. *Boom.*

Right now, I'm paralyzed in the blind spot. The blinker is on; it's the same color as the golden-hour sun reflecting in Jessa's eyes as she winks at me over the grill.

Do I speed up or slow down? Do I even want to avoid a collision with them?

"Bring this over to the table," she says, handing me a plate of food.

I nod as I grip the warm ceramic.

"Good girl," Jessa murmurs.

It's not fair, how she throws around those two words so casually. My ears heat, and her devious smirk flashes. She knows what she's doing—and it's clear she relishes seeing me squirm as I pivot on my heel.

The potent scent of grilled hotdogs and burnt cheeseburger edges waft up as I place the dish down on the picnic table, then proceed to slap buns on empty paper plates as everyone calls out their orders.

All the while I'm lusting my ever-loving mind out.

When did our dynamic change, exactly? It's more than the usual flirty quip that we throw back and forth. Jessa's hand curls around my waist every time she squeezes past me, nails scraping over the strip of exposed skin between my tank top and shorts. Harley plasters himself against me from ankle to shoulder every time we sit; his thumb finds my knee and runs back and forth mindlessly, sometimes even daring to trail up my thigh.

And they both give me these *looks*.

Darkened, hazy eyes. Damning smirks and sweet smiles.

Dangerous, unspoken questions flutter in the air between us.

Is this new, or has it always been like this, and I'm only now noticing it? Or am I hyper aware of their every move because Steph and Erica are watching?

Erica waggles her eyebrows at me as I drop a hot dog bun on her plate. I know that eyebrow waggle. It's her 'mischief is about to ensue' waggle.

I'm so fucked.

"So," Erica drawls, lips puckering around the straw to her drink. Harley had transformed from librarian to bartender upon our arrival, whipping us all up cocktails from the makeshift bar in their kitchen. Her mouth pops off the straw, and a refreshing click of her tongue sounds. "How did you all get together?"

I shoot her a glare as I settle on the wooden bench. She's a habitual shit stirrer, and I'm not stupid enough to miss her choice of words. It wasn't 'how did you guys meet'. It was 'how did you get *together*'.

She thinks we're fucking.

"Jessa and I have been friends since we were kids," Harley answers without skipping a beat, completely unfazed as he scoops a dollop of potato salad onto his plate. "But we only became a couple a few years ago."

"And you have another friend who lives with you? You all bought a house together?" Erica asks. "That's a big commitment."

"He's not *with us*, if that's what you're asking." Harley's cheeks go pink at the mention of Ori. "He's family though. That's why we all live together."

Erica hums, taking her time gulping down her mix of fruit juice and liquor. "So, how does Alice fit in with all this? She's not just some unicorn for you, right?"

"*Erica*," I warn in a low murmur. "Stop interrogating them."

"These are important questions," she argues. "You're painting them. You haven't even painted *us*." She turns to Steph, pleading. "We only want to make sure they're serious."

Steph throws her hands up in the air as if to say: *it's out of my wheelhouse*.

"It's alright," Jessa says, back from the grill. She reaches over my shoulder, between me and Harley, depositing the final side on the table: five ears of roasted corn on the cob. "I don't mind being interrogated if it means we get their approval at the end of the conversation. Right, Harley?"

Harley hums his agreement as his teeth sink into the one veggie burger Jessa grilled.

Jessa drops into the empty spot to my left, her smooth thigh pressing into mine. I tug at the fabric of my shirt in an attempt to reduce the flush I know is creeping over my chest. I can't even shift away to give myself some breathing room, otherwise I'd smush into Harley.

"I'll be honest with you both. We want to be with Alice in whatever capacity she'll let us," Jessa continues. She busies her hands, but instead of serving herself, she grabs my plate and starts serving *me*. "We're aware of Ryan and how important honoring his memory is. We'd never take advantage of someone's grief. And we're certainly not going to pretend we can replace him."

Jessa punctuates her words by dropping a full plate in front of me. Her hand finds my knee and squeezes once.

Comfort; protection; love, it offers.

"It's not what you're thinking, Erica," I blurt out. "We're not fucking,"

Steph coughs, choking on whatever food she shoved into her mouth.

"Yet," Jessa teases confidently, then leans down to whisper in the shell of my ear, "Eat."

Erica whistles in shock, but there's respect in the gentle purse of her lips. She waggles a finger at Jessa. "I like her."

I groan, the sound muffled as my palms scrub over my embarrassingly rosy face. "You guys don't need to have this conversation. You're not my parents."

"No, but we promised Ryan we'd take care of you," Steph says, finally making her voice heard in this conversation.

"What?" My hands fall from my face, gaze pinging between my oldest friends. Steph shrugs, awkwardly tucking her long hair behind her ears. Erica's bright brown eyes sparkle with heartfelt mischief in turn.

"I promised him I'd pull a 'I've got a shotgun and a shovel and no one's gonna miss ya' protective dad moment if something ever happened to him and you dated someone again," Erica says, then snorts. "Sorry. *Someones*."

Erica smirks, but it's Steph who meets me with a somber smile.

"I don't think he wanted us to tell you that he made us

promise that, but yeah. He did. It was way back in flight school though, after that one crash. You remember right?" Steph says, and I nod.

It's hard to forget the fear I felt in the days after, wondering if his helicopter would malfunction like his peer's had. It was the first time the danger of his job became *real*.

"He loved you," Steph says.

"I know."

"But he also knew his job had risks."

"I know," I repeat, though my voice cracks.

The table goes quiet at that. The mood doesn't sour as much as it sobers up, our livers processing the liquor in our cocktails at lightning speed. Everyone's attention is on me, and I hate it. Four sets of eyes, boring eight holes through my skin and to my messy soul.

"Do you?" Jessa asks, breaking the tension. "Have a shotgun and a shovel?"

Erica huffs a sad laugh. "No, but I'm sure I could find someone to do our dirty work for us if you ever hurt our girl."

"I fully expect you to string me up like a rabbit if that ever happens," Harley says.

My eyes widen on him. "*Harley*," I whisper, but his hand finds my knee again, squeezing a reminder of his intention as Jessa had.

"We won't hurt her. That's a promise," Harley adds.

"Seconded," Jessa says.

THE FIRE CRACKLES LOW, tossing glowing embers into the night sky. They're shooting stars that find themselves trapped and desperate to rejoin their friends; they make a valiant effort, reaching higher than I could ever, but still don't make it up to space.

We're all lingering in the satisfied afterglow of dessert; melted chocolate and marshmallows sandwiched between crisp graham crackers settle in our stomachs. It's quiet, but not uncomfortably so.

Jessa, Harley, and I each take up individual chairs around the fire pit while Erica and Steph are cuddled together on the cushioned two-seater. Smoke unfurls from their lips as they exchange a joint between their manicured fingers.

They offer it to Jessa next, who takes a hit. As she lets the smoke flow out of her mouth, she stands. "I'm going to get more firewood from the shed."

"Thank you, esteemed fire-keeper," Erica drawls, shooting a salute Jessa's way.

Jessa passes the joint to Harley before disappearing around the other side of the house. Harley pulls it to his lips, but it's almost dead, having made a few circles around the group already.

Our fingers graze when he hands it to me to finish off. I shiver, even though I'm warm from the fire and the drugs. His attention flicks from our hands to my face, and I'm lost in the way the embers reflect in his glasses.

I tuck the joint between my lips and suck. His head tilts, and the reflection clears, revealing heated eyes behind the panes of glass. The natural light source brings out his otherworldly coloring—fiery eyes and lunar white hair. It's a wonder, how I ever assumed he was human in the first place.

I shiver again, under his intense gaze. My lips pop off the dead joint, and I swallow down the last of the bitter smoke.

"Are you cold?" Harley whispers, leaning over the arm of his chair. "Do you want to go inside and get a sweatshirt?"

I shrug, flicking the bud into the fire. "Can it be one of your cardigans?"

Harley nods, and his tongue darts out to lick his lips. Palpable desire fills the air between us, and I hope the way I shift in my seat doesn't look too much like I'm squirming with need.

Harley glances over at Steph and Erica, who are now making out across the fire.

"C'mon," he says, pulling me out of my chair and leading me into the house.

Their house is a newer build than my grandma's, but it was designed with old charm in mind. Fresh paint in dark colors. Detailed molding. Hardwood floors.

We clamber up the stairs, our thumping steps dulled by the carpet runner, and stop in front of a closed door at the beginning of the hall. Harley lets go of my hand, and I despise the rush of air against my palm; the loss of warmth; the slightly humid tack to the skin. My fingers curl inwards, nails digging into the flesh, but they relax when Harley swings open the door with a dramatic flourish.

"Come right this way, mi'lady," he drawls in a terrible fancy accent, peering at me over the frames of his glasses.

I play into our bit and roll my eyes. His smile grows— balloons really—to the point that I could pop his pronounced cheeks like one.

I stroll into his bedroom and am hit with the scent of *him*. Books. Cinnamon, fresh, like he had a candle burning not too long ago. Old wood and that house mildew that some would find gross, but I find endearing.

Harley follows but doesn't shut the door behind him, shooting off to the walk-in closet and disappearing between the rows of clothing. The sharp swipe of hangers over metal poles fills the room.

I explore as I wait. A big bed takes up most of the space, with two nightstands on either end and a dresser with a TV across from it. Bracketing the dresser are bookcases. Some shelves are filled with old, clothbound classics, some house newer releases with colorful sprayed edges facing out, and some are home to library books, sheathed in plastic with their barcode stickers peeling on the spines.

I trace my finger over all of them, and the differing textures scratch a sensory itch I didn't know I had.

Maybe, in my next series, I could play with texture. I'm partial to a smoother canvas—I like my paint to blend unless it purposefully isn't meant to. But an experiment could prove fruitful.

My tongue traces over my faint smile, tastes the possibility of a *next*.

Look at me, thinking about the future of my art.

Maybe I should do drugs more.

"Here," Harley says, popping out of the closet wearing a brown cardigan and clutching a matching one between his long fingers. "I have two of these, so we can match."

Or maybe *they're* the drug. I should do *them* more. Or *start* doing them.

I giggle to myself.

Harley's head cocks to the side with curiosity. "What's so funny?"

"Nothing," I say, stifling my laughter.

"Nothing?" he repeats.

"Nothing," I tut, like I'm keeping a secret.

Harley hums. "Here." He spreads out the cardigan, holding it so I can slip my arms through.

I turn around, stabbing my hands through the sleeves, and Harley pulls it up the rest of the way. He adjusts it so it sits right on my shoulders and runs both hands down to my wrists. He hums again, noting how the sleeves land past my fingers. He pushes them up, gently, one by one. The soft cashmere fabric brushes pleasantly over my forearms, as do his fingers, as he rolls the sleeves to my elbows.

"This should warm you back up," Harley whispers, and his

breath is *right there*, on the back of my neck, where the earthquakes of my flesh originate.

That's not what's making me shiver, I think, hoping he can read my mind.

I spin around. "How do I look?"

I hook my hands into the pockets and pose dramatically—as if I'm a model on the other side of a camera lens. It's silly, but it feels good to indulge my whims.

It also feels good to be looked at with such dopey, blatant desire.

"You should keep that," Harley says, nodding to himself like he's answering a question from his head. "It looks good on you."

"It's too big," I say.

"It's mine," he counters.

"Fair."

"You should keep it," he repeats.

"If you insist."

"I do."

Harley is a strange mix of always nervous and sometimes confident. He isn't only one thing at a time, which is very human of him, considering he's not. He's like me; there's a cautiousness to every choice, and a carelessness in the way he executes them. As if once he's committed to something, he can't help but throw himself into it.

Right now, I want to throw myself into him. But I'm cautious with the *how*.

"You're cute," I say, because it's the truth.

"So are you, in my clothes," he volleys back, no hesitation.

Can't he just kiss me already?

He's so close. And he looks like he wants to. There's no mistaking the flickering caress of desire by his eyes, as if they're his lips and they're kissing every inch of me.

His hand reaches up, and I hold my breath, waiting for the

moment where he pulls my face to his. Except his fingers simply brush a curl from where it lays against my cheek and tucks it behind my ear.

Then he grabs my hand, and he's pulling me back downstairs. My mind is slow to catch up to my body, but once it does, we're already in the kitchen, headed straight to the backdoor.

"Harley." I dig my heels into the tile, pulling him to a stop. He turns around, brows knitted in that cute and confused way of his, as if I'm a puzzle he's trying to solve.

"What?" he asks.

"Are you not going to kiss me?" I ask.

His lips part as he blinks, his mind working double-time to process my question. The moonlight streams through the kitchen windows and sliding glass door, casting us in a cool glow.

"Do you want me to?" he finally asks.

"I thought the cardigan ploy was to get me alone so you *could*," I say, stepping closer.

"It wasn't a ploy, it was to make sure you were warm."

"I wouldn't have minded if it was."

"Really?" His throat bobs.

I nod. "Kiss me."

"Are you sure?"

"Harley, if you don't kiss me right now, I might actually die."

His head falls back with a groan. "I love how you speak in hyperbole."

I fist his cardigan, uncaring if I stretch out the cashmere, and pull him to me.

Boom. Crash. Pow. Whatever other noises cars make when they hit each other. I'm okay with being charged with vehicular manslaughter though, if it means I get to be kissed like this.

Fuck, he's a good kisser.

Not like I have that many people to compare it to, but still.

Harley's lips are so soft, I could be kissing clouds. They're tentative at first, but their confidence grows exponentially with every caress. A tortured sigh rushes out of his nose as my teeth graze his bottom lip, balmy breath coating me in his mounting desire.

My nails, even with the barrier of his cardigan against my palm, dig into my skin to the point of drawing blood. I'm tugging him closer and closer—he can't get fucking close enough.

We stumble backwards and Harley's arms catch us against the counter, bracketing me. His body is flush to mine, and he shamelessly grinds his hardening arousal against my hips.

I love it, crave it—the way he's unraveling. Arousal strikes me so hard I'm almost knocked off balance. I lean my back into the counter, urging him to press me against it.

To devour me. To fuck me. We could absolutely fuck like rabbits right now and I—

I snort, unintentionally breaking our kiss.

Fuck like rabbits. I stifle my laughter with a hand over my mouth.

He's a rabbit shifter. Oh my god, I'm fucking hilarious.

"What's so funny?" Harley asks for the second time tonight. It's not an annoyed question, it's asked with genuine curiosity. He enjoys learning how my brain works, clearly loves the way it hops between topics, drawing connections where others might not.

"I'm just giggle-happy," I say, biting into my lip.

The pain helps to bring me back down to earth, but it also makes me hornier. I soak in Harley's slightly unhinged appearance: lips puffy from our kisses and glasses fogged. I release his cardigan, leaving the fabric indented with my handprint, and gently remove his glasses. As I draw them to me, I notice the tiny smudges spread across the glass.

"Why are these so dirty?" I ask. "You can't possibly see through them."

He hums, nose bumping into mine teasingly. "Sometimes the world is more beautiful when you see it less clearly."

A beat passes between us, one where we both realize how ridiculous his statement is. That beautiful blush fills his cheeks, and he clears his throat.

"Actually, that's a complete lie." He cringes. "Dirty glasses are the worst. It's just too dark to care right now, and I'm trying to woo you with fancy words. Is it working?"

I place his glasses on the counter. "I'm going to steal that one liner for an art piece I think."

"Steal away," he says, then on a whisper adds, "You could take anything from me and I'd be happy about it."

"Then that isn't stealing," I chide, reaching up to boop his nose twice. "That's sharing."

Harley releases a strangled, desperate sound. "Is it? I must need to refresh my vocabulary."

"Do you like the idea of that?" I ask.

I don't know what it is about Harley, but he makes me bold. I'm addicted to pulling reactions from him; the tick of his jaw is great, but I want more. I need that decadent shade of peachy pink in his cheeks to spread down his neck, so I can study it. I still haven't mixed it perfectly on my palette, only managed a good enough version for now.

"Do you like the idea of sharing me?" I press.

He nods, but the flush isn't deep enough. I let my fingers toy with his belt loops, and his hips press harder against mine on instinct—chasing my touch.

"... of being shared?" I add.

There. That's the bloom I'm looking for. Blossoming on the tips of his ears. Crawling down the taught tendon of his neck.

Memories of Jessa flash through my mind. *But you are my good boy*, she once said to him at the beach. It finally clicks as to why he hasn't initiated more—why he didn't kiss me first.

He's waiting for permission.

"Ask for it," I say, running my hands up his chest to hook around his neck. His breath stutters under my touch. My lips graze his as I speak. "You haven't touched me yet. Ask me for it."

Harley's entire body melts.

"Can I touch you?" he mumbles into my mouth, a tortured rasp. "Tell me what you want me to do."

I hum around his bottom lip, suckling it. "Make me feel good."

That's all he needs to undergo a transformation. All the hesitance is gone.

Our lips resume their forceful collision as I'm lifted onto the counter. My body is eager, matching his frantic energy. My legs wrap around his waist—narrow but solid—and my hands run through his hair. The messy strands on top are silky soft, but the sides and back have the same texture of a blending brush.

Suddenly, I'm burning up. Why did we put on sweaters when we could have been doing this from the get-go?

I groan. He groans too. Our kisses turn sloppy. Our breath runs ragged. Our bodies grind and rub and it's pushing me towards release. I've never come from dry humping someone before but tonight might be a first.

Harley's hands slip under my tank top, tracing over each divot in my spine.

"Is this okay?" he asks in between breaths and kisses.

"I told you to make me feel good," I murmur my frustration. "Everywhere is free game, Harley."

"Fuck," he groans, and I use the opportunity to lick into his open mouth.

Our tongues dance briefly before he pulls back to kiss along my cheek, my ear, down my neck.

"I just want to make sure." His words puff against my pulse.

I grip his hair tightly and pull. He squeaks and looks at me with wide, lust-filled eyes; his pupils have taken over his irises completely.

"Stop overthinking this," I say firmly. "I wouldn't say yes if I didn't mean it. Okay?"

"Okay," he whispers.

"Now, I haven't orgasmed in two years. And I'm fucking desperate," I say, and he visibly gulps. "Don't stop until I come in my already soaked panties or, if you so choose, on your fingers. Because you have really nice fingers. And I think they'd feel fantastic inside me."

Harley's head drops into the crook of my neck. His teeth start nibbling, licking, sucking on the expanse of skin, making me squirm. I tighten my grip in his hair for emphasis.

"Is that clear enough for you?" I ask, breathless.

"Much clearer than my glasses," he mutters against my neck, swiping his tongue up my jugular.

I laugh. He laughs too, his body shaking against mine, though it quickly turns into a moan as I grind my core against his arousal.

"Come here," I beg on a whisper, pulling his lips back to mine. "Keep kissing me."

We don't talk again after that. Our bodies speak for us.

Hands. Tongues. Lips. Teeth. It's like building a fire. Start with the kindling. Layer on the sticks. Once it's strong enough, drop on the logs to catch. They do, and then it's a blaze.

Jean on jean rubbing together, soaking through. Nails on skin, raking out raised red lines of our pleasure. Popped blood vessels in the shape of our lips and bruises in the shape of our fingers.

I hope he leaves a mark. I hope he lasts. I need proof of him on me like I need air to breathe.

As if he can sense how close I am, Harley's hand shoves into my shorts, not even taking the time to unbutton them. He runs two fingers through my wetness and murmurs expletives I can't make out as he suckles on my earlobe.

All it takes is a few strokes of his nimble fingers over my clit to set me off. My pleasure triggers his. All the sweet noises run from our throats.

Harley kisses me through the come down, then gently eases his hand out of my pants.

And when he lifts his fingers to his lips and sucks them clean, I'm breathless all over again.

Harley wraps me in a strong embrace and we nuzzle into each other, heads falling to each other's shoulders as our breathing steadies.

From this angle I have a perfect view of the wet spot on his crotch. I pull back and snort, though I have the decency to cover my mouth to *try* to stifle it. His hands find the counter on either side of me; he looks down at himself and huffs.

His gaze lifts to meets mine, and we both stare at each other with dopey, unbelieving smiles.

Did we really do that? The air carries our thoughts between us.

Yes, and it was fucking erotic, the buzzing cicadas outside answer.

"Are you fucking kidding me?" Jessa's voice cuts through the kitchen, causing both of us to tense.

Harley looks over one shoulder, and I peer over the other. We both gape as Jessa throws her head back, releasing a frustrated sound from the threshold of the sliding door.

"I missed our first secret sexy time?" she groans. "No fair."

WHEN STEPH, Erica, and I leave, Jessa and Harley both give me see-you-later kisses on my cheek. Sweet. Innocent. So different from the ones Harley plundered from me an hour before.

We're halfway back to my house, three idiots walking in the middle of the road—but it's midnight in a small town, so it's fine—when Erica throws her arm around my shoulders and shakes.

"So…" she slurs. "They're hot, Ali."

I smile. "Yeah. They are."

"They seem nice," Steph says, turning around so she can face us as she walks backwards.

"They are," I repeat.

"Ugh, give us details," Erica says, shaking me again. "Where did you and Harley sneak off to? Was he so overcome by your beauty he had to ravage you? Give us *something*."

I push her away, shaking my head. "Something like that."

"You're killing me here!" Her frustrated cry echoes down the street, but it's accompanied by laughter.

My laughter.

What a nice sound I've become reacquainted with.

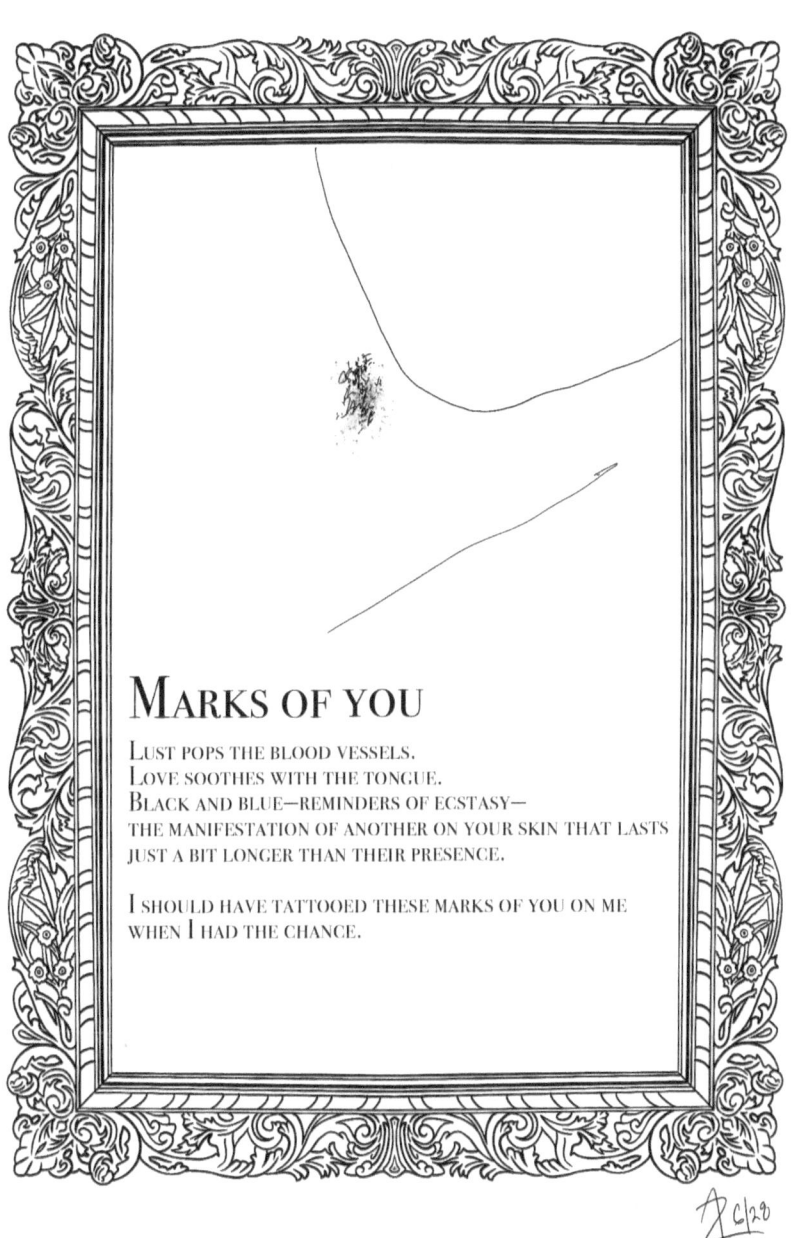

Marks of you

Lust pops the blood vessels.
Love soothes with the tongue.
Black and blue—reminders of ecstasy—
the manifestation of another on your skin that lasts
just a bit longer than their presence.

I should have tattooed these marks of you on me
when I had the chance.

26

HOW TO TRAIN YOUR DRAGON... TO FIGHT YOU

ALICE

Ori hasn't been to training.

He stopped coming after I ran into him at the bagel shop. One miss, *fine*. Two skips, sure, maybe he's exceptionally busy with wedding season. But *five*?

Given we're pressed for time, every second counts. We meet every morning, except for recovery days or like this weekend, when Steph and Erica visited, so it's a slap in the face on his part to no show with no notice.

The only benefit of him not coming is I feel less embarrassed when I lose against Jessa.

It's different than fencing, a combination of swordplay and hand to hand combat, and the practice weapon she's given me is bulkier than the sabre I used to wield in high school, so it's taken some getting used to. But the basic principles of reading your opponent are the same, and I've progressed farther than Jessa thought I would by now.

I'd be lying if her proud smile and murmured praise hadn't

turned me on from the beginning. But ever since the other night with Harley, my body's been a live wire, and shocks zap my nervous system every time she gets close.

And she gets *close* during training. It's some twisted version of foreplay.

"Good footwork," Jessa says as I dodge one of her swings.

My heart flutters in my chest at the compliment, but then she switches up her movements in a way I can't anticipate. I'm knocked onto my ass, and I grunt at the impact. I've quickly learned that grass doesn't soften your fall like you think it will.

She offers me a hand. "You're decent at dodging a human, but you'll have to move faster than that if you don't want to get swiped by a dragon claw."

I'm simmering with annoyance as Jessa pulls me to my feet —not at her, but at *him*. The beast that *I'm* putting in the work to help. The beast whose crown *I'm* going to win. And he can't even show up and *pretend* to care?

"How am I supposed to know how fast a dragon can fight if I don't ever train against one?" I huff.

Jessa hums knowingly. "Let's take a break."

I lay on my back, my annoyance subsiding as my heart rate settles. My hands slip through the slightly waxy blades of grass at my side, and I mindlessly rip some from their roots, letting them float away in the wind.

Jessa's water sloshes in her bottle, and the faint metal clanging fills the air between us as she drinks and reseals the cap. I close my eyes, and summer sounds take over my brain; birds chirp in their trees, wind rustles the leaves, and the eerie tune of an ice cream truck passes through the neighborhood.

"He's stubborn," Jessa finally says.

I lift my head and crack open one eye, careful to look only at her and not at the sun.

"Who?" I ask, even though I know.

"Almost as stubborn as you," Jessa says, shaking her head. "Ori." She heaves a sigh through her nose. "You know anything about why he might be acting up again?"

I chew the inside of my cheek. I may not have told her or Harley about our run in the day after my anniversary. I had gone out to grab us all breakfast as a thank you, after Harley fell back asleep in my studio while I painted through the early morning hours.

"I saw him at Strathmore the other day," I say slowly. "We... talked."

"You talked."

"Yeah?"

"You don't sound sure about that, Trouble."

I frown as I sit up. "Don't use that nickname in such a scolding manner."

"Why not?" Jessa taunts, a lopsided smirk cutting a dimple into one cheek. "You do something bad, *Trouble*?"

I shrug. "We talked."

"About what?"

"About *things*," I mumble. "About *him*." She raises one black brow, egging me on. "About what happened the day I left."

She sighs. "Well, that explains the past week, at least."

Jessa runs a hand over the slicked-back part of her ponytail, avoiding messing up her surprisingly sweat-free bangs, and pulls the long swath of hair over her shoulder. Her fingers toy with the red and black ends.

"You two will keep on clashing unless we come to some kind of understanding," she mutters, as if pondering things through. "We need to force his hand. Make him admit he cares enough to help you."

I scoff. "He clearly doesn't care."

"I beg to differ. Might not be in the way any of us think he should care, but he does. You have to remember that he's *meant* to work with you," she says, rubbing at her chest, right over her heart. "You don't understand what it's like having a beast inside of you. They make everything more intense. And when they're upset, they make you do irrational, stupid things."

"That seems more like an excuse than an explanation," I argue. "We're all adults. He should be able to talk it through if he has an issue."

"You can view it however you want, but I know he's only acting this way because he doesn't want to get hurt again," she says.

Now that, I can relate to. How many of the military friends I'd gained over the years had I pushed away because I didn't want to be reminded of the hurt? Too many.

I tie a blade of grass into a knot instead of answering.

"I have an idea on how to force his hand though," Jessa says, a devilish crinkle forming at the corner of her amber eyes. "Do you trust me, Alice?"

I eye her suspiciously. "Yes."

"Wanna play a game?"

I WASN'T EXPECTING for Jessa to take me to Arcadia, but here we are, at the familiar edge of the flower-filled Meadow.

"Are you going to explain how being here helps us get Ori to train with me?" A bit of snark is laced in my tone, and Jessa shakes her head at it.

"You know about Spanish bull fighting?" she asks. "I learned about it in the early years of scouring the human internet after we moved to Meadowbrook."

"Not really..." I murmur.

Jessa starts to pace in a circle around me, eyeing me up and down as if I'm her next meal. I haven't gotten to see her in Arcadia before, but there's a predatory grace to her here that was missing minutes ago, across realms.

"I'll summarize. There's three main parts of the fight. First, you release a bull into a ring and you test him. You know, the whole waving a red cape image?" Jessa says. "You study his movements. It makes him less dangerous when you know how he reacts to stimuli."

I spin in a circle, tracking Jessa. The hair on my neck rises; the simple action of her walking fills me with nerves—the good kind.

"Then, you tire him out. You poke him where it hurts. You weaken him and his resolve, until he doesn't want to fight anymore," Jessa continues. "Essentially, you break him of his stubborn nature."

She stops and scans the woods behind me. Her pupils dilate, then narrow into slits, and I blink hard, thinking I'm imagining it.

But I'm not. Her eyes have shifted.

"Jessa..." I murmur.

"The third part of it is twofold: you show your skill in maneuvering the bull around the ring, controlling it. And then you go in for the kill. Of course, we're not going to kill Ori. But I do plan to murder this attitude he's developed." Jessa steps forward, and I instinctively take a step back. She smiles. "You trust me, right?"

"I do," I say. "You having to ask me a second time in fifteen minutes makes me a bit concerned though..."

"We're going to taunt him, babe," she says, closing the distance between us. Her thumb and pointer grip my chin, gently tilting my head up. "And you're going to be the red flag."

I blink up at her, still not fully getting it.

Her thumb slides along my bottom lip, and my pulse skips as her nail digs into the flesh, tugging it down.

"I'm going to give you a head start of one minute," she whispers.

My muscles tense, anticipation thickening the air like humidity.

"A head start," I repeat.

"Mhm."

"Because..." Her hand glides along my jaw, anchoring at my nape. The touch is distracting in the best way, although it makes it hard to focus on understanding. I glance around the clearing, starting to put some of the pieces together. "Because we're going to play a game?"

"Yep."

"I thought you don't play *games*," I say, hushed.

"Not pesky emotional ones. But sometimes I enjoy playing with my food before I eat it."

"And I'm the food?"

"For me. For him you're the red flag."

"Tracking," I drawl. "So, I should think of this as an evasion exercise."

"Sure. But, if you *wanted* to get caught I wouldn't complain," she teases. "We still haven't talked about you sneaking off with Harley the other night. You're allowed to do that, don't get me wrong, but I'm jealous. He got to taste what I'm desperate to sink my teeth into."

My tongue turns to cotton in my mouth, and I swallow around nothing but arousal at the dangerous, silky tone of her voice.

Okay, this is really happening.

Jessa's about to chase me through magical woods, and that will also somehow help us get Ori back to training.

Honestly, in the grand scheme of crazy, it isn't the most outrageous ask.

"If you hate this, tell me, and I'll stop," Jessa says, leveling with me. "I want you to want it."

I take mental stock of my body. Gooseflesh? Risen. Heartbeat? Pounding. Underwear? Definitely damp.

Yeah, I think I want it. New kink officially unlocked.

I inch away, and Jessa's hand falls from my nape. She watches as I slowly walk backwards, and a beaming grin grows with every foot I put between us.

"Run, Trouble."

When I spun on my heel and sprinted into the woods, I didn't think through two very important things.

One: Jessa knows these woods. Like, she could probably draw the trails from memory if you slapped a sheet of paper and a pen in front of her. Without making a mistake. No white-out necessary.

Two: Jessa said she could shift into a big cat. And by big cat, she meant a giant white tiger.

I'm going to pass out—I don't think humans were made to sprint for this long—but I'm also incredibly turned on.

It's clear she's toying with me. Letting me stumble off the clear path and trip over roots and bushes. Letting me fall and get back up. Letting me get away.

It's not the fear that's causing my pulse to jump out of my neck, and it's not the physical strain. It's the inevitability. It's the question of what will happen when she does decide to catch me.

I hope she kisses me.

Fuck, I sound so desperate in my own head.

The other night, I could blame this urgent need on the substances coursing through my bloodstream, though I would never discredit the connection Harley and I have. The drugs simply emboldened me.

This time, I emboldened myself.

Look at that. More progress, trying something new.

The crackle of twigs behind me pulls a yelp from my throat.

It echoes unanswered by the trees. I glance back and catch the blur of her graceful, furry body darting between the ancient trunks.

"Shit, shit, *shit*," I chant, getting higher pitched with each iteration of the profanity. A hysterical laugh bubbles in my throat.

And then I hear the roar.

As I see the dreadful shadow of a beast pass overhead, something tackles me from behind. I fall, somehow landing on my back, cushioned by a soft patch of moss. My chest heaves with my harried breath, and I take in the feline snout looming above.

Jessa.

Her fur is mostly snow-white, but there are darker markings that start above her brow and extend down her back and limbs. From far away they look black, but the stripes are actually a deep, blood red. Amber irises glint with mischief; they trace over my face with knowing precision and a spark of humor that's purely Jessa. Her paws bracket my head, each the size of my face, and her pink tongue hangs out between sharp teeth as her shifted form pants in my face.

Her beastly head dips down, and she licks my cheek. *Twice.*

"Gross," I groan out between huffs of laughter. I press my hand to the soft fur of her cheek and push her head away, only for her tongue to lap at my fingers. The texture is both wet and rough, the fine prickles tickling me. "Jeeze, Jessa, stop it."

There's a visible shimmer in the air, and a tingling sensation washes over me as she shifts.

"Gotcha." She giggles when she materializes.

There's pure delight in her expression as she gazes upon me. She's in the same position as her beast was, hands on either side of my head, thighs straddling mine. Her head falls to the crook of my neck, and her nose runs over my skin, greedily sucking in my scent.

"Damn. You smell fantastic." Jessa's tongue darts out to lick the pulse thumping in my throat, and I yelp with surprise. "Harley never wants to do this with me," she mutters, teeth nipping at the soft flesh beneath my ear, and my surprise quickly turns into arousal. "Can I kiss you now?" she asks, breathless, pulling back to press our foreheads together.

When have I ever seen her breathless before? I don't think ever.

I nod.

"Words, Trouble," Jessa chides.

"Y-yes," I stutter.

"Good girl."

Jessa doesn't kiss, she claims. Her lips are soft in texture, but that's where the softness ends; she's all power and lethal dominance as she slants her mouth against mine.

I moan, embracing the adrenaline coursing through me and turning it into pleasure. She takes the opportunity to lick into my mouth, deepening the kiss. My hands find her neck—they lace into her hair at the base of her ponytail—and I taste her resulting smile.

Her hand slides over my body, gripping my hip, then palming my breast. Arousal has me squirming underneath her, and I arch up into her touch.

"What the fuck is going on here?"

I yelp at the quintessentially masculine, raging rasp that bangs against my eardrums. My first instinct is to break our kiss, but I can't move, pressed down into the earth by the woman above me. Jessa is unperturbed by our visitor, and she takes her time ending our kiss. She suckles my bottom lip, dragging it between her teeth as she pulls away.

"How nice of you to join us," Jessa murmurs, glancing over her shoulder. "Did you come to watch?"

A dragon's growl vibrates the forest floor. I still can't see him, Jessa's chest in the way, but I know he's close.

"*Jessa,*" I warn with a whisper.

"Let me handle this, babe," Jessa whispers, planting a soft kiss to the corner of my lips.

But the tender moment is ripped apart as Ori appears, grabs her by the collar of her shirt, and throws her against a tree.

"You know these woods are dangerous. Why would you bring her here?" Ori shouts, clearly incensed. His hand wraps around her neck—his body trembling with barely concealed rage—and yet, Jessa has the audacity to smile at him.

"Umm... because I wanted to chase her while shifted? And then finger-fuck her in the dirt?" Jessa taunts. "Is that not allowed?"

"I thought she was being chased by some predator!"

"I *am* a predator."

"One that would hurt her. My beast didn't realize it was *you* in the haze—" He cuts himself off. "Stop smirking at me. Why are you laughing?"

"No reason," Jessa says, biting into her lip to stifle her laughter. Then she glances at me and winks.

"Were you... coming to save me?" I ask quietly, but it's clear he heard me, because his back stiffens. "You were going to save me from whoever you thought was chasing me?"

"No," Ori says without looking at me.

Jessa snorts. "Liar."

"*No,*" Ori repeats.

"How did you know I was in trouble?" I press, rolling up to my knees and standing. "How did you even know it was me out here?"

"I know your voice," he grits out. "And your scent."

"Don't let her know that, it makes it sound an awful lot like you *care,*" Jessa says.

"Of course I fucking care! I'm not a monster!" Ori pushes off Jessa and begins pacing; one hand weaves into his black tresses while the other waves madly at me. "I don't want her to die!"

"If you don't want her to die, then you should be helping her prepare," Jessa booms, straightening to her full height. "She can't kill Enzo if she never trains with a dragon!"

"I *can't*."

"Yes, you can."

"There's not enough time, Jessa, even if I could—" Ori growls, pivoting towards me. "I thought you'd give up and leave by now." His eyes are crazed, vibrant. "Why do you want to risk yourself? You understand Maven's insane, right? They must have told you what she did. So, why are you doing this? Why are you *here*?"

A beat passes between us, heavy and thick.

"They feel like home." My breath stutters against a sudden swell of emotion. "And this place means something to them. Why wouldn't I want to help, knowing that?"

Suddenly, Ori's face shutters, devastation wracking his strong features.

"Fine." He turns to Jessa. "Take her home, Jessa. No more trips to Arcadia. Especially for whatever"—he waves his hands around—"that was." He sighs, one hand scratching over his beard.

It's grown since the day I visited his shop. Thickened. It's still well-kept, but it's got a roughness to it now.

It suits him.

Rugged. Masculine. A touch of ferality lurking under the surface.

My thoughts drift to my dream—my memory—of riding on his dragon's back. How free it felt to soar through the sky.

His tormented gaze meets mine, narrowing, and my cheeks heat with embarrassment.

"You will continue training with Jessa on swordsmanship, but I will work with you on dragon-specific dueling," he says.

My face lights up, but quickly falls when he adds, "With the condition that if I don't deem you fit by our birthday, we'll forfeit. It's not a lie to say I don't want you to get hurt, but more than that, I refuse to risk Harley and Jessa."

"You promise?" I ask, quirking a brow. "You're not allowed to ditch like you did this whole last week."

Ori's jaw grinds. "I don't trust your promises, remember?"

"A deal, then."

"Deals are meant to be reciprocal in nature."

"Then let's say I owe you." I shrug. "One favor to be called in at any time." I offer my hand. "Shake on it."

Ori stalks over to me, stopping close enough that his heat hits my fingers. He stares at my hand, contemplating. I think for a moment that he's going to refuse, if only to be a dick. But then he caves.

His hand wraps around mine, and at the first brush of our palms, my breath catches. It's lightning, sizzling the nerves across my entire body. I barely register the scrape of his rough fingertips, or the surprisingly gentle pressure of his squeeze, as I focus all my energy on not trying to seem so affected by a simple handshake.

But nothing about this beast of a man is simple. I can tell that much just by looking at him.

"We'll start after the fourth," Ori says, releasing my palm from his massive grip. "I have matters that need tending to first."

"Great," I say.

"Good," he says, as if he *has* to have the last word. "I'll be in touch."

Ori turns and walks away. Magic fizzles in the air, a shimmer overtaking his body as he shifts. And then his glittering white dragon soars beyond the trees.

"Well, that went great," Jessa says with a chipper smile on her face. "Much better than I could have hoped." She grabs onto my shoulders and squeezes affectionately when I roll my eyes. "Anyway... do you want to resume where we left off or go home first?"

It takes me a second to realize what she's talking about, and I shake my head. "You're not *finger-fucking* me on the forest floor, Jessa."

She hums cheekily. "As usual, there's a 'yet' missing at the end of that sentence, Trouble."

27

FIREWORKS

ALICE

I'm not feeling exceptionally patriotic as the fireworks boom overhead. When you marry someone in the military, there's a certain level of unpacking you have to do about how complicit you are in the world's horrors.

The 4th of July always churns the sludge at the bottom of the river, clouding the waters around what—in theory—is meant to be a fun little beach holiday.

Even when your partner's job is decidedly *positive*—even if they have a list of folks who they've literally scooped out of the ocean or rescued from a mudslide in some European mountain range—they're still a part of the machine.

You can argue that they're changing it from the inside. Don't you want a kind soul to be in charge of the big red buttons? Someone who actually cares?

You can also argue that taking the military-industrial complex's money and using it to patron art and advocacy is the biggest 'fuck you' you could give to a government that continues to strip away folks' rights.

Ryan liked to remind me of this when I'd cry about the news.

He'd gently take my phone away from me, place it on the table, and hold me. Ground me. Tell me that I'm only one person, and that I have a specific set of skills that I can use to make a difference.

As an artist, I can do more than people would think. I can connect. I can take a stand. I can change a point of view. I can comfort. I can make folks feel seen—I can make them feel heard.

I can remind them they're not alone.

I'm not alone now, which is nice; Jessa, Harley, and I lay on their roof, watching the fireworks pop and fizzle. My gaze follows the sparks that hang onto glowing life with everything they can, only to die out a few seconds later.

The past two summers, I escaped to the desert to outrun these booming reminders of my loneliness. I replaced the nagging questions of how pointless it all is with the nothingness of the Mojave sky. Unscathed blue. Searing sun. Refreshing cowboy pools and the sound of dust breezing by.

It might have made me a coward, but at least I didn't feel so fucking sad.

Jessa's hand curls around mine, fingers slotting into empty spaces that are meant to be filled. "You're thinking awfully loud."

I turn my head and our noses almost brush. Her lightly tanned, white skin glows pink, orange, and red in quick succession with the fireworks bursting above us. Her bangs sit askew, half stuck to her forehead from the persistent humidity.

"So loud I can hear you from down here," Harley says, raising an arm and pointing at himself. His head rests on Jessa's stomach, and it bobs up and down with her silent laughter.

"What's plaguing you, Trouble?" Jessa asks.

"Do you want the short answer or the long answer?" I mutter.

"Whichever you're willing to give me," she says.

I wait for the next popping of color to subside, watching it play out on her skin and in the reflection of her concerned eyes. "Can I ask you a question?"

"You already did."

I chuff, turning my gaze away from her smirk.

Another pop.

Another boom.

Another crack and fizzle.

"Would it be so bad to stay here?" I ask in the break.

"You mean in Meadowbrook?" Jessa asks.

Her hand twitches in mine. Another pop. Another boom.

"Yeah," I say.

Ori's words have sat heavy with me—that he refuses to risk Harley and Jessa. At the time, it didn't fully register; I was high on adrenaline and frustration at his lack of communication. But now, I hear the fear behind the words, the struggle in the syllables.

He'd choose them over an entire kingdom. Over duty.

It strikes a chord deep within me, one I try not to think about, but today is hard to ignore.

"I've been to Arcadia a few times now, and it never seems like anything is actually wrong?" I add. "What am I missing?"

"You've only seen the Wandering Woods, Alice..." Jessa says, trailing off.

Another crack and fizzle. This one has a different shape than the rest, more oblong than circular. It's nothing to write home about.

I turn on my side, placing my hand between my face and the blanket that does little to cushion against the shingled roof.

"Explain," I demand.

"Maven and Enzo are controlling and unhinged. They don't

care about the people, only themselves. They think everyone lives to serve them. You haven't seen the towns..." she says. "I snuck in once. It reeked of terror. Maven has Enzo make a spectacle of those that openly defy her. Dragon fire is a terrible way to go."

Jessa's lips purse as the fireworks pick up; the annoyed scowl is frustratingly cute, and I reach out to smooth the line between her brows. Her face slackens, expression softening.

"We have a duty to our people, Alice. They shouldn't have to live in fear. And if we have the means to save them, how can we not try? How can we disappear and live our lives like they don't matter?"

"Fuck duty," I say. Anger blooms in my chest, sudden and fierce. "And fuck responsibility."

Jessa flinches at the vitriol in my tone. Harley even sits up, concerned expression directed my way.

The fireworks pick up again, in tune with my inner turmoil. The booms are deafening, ringing out every other second. A deluge. An avalanche. They mirror the thoughts and memories blasting apart behind my lids as I squeeze my eyes shut. Crackling debris strings together, a near constant static that fills my eardrums. Panic pushes up my throat and chokes me.

The show ends.

There's a brief moment of shocked quiet. Then, the crickets take back the night.

"Alice... do you not want to compete in the tourney?" Harley asks.

Jessa removes her hand from mine and sits up. Her expression is serious but not angry, and yet a thread of guilt weaves though my ribs as if I've been reprimanded for expressing doubt.

"It's okay if you don't," she says. "But I'm confused. The other day, you—"

"No, I still want to fight for you, I just—" I groan, my hands rubbing over my face as it tilts to the smoke-filled sky. "I'm thinking about Ryan. He would say the same shit, always droning on about his duty to protect. I hated the connotation, but I also secretly loved that he was chivalrous. How could I hate that I had a husband who cared deeply about others?" My hands fall to my lap and wrap around my middle. A painful ache emanates from my center. "Why couldn't he have been a doctor or something?" I whisper. "There are a million other ways to save people."

The breeze blows a curl across my face.

"*Babe*," Jessa chides. Her gentle fingers tuck the stray strand back into place behind my ear. "What's really the matter?"

Tears well in my eyes, and when I blink, they cascade down my cheeks. Jessa's thumbs catch them, and though blurry, I can tell she's stricken by the sight of me crying.

Harley crawls over on his hands and knees when the sobs hit. My chest heaves, and emotions I've long stored away break free. Two heartbeats press into me as I'm sandwiched between one hard chest and one plush one.

"Talk to us," Harley whispers into the crook of my neck. He places a tender kiss below my ear.

"It's so stupid," I say through hiccupping sobs. "I can't even be mad at him because it always made him so happy."

They don't interrupt; only their hands respond to my words, running over my body with intent to soothe.

"He was a rescue pilot," I explain, swallowing my tears. "Helicopters are dangerous. We both knew that, but he loved flying. He loved the adrenaline rush. And he loved that he got to help people in such a tangible way." I swipe at the snot dripping from my nose with the sleeve of my sweatshirt. "Do you even know how many times people need to be rescued in the middle of the ocean? It's not a lot but it is more than you'd think."

Emotion gets caught in my throat, and I have to breathe for a moment before continuing.

"But he didn't save the person who mattered most. *Him*," I choke out, and the hands on my body pause. "I'll never know exactly what happened that day. I think my brain shut down when the officer and chaplain came to our apartment and broke the news. And any information I read about the crash after that never fully digested. All I know is that there was an equipment malfunction and they hit the water."

I detangle myself from Jessa and Harley's hold, sitting up.

"He had that same strong sense of duty and responsibility for others that you speak of. But he also made a vow to me. *To come back to me*. And he *didn't*. So, fuck responsibility, and fuck duty. Now that I think about it, maybe Ori's the only smart one of us. Survival is more important. Maybe, if Ryan thought about that more, he'd still be here," I say, all my twisted bitterness floating to the surface. "You know how many people called him a hero after he died? Thanked me for his service and sacrifice? It made me sick. I didn't care about heroics. I didn't care about service. I cared about *him*."

"I'm sorry," Jessa says. "I know nothing I say right now can stop the swell of all that you're feeling."

I sigh, batting at the last few tears that fall down my cheeks. "It's okay."

"It's not," Harley says, reaching out and grabbing my hand. My tears grow tacky between our palms as his thumb traces over my knuckles. "You shouldn't have had to go through that."

"No, I shouldn't have," I agree, staring at our hands.

Two fingers lift my chin, and I'm met with Jessa's sharp features.

"I hear all your fears," she says. "But this is not the same situation, okay? Nod if you understand."

I nod.

"Shouldn't we be the ones worried about you, considering

you're the one that will be fighting to save us?" she asks in a raspy murmur. "I'm not planning on losing you now that I have you."

My eyes dart from her to Harley. He shoots me a soft smile and nods his agreement.

Jessa does have a point.

"Look at me when I'm talking to you, Trouble." My throat bobs, a tickle of something else infiltrating all the anger and sadness stuck in the space where my neck meets my jaw. Her nostrils flare and she sucks in a deep breath; as if she can read my mind, her thumbnail digs into my bottom lip, tugging it down. "Do you need to get out of your head?"

I nod.

"Make you remember that we're here and that we're not going anywhere?"

I nod again.

"Then let's go inside."

28

NUMBERS, DATES, AND OTHER FILTHY THINGS

JESSA

August twenty-seventh. Alice and Ori's birthdays.

Ninety-four. The number of days she was with us before she disappeared.

May eleventh. The day Alice walked back into our lives.

Seventy-two. The number of freckles that sit between the plump endcaps of her smile.

June thirtieth. The day I kissed her for the first time.

I've always been fond of dates and numbers in the same way that I am *not* fond of the wishy-washy games people play with other's emotions. Numbers are what I strive to emulate: they are clear; they are consistent; they are predictable; and they are all the other synonyms for reliable that Harley can recite from the thesaurus he keeps on his bookshelf.

July fourth. The day I finally get to taste her.

My poor girl is hurting. She feels so deeply—a trait I admire, but I also know it's the reason she's in pain.

Caring leads to pain; they're born of the same vows you

make to another at the altar. To commit to love is to one day commit to grief.

I push open the door to my bedroom and guide Alice in with a hand on the small of her back. "Sit on the bed, Trouble."

"Okay," she whispers.

Gods, I relish the sound of her voice, all breathy and sweet.

Harley and I exchange a look—we've talked many times about how we'd share Alice. Sex is a large part of our lives, but tonight isn't about sex. It's about lessening the weight bearing down on her. It's about making her forget her pain. It's about giving her reprieve.

"Harley hasn't touched you since the other day, has he?" I ask, tracing feather-light fingers across my sweet boy's shoulders. Harley shivers, and I embrace the smirk that crawls onto my lips.

"No," Alice says, shifting awkwardly on the edge of the bed.

"We're going to change that," I say, curling my arms around Harley's middle and trailing them up his chest. "If you don't like where this is going just say so, okay? Same as with the woods."

Alice nods, and watches with rapt attention as my fingers pop the buttons of his shirt. One by one, I take my time undressing him for her. He's not wearing an undershirt, which is unlike him, but maybe he hoped tonight would end like this, and decided not to bother with it.

My nails scrape over the skin I expose and Harley's abdomen shudders as I reach the last button, flicking the shirt open. I trace over his ribs and play with the faint trial of hair leading past his belt.

I plant an open-mouthed kiss on his neck, then drag my lips up to his ear. "Look how she's watching you melt for us."

If he wasn't already hard, he would be now. I palm his erection over his pants, and he sucks in a stuttered breath, arching into my touch.

The sound causes Alice's thighs to press together; I don't blame her for squirming. Harley's responsiveness is erotic.

"Do you want to taste her?" I ask him, loud enough for Alice to hear. Her shocked expression rises from the tent in his shorts to the hand I gently wrap around his throat. Alice visibly gulps her arousal as I squeeze my claim into his pulse. "Do you want him to eat you until you're screaming his name, baby?"

"*Fuck*," she whispers.

"Yes, exactly." I chuckle, releasing him. Gripping the cotton lapels, I slide his shirt off and push him towards the bed. "Do a good job and you'll get a reward. No touching yourself until the end."

Harley utters a curse, both in desire and frustration as he takes off his glasses, sets them on the nightstand, and kneels before Alice.

He knows the rules. Ladies come first.

"Yes, ma'am," he says aloud, knowing I need his enthusiastic consent. He gazes up at Alice tenderly. Reverent hands run up her shins and stop at her inner thigh, where they finger the edge of her shorts. I find myself softening at the sight of the two of them.

"Is this okay?" he asks.

Alice nods. Her eyes flick to me quickly, and I raise a brow.

"Yes," she says out loud, correcting her behavior before I have to say anything. "Can I kiss you first?"

"Of course," Harley says, beaming up at her. Her hand runs over his jaw, tracing the sharp cut of it. "You can always kiss me. I encourage it."

A giggle accompanies her smile as she leans down to claim his lips. It's affectionate at first. Slow. Innocent. They savor the taste of each other.

I perch my ass on the edge of my dresser, enjoying the view. I'll let them work each other up, and then I'll swoop in and steal her pouty lips from Harley.

"Don't forget you have a job to do, babe," I teasingly scold him.

He doesn't break their kiss to answer me, using his hands to reply instead. Her sweatshirt zipper slides down her chest; the garment is ripped off her arms and tossed into a dark corner of the room.

An urgency sizzles the air as Alice scoots closer to the edge of the bed, giving Harley better access to the rest of her clothes.

Next goes her shirt. Then her shorts. I don't pay attention to where he flings either—we'll find them in the morning. He leaves Alice in only a lacy black bra and simple blue cotton panties. The mismatched nature does nothing to lessen how sinful she looks.

Harley must agree, because his hands can't get enough of her—they devour her curves, dig into her spreading thighs.

Their kissing intensifies. Alice takes a bruising grip of Harley's hair, tilting his head back. A divine, wanton moan vibrates his throat as she plunders his mouth, tongues tangling, taking from him what she wants.

It gives me far too many ideas for the future.

I push off the dresser and crawl onto the bed. Alice doesn't notice me sidling up to her, she's too enthralled by Harley's lips. My own meet the juncture of her shoulder and neck, a chaste peck that causes her to squeak and break their kiss.

I check in with Harley with a glance. His glazed expression sparkles with hunger. But he's my good boy. He'll wait.

I turn back to Alice.

Our noses brush as I lean in. One kiss to her cheek. One kiss to the corner of her mouth. Her hitching breath teases me, and an exhilarating moment passes where I watch her crystalline irises dilate. Lashes flutter shut in submission. She's waiting for a real kiss. But she's not getting it yet.

"You're beautiful, all flushed and wanting," I whisper, pressing my forehead to hers.

Her lids pop open. My nostrils flare, scenting her sudden burst of arousal. Sweet as sugar, it's a call for more.

I answer it, never breaking our stare. Two fingers hook between Harley's parted, puffy lips, pressing down on his tongue, and drag his face between Alice's thighs. Harley groans against her core, and she gasps.

They're both so fucking perfect.

Harley tongues her over the soaked cotton, and her tiny moans coat my lips as I tease my kisses on her jaw. Then the spot under her ear. My hand weaves gently through her curls and fists the root of her hair.

"Take off her underwear and eat in earnest," I say, knowing the command will reach Harley. Alice shifts as he tugs them down her hips. Then, only to her, I whisper, "I've been dreaming about tasting you on him."

"Jesus," she moans.

I hum. "Close, but not quite."

I release her hair and shift to better position myself, kneeling half to her side, half behind her, so she can lean her weight into me. The angle also gives me a much better view of Harley eating her gorgeous cunt.

"Try again," I murmur in her ear. My palms slide across her stomach, and she shivers.

"*Jessa*," she half-scolds, then moans as Harley swirls his tongue over her clit. "Fuck, Harley, that feels good."

I chuckle, admiring his work. He's a wonder with his tongue —I know from many, *many* personal experiences.

One of his long fingers dips into her core, then two, slowly pumping while his tongue flattens over her sensitive bud; it truly is magnificent, watching him pleasure her.

"He's such a good boy, isn't he, Alice?" I taunt, knowing he loves the praise. I resume nibbling on her neck, watching the hickeys form in real time; my teeth rip red roses from the pale expanse. "Talk him through it. He loves that."

I tongue the deepening flush on her neck as she nods, filthy words dripping from her tongue like I'm sure her pussy is dripping all over his chin. Her fingers weave into Harley's hair, and she physically pulls him closer to her core.

"More," Alice rasps. "You lick me so well, but you can give me more. Yes, like that."

Her tone is tentative, nervous, but grows more confident as Harley's groan of approval hits our ears. It's sweet music, a sensual lick of base setting the pace of Alice's pleasure.

"Your fingers are perfect. I love the way they fill me up," Alice continues. "Curl them. *Fuck*, yes. Exactly. You're such a good listener."

"Good girl," I praise. "You're a natural."

Alice shudders—either from Harley licking her needy cunt as if it's his last meal or from me licking a line up her jumping pulse. It thumps under my tongue, erratic. She's getting close.

"Now focus on coming, okay?" I say.

I grab her chin and capture her lips. They're puffy and slick, and they open for me without my tongue needing to ask for permission. Her moans vibrate against my teeth as I draw her bottom lip between them and bite. My free hand runs over her breast, rolling her nipple between my fingers.

Alice cries out, and I greedily swallow her ecstasy as she comes. I kiss her through it, until our lungs demand we break for air.

She glows with a freshly fucked daze that I commit to memory, gazing at me like I've hung the moon.

It's dangerous. A girl could get addicted to that expression.

I reach for Harley and he meets me halfway, rising on his knees. I latch onto his glistening mouth, licking into it in obscene fashion. My smile bumps into his grin as our tongues tangle, and I lap the taste of Alice off him with a moan. The perfect amount of sweetness and bite, her arousal is going to be added to the list of treats I crave late at night.

I release Harley and peck his nose.

"Good boy," I say. "You can touch yourself now."

"Thank fuck," he says, letting out an exasperated sigh.

His hand dives into his pants and with no more than five quick strokes he comes. He deflates, flopping onto his back with a breathless chuckle.

"That was awesome," he says, grin dopey and eyes shut.

"That... was the hottest thing I think I've ever done," Alice murmurs, sinking back on her elbows in shock.

"That's only the beginning of all the filthy things we can do," I say, smug at the state of her kissed-raw lips.

How she can be shocked after uttering all that filthy praise to Harley is beyond me.

We quickly clean up and change into comfy pajamas, and once we're all settled in bed, Alice uses Harley's chest as a pillow, slotting under his arm as if she was meant to fit there. I spoon her from behind, arm draping over her waist and fingers lacing with Harley's as we cuddle our girl to sleep.

"Next time, I want to taste you from the source," I murmur, placing a languid kiss on the spot just below her ear. "I want to hear my name falling from those pretty lips when you come."

"Okay," Alice yawns, patting my arm that circles on her waist. "I don't think that will be hard to make happen."

29

DREAMSCAPE, PART TWO

ALICE

"I think Harley has a crush."

"What? On who?" My attention whips to Jessa. She's got this sneaky squint to her eyes as she stares at the boys who wade in the shallows, each holding a long fishing pole.

"Don't you think?" she adds, leaning close. "Why else would he let Ori teach him how to fish. Harley doesn't want to fish." Her nose scrunches on the last part, as if the idea of fishing insults her.

"You think he likes Ori?" I ask.

"That's what I said."

"Oh."

"So?"

"So, what?" I ask, confused.

"Does it make you mad?" Jessa presses.

I shift on the large sheet Harley laid out for us, sticking my feet out of the shade and into the sun. My toes wriggle against the strange airy-yet-solid texture of the cloudy expanse.

"Why would that make me mad?" I ask, genuinely confused. "People can like whoever they want."

Jessa sighs, scooting closer, her feet joining mine in the sun. We painted our toenails black the other day, and we already have matching chips in the polish.

"Because," she says, voice teetering on the edge of annoyance. "You like Ori."

"What?" I say, too loudly. At the same time the boys look back at us, Jessa slaps a hand over my mouth.

"Shhhh," she hisses. "They have good hearing."

Harley cocks his head, shooting us a thumbs up—his way of asking if we're okay. Jessa drops her hand from my face, and we both plaster on stiff smiles, waving back. It takes a second for him to turn his focus back on the water, but Ori helps with that, snaping in Harley's face.

I speak through clenched teeth, "I don't like Ori."

"Yes, you do," Jessa says, like I'm a big old dummy. "You're his fated Champion. You're supposed to fall in love, just like his parents did. Plus, I can tell."

"No, you can't," I mock back. My arms cross over the frilly bathing suit Ori's mom got me. "Clearly. Because I like you all the same."

Jessa's mouth puckers and her eyes squint as she stares me down. I mirror her, doubling down. I'm not lying, so it's easy to hold my ground.

Finally, Jessa huffs and flops backwards, landing on the striped sheet with a dull thump.

"Dang it," she groans. "You're too nice."

"Am I supposed to be mean?"

"No," Jessa says, waving a raised hand in the air. "I thought you'd have more of a reaction though. I heard humans get weird about this stuff."

"I don't care if any of you like each other." I shrug. "So long as you guys keep being my friends."

Jessa's head pops up, one eye squinting at me. "What about if one of us likes you?"

"Do you?" I ask.

"I like you all the same," she says, quoting me back. Then her nose scrunches again, her lips pulling back like she tasted something sour. "Well, except Ori. He's too grouchy."

I laugh. "I like grouchy."

"Today, we're going to discuss the arena itself," Memaw says, scratching a lopsided oval on the blackboard with chalk. I shiver at the grating sound. "And how it changes based on the trial you're in."

The old woman turns around, toothpick dangling out of her mouth. She always has something tucked between her lips; the queen doesn't want Memaw smoking inside, so whenever we have our lessons or a big dinner all together, she chews on those. Or gum. I didn't think Arcadia would have gum, but it does.

"One of you remind me what the tourney is," she asks without asking. Her questions always come out like commands.

Maven's hand shoots up, and Memaw nods in her direction.

"The tourney occurs when the Heirs and Champions turn thirty. This competition determines which pair will preside over the crown of Arcadia and all the power that comes with it," Maven says. She speaks matter-of-factly, as if she's reading straight from a textbook. "There are three trials that determine who's fit to rule. However, there are multiple ways to win. You can go through all three trials and come out on top," Maven rattles on, ticking off her fingers. "Or someone can forfeit. Or if a pair isn't complete at the start, they automatically lose."

"What a comprehensive answer," Memaw deadpans, then looks at me. "Anything you want to add, Alice?"

"Uh..." My lips part to add what Harley showed me in one of his books. That Arcadia's magic is influenced by those who wear the crown; their intentions can allow the land to flourish or cause it to rot. But I decide against it, remembering how Maven reacted the last time I 'showed her up in front of grandma'. I shake my head. "No. Maven covered it all."

Memaw frowns. "Alright."

She turns back to the board and starts scratching out words in cursive; chalk dust floats to the floor with every curve, loop, and stroke. When she's done, she taps the board with the chalk three times, dotting down the list she's made.

"The arena doors open at midnight leading into your birthday and close at midnight twenty-four hours later. Once those doors are closed, no one can come in or out until the tourney is over," Memaw says. The chalk strikes the board again, screeching down in a long circle around two of the bullets she's written. "Three trials. One for the Champions. One for the Heirs. One for you both."

There's a beat of silence where Memaw stares at us scrutinizingly with her wrinkle-framed eyes.

I tentatively raise my hand. Memaw nods her permission to speak. "Are you going to tell us what they are?"

"Yes and no," she says, dropping the chalk on the metal ledge at the bottom of the blackboard. She begins to pace, plucking the toothpick from her mouth with two fingers. It's waved around in the air like one of her weird-smelling cigarettes. "The arena changes for each trial, picking what it thinks is most appropriate for the crown's candidates. Usually, it tests the Heirs and Champions on what they're lacking, to see if they can overcome their flaws. The combined trial is meant to test compatibility. All three may be physical or mental, so we'll prepare you for both."

"I hope the combined trial is a duel," Maven says.

"Why would you hope for that?" I ask. "You want to fight me?"

Maven scoffs, her dark red bangs puffing out with the huff of air. "Of course. I love fighting."

I shrink in my chair. "I don't."

Maven doesn't comment, but I can tell she heard me. She listens to the rest of the lesson Memaw gives with a smirk on her face. It's like she thinks she's better than me—knows it.

The thirty minutes pass slowly, and I count each one of the ticks coming from the desk clock to distract from the scrape of chalk on blackboard.

Puzzles. Riddles. Croquet. Obstacle courses. Chess. Memaw explains the different types of trials we might encounter. Some are stranger than others—what does croquet have to do with ruling a kingdom?

Duels are brought up again. Memaw makes note about how I'll begin training with Jessa's father soon. Maven preens about how her lessons are going, and Memaw stares at her with disinterest but doesn't stop her from blabbing on about how she's graduated to a real sword from a wooden one.

Memaw moves on to other categories. Magical beasts. Archery. Mazes. Magic.

I try to pay attention, but end up doodling in the notebook Ori gave me instead.

Memaw ends her lesson and leaves; I'm too focused on finishing my drawing to care. Or to notice that Maven is looming over my desk with a scowl. Her pale white hand slams down over my notebook, making my pen swipe a haphazard line across the sketch.

"What the heck, Maven!" I whip a glare at the girl. Her pink lips are tugged into an unnerving, tight smile. "You ruined my drawing."

"You can make a new one," she says. "We need to talk."

"About what?" I huff, crossing my arms and slouching in my chair. The stiff wooden back digs into my neck.

Maven lifts her hand off my notebook, and sneers down at my doodle. "What's this supposed to be?"

"It's a dragon..." Sort of. It's not very good, but Nana says that you have to practice if you want to get better at art. I snatch the notebook back from her and hug it to my chest. "What did you want?"

Maven sighs, and all the pretend niceness falls off her face. Jessa told me about it a while ago—how she thinks Maven is pretending to be their friend. I didn't believe her at first, but the longer I've been in Arcadia, the more I think Jessa's right.

Maven gives me the creeps.

"Do you want your family to die, Alice?" she asks.

"What?" I squeak.

"Because that's what will happen, if you stay here. Champions don't get to have families back home."

"No," I say. "If that were true, the queen would have told me."

She's asked me about my family many times, and I'd told her all kinds of stories about Mom and Dad and Nana. She never once said anything about them dying while I was here.

Maven rolls her eyes. "Of course they'll die, stupid. You're going to be here for, like, forever if you compete in the tourney. And if you win and get crowned, then you'll definitely never see them again."

I blink up at Maven, confused. "I don't understand."

"All the Champion's families die. That way, you're alone. And you have no reason to leave." She plants both hands on my desk, leaning forward. I try to lean farther back, but I'm already scrunched so low in my seat, there's nowhere else to turn to. "I got here first, and mine are already dead, Alice. So, you should leave Arcadia before it's too late for you."

"B-but what if I can't come b-back?" I stutter.

Maven starts to sneer something at me, but the heavy slam of the door against the wall cuts her off.

"Alice, there you are," Ori says. He strides into the room like he owns it—which I guess he does, since he's an Heir. He's only an inch taller than me, and the same height as Maven, but he seems bigger now. His attentive navy eyes don't waver from me as he steamrolls Maven's dark presence. "C'mon, we need to leave if we want to make it to the Lake for sunset." He finally glances at the red-haired girl. "Oh, hey Maven."

Maven is frozen, bent over my desk and staring daggers at Ori. I take the opportunity to slide out of my chair.

"I think Enzo was looking for you," Ori adds once I'm at his side.

"He's always looking for me," Maven says.

An awkward moment passes where they glare at each other.

"Well, bye," Ori says, grabbing my hand and dragging me into the hall.

"Thanks," I say when we're far enough away that I know Maven won't hear.

"No problem," Ori says. He doesn't look at me; his focus is trained on our route through the maze of castle halls.

"You're always saving me," I say, shyly. "I feel bad."

I've gotten lost in the Woods too many times to count, and he's had to come find me and bring me back to the castle. He often backs up my opinion when our friends are arguing about where to go that day. And he never lets me be alone with Maven.

"Don't. It's my job," Ori says, in that grumbly way of his, but there's a fondness that lingers after the words are spoken. His ears go pink. "I'm your Heir. You're mine to protect."

30

MORNINGS AFTER

ALICE

It's warm, is my first thought as I wake.
It's too warm, is my second.
Why are there eyes on me? is the third.
My lids snap open.

Ori leans against the doorframe with his arms crossed over his muscled chest; he's clad in those same Arcadian fighting leathers he wore to our first training. A pauldron curves over one of his pronounced shoulders and an embellished chest plate lays flush against his wide center, both strapped over a billowing white shirt, brown pants, and matching leather boots. It's all very fantastical, as if he's about to go to the Renaissance Faire.

Time stretches out languidly between us, much like my muscles ache to do, but I stay still, and silent, waiting for him to say something.

His gaze trails down my body, taking in the way my legs are tangled with Jessa's and my arm is curled around Harley's waist. It snags a few times, getting caught on my rucked-up nightshirt, which exposes a sliver of my belly, and my fingers, which curve over the soft skin of Harley's Adonis belt. And though his expression never shifts during his appraisal of us three, the energy emanating off him does. It deepens from a stormy gray to midnight black.

Thirty more seconds pass—I count them in my head to be sure, because it feels like an eternity before he pushes off the molding.

The floorboards creak.

Ori freezes, eyes narrowing over Harley's sleeping form. His jaw grinds, rippling the beard that accentuates his chiseled features.

"Get up," he finally says. It's a gruff whisper. Raw, like he hasn't used his voice in days. "We're training today."

He waits for me to move, but I just blink up at him in my post-sleep haze. He can't be serious right now, can he?

"*Alice*," Ori growls impatiently, and I hate how my body clenches at the sound. Every muscle tightens, and a shiver passes through me.

I suddenly *need* to get out of this bed. I quickly—but cautiously—slip out of Harley and Jessa's hold, and crawl off the end. Tiptoeing around, I begin to collect my discarded clothes.

"Leave them. I have something for you to change into down in the kitchen," he says, quiet enough not to wake Harley or Jessa.

I pause, one hand curled around my shorts. Ori waits for me to challenge him, but I sigh, deciding to pick my battles with him sparingly.

"Fine. But let me text them we're leaving. I don't want them to freak when they wake up and see that I'm gone."

"I left a note on the fridge," Ori says.

"I want them to have a note from *me*," I explain, expecting him to understand. But his stoic expression says otherwise. I stifle my groan, tossing my shorts back on the ground and padding past him with my phone. "I can't just ignore them the morning after. I'm not some college fuckboy."

"*You're fucking them now*?" Ori asks, way too loud, as he follows me down the hall.

"*Shhh!*" I hush over my shoulder. "*What the fuck is wrong with you? They're sleeping.*"

Ori's nostrils flare in frustration, and as we descend the stairs, he mutters things I can't make out, but I'm pretty sure I catch an annoyed '*smells like sex more than usual*'. Otherwise, he keeps his mouth shut until we're in the kitchen.

I slide onto a stool at the island and finish prepping my text in our group chat, while Ori grabs a brown paper bag from the counter. He turns it over on the granite, two wrapped bagels falling out.

"Are you fucking them?" Ori asks, tentatively, while he reads the handwritten label on each bagel. He slides one to me, and I stop it from flying off the ledge.

"What if I am?" I ask. "Do you have a problem with that?"

"No," he says, too quickly.

I lift the bagel and inspect the waxed paper. "What is this?" I ask. It's got the Strathmore sticker holding it closed, and it's still warm, which means it's fresh.

"It's a bagel," Ori drawls sarcastically.

I roll my eyes. "I know it's a bagel."

"Then why did you ask?"

"I'm only confused as to why you are giving it to me." I open it and find a perfectly crusted, yellow egg-everything, smeared with veggie cream cheese. It's not just *a* bagel. It's my favorite.

Ori unwraps his own and rips into it. A single bite from his pearly teeth takes out a quarter of it. "Just accept the peace offering, Alice."

My lips purse. I don't want to admit it, but this is as good a peace offering as any, if not better. And definitely unexpected.

I take a bite and sigh, closing my eyes. I missed the hell out of these when I was in California. You can't get them fresh anywhere else, and there's nothing better than a warm one, right out of the oven, crisp on the outside, doughy on the inside, with an inch of cool cream cheese sandwiched in the middle.

As I chew, I can't help but circle back to Ori's reaction to my sex life. "You know, it sure sounded like you have a problem with me fucking them."

Ori's sigh is great, and I hear the fridge open and close. "They're their own people. They can do whatever they want."

I crack an eye and see his back is still turned, pouring milk into the steamer cup attached to their coffee maker. Next to him, a sticky note flutters under a blast of air conditioning, slapped at eye-height on the fridge. I can't make out the text written on it, but I can see the larger letters of his name scrawled out at the bottom.

The steamer squeals. Milk bubbles.

I don't fully understand my visceral reactions to this man, or why we can't seem to do anything but argue. But it's obvious he cares deeply for Jessa and Harley, and in that, we are the same. If he's going to extend an olive branch, then I should accept it.

"Peace offering accepted," I say, licking the cream cheese squeezing out the side of my bagel. "Egg everythings are my favorite. Did Jessa tell you?"

"It's what you ordered at the store the other day." Ori turns around, perching his ass against the counter. His arms cross—or, half cross. One hand still holds his bagel, while the other grips his bicep. And then he stares.

Attentive. Watchful. Slightly amused and puzzled as to why. It's as if he's allowing himself to see me for the first time, even though he's seen me plenty—took one hell of an eyeful not five minutes ago.

A standoff ensues, as we each nosh until we're licking our fingers of crumbs and cream cheese.

The coffee steamer beeps, marking an end to the stalemate; Ori pours himself his latte while I clean up my mess. I crumple my discarded waxed paper into a ball, swipe any loose seeds into my open palm, and hop off the stool to toss them in the trash.

"This what you brought for me?" I ask, pointing at the garment bag I noticed hanging on the open bathroom door. I stride over to it, grabbing the zipper and pulling it down. "Is it some kind of sacrificial outfit for you to kill me in to appease your dragon?"

"Arcadian fighting leathers," Ori chides as I part the garment bag, catching a whiff of smoky leather and taking in the custom outfit that should belong on a movie set. "They're mandatory for the tourney. Better for you to start training in them now so you're comfortable by August." He takes a sip of his coffee, and over the rim, he casually adds, "I made them for you."

"Wait, what?" I gawk. "You made this?"

"I'm a tailor," Ori says, turning away to add sugar to his cup. "I make clothes for a living. Don't overthink it."

31

THESE TORTURED SIGHS OF MINE

ORAZIO

I'm overthinking it.

The leathers fit her immaculately, and I silently give myself a pat on the back for being able to pull this build off without having easy access to her measurements. I had stolen a look at the dress she wore to the gala, offered to pick it and Harley's suit up from the dry cleaners on my way home from work. While it gave me a starting point, I still had to guess in some places.

Harley had thanked me for the help, giving me that wide smile of his—the one that pushes his glasses up with his cheeks—but that smile made me feel guilty.

I'd been ignoring them. And I should have been offering to help regardless of my need to distance myself from *her*.

I should have realized that she makes them happy. Genuinely. More than I have. More than I ever could. It only took me finding her in the Woods with Jessa, after my dragon nearly burned down the forest thinking his fated was in danger, to realize that.

To make matters worse, she *wants* to make them happy.

That's all I ever wanted too.

They're going to freak when they see her in her leathers.

Alice looks... good.

Too good, I realize as she tugs at the layered fabric and leather gorget around her neck. She clearly thinks her armor is too tight, but they're meant to be snug, to shape to your body over time as the leather is stretched and heated with repeated use.

The pauldrons curling around her shoulders widen her stature, and the cinched breastplate accentuates her waist before an added layer peplums out over her hips, helping to support the sword belt strapped around her. Her figure flares out at her thighs; I had cut the breeches wide for easy movement. They end tucked into knee-high boots that mold to her strong calves.

With her wild golden curls flowing down her back, she looks ethereal.

Like a Champion.

Like she belongs here.

Like she's mine.

My clothes wrapped around her body. My land underneath her heel. My throat, soon to be at her sword's mercy.

These are stupid, reckless thoughts.

My beast prowls under the surface of my skin, too easily tempted by her presence, and I force him down.

"You know, it would be nice if we could be friends," Alice says as I lead her through the Woods. My boot almost catches on a protruding root, and I narrowly avoid tripping.

"Watch your step," I grumble.

"I remember more now," she adds, her voice tapping my back for attention. "Not everything. But enough to realize you do mean well..."

I grunt, half listening. My ears are trained on the sounds of the forest and my nose primed to scent any unwanted presence. I'm taking a calculated risk bringing her here, though the Wandering Woods are relatively safe, so long as she has me with her. The natural beasts that prowl are the least of my worries—the Woods like me. Always have. It's why I can navigate them so easily. They shift the paths around me to my benefit.

It's only if she's alone, or if we stay too long—if our scents grow too strong and Enzo realizes who he's tracking—that she's in real danger.

"And that you're just the group's resident grump," she continues. "I don't *mind* grumpy."

"Alice," I growl her name on a sigh. I hate saying it aloud. My tongue licks around the sugary syllables too easily. "I need to focus on our surroundings. Unless you want a true trial by dragon-fire, stay quiet until we get to the clearing."

"Oh," she whispers. "Sorry."

It doesn't take long for us to reach our destination. It's one I use often to recover in, after my—admittedly ill-advised—rampages against Enzo and Maven's forces. Sometimes my mind gets too crowded with thoughts for sewing to clear it, and I must purge the unsettled anger within my beast in a more violent manner.

The soles of my boots crunch over brown, scorched patches of grass marked into the green, all the moisture burned out of the blades from my dragon's unnatural heat.

It won't burn anyone or anything I don't want it to; I should probably care more about the field and not stamp the land with my mark. But the idea of never coming back does haunt me, despite what Jessa and Harley might think, and so I leave a part of myself in the only way I can.

"So…" Alice says. "How's this going to go? Are we going to run drills?"

"No," I say, leading us to the center of the clearing.

"Okay."

"If we're going to do this right, we need to establish some ground rules."

"*Okay,*" she drawls.

My attention slams down on her like a gavel. "Rule one: don't give me attitude."

"I'm not giving you attitude," she says, raising her hands placatingly. "However, I am questioning if you know what you're going to teach me today, since you haven't given me any indication."

I release a slow breath through my nose, eyes darting away from her crystal irises to the center of her forehead. I can't look her directly in the eye for long, or else my skin starts to squirm.

"Dragon scales are mostly impenetrable due to the magic imbued in them. The only ones who can pierce this magic and do lasting damage—"

"*Super smooth transition.*"

"—are other dragons or Champions," I grind out, jaw ticking. "But even so, the scales and hide are thick. Most cuts won't physically break through, which is why you have to target our most vulnerable areas."

I point to various parts of my body as I continue.

"The obvious one is the head. There's a lot of soft tissue. A well-aimed stab through the eye could prove fatal. But where our scales thin to allow us better movement are also good targets. They're also easier to reach than the head. These include the ankles, knees, elbows, armpits—" She snorts, and I freeze. "What's so funny?"

"I'm sorry, but the image of me stabbing a dragon's armpit is simply hilarious."

"I'm not laughing," I deadpan. "Therefore, it cannot be that hilarious."

I unsheathe the sword strapped to my hip and shove it at her. She fumbles with the hilt, almost dropping it.

"Show me where else you think you should aim if you want to kill me," I demand.

Alice shifts on her feet, adopting a decent starting stance; Jessa's taught her well. Her feet plant themselves wide for stability as she holds the metal blade with one hand, though the point of the blade droops towards the ground, rather than at me.

"You want me to poke you with the sword where I'd try to hit you?" she asks with uncomfortable confusion. "You trust me not to cut you?"

"If the arena decides to put you in a duel, the sooner you get first blood, the better," I say, grabbing the blade with my hand. The cold steel bites into my palm as I press forward and lift it to my neck. "Rule two: aim to kill."

She jerks the sword back, letting the tip of the blade fall to the dirt. "I'm sorry, did I hear that right?"

"I didn't bring you out here to fuck around, Alice," I grit out around clenched teeth. Magic skitters across my skin, glittering whites and iridescent blues that match my dragon scales. My beast sees her panic, scents the burst of burnt sugar wafting off her, and demands to be freed. "Show me you can do this. Show me you can handle fighting a dragon. Otherwise, I'm not going to entertain this any longer."

It may make me a coward, but I will not see her die. I won't allow Jessa and Harley to mourn us because of a misplaced sense of confidence that we can win the tourney. I refuse to subject them to that.

Maven may have left a scar across my chest, but waking up in Meadowbrook and witnessing the fear and relief in their eyes that I was alive, saw me scarred far worse. Never again will I be the source of such agony.

"Wait, wait, wait," Alice says, breath coming in quick bursts. "You're jumping from one to one-hundred real fast. I don't know if real swords and real dragons and real injuries are typically on the syllabus for *day one of dragon fighting*."

"Rule three: teacher knows best," I taunt. "If I say attack, you do that."

"What if I cut you and your dragon goes berserk? I don't want to be a mid-morning snack," she squeaks.

I loose a tortured sigh. It's a ridiculous sentiment, that my dragon would nosh on a human for a snack—let alone consume the Champion fated for him.

Though, the sudden thought of consuming her in another way...

My ears go hot. *No. Nope. Why the fuck would my brain conjure that image?*

It's all the damned sex pheromones those three left in the house.

"Yes, I might sound like a wishy-washy hypocrite right now. I know I was the one who basically begged you to do this," Alice continues. "But I'm only being honest. My bravado got me this far and right now it has flown right out the—"

My hand swipes over my bearded jaw as I growl out, "I'm not going to *eat* you."

"But what if I *hurt* you?" Alice shouts, and my heart skips a beat at the declaration.

She sounds so genuine. So worried. So *concerned*. But the thing is, she's already hurt me, more than anyone else has. It doesn't matter that it wasn't intentional—that whatever wild magic Arcadia wields made her forget her promise. My heart broke the day I realized she'd committed herself to anyone other than us—other than me.

I close my eyes, head falling back as I mutter a string of curses and muddied words.

Is there a part of her that wants to protect me as I have her? It's too torturous a thought to answer.

Still, she wanted this. And she needs to understand the stakes.

"I dare you," I murmur.

"What?" she asks, exasperated.

My head snaps forward, growling, "I said *I dare you to*."

"Oh."

"Now, remember our ground rules."

"Wait—"

Magic fizzles over my body and I give in to the shift.

My white-scaled dragon is magnificent, but frightening. I can see the awed terror reflected in the cool glint of Alice's eyes. I stretch out my wings, and a gust of hair hits her as they flap, blowing her curls in wild directions. The grass pressed under my iridescent talons sizzles. My tail whips, almost of its own accord, swiping close enough to Alice that she stumbles back with a shriek.

"I'm not ready!"

Steam unfurls from my nose as I loll my head from side to side. I can't speak in this form, but I hope she gets the message.

Fight me.

My pupils turn to slits, narrowing on her, and my lip curls to reveal a row of gruesome, sharp teeth. It's a twisted, taunting smile.

Rage, Alice. Show me all that anger you hurl at me as pretty words with the swing of your sword instead.

I know it's in there. I remember it from when we were kids. Loved that she matched the energy coursing through my veins, rivaled the wild nature of Arcadia.

There's never not been fire in her words or dragon breath in her lungs.

Prove me wrong. Show me you can hold your own against my brother.

"Jessa's going to be real pissed when I tell her about your

unorthodox teaching methods," Alice yells, waggling a pointed finger as if to scold me.

I scuttle forward, and she stumbles back again, this time tripping and falling to her ass. The sword lands in the grass, and she raises her hands to protect her face.

My steamy breath hits her, parted by her delicate fingers. A rumble forms deep in my throat, causing her to drop her hands and glare at me.

Her hands curl into the field, tearing out fistfuls of scorched grass; she tosses the blades in my face.

"I said I wasn't ready, asshole!" she shouts. "Now you're just pissing me off on purpose."

I chuff, shaking the ticklish grass from my snout and flashing my gnarly teeth again.

Then something changes. In her. In me. In us.

Her frustration burns through her panic, and her glare turns determined. Deadly. A myriad of thoughts pass over her expression, twisting her lips into a fierce frown.

Does she realize now, that if I were my brother, she would already be dead?

She won't get a chance to not be ready. She won't get to talk. She won't get eased into a fight. Enzo and Maven will strike without preamble.

"Fine," she sighs, rising from the ground and extending to her full height. She's tiny, especially compared to my shifted form, but her aura is massive. It's not a tangible thing, but the energy radiating off her pulses. "Don't give him attitude. Teacher knows best. Aim to kill."

Alice repeats my rules. Raises *my* sword, donned in *my* leathers.

The sight pleases my inner beast.

32

I DON'T NEED A PRIZE IF I HAVE YOU

HARLEY

Ori and Alice have developed a truce. Over the past two weeks their banter has evolved from toxically passive aggressive to... playful? At least, that's what I think is happening. I'm not 100 percent positive.

"Dude, what are you doing?" Alice groans as Ori repeatedly misses shots at the carnival booth we've stopped at. The plastic rings he tosses ping off the glass bottles, flying into the back of the tent. "You have to throw it with an arc, so it lands on top of the neck, otherwise it's going to bounce right off."

"If you have so many opinions, why don't you try?" Ori snaps.

"Okay," Alice chirps, sticking her hand into his bucket of rings and plucking out a few. "But you're not allowed to be mad when I'm better than you at this."

"Uhuh," Ori says. "I'll believe it when I—what the hell!"

"See? Told you." Alice preens, having immediately gotten

one on the target. "Ugh, stop making that face. It almost makes me feel bad for you."

"I'm not making a face. This is just my face."

"No, your normal face is a scowl. This is a pout. Sad doesn't look good on you, Ori."

"Whatever," Ori grumbles. His hand dives into the bucket. "That first shot was good luck. I bet I'll still get more than you."

"Big talk, Beast," Alice says. "You're on."

"Ori, you got this," I interject.

"Hopefully," he says, glancing back. A ghost of a smile tilts his lips; it's one I haven't seen in a long time. The kind that lights up his eyes, even if he's trying to hide it.

Jessa's breath hits my ear as she leans in, wrapping an arm around my shoulders. "Are you enjoying the show?"

I snort. "Sure am."

"You think it's foreplay for them? The bickering?" she whispers.

I mash my lips together, holding back my laugh. "I don't know. But he's smiling. I wish I could get him to do that."

"No, no, no," Jessa chides. "Shut that shit down right now. Your relationship with him will always be different than his is with Alice. But that doesn't make either less important or beautiful."

"There aren't *any* relationships to compare, Jessa." I sigh. "At this rate we'll be eighty by the time he makes a move on either of us."

"It'll happen when it's meant to," Jessa says, squeezing my shoulder. "Now, we're here to have fun, not mope. Eat up."

Jessa holds up a basket of onion rings and garlic fries, having been voted resident food-getter for our time at the county fair. It's one of my favorite parts of summers here, and it always rolls in around my birthday. I had asked Alice to join in on the celebration this year, much to her delight.

I snag one of the fries from the basket and pop it in my

mouth. "Honestly, I can't think of a better birthday present than a steady stream of fried food that's hand delivered to me by the love of my life."

Jessa chuckles around crunching bits of fried goodness. "Be ready to amend that statement. There might be something extra planned for later on that you'll enjoy even more."

"Yeah?" I take in her knowing smirk. "Was this surprise a team effort?"

She shrugs. "Could be. But it was *his* idea."

Heat blooms on my cheeks. Despite his outward persona, Ori is a very thoughtful gift giver. Over the years, he's gotten me rare editions of classic books I enjoyed, repainted my entire room while I was at work, and even used me as the model for his final build for his apprenticeship, gifting me the suit afterwards. It's my favorite of the ones he's made me over the years.

"Harley, come here and pick out which prize you want!" Alice beckons me over.

"You won?" I ask, sidling up to her and a grumbling Ori.

"Yep. Be prepared to leave here tonight with a minimum of five prizes," Alice says confidently.

"Five?" Ori balks.

"Five is too many," I say.

"*No*," Alice drawls. "Five is a very reasonable amount to make you feel special. Now pick which one you want." She points to the plushies hanging off the top of the booth. "The unicorn, the blue raccoon, or the teddy bear."

Ori's competitive streak bites him in the ass.

He can't help himself, and he challenges Alice over our snack break to a best-of-five carnival game competition. He loses in a whopping 3-0 shutout, failing at the water guns, skee-ball, and darts. At the same time, Alice wins me an avocado plushie, a tiny unicorn, and a Velcro monkey that Jessa fastens around my neck.

Ori doubles down when we break to ride the Ferris wheel, and Alice raises the stakes: if he doesn't win at least one of the last two games, then he has to do the dunk tank.

He loses both.

And that's how we end up with Ori stripping in front of the entire town.

"You can't do it half-naked," Alice seethes. "That defeats the whole point of doing the dunk tank! Your clothes are supposed to get wet!"

"You never said I had to do it clothed," Ori says, reaching for his nape, grabbing a fistful of shirt, and pulling it over his head. The move's obscene when it shouldn't be, revealing the bulky muscle underneath. "I paid a lot of money for these. I'm not letting them get a soak in chlorine."

He folds his shirt methodically, handing it off to Jessa, who's trying to hold back her laughter and doing a terrible job at it.

Alice harumphs at my side, but stays silent as he shucks off his shoes, socks, and pants, drawing a crowd. His massive figure, chiseled and pale, and draped only in a pair of black boxer-briefs, acts like a neon sign for the single adults in the crowd. Someone even whistles as he climbs up to the dunk tank platform.

I don't blame them. His thick thighs and round ass are the thing of dreams.

"You two are drooling," Jessa snickers. "See something you want, Trouble?"

Alice flinches. "What? No. I wouldn't ogle him. That would be inappropriate."

Jessa winks at me as Alice scurries away to grab the three balls from the dunk tank worker.

"Here you are," Alice says, offering me one of the balls to

throw. Ori is finally settled in his seat, his arms crossed and a scowl on his lips. "Birthday boy gets first shot. Make it count."

My body tenses under the pressure and extra eyes watching us, but I catch Ori's eye as I wind up to throw, and he shoots me a smirk. It immediately calms me.

I point to the ball, mouthing, "You ready to get wet?"

His shoulders shake with begrudging laughter. "Do it," he mouths backs.

I throw and—in a birthday miracle—hit my mark.

Shock colors Ori's expression in the split second he's airborne, and then he crashes into the water with a magnificent splash. The crowd erupts in jeers and excited shouts, and I find myself smiling as Alice and Jessa clap me on the back, murmuring how perfect I was.

Ori surfaces, shaking his black hair out and pushing it back with both hands. The action has me clenching my stomach, because he's so damn hot without trying to be. Especially as he lifts himself onto the exit platform, with water sluicing down his toned back, and his underwear suctioned to *everything* below the belt.

"You're drooling again," Jessa taunts, tapping my chin. She shoves his clothes into my chest. "Go help him get dressed. Alice and I are going to grab us fresh lemonade."

As the crowd clears, I hurry behind the dunk tank, where the worker hands Ori a towel before resetting the machine for the next unlucky soul. I stand there awkwardly as Ori swipes it over his hair and down his body, drying off.

Then he wraps the towel around his waist and magically shucks off his wet underwear without flashing me.

"Can I have my pants?" he asks, one hand outstretched to me and one hand holding the towel around his hips.

I hand him his clothes, one by one, and remain quiet as he covers up. It isn't until he's retying his shoelaces that I speak.

"Thanks for coming today," I say. "It means a lot to have you here with us."

Ori quirks a confused brow. "Why wouldn't I celebrate your birthday with you? We always do it together. And this is a big one."

I shrug. "You've been... absent lately. More than usual."

Ori's fingers pause midway through looping one lace around the other. "I'm just keeping out of the way. Giving you guys space. To be with her."

"You don't have to do that."

"I know."

"Do you?" I ask.

Ori sighs. "I don't want to ruin your happiness, Harley." He shoots me a resigned, scrunched smile. "It's better if we all stay friends."

It's a lie. He knows it as well as I.

33

I WISH

ORAZIO

"You ready for the best part?" Jessa says, leading Harley by the hand through the field. His eyes are squeezed shut behind his glasses, and he laughs with a wide smile cutting his cheeks.

He looks good like this. Happy.

I once thought I could be the reason behind their joy; sometimes I contribute to it, like now, but I wish it could be more.

Harley doesn't understand that I'm a broken man; that it's not a matter of not wanting him, it's that I cannot give him all of me when half of my heart is missing.

Would that not be a disservice to love? To not give him all that he deserves? I've always thought it better to disappoint him with none of me than torture him with half.

"Okay, open your eyes," Jessa says.

His bright, burnt umber irises trace over the checkered blanket, spread wide over the grass and placed at the edge of the field, half under the shade and away from the rowdy folks closer to the concert stage. A picnic basket sits open, full of simple dinners for the vegetarian—sandwiches, fruits, bread, and jams—carefully chosen to counter all the fried snacks he inevitably would eat at the main fair.

The past two years he's complained of a stomachache on the way home. Hopefully not this year.

"You guys set up a picnic for the Sunset Series?" Harley asks, though he knows the answer.

I had snuck away after the dunk tank, telling them to enjoy some rides while I dropped my soaked underwear in the car and came to set up. He flops onto the blanket, drawing his hands behind his head. The action rucks his shirt up, exposing a sliver of his pale stomach.

"Hell yeah. Close enough to hear the music, but not too close that we're sitting on top of another family," Harley continues.

Jessa sits cross-legged next to him, grabs a beer from the basket, and cracks it open. "Want one, babe?"

Harley holds out his hand, sighing contently when she hands the can over. He takes a gulp, and condensation on the can drips onto his neck, rolling down his bobbing Adam's apple. Their eyes are locked, as if having a silent conversation; Jessa smirks, and Harley's scent grows stronger in the air.

It's not as sweet as Alice's sugar and vanilla, but it's just as dizzying—cinnamon and a twinge of old paper that reminds me of the castle library he loved to get lost in back home. I shift on my feet, crossing my arms over my chest and trying not to draw attention to how effected I am by him.

Jessa cracks a second beer, turning to Alice. "You want one, Trouble?"

Alice stands at the edge of the blanket with a pensive look on her face. She mirrors me, arms crossed over her chest. The white linen button down she has on underneath her overall shorts is wrinkled from pushing it up her elbows all day. Platinum glints around her neck, dipping below the open collar, as it always does.

I don't think I've ever seen her without them on, and while I've gotten used to the reminder of her betrayal, seeing them doesn't hurt any less.

All of a sudden, she brightens. It's a quick shift, the one second it takes for a switch to flip. But I caught the darkness there, right before the light turned on.

Her smile is tight, though her eyes gaze softly upon the duo on the blanket.

"Yep," she says, popping the p and making grabby hands as she sits on the blanket.

"Ori?" Jessa asks, hand poised above another can.

"Nah, I'm driving remember?" I say, easing to the grass and resting my forearms on my bent knees. "Toss me a water."

"We're going to be here long enough that you can have one beer." Jessa rolls her eyes, but Harley smacks her thigh.

"Let him self-sacrifice if he wants to," he teases, though his attention is trained on me. "More for us in the meantime."

I shake my head, catching the water bottle Jessa throws my way and cracking the cap. The words are pointed, and I'd be stupid not to catch their hidden meaning. He's openly inviting me into their forming pack—but that's not something I can entertain.

I told him earlier that it's better if we all stay friends. *Friends* I can handle. *Friends* means I won't break my heart again.

Later, after the food has been picked through and all the beers drained, Harley, Jessa, and Alice fall into a cuddle pile. Harley is at the center, arm wrapped around Alice's shoulder, while the other rests on the strip of exposed stomach between Jessa's shorts and cropped T-shirt. Jessa's using Harley's lap as a pillow, and her hand is gripped around one of Alice's. They're a true tangle of limbs.

Then, Harley and Jessa fall asleep. I don't know how they

can do that, nap anywhere. I could never be comfortable enough to let my guard down in public, though part of it may be the soft singer-songwriter opening act crooning on stage, lulling them into peaceful rest.

I haven't been getting a lot of that lately.

I wish I could join them.

But my beast is raging in my chest. Not in anger, but something darker. There's a ferality caged by my ribs, one spurred on by their combined scents. I'm not usually around all three of them at the same time, and it's harder to ignore than I thought it would be. It doesn't help that their joy and subtle flirting make the scents stronger, either.

Now that they're asleep, I let my head fall to my knees and sneak a greedy breath.

Harley's cinnamon combines with Alice's sugary vanilla to create a snickerdoodle cookie, fresh out of the oven. My mouth waters and my teeth grind as I try to focus on the scent that riles me up the least.

Jessa's is subtle, but it wraps around the other two like a cocoon. It's deeper than Harley's cinnamon, a mix of amber and clove, with a hint of ginger. It's safe. Complimentary. Pleasant, but not addictive to me in the way the other two are.

I need to get a fucking grip.

"Dude," Alice whispers. "Why are you still over there?"

"What?" I ask, snapping my head up. Alice is staring at me from her place tucked under Harley's arm. My shoulders tense, and my pulse races, as if I've been caught doing something I shouldn't.

"Come here," she huffs, her free hand waving me over. "You look uncomfortable."

I shake my head, tightening my arms around my bent knees. I won't admit to her that it isn't the most comfortable position, sitting hunched on the grass, but the alternative is much worse.

"Why not?"

"There's not enough room."

"There's plenty of room." She pats the open blanket next to her. "I swear, I won't bite."

When I only give her a deadpanned stare, she clicks her tongue impatiently.

"I'm trying to be nice." Alice's hushed voice sends a shiver down my spine. "I'm sorry that I beat you at all the games. But don't be a sore loser and pout all night. Harley will be happy when he wakes to see you with us."

It's the right thing for her to say, because I find myself crawling onto the blanket after her birthday guilt trip. I stretch out, and my limbs thank me as I do, though I ensure there's a considerable distance between the trio and me.

It doesn't stop their heat from tingling my skin, though.

"Happy?" I grumble.

Alice hums, gazing off at the concert. Her free hand scratches at her collar, fiddles with the chain that holds her rings, then drops back to her side. "Nearly there."

It's a loaded two words. My tongue pushes a question against my clenched teeth, but I manage to hold it back.

Something soft brushes my hand, and I freeze at the shockwaves shooting up my arm.

Alice's pinky brushes mine.

"Friendly advice?" she whispers, and my gaze lifts from our touching hands to her kind crystal eyes. "Stop fighting it."

My throat constricts as I whisper back, "What?"

"*Him*," she says. "I see the way you two look at each other."

My head shakes. "You don't know what you're talking about, Alice."

"Maybe not. Or maybe I do," she titters.

But she doesn't understand. She doesn't *see* as she should.

"It's not him I'm fighting."

34

NEARLY THERE

ALICE

I dab the final highlights onto the canvas. I'm getting down to the wire here, still missing a few pieces to make the collection whole. But even if the gallery was tomorrow, I'd have something to show for myself, and that fact straightens my back with pride.

The quick, piercing ding of the doorbell cuts through the music drifting from my speaker. I jerk at the sound, and I'm glad my instinct is to pull into myself, otherwise I'd be spending the night carefully scraping a giant slash of off-white from this canvas.

I blow out a relieved sigh and set my brush onto my palette. The doorbell dings again, and I rush from the room, letting my music run on loop in the background.

My feet stomp down the old stairs, punching the air with noise. A small smile curls my lips, because I used to tiptoe around this house. Now, I make a scene when I move from room to room.

I slam my cabinets shut with purpose, rather than leaving

them ajar. I sing in the shower. I raise the music on my speaker to fourteen or sometimes sixteen volume—not capping it at ten. And I don't shy away from the creaking floorboards unless there's a special someone dozed off in the corner of my studio.

Making noise is my new way of taking up space.

What a difference a few months can make.

I pull open the front door, revealing Jessa, who leans against the porch railing. She pushes off it with a smirk, immediately closing in to curl a hand over my waist and drop a chaste peck on my cheek.

"Hey, Trouble," she murmurs, and happy shocks skitter down my skin. "Harley's working late. Hope it's okay that I help you tonight instead."

"Oh, okay," I say, slightly bummed. It's kind of become *our thing*—me working and him watching. "Do you think he'll stop by after?"

One of Jessa's hands rises to her chest, rubbing over her heart. "Ouch, way to knock me down a peg," she feigns offense, but there's humor in her lilt. "Am I not good enough for you all by my lonesome?"

"What? No, that's not what I meant," I panic. "I just—"

"I'm pulling your leg, Alice," she says. Then, she winks. "I already know I'm your favorite."

I mash my lips together, slightly embarrassed by my initial reaction, but I play into the bit anyway. "I see. I won't tell Harley about this upset in the partner rankings."

"Please don't," she teases. "He sounded sad enough when he asked me to come in his stead." She nods to the dark house beyond my shoulder. "You going to let me in?"

"Oh," I squeak, stepping back. "Yeah, here."

Jessa brushes past in that graceful way of hers—her steps never make a sound unless she wants them to—and finds her way into my kitchen. She shucks a tote from her shoulder and pulls out two bottles of wine.

"Where are your glasses?" she asks, beginning to rummage through my cabinets.

"That one," I say, pointing at the farthest cabinet. "And the bottle opener is in the drawer below."

"Thank you," Jessa drawls.

With practiced hands, she gathers the supplies and pops the cork on one bottle. Dark red wine pours into twin crystal glasses.

"Tonight is girl's night, and pizza should be here in ten," she continues. "I felt like we were due for some much-needed alone time."

Jessa pushes one glass towards me, her fingers split around the stem. I take it, relishing the spark that passes through me when our hands brush, and sip. Dry cabernet rolls over my taste buds, making my mouth tingle. My tongue darts out, cautiously, to chase the flavor on my lips.

"Are we... doing too much all together?" I ask, suddenly self-conscious.

"No," Jessa says. "I love when it's the three of us. But between Ori stealing you away to Arcadia, and Harley and you holing up here to paint, you don't make it to the café as much. Outside of training, I don't ever get you to myself."

I glance at the ceiling, where my studio sits above us. My music filters through the non-existent insulation. "I'm sorry."

"It's fine. You're stretched thin. I'm not mad," Jessa reassures me, taking a large sip of her wine. "However, I do think it's time that I get to participate in the full artistic experience of the famous painter, Alice Raine."

"You know I don't actually paint Harley naked, right?" I say, laughing.

Her thumb swipes a runaway drop of maroon from the corner of her mouth. "A girl can fantasize, can't she?"

~

FOUR GLASSES OF WINE, one fresh underpainting, and a half-eaten grandma pie later, Jessa pulls me onto the daybed in the sunroom.

I only ever come out here at night; it gets too hot during the day. With the glass walls and ceiling, the direct sunlight my backyard gets is magnified, causing it to swelter. Whoever designed it should have made it screened in, so we could open the windows and let a breeze flow through. But night has descended, so it's not terribly hot, even if the staleness of the sunbaked air lingers.

We lay on top of a thin and scratchy throw blanket, one that I should have thrown out when I moved in but never got around to, and I curl into Jessa's side. She gladly accepts me as my head nestles in the crook of her shoulder. Her leg hooks over my hip and one of mine slots between hers, weaving us together.

I've got an alcohol buzz—our drained glasses sit on the side table—and my skin tingles in all the places we're pressed together. It's calming, and I lean into it, trailing a finger over her tan, muscled thigh. Under the hem of her shorts her sun-kissed skin lightens, the highest point of her thigh whiter than the rest from how much time we've spent training outside.

Crickets chirp, and katydids buzz, droning out the distant squeals of my neighbors' summer parties.

"How are you doing?" Jessa whispers.

I hum, a high pitch of tentative pondering. "That's a vague question."

Her chest shakes, and I snuggle closer.

"How are you feeling right now?" she clarifies. I can hear the smirk in her words.

"I missed cuddling," I murmur. "As much as it makes me overheat in the middle of the night, it's so much better than being alone. Will you stay over?"

Jessa shifts, lifting one hand to graze along my cheek. Her

amber irises glow in the moonlight, as does the white patch of hair in her bangs. The darker, loose tresses embrace the shadows of night, curling around her neck and flowing onto the pillow we rest on.

"You want to sleep with me, Trouble?" she teases.

"I haven't wanted to fuck anyone in years and now I want to fuck you both constantly. I'm incredibly horny and it's incredibly frustrating." I've loosened my filter considerably over the last few weeks, and the wine we've consumed only bolsters my lack of inhibition. "Please?"

Jessa's thumb slides back and forth, before pushing a curl back from my face.

She shifts again, curling closer to me and bracing her weight on her elbow. It gives her better access to me, and her fingers pinch my chin lifting it up.

"Hm..." Her eyes flick between mine, as if they're gauging how many of my words are truth and how many are drunken ramblings. Jokes on her—they're both.

Her thumb catches on my bottom lip. It tugs, dragging it down. If I had any lip-gloss on it would smear down my chin with the action.

Is that what she's imagining, as her gaze follows her nail? As it releases my lip and my tongue chases the taste of her as it did the tang of wine earlier?

"You know you mean more to me than sex, right?" she asks. "You feel good in my arms right now, as is. I don't want to ruin that peace."

Emotion swells within me, surging like a rising tide. It all gets caught in my throat, as it always does. I choke on it because —I suddenly realize—I feel at peace here too.

With her. With Harley. Even with Ori. As much as we bicker, his grouchy ass can be fun to play with, like at Harley's birthday.

They don't only distract my mind but soothe it.

When was my last truly bad day? The kind where I can't get out of bed. When I can only manage to nibble on crumbs from my cabinet. Where I'm lost to the catatonia, and stare out at nothing, but feel *everything*.

My anniversary, weeks ago, back in June.

They haven't been fully devoid of bad moments, but I can't recall whole days being swept away by the riptide of my mind. Maybe I've become a stronger swimmer; maybe I've been training with Jessa and Ori in ways I didn't realize. Can I now outlast the undercurrent of my emotion when it tries to pull me under?

Hope. *True* hope. That's what this is.

Fruity and dry, like the wine in my belly.

Decadent, like the swipe of Jessa's fingers over my skin and the praise she murmurs into my crown. Like the tentative grip I take on her strong calf, keeping her leg wrapped around my hip.

I let go and fall into it, consciously now. Though I think I've been swimming in these new waters for a while.

I'm going to have to paint this.

"You're not ruining it," I say, turning my head to kiss her palm. "And you mean more to me than sex too," I add, detangling myself from her hold. Jessa tries to sit up, following me in her confusion, but I push her back down onto the daybed. "Don't move."

"Okay..." Jessa drawls with suspicion, settling back on the pillow as I pat at the scratchy blanket.

"Fuck, where is it?" I grumble. "I need to get a reference so I don't forget."

"If you're looking for your phone, it's still on the speaker dock upstairs."

"*Damn it*," I groan, crawling over Jessa and hopping off the mattress. "Fine, I'll do it the old-fashioned way." I point a finger at Jessa. "Do. Not. Move."

Her brows disappear under her bangs. "Heard, Trouble. But if you don't start asking for things nicely you're going to regret it later."

Well, that doesn't exactly sound terrible.

I pull open the drawer of the coffee table out here, snickering when I find a spare sketchbook and pencil inside. Jessa's predatory eyes track me with curiosity as I drag one of the wicker chairs next to it to the daybed. The legs scratch over the floor noisily. A devilish smirk grows on Jessa's lips as I position it at the foot of the bed, and plop down.

The itch in my fingers is too strong to ignore. I flip open to a random blank page and start sketching. A graphite form takes shape, slowly. With each stroke of my pencil, I mirror Jessa's lounging form, and generally mark out where I would be, still curled around her.

Glancing through my lashes, I take in the moonlight highlights on her skin, the shadows in the folds of fabric bunched around her waist, and the way her hand fists the blanket.

All the while Jessa stares back at me, heat blazing in those amber eyes.

The air is thick by the time I finish, flopping back in my chair.

"Okay. I'm done," I say.

"You got what you needed for your gallery piece?"

I nod.

"Good, now do another," Jessa says, sitting up.

Her demeanor changes, transforms—her dominance taking over the room. It's like on the Fourth of July; it loosens my shoulders, allows me to let go of all my burdens, to *breathe*, as she holds them for me and leads.

"It's hot watching you sketch," she continues, whipping off her tank top and tossing it aside. "With your eyes focused all on me." Next goes her shorts. She flings them across the room, and the jean smacks onto the floor. "You want to sleep with me, Alice? Then draw me first."

"Okay," I whisper.

"What was that?" she teases, unclipping her bra and dropping it off the bed. "I couldn't hear you."

"Okay," I say louder.

"Good girl." My core clenches at the praise, and I suck in a stuttered breath as Jessa leans back, shucking off her panties and baring herself to me. Her brown nipples firm to pointed peaks, and her pussy glistens, showing how much she enjoys this. "When you're finished you can have your reward."

My fingers tremble as I flip to a new page. The pencil glides over the paper with a fury, my fast heartbeat setting a fervent pace. Her body is divinely sculpted, strong and muscled from her training, but not bulky in the way Ori is; she's all angular length when you break down her shapes. Long legs and a shorter torso. A waist that doesn't curve in like mine does before it flares out into wider hips. Hers are narrow.

Broad shoulders that can swing a heavy sword with ease. Confident hands that can draw out the most content of sighs with how they hold me. Soft lips that plunder mine like I was meant to be hers.

Jessa doesn't touch herself as I draw, she only poses, still as a statue, and stares. Which is almost worse, because it feels so wrong—and *so right*—that she could elicit such desire in me from simply existing.

My thighs rub together, and the friction of my shorts and underwear on my clit helps to keep my need at bay as I add the final touches to my sketch.

"I'm done," I say as I hold the sketchbook up, my chest heaving.

Jessa's deviant grin grows. "Good girl." She pats the space next to her. "Bring it here so I can have a closer look."

I stand immediately, but she clicks her tongue.

"Uh-uh," she tuts. "Crawl."

I'm so aroused that I don't give the command a second thought. Her silky voice is a siren's call, and I'm caught under its thrall. Her pleasure at my obedience is clear as she drinks in my movements, crawling around her legs to kneel at her side.

"Here," I say, handing it over.

Jessa doesn't only glance at the drawing—she studies it. It makes my chest tight, knowing my art isn't a gimmick for sex. She truly cares for everything I create.

"You are so fucking talented, it's unreal," she says, hushed and awed. "We should frame this and give it to Harley."

I snort.

"I'm serious, he would love it." She closes the sketchbook and sets it on the side table with our discarded wine glasses. "Come here."

Her hand cradles my jaw, pulling my face to hers before sliding around my nape and anchoring there. Our lips tangle, and my heart skips at the familiarity of it all. Not with her—but with Ryan. How many times had he pulled me to him, just like this? Tenderly and hungry at the same time?

I melt into Jessa, open myself to her.

We kiss, the tension between us mounting as she strips me of my clothes. Soon, her hands find my hips and she guides me to straddle her thigh. The relief is immediate as she grinds me down on it. I'm already dripping from the build-up, and she groans as I mark her skin with my arousal.

She breaks our kiss to speak, but doesn't stop her other ministrations, one hand coming up to roll my nipple between her fingers. "I wish I had my strap. I'd fuck you so good right now, Trouble."

"Next time," I murmur between our open-mouthed kisses. "Girl's night should be a weekly thing."

"I think that's an excellent idea." Jessa chuckles, nipping at my jaw and down the column of my neck. "I guess for now I'll settle for you riding my face. How does my tongue on your clit sound for your reward for being so good?"

"Fucking hell," I mutter as her mouth latches onto my breast, tongue lashing my nipple. "I think that'd be satisfactory."

Jessa's velvety laugh fills me with warm joy before she kisses down my body, causing me to burn up from the inside. She maneuvers us so she's flat on the daybed, and I'm kneeling above her face.

My fingers push her hair back, tender and loving, and her eyes sparkle with pride.

"Thank you." The words tumble from my lips, sudden and breathless, and in awe of this moment. Yes, it's sex, but there's weight behind it. Emotion and connection that I've missed sharing with someone.

"Thank me by coming," she says.

Then her tongue is licking long stripes across my core. And I forget about the world.

My eyes fall shut and I lose sense of time as she works me to my orgasm. Her tongue is different from Harley's, rougher in its swipes across my clit, but no less pleasurable. It doesn't take long for my hips to grind on her tongue of their own accord.

"Please, Jessa. Fuck, I'm so close."

Her thumb joins the mix, rubbing consistent circles over my clit as her tongue dives into my core. The sensation is wildly different than what I'm used to and that, paired with the delicious bite of her nails digging into my ass, I'm pushed over the edge.

Jessa laps up my release as if its nectar, humming her approval.

I slide down her body, boneless and sated, and claim her lips. She tastes like me, and it's filthy in the best way.

"You taste so sweet, Trouble," she murmurs. "I could eat you all night."

35

YEAH, SEX IS GREAT, BUT HAVE YOU TRIED FALLING IN LOVE?

ALICE

I think I'm addicted to them.

It's an issue.

Well, it's not an issue in that it's been bad. It's been fantastic. My body's insatiable, like it's making up for my—entirely warranted—two-year dry spell. I haven't orgasmed this frequently in... ever. Ryan might have had a great sex drive, but he wasn't two people.

It's only an issue in that while our mouths and fingers have been all over each other's bodies, Harley and I haven't *fucked* yet. And that shouldn't *be* a problem, except for the fact that my mind seems to think that it means there's something wrong with me.

My leg bounces underneath the table of this restaurant, shaking it enough to rattle the candle votive against my untouched water glass. Condensation runs down the clear panes, soaking the white fabric with an ugly damp splotch.

We're at some new vegan place that Harley wanted to try with all of us, but I was the only one available to make the open reservation time. Our conversation has lulled as my anxious thoughts took charge, speaking over both of us.

"Alice, are you okay?" Harley finally asks.

"Why haven't we fucked yet?" I blurt out.

To his credit, Harley doesn't choke on the bread he's chewing on. His jaw only stops grinding, and the strong column of his throat bobs once with his swallow. The muscles tense under his pale skin, making the long lines run taught.

"Did you want to?" he asks, cautiously.

"Well, *yeah*," I say, awkwardly glancing down at my half-eaten lasagna. I lean forward, whispering so our conversation stays private, "Do you not want to?"

Harley's eyes go wide. "No!"

"No?"

"No—I mean, *yes*. Of course I do," Harley stumbles over his words. He levels with me, both hands braced flat on the table, staring through his round glasses. "What kind of question is that?"

"I don't know, a real one?" I say, finding a bit of humor in his crazed and flushed expression. Our faces are inches from each other as we murmur back and forth. "You haven't even *tried*."

"Well, I—uh…" It's as if his brain buffers. "I didn't know it was an option."

"Why wouldn't it be an option? It's been weeks. You eat me out, like, every other day. And your fingers have been so deep inside me you could probably tell me where all my organs are."

Harley blows out a nervous breath as he pushes his glasses up with his middle finger. "Because you didn't say anything about it. And Jessa's trained me to only have penetrative sex when she asks for it."

"That makes it sound so clinical," I say, my nose scrunching. "It also makes it sound like you're a dog."

"I'm a *good boy*, Alice, I basically am a dog," he jokes. "Though, I'm not complaining about it. I get lots of treats."

My elbow finds the table, and my forehead falls into my hand. "I don't even know what to say to that."

"Everything okay here? Do you guys need a to-go box?" the waitress's overly cheery voice rings out. Both Harley and I jolt back in our seats, like two kids who were caught sticking their hands in the cookie jar. "Maybe a look at the dessert menu?"

That lovely flush crawls up Harley's neck as his attention flicks between the waitress and me. His tongue pokes his cheek as his expression darkens.

"No, just the check please. We have dessert at home."

My back hits the front door the second Harley slams it shut. It's dark—none of the lights in the house are on because no one is home yet, both Ori and Jessa working late—but it doesn't matter, because I'm closing my eyes anyway.

His lips slant over mine, pillowy and giving. I nip and he groans. My tongue leads and his follows. It's delightful, how responsive he is; how he takes everything I'm willing to give with enthusiasm.

"Bedroom?" Harley whispers, breathless, when I kiss down his long neck.

"Nope. Couch. Now," I growl, biting into the flesh.

"*Fuck.*"

His throaty noises of approval rumble against my lips, and I swallow all of them as he lifts me up. My legs wrap around his hips, and he carries me to the couch, his lean limbs deceptively strong.

I fall onto the firm cushions and Harley crawls on top of me, fusing our mouths together. He slots easily between my legs, and my skirt rides up as we grind into each other—his erection hot and firm beneath his slacks, rubbing gloriously against my underwear. I normally don't wear skirts, but Jessa encouraged me to wear it tonight, noting how cute I looked.

She's always meddling, but I'm not complaining at the results.

"Clothes off," I demand in my best imitation of Jessa's dominance, kissing my way over his stubble and nibbling on his ear.

"Yes, ma'am." Harley chuckles his aroused amusement.

His hands are fast and efficient in ridding us of our clothes, and then it's a frenzy of touch.

Harley is *everywhere*.

His tongue swirls over my peaked nipples, teeth biting into them when my back arches into the sensation. His thumb circles my clit while he teases my core with a single curling digit. His erection presses into my thigh, smearing it with pre-cum.

My fingers weave into his white tresses, nails digging into his scalp, and his mouth pops off my breast, dazed expression turning confused behind his skewed glasses.

"Let's get these to safety before we go too crazy," I murmur. I pluck the glasses from his face, close them, and toss them as gently as I can onto the coffee table. My fingers find his hair again, and I push his face into my tits. "Resume."

Harley hums, nibbling the flesh of my breast before trailing down my stomach. I sigh into the sensation of his tongue lapping at my skin, of it circling my clit—but it's not *enough*.

Even as his fingers curl inside of me, pushing me towards the edge, I want *more*.

"Harley," I say, breathless.

My fingers tighten their grip in his hair; his begging gaze meet mines, though he doesn't lift his mouth from my core. It's obscene, the look of him desperate and heady between my legs.

He gets off on giving.

I could suffocate him with my thighs, and he'd be happy to die so long as the juice of my orgasm coated his tongue.

"Stop," I say, trying to force all the cool haughtiness I can into my voice. I release his hair and push up on my elbows. "Get up."

Harley whines his disapproval, but he's quick to comply, scuttling up and standing next to the couch. My throat bobs, much like his erection does against his abdomen. I could easily lick over his crown and suck him down my throat if I wanted. But that's not where I want his cock.

Rising to my knees on the couch, I trail my nails up his chest and hook my arms around his neck.

"I want to ride you," I say, pressing a chaste kiss to his lips. He curses under his breath and I giggle. "Now, sit."

"Yes, ma'am." Harley flops back on the couch with that wide, beaming grin that crinkles the skin around his rust-colored eyes. Though it falls, too quickly, when I hook my legs over his hips and notch him at my entrance. "Wait."

My hand freezes, gripping the base of his cock. "What?"

"Condom?"

"I have an IUD. So unless you want one, I'm okay to go without." I rub him back and forth over my slit, coating him in me, causing his head to fall against the cushions.

"Nope. All good here," he mutters. My hips tilt, and I slowly lower myself, inch by inch, onto his cock. "*Fuck.*"

The stretch is noticeable, but manageable. Harley's more long than he is girthy. My hands brace on his shoulders, and my nails dig crescents into the freckled skin as I bottom out.

We pause, breathing together, as I lean forward, my nose nuzzling his.

"Good, because I love the idea of being filled with your cum," I whisper bravely. "I kind of have a breeding kink."

A strangled sound rips through his throat as his hands find my hips, gripping tight and guiding me along his shaft.

"You never fail to surprise me," Harley murmurs as we come together.

It's slow, and sensual, and so much more than sex as we stare into each other's eyes, foreheads pressed together.

"You feel incredible," I murmur back.

"Incredible," Harley echoes. "So tight. So wet."

"Kiss me," I say, or command, or beg. I don't think it matters which intention they fall from my lips with, because Harley would answer the call no matter what. "Kiss me, Harley."

I don't have to say it a third time.

Lips turn puffy. Tongues tangle. Teeth bite. My arousal builds with every frantic swivel of my hips. One of Harley's thumbs falls to where we're joined, rubbing torturous circles around my clit.

The pleasure crests, and I tighten around him, the faint flutters of my budding orgasm making an appearance.

"*Fuck*," Harley groans into my mouth.

I ride him with increased intensity, and his thrusts match me with fervor. They're still decidedly *gentle* in comparison to some of the times Ryan would pound into me from behind. But he's not Ryan. And this isn't some feral claiming after weeks of being apart.

This is Harley. My soft, uniquely beautiful, kind stranger, whose blushes inspire my muse, and whose presence fills me with the comfort of being seen.

There's too much emotion; it's tucked in the divot between Harley's brow, splattered in the freckles on his cheeks, shining in the depths of his blown-out pupils. I'm sure he sees it in me, too, by the way his teeth dig into his lower lip, drawing blood.

I lick it away. The metallic tang of him fills our mouths as our kissing turns sloppy.

My heartbeat fills my body, thrums in my neck, pulses on my tongue as it dances with his.

We grind and thrust and kiss and bite and moan until we throw ourselves over the edge.

I flutter around Harley and his warmth fills me in spurts.

We fly high in the ecstasy, and when we come down from it, I linger in the afterglow, wrapped around him. Full. Whole. Sated.

His hands are pressed firmly into my back, and my sensitive nipples brush against his chest with every heaving breath I take. Eventually, the aftershocks cease, his cock softens, and we have to part.

Harley sets me down on the couch, telling me to hold still before hopping off into the dark house.

He comes back with a wet washcloth. Sitting between my spread thighs, he watches as his cum drips out me. I almost tell him to push it back in, just to see him blush again, but his dopey grin is too pure, so I let him do what he wants and clean me up.

But when I gasp at the rough cloth swiping over my throbbing clit, his grin drops. A hungry look takes over his face, tongue swiping over his teeth. His head dips, too fast for me to realize what he's doing, and licks along my seam.

I yelp, smacking his head.

"Stop that," I scold, though there's no bite to it. He licks his lips and tries to go in for another taste—to lap up the mixture of us leaking from me. I dig my nails into his scalp and pull him up to me, despite his pouting groan. "As hot as the idea of you down there is, I cannot do a round two right now."

Harley hums, as if he wants to challenge me. But with a quirk of my brow, he quiets, wrapping his arms around my hips and resting his head on my belly.

"Cuddles though?" he asks.

"Absolutely."

Eventually, we move from the couch. Harley carries me upstairs—despite my protests—and dutifully dresses me in one of his shirts and a pair of boxers before pulling us into bed to wait for Jessa to come home.

The world is quiet as we lay in the dark of his bedroom,

save for the bugs outside and our contented sighs. Harley latches onto me, nuzzling into my chest as if it's his favorite pillow. My fingers trace his exposed spine lazily, playing with the elastic of his boxers when they reach the bottom and with the short crop of hair at the base of his neck when they reach the top.

"Gods, I love you," he murmurs.

My fingers freeze in the valley between vertebrae.

"Really?" I ask.

"Mhm."

My palm spreads out on his back as a means to steady myself. A throbbing beat fills my ears, my own heart drumming up a panic.

"Harley?"

"Yeah?"

"You're not just saying that because you're sleepy and orgasm drunk, right?"

"No, Alice." Harley lifts his head so I can meet his half-lidded gaze and see how serious he is. "And don't worry, I don't need you to say it back."

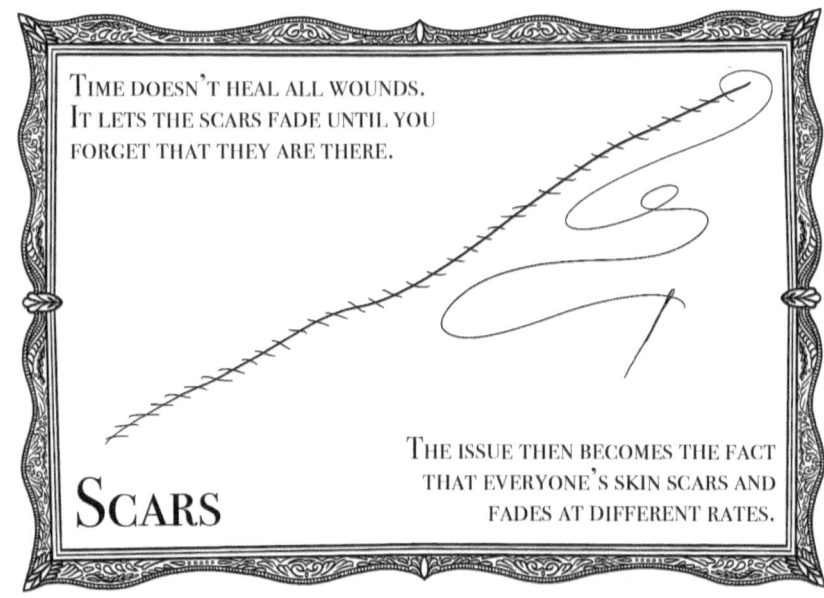

Time doesn't heal all wounds. It lets the scars fade until you forget that they are there.

The issue then becomes the fact that everyone's skin scars and fades at different rates.

Scars

36

STABS AND SCARS

ALICE

"Are you a voyeur?" I whisper-yell, untangling myself from Harley's sleeping form. "Because I'm starting to think that you are."

"I am *not* a voyeur," Ori whisper-yells back, face contorting into a sneer. He holds up my phone. "It's not my fault you keep leaving your phone downstairs. The alarm wakes everyone up but you."

I pointedly look at the sleeping form of Harley at my side, and Jessa on the other side of him. Jessa's breath hitches, but she doesn't stir.

Uhuh, everyone is totally awake right now, I say by tossing a quirked brow at the dragon taking up the threshold.

He kicks off the molding and leaves with a miffed scoff. I scramble off the bed, following Ori to the kitchen to start our strange new routine.

He's already got two bagels set on the kitchen island for us when we enter. I still don't know if our shared breakfasts are meant to be consolatory because I keep failing; I haven't managed to cut him once while he's in dragon form. Or if it's meant to negate my claims that his dragon seems hangrier than normal... How could he be hangry if he's just eaten breakfast, right?

The third option, which is becoming increasingly more likely, is that he's just being nice.

Between this, the way he thoughtfully planned the picnic for Harley's birthday, and the memories that have resurfaced of the dragon shifter, I'm starting to wonder if his constant crotchety attitude is a mask he clutches to.

What is he hiding behind it?

I swipe my bagel off the counter, the yellow-orange tint of the egg-everything showing through the waxy paper. Ori gets a plain. With butter. Like a fucking psycho.

"I'm not a voyeur," Ori grumbles, dropping my phone on the island before grabbing the shaker cup next to his bagel and taking a sip of a grossly thick protein shake. "I don't watch you guys sleep."

"Well, I keep waking up to you staring at me in bed with my boyfriend and girlfriend. It's starting to get weird." I rip open the bagel and take a large bite, sighing at the toasted notes of the seeds and the creamy veggie spread.

"If you stopped sleeping over, then it would be less weird," he says, meticulously unwrapping his bagel and sitting down on one of the two stools. "I would come knock on your door, like a normal person. No bedroom wake-up calls."

"Uhuh," I say, licking cream cheese spilling out between the halves of the bagel. His gaze snags on the action before quickly turning away. "Or you could text me, *like a normal person*."

"You're not this combative with them, are you?"

"Of course not, I'm an angel for Harley and I'm only slightly bratty for Jessa, but she loves it." I round the island and grab a cup from the cabinet—because I know where things are here now—and fill it with water from the sink. I gulp down the cool liquid.

Ori stares at me as if I've grown three heads.

"What?" I ask.

"Nothing." He shakes his head and refocuses on pulling bite-sized pieces off his bagel and shoving them in his mouth. For such a gigantic man, he's awfully delicate with his fingers.

I narrow my eyes at him.

"*What*?" I repeat.

"You smell like them, okay?" Ori says, shoulders rising to his ears. "You're all over them, and they're all over you. And all of you are all over the house. It reeks of sex. Did you and Harley fuck on the couch last night?"

"Maybe," I mumble around a bite of doughy goodness. "What's it to you?"

"It's. Nothing." Ori says the words like they're each their own sentence. Clear. Pointed. Avoidant. "It just... it sets my beast off."

"I said this at Harley's birthday, but if it wasn't clear, you know you can have him too, right?" I ask. "One of the first things Harley told me after I found out about Arcadia is how he hopes you'd recognize and return his feelings. Jessa's okay with it. *I'm* okay with it." It's strange to admit, but it's the truth. "We're chill. Just don't give him a dragon STD, I don't think my OBGYN will know how to treat it if I catch it from him."

Ori's head drops into his hands with a murmured curse. His strong fingers, thicker than Harleys, rake through his black hair, messing up the perfectly styled locks as he stares at the counter. "You're not understanding."

"Then explain it to me." When he doesn't immediately answer, I slide onto the stool next to him and continue, "I give you a lot of flak, Ori, but you're not a bad guy. I don't know that part of your past, so I don't know if you did something wrong or if you just weren't ready to accept his love back then. But stop torturing yourself."

He lifts his head—but instead of the distant, dulled navy hue that I'm used to, they're vibrant with grief.

I've seen these eyes before, but on me, in the mirror. It's guilt. It's loneliness. It's paralysis—the cage of one's own mind barring you from doing *anything*, no matter how much you want to move.

There's a single beat where we breath in each other's air. It's charged with shared knowing. My lungs burn with my intake of breath, and each exhale is accompanied by gooseflesh rising on my arms. It's like we're on the edge of a cliff, waiting for him to push us off it.

We're more alike than I ever realized.

"Our birthday is in two weeks. If you don't break through my scales today, I'm calling the tourney off." Ori's potent gaze retreats, pulling us back from the cliffside. "Get changed into your leathers and meet me outside in ten."

ORI DOESN'T TALK to me after that. Not when he slams the front door and I tease him that he's going to rip it from its hinges if he continues to manhandle it. Not when we go to Arcadia and wind through the pine-scented woods. And certainly not when he shifts into his dragon form and charges at me with no preamble.

The fight... isn't good.

I'm sloppy. My blade doesn't hit my marks, though that isn't exactly new. My leathers feel heavier, tighter, and my feet drag along the grass as I dodge the swing of Ori's barbed tail.

Frustration fills the clearing, emanating off both of us in hot waves that distort the air; he's pushing me harder than ever and I'm failing.

I *hate* failing.

"You know, I thought we were friends now!" I shout my aggravation at the iridescent dragon as he regroups across the field. "This isn't very friendly behavior!"

His wings bristle as he chuffs. A puff of fire escapes his nose, and I instinctively step away. Slitted eyes lock on me, and his wings spread wide.

"What are you doing?" I mutter.

Ori launches into the air. He's only ever scuttled around the field on all fours during our sessions. The serpentine body is nimbler than I thought it would be.

"Fuck!" I yelp, running towards the cover of trees. "What the fuck, Ori!"

His rumble sounds overhead, and my curses slur together as his shadow passes over me. Talons grip my shoulder, wrapping under my arm and around my torso, and pull me into the air.

I scream. An embarrassing, high-pitched squeal.

"Put me down right now or so help me, Beast, I will—" I cut myself off with a frustrated snarl when his deep chuff vibrates through me. I look down and realize he's fucking around with me. We're barely six feet off the ground, and he's circling the field. "You want me to stab you that bad? *Fine.*"

From this angle, I'm able to access the softer patch of his underbelly, where the scales part into iridescent hide. When fighting on foot I have a hard time reaching these joints, so I've been aiming for his head or the thinner leather of his wings.

I jab, with all my strength, right into the dragon's armpit.

Ori roars in pain, and my heart stops at the terrifying sound. I rip the blade out with a panic, and it splatters a red line over the flesh of his inner leg.

Then the asshole drops me.

I fall, six feet to the clearing, casting my sword away so I don't impale myself, and manage to land in a way that doesn't break any bones. It's as if some warrior instinct takes over my body and urges it to roll on impact, saving my ankles and wrists from devastation.

Groaning on my back, I blink away the spinning dark splotches as the dragon's shadow passes over me—but then the shadow turns into a bearded face, and I'm hoisted upright.

"Are you okay?"

I stagger, the world spinning from being tossed about; Ori tries to steady me, but I slap his hands away.

His shirt is tattered—strange, how it shifts back all cut up from where my sword hit. As if all my whacking at him in the lead up to our brief flight had shredded the fabric instead of his skin.

His gruff voice hits my ears, but I can't focus on the words, because a giant slash pours rivulets of red down the valley of his bicep.

"Shit. *Fuck.* Fucking hell," I say, rushing forward. "I stabbed you! Oh my god."

"Alice, I'm fine. Are *you* okay?"

Curses spit from my mouth as I search for something to stop the bleeding. There was a time when Ryan cut the tip of his finger off in the kitchen, and blood was *everywhere*. We didn't have any bandages, so I had to use paper towels; took the whole roll with me to the ER so we didn't make a mess in the waiting room.

We don't have paper towels here. We also don't have any bandages.

That's stupid. Why have we never brought a first aid kit to these sessions?

Did Ori expect me to never land a blow?

I catch the edge of his tattered shirt and rip it from his waist, frantically wrapping it around the wound on his arm.

"Alice, *stop*. I'm fine," Ori says, shaking my shoulders to snap me out of my panic.

"You're not fine, I *stabbed* you," I say, hands trembling as I mess up a knot.

"And I dropped you six feet out of the air," he seethes. A strong hand weaves into my hair, pulling my head back. I freeze, blinking up at his angry expression. "It's fine."

His other arm circles around the back of my head, and his finger tugs at the white—turning red—fabric. My grip goes white to match, refusing to release the pressure around the wound.

"Stop saying it's fine," I grit out.

"It'll heal," Ori says.

"But—"

"*It'll heal*," he repeats. "Look."

I stare, in wonder, as the wound stops bleeding and the flesh slowly knits together to form a puckered pink line. It's not quite scabbed over, but it isn't in need of stitches anymore.

"You didn't tell me dragons had supernatural healing abilities," I say.

"You didn't ask."

"I didn't *know* to ask."

Another moment passes of still observation. Suddenly, I'm far too aware of the way he's wrapped around me, infusing me with the remnants of his dragon's heat. His chest, which has a manly thatch of black hair spreading out from his sternum, presses against my breastplate. It's a strong embrace, and I feel so *tiny* compared to his thick body. Not in a *oh-I'm-a-dainty-princess* way, but in a *I-didn't-realize-muscles-could-have-muscles* way.

"I'm sorry I dropped you," Ori says, his deep voice vibrating between our chests.

"You should be apologizing for picking me up in the first place," I mutter, peering at his harsh expression through my lashes.

"I'm sorry."

I never get this close to him, so it's the first time I notice the faint worry-lines forming on his forehead and around his eyes.

"I'm sorry I stabbed you," I counter.

"I dared you too, remember?"

"Yeah, but I did it because I was mad."

"Are you not mad anymore?"

"I'm still a little mad, but not in that way." I snicker at myself, noting the double meaning hidden in my words. Hadn't I said something similar to Jessa the first time we met? I shift in Ori's fierce hold. He tightens his embrace, thick fingers curling at the back of my neck, and I suck in a gasp. "Um, do you need to be holding me so tight for whatever magic to work or..."

Panic flashes in Ori's widened eyes. He lets go, practically throwing me across the field, and paces away.

"No," he rasps. He clears his throat, clearly uncomfortable. The sparkling magic of his pending shift skitters across his skin. "Let's try again, but this time do it while we're on the ground."

I manage to stab him three more times during our session, and I only freak out after the first two; whatever mental block I had has cleared.

Afterwards, Ori walks me home in silence, with four puckering wounds spread across his bare arms and chest. I stare at the marks of me on his skin, red and ugly, as we trudge through Meadowbrook Park.

The familiar urge to paint twitches my fingers, and I resign myself to my fate.

I paint well past sunset.

37

EVASIVE MANEUVERS

ALICE

I toss and turn all night, falling out of nightmares and into memories.

Ori is at the center of every one of them.

In some macabre rendition of our training, my subconscious has me stab him with a blade straight through his chest. He reassures me he's fine, but red pools between his teeth and drips from his lips as he coughs.

I scream. The dream ends. Then it repeats, slower, each time, until it doesn't.

Maybe I wake up, turn over in a haze, and the sensation of fresh pillow on my cheek resets my slumber. Because suddenly, we're kids again, and I know it's a memory.

I'm gripping his hand tightly, pulling him to the water of the Lake in the Sky. Ori fights the entire way, digging his heels into the clouds before the shallows.

"Alice, it's cold."

"Don't be a coward," I urge, pulling him farther into the lake. "Come on."

I wince at how freezing the water is on my toes, but I know that once it's up to our chests, our bodies will get used to it.

It's like playing tug of war with Ori's hand, though; we go back and forth, one step into the water, one step out. I huff, frustrated with his stupid frown and lack of trust, and let go. Ori stumbles, falling to his butt.

"What the heck, Alice!"

My hands find my bathing-suit clad hips, pressing into the ruffles that line the sides. "If I get eaten by a sea monster out there, then it's your fault."

I turn, stomping into the chilly lake. My arms wrap around my middle as the water soaks through my bathing suit and I hurry to the deeper waters. The faster I'm fully submerged, the faster I can rid myself of the sensation of the stretchy fabric suctioning to my skin.

"There are no sea monsters in a lake. It'd be a lake monster that eats you!" *Ori yells.*

"I'd be fish food either way, dummy!" *I call over my shoulder.*

I lift my feet off the ground and bob with the water, treading past where the waves break. Splashing sounds behind me, and I swim in a circle to catch Ori's head surface a few feet away.

The scowl on his face is normal; what's not is how deep it cuts into his cheeks. It's been doing that all week.

"You've been pouty all morning," *I say.*

"No, I haven't," *Ori says, too quick.*

"Yes, you have. More than usual. Except now this is your usual."

"That doesn't make any sense," *he says, dipping under the water. When Ori resurfaces, he shakes his wavy black hair out, spraying lake water all over me.*

"Rude," *I say, splashing him back.*

"You're the one who wanted me out here," *Ori snaps. He licks his lips, grimacing before spitting into the lake.* "So salty. Ugh."

I roll my eyes. "Yeah, well, that doesn't mean I want you to spray water on me like a dog."

We swim in silence for a minute, until I finally gain the courage to ask what I really wanted to come out here for. It's more private, and since the others have good hearing, the waves help to block us out.

"Why are you sad?" I ask, sinking partway under the water and blowing nervous bubbles.

Ori looks away, out at the clear blue horizon that meets the lake. "Do you want me to lie or do you want me to tell you the truth?"

My lips rise out of the water. "The lie first. Then the truth."

Ori chuckles, though the laugh is short-lived. "You're weird."

I shrug, and a ripple flows from me to him. His hand breaks it, gliding though the water like a shark's fin.

"Everyone here has a best friend. Enzo has Maven, even though she's weird," Ori says.

"Weirder than me?"

"You're... cool weird. She's mean weird." Ori sinks deeper in the water; it laps at the bottom of his chin. "Harley has Jessa. The other kids in town have paired up too. And I'm just there. Even though we all grew up together."

I hum. "That's an easy problem to fix."

"How?"

"You can have me, duh," I say, holding both hands above water to show a six count. "That makes three even pairs of two for a total of six."

Ori's lips purse, as if he can't believe me. "Really?"

"Mhm. Are you bad at math or something?" I swim a circle around Ori, who treads in place. "I don't have a best friend back home, so the job is open."

"Being a best friend isn't a job. Being a baker is a job," he says. "Being an Heir is a job."

I scrunch my nose. "You're supposed to always be there for them. You have to hang out with them regularly and sometimes have sleepovers. You have to compliment them, even if you don't like their new haircut. And you have to ask them why they're sad when they look sad. There's a lot you have to do as a best friend. I know because I saw it at school and took notes, just in case I got one. Tell me that doesn't sound like a job."

"Oh," Ori says, brows furrowing. He stares down at the water again, studying his pale hands as he glides them under the rippling surface. "Okay, that makes sense."

"Will that make you happy again?" I ask, swimming closer.

"What?" he says, looking up.

"Will me being your best friend make you happy?"

"I don't know," he says. Then quieter, "Probably."

"Okay," I chirp. "You're already my Heir. Might as well add best friend to the list." I purse my lips, hiding my conniving smile. "Also," I drawl, "best friends share food. And I want some of those sour gumdrops you snuck from the pantry when we're done swimming."

"That seems reasonable," Ori says, utterly serious. "But I like the purple ones the best, so is it okay if I only give you the red ones—" Ori cuts himself off, taking in my face, which convulses with silent laughter. He must realize I'm pulling his leg, because I'm suddenly doused in a wave of water.

I scream, but it's all giggles as I dive into the lake to escape Ori's wrath. I pop back up closer to shore, and he starts swimming towards me.

"Alice!" he calls out.

"First one back gets the purple gumdrops!" I yell, maniacally.

I WAKE UP WITH A JOLT.

My heart races like it did twenty years ago, as if I was chased through the clear blue waters of a lake that defies all laws of physics by a boy who could turn into a dragon.

It would be a great dream to tell people, if it was only a dream.

I glance at the sleeping forms at my side; last night Jessa and Harley had their date night but asked me to come over after. I'd slipped into their bed well after dark with paint-stained fingers, having worked all night to finish the second to last piece for the gallery.

It's of Ori and I—of me tying a scrap of cloth around his wound.

Ori's a riddle; I think that's why I keep poking him. 90 percent of the time he reacts to me with a variation of annoyance, but the other 10 percent he acts sweet, on the verge of caring. It makes me want to solve him. I love a good puzzle.

At least I used to. I stopped doing them around the same time I stopped painting.

I can already tell by my erratic pulse that I'm not going to fall back asleep, so I slip from the bed, pad into their kitchen, and grab my phone from its charger on the counter. It's an ungodly hour, so early that it won't be time to train with Ori anytime soon.

I could wait for him. Or, better yet, I could call him on his bluff and go home, make him come knock on my door to get me for our session. And then I could make him wait under the guise of not hearing him banging on the front door while I'm all the way up in my bedroom.

My head shakes as I perch on one of the island stools.

Nah, that would be overkill.

I've come to enjoy our early morning banter, in a strange twist of fate.

I glance at my phone again. August tenth. A little more than two weeks until my birthday—*our* birthday—and my gallery deadline.

What if I don't finish piece 100?

Static fills my ears. It's a switch flipping. A bulb blowing out as the anxiety rolls in.

Sometimes it's as simple as one brief thought to send you into a spiral of your own making.

What if I forget his face before I can immortalize it in paint?

It's going to be a bad morning.

I pitch forward off the kitchen stool, stumbling as I climb back up the stairs to pull on the shorts, T-shirt, and sneakers I arrived in. My hands shake as I try to tie the laces, and I give up, shoving the strings down the side of my sneakers. The aglets poke against my socked foot, but I push through the annoying sensation as I leave their house.

It's not one of *those* bad mornings. The ones that are characterized by stagnancy and blank stares, by the smell of stale bedsheets and dirty dishes stacked in the sink, or by cyclical thoughts and hours that pass like seconds.

No, this is one of the bad mornings where you're overcome with the need to *run*. To flee. To leave everything behind. To remake yourself and pretend to not be who you are anymore— because it's *too much* to bear all by yourself.

I can sell my Nana's house, and my car. I can change my name and get a new ID. I can cut my hair off, chemically straighten it, dye it a different color, just so I don't have to think of how he'd twirl a curl around his tanned finger.

I can escape all these things that remind me of him, but if the past two years have taught me anything, it's that I can't escape my grief.

It's in my shadow, and it follows me everywhere. Even at night, it's still there, I just can't see it clearly.

The need and the want and the yearning hit me, twisting painfully in my gut.

I need air. I need clarity.

I yank open their front door and step into—

38

HIM

ALICE

Arcadia.

I haven't fallen into the other realm in months, and it's disorienting.

I also haven't landed anywhere but the Meadow. But tonight is different. My shorts soak through from where I've landed, dropped in a luscious clearing glistening with early morning dew. It's smaller than the others I've been to in the Wandering Woods, only a few feet of grass surrounding a circular pond.

"*Alice?*"

I freeze.

I know that voice.

"*Is that you?*"

It's foggy in my memory, but my heart recognizes the timbre.

A shaky breath rattles my lungs.

"Ryan?" His name could barely be described as a whisper on my tongue.

I slowly pan across the clearing, but everything is perfectly picturesque, not a person in sight. Nor an animal or insect. In fact, the world is eerily quiet.

"*I'm over here, babe. Come to the water.*"

I hold my breath in disbelief as I crawl to the edge of the pond. One hand stamps the dewy grass after the other, and my bare knees are imprinted with the blades.

The thing people don't tell you about being apart from your person for longer than a few weeks is that you start to question everything you remember about them.

Was his voice always that deep? Was it smooth, or did it sometimes get rumbly? You're thankful you have recordings saved on your phone to remind yourself of the exact intonation, because the sleepy goodnight from him you conjure in your head isn't quite *right*.

Was his touch gentle, calloused? Was it ever bruising, but only in the moments you wanted it to be? Warm when you were cold and cold when you were warm, always managing to anticipate your needs before you could voice them?

Yes, you reassure yourself. Yes, he would tuck his cold hand between your thighs when you complained. Yes, he let you rub your cold feet against his overheated ones. Yes, you would run your hand through his chest hair when you snuggled, and you'd follow it down to the belly rolls he got when he curled up to sleep.

His skin was always so soft, despite never moisturizing.

But *was it*?

I don't know if everyone is like this. Maybe my brain processes things differently. Some days, remembering is all I can do, and yet I can't grasp it.

It's smoke. Vapor. It's running and not moving in a dream, a slow-motion clip set to loop. An eye twitch that only happens when you're alone and stops when you go to the doctor.

I stop at the edge of the moonlit pool. The surface is smooth, glistening like glass, with not one ripple in sight to mar its beauty. My fingers dig into the dirt as I lean my trembling body forward and—

A scream flings from my throat. It rings out into the nothingness of night as I scramble backwards.

"*Babe, it's just me,*" Ryan says with a laugh. "*Is my bedhead that scary looking?*"

A violent roar rings through the air. It sounds far away, but it echoes between the tree trunks surrounding me all the same. I glance at the sky; there's no dragon flying overhead. Only stars, twinkling happily.

Surely, I must be hallucinating this time.

"*Alice?*" Ryan's voice calls out again, full of concern.

"Ryan?" I croak. "Is that really you?"

"*Of course it's me,*" he says.

"Tell me something only you would know," I manage to whisper. My body trembles, both from the cold air and the shock. "Something from the last time you were home."

"*Well, we were crying. And you were butchering onions like they'd personally offended you. Really, what did they ever do to you?*" Ryan asks, laughing.

Tears that have been welling in my eyes pour over, trailing down my cheeks. I stop shaking enough to move, and I pull myself back to the ledge of the pool, gazing into the crystal waters.

I haven't seen his smile in years. Only snapshots of it in pictures, when I could stomach looking. Only imprints of it in my mind, when I dared to recall.

He looks as he did the day I dropped him off at the pier—peacock blue T-shirt. Rumpled brown hair, long enough to test regulations but short enough to get away with. Red-rimmed umber-brown eyes, sparkling with adoration.

"They had the audacity to be the only vegetable in the kitchen when I needed something to channel all my worry into." I shake my head, blinking hard, but when my gaze refocuses on the water, he's still there. My hand reaches out but pauses halfway to the stagnant water. I pull it to my pounding heart, whispering, "How is this possible?"

"*Magic.*"

That seems a good enough explanation as any. How can I argue when I've spent all summer discovering the curiosities of it?

Ryan tilts his head, a frown forming on his lips.

"*I'm sorry I broke my promise, Alice. Can you forgive me?*"

"No," I croak out with a sniffle. "Yes." I swipe at my cheeks, palms coming away wet. "I miss you so much it's hard to say either with any certainty."

He sighs. "*Come here, babe.*"

A sense of peace wraps around me, like a fresh blanket out of the dryer. I'm sobbing, but it's muted in my ears.

"*Let me make it up to you,*" Ryan says, drawing me closer.

I reach out to the water, to his reflection. But just as my finger touches the glimmering surface, the smallest ripple distorting Ryan's reflection, I'm yanked away.

Thick arms wrap around my waist, pulling me against a hard body.

All the calm is ripped away too, and the devastation of my loss hits me all over again. The stitches tear open, and the wound bleeds.

"No!" I scream in agony. I reach out, try to grab onto him, but the water ripples, and Ryan's visage disappears. Sinks into the pool's depths like a stone.

"What are you doing here?" Ori's gruff voice hits my ear, along with his hot breath.

I push against his arms, but they're locked around my torso.

My emotions are a violent pendulum between rage and melancholy. A curse is poised on the tip of my tongue, ready to lash Ori for his interruption, but then I swing the other way, wailing, "Where did he *go*?"

"Who?" Ori asks.

"*My husband!*" I growl, or cry, or scream. It's a raspy mess in my throat.

"No, Alice, that's not—" Ori grunts as I elbow his ribs with all my strength.

"Let me go to him. He was *right there.*" I fight against Ori's hold, but the more I struggle, the tighter he grips me, drawing us both away from the pool. "And now he's *gone. Again.*" My nails scrape over his forearms; they're not sharp enough to draw blood, but red lines rise in their wake. "I didn't even get to say *goodbye.*"

"Alice, listen to me, he's not real."

"You don't know what you're talking about," I snarl.

"Yes, I do. I almost drowned here too, when I was younger," Ori grits out as I kick my legs into his shins. "Stop fighting me. The pond tricks people with what they want most. It's a living beast." I bite into his thick bicep as he walks us out of the clearing. "Ouch, fuck. *Stop fighting me.*"

"You sound fucking crazy. A pond can't be alive," I say. "A pond doesn't play tricks. Humans do."

Ori manages to maneuver me over his shoulder, despite my protests. One arm bands across the back of my calves while a calloused hand grips my thigh. The moonlit field with the pond disappears, and the woods shift, closing off the path.

"Let me *go,*" I scream.

"No."

I hit his back with all my might, but it's like tenderizing a tough cut of meat with a spoon. "Let. Me. Go. Or. So. Help. Me. I. Will—"

His large hand smacks my ass, and I yelp. "*Stop fighting.*"

"You did *not* just smack my ass, you insufferable douchecanoe!" I yell, slamming my fist into his ass. "We might have graduated to friends but that is not okay!"

"I did and I will do it again," Ori growls as his fingers dig into my thigh. The vibrations of his reprimand raise gooseflesh on my skin. "You could have died, Alice! So shut the fuck up, stop fighting me, and calm yourself down."

I scream. I growl. I let it all out—and he takes it.

My pain, my sorrow, my rage. I smack and curse the unfairness of it all into his back. I hiccup and hyperventilate and watch as the woods shift behind us, until my emotions finally simmer into something tolerable.

"How did you know where to find me, Ori?" I finally ask, voice low and raw, as I press a hand into the back of his T-shirt for balance. My head is swimming from being inverted for so long. "It's three in the morning. You should be asleep back in Meadowbrook."

"Why do you *think*?" His question is barbed, pointed, like his dragon's tail.

"You're always so fucking vague," I grit out.

"Because I don't sleep when you stay over, Alice," Ori says, flinging me off his shoulder. "Because I *lied* to you. The three of you fucking does bother me. But it has nothing to do with Harley or Jessa, and it doesn't have anything to do with you being romantically involved with them." I stumble as the blood rushes from my head, gray splotches blooming in the corners of my vision. Ori steadies me with two hands on my shoulders as he growls in my face. "It's because I can smell your arousal everywhere, and my beast wants a taste."

My face contorts. "*What*?"

"I'm jealous, Alice!" Ori snaps, hands leaving my shoulders and flying out at his side. "Is that what you want to hear? That I fell in love with you as a child, and when you left and never came back, it broke my heart? That ever since then, the 'what if' of you has plagued me?"

He steps back, hands raking through his hair as he paces.

"That I convinced myself I hated you, tried to give up on the idea of you, just so I could fucking survive after

Maven and Enzo took everything else from me? That I watched my two best friends fall for each other, and that was fine, because I want them to be happy. But when they wanted me too, I had to say no, because I can't love them right with half of my heart missing? And now, I've watched you all fall for each other, and it's making me insane, because I know *you* don't want me? Does that make you feel better?"

"No, actually, it doesn't," I say, exasperated. "Why wouldn't you tell me any of this sooner?"

"Because you rejected our bond. You rejected me. You married someone else," he says, arms flinging out to his side again, leaving his black hair messy and wild. "And I don't know how to deal with that."

"I didn't even know who you were, Ori. I didn't fucking remember!" I shout. "You can't blame me for falling in love."

Ori's hands scrape over his face, his expression morphing from tortured rage to tired melancholy. "I only wished it were me, Alice," he says, quietly, then with more confidence, "I still wish it were me. You were supposed to be *mine*."

"Well, I'm not." I huff a laugh, though it's devoid of humor. "You can't say that shit and expect a good response, Ori. I'm not a mind reader. It doesn't matter if we have some magical bond —which I will admit, I find myself drawn to you. But you haven't made your interest clear, nor have you tried to get to know me like the others have."

Ori flinches, as if I've slapped him across the face. Devastation wracks his strong features. "You're drawn to me?"

"You're objectively attractive and I have eyeballs, dude! What the fuck!" I screech. "I also have ears. And so do Harley and Jessa. And it sounds like you haven't told anyone any of this ever." I take a breath, hold it for four seconds, and let it out, slow. "I'll let you in on a little secret. I don't know if I can *be* anyone's, anymore. At least not fully."

The idea is too big; too much; too scary to commit to, even if I am actively falling in love again.

"So, we're in the same fucking boat," I say, my voice cracking. "I was supposed to be *his*."

A damn breaks inside of me, and I'm unable to stop the flood. All of me spills from my mouth.

"And I'm sorry that these words are hurting you. I can see it in your face—I'm sorry they're not what you want to hear. But we don't always get what we want, especially if we don't ask for it," I continue, in a tortured rasp. "I had *everything*. I did it all right. I found my person at seventeen. I chose to build a life with him. I moved across the fucking country. Multiple times. I managed, when he had to leave for six weeks here and eight weeks there, and I managed when he had to leave for five months. I fought off the bitterness. I battled the gloom. I tried to 'find the joy' in the experience of being married to someone whose job took them away from me."

The words are sour on my tongue, and I spit them out.

"Because I loved him more than the inconvenience. But after that last time..." My throat catches on itself, but I don't hide the struggle from Ori. No, I stare right into his damned *navy* eyes. I glare right into their haunted cast. "After that, he was supposed to be home for a few years. And we were supposed to have kids. We were going to have two. And he'd be there. And we'd be happy. And we'd grow old together. We were supposed to *grow old together*."

"Alice—"

"I'm not done talking," I snap. "He *died*." I swallow the word, along with my dread. "Forever became an awfully hard pill to swallow when it finally hit me that he wasn't coming home. And now, I see his ghost everywhere. I see what I was supposed to have. What I *did* have. And it hurts."

I close my eyes.

"I see him in the rain and in the flowers. I see him in the

untouched cup of water I leave on the nightstand before bed. I see him in the blanket from college draped over the couch that I can't get rid of. I see him in the paints he bought me for when he was gone. I see him in the checkout aisle when I pass by a pack of spearmint gum. I see him in Jessa's flirtation. In the way she pulls confidence out of me I didn't know I had. I see him in Harley's kindness. In the way he makes me feel safe. I even see him in you. And that's the worst part." I suck in a stuttering breath and hold it like I hold Ori's devastated gaze. "I see him *everywhere*. In *everyone*. In *everything*. *And it hurts*. It's pervasive. It's unyielding. And it's *forever*."

39

MOMENTS IN THE WOODS

ALICE

Silence. The woods don't buzz or chirp, not even a nighttime breeze passes through to rustle the leaves as we stare at each other. It's just us, and our raw, open wounds dripping blood onto the dirt.

"Alice, I—I'm sorry."

"It's okay."

"No," he says, thick black brows scrunching together. "No, it's not. I—"

I hold up a hand, cutting him off. Surprisingly, it works.

"I need a moment, Ori."

"But—"

"*Please*. I just—I can't do any more of this right now."

I'm completely and utterly drained. My tank is empty; I'm running on fumes. It's as if I've finally purged everything I've been holding in for years.

"Okay." Ori heaves a breath, his baggy T-shirt clad chest expanding.

The patchy logo on it is unreadable, having melted off from too many runs through the laundry, and his polyester gym shorts hang loose around his hips. It's a strange detail to focus on right now, but it strikes me as odd, seeing him in such untailored clothes, and pondering it grounds me. Even when we went to the county fair, he was in pristine business casual.

Is this what he sleeps in?

I turn my back on Ori with the intention to sit against one of the thick tree trunks lining the trail. But as soon as I take one step off the dirt path, the forest shifts, and Ori's panicked voice calls out.

"Alice, wait—"

The brush closes in around me, and I grab the nearest branch to steady myself as the ground moves under my feet.

Magic whirs, a blur of forest green; branches snap and roots curl, and suddenly, I'm lost.

Mentally, emotionally, physically. I couldn't tell you who, what, or where I am. All I know is the tacky feel of drying tears on my cheeks, a lingering pain in my chest, and the panic flooding my veins.

I stumble, searching for Ori, calling out his name, but my voice bounces off the shadowed trees and back to my own ears. I spin, but there's nowhere to go, I'm surrounded on all sides except one, and the brush is too thick and thorny to part myself. The trail ahead doesn't diverge or split. It's a straight line forward.

It seems Arcadia doesn't want me to wander.

The only thing I can do is humor the land, and so, I walk.

Sunrise fog floats from the earth, curling around my ankles as the cool soil wakes. The leaves shiver as if they're clairvoyant, hearing the roar that shakes the air a second before it hits my ears. I recognize it as a dragon's call, but it's different from the ones Ori hurls from his massive throat. It's full of pain.

My shoes pause in the dirt, taking root as my body stills.

Every hair on my body stands on end, warning me to not move. Call it survival instinct or call it fear, I listen to it either way.

I only continue my journey when a calming breeze pushes me forward with a cool palm against my lower back.

Soon enough, there's a break in the canopy.

The wind rushes, drawing me into the clearing, and there, tucked in the center, is a curled dragon. Except it's not *my* dragon.

This one is red. Burgundy scales shimmer and shift along its wings and hide. Its tail is sharper than Ori's, more suited for slicing than smashing. The grass below it sizzles, burnt blades marking a perfect outline of the beast. It doesn't notice me, not at first, as it licks at its extended wing... which is bleeding.

I inch backwards, slowly, but my sneaker lands on a root in the path. As my weight pushes down and my heel slides off, striking the dirt, it makes just enough noise for the dragon to swing its massive head at me. Slitted pupils dilate within yellow-hazel eyes.

The dragon flinches at the sight of me. It scuttles away, curling into itself defensively.

I back up too, except my back hits the hard trunk of a tree instead of the clear path out of the field. I murmur a curse as I twist to see my escape blocked by the shifting forest.

The dragon growls, low and single-toned, like a cat. A warning.

I raise both hands in the air, hoping it communicates my intention of not getting into an altercation, as I scan the tree line for a path out.

There—beyond the dragon, a new trail has parted the forest.

"I've enjoyed strolling in you," I mutter to the Woods at my back. "But now you're being meddlesome."

The leaves rustle with a sudden breeze, as if they're laughing at me.

The dragon bristles with the wind too, wings shaking out as if it's getting ready to charge.

"I'm lost!" I call out. "I mean no trouble."

Its wings freeze, then tuck back to its side. The beast tilts its massive head, bearing its sharp teeth as it studies me.

"Can I pass?" I ask, taking a tentative step forward.

The dragon flinches again, which is better than frying me on the spot with its fire.

"I don't have any weapons," I reveal, slowly inching along the curved tree line. It's skittish; if I keep talking to it, there's a chance I can slip far enough around the clearing to make a clean break to the path. "I've only got my sparkling personality with me today. Which some say is as sharp as a whip."

My words float through the field, and the dragon cants its head to the other side. Its eyes narrow as if... as if it's recognizing me.

"*Shit*," I whisper, squeezing my eyes shut in silent prayer.

If this dragon is who I think it might be, since Ori hasn't mentioned the possibility of any other family members flying around Arcadia, then I *really* don't want them to recognize me.

"Alice?" a rusty, deep voice says.

Fuck.

I dare to peak through my lashes at the man attached to the voice. His hair is long and black, falling in waves to his collarbone. He pushes it back, running a shocked hand though the strands.

"Is that truly you?"

He's muscular and tall, like Ori, though slightly leaner. The pale expanse of his bare chest is littered with scars; some are faded, the raised tissue extending past the waistline of his breeches, and some are fresh, still pink and healing along his pectorals. Blood actively drips from a wound on his arm.

"Are you the one I've been tracking?" he rasps. His tongue wraps around the syllables slowly, as if he hasn't spoken in weeks. And maybe he hasn't... if he prefers to spend his time in his dragon form.

I take a measured step back, even though there's nowhere to retreat to. But every warning the trio back home has given me about Enzo and his Champion rings in my ear. I might remember a sweet and shy boy from my time here as a child, but Enzo isn't a child anymore. And we've *all* changed.

"I don't know who you're talking about," I say, cautiously.

Enzo's firm footsteps crunch over the grass. I make to retreat, not caring if my legs and arms bleed from the thorny bushes, but he's too fast, and I'm slammed against the rough bark of a tree with a hand on my throat. It's forceful, enough to keep me in place, but he doesn't squeeze. If anything, his fingers err on the side of gentle-giant-who-doesn't-know-his-strength as he pinches my jaw, turns my head, and sticks his nose to my pulse.

He inhales deeply.

"It is you," Enzo says, in awe.

His bright hazel eyes flick over me fast, before he rips himself away. I crumble to the ground as he stumbles back, both hands lifting out placatingly.

"I'm s-sorry," he stutters. "*Fuck.*"

Both his hands weave through his hair as he starts to pace, panicked and frantic. It's awfully similar to the way his brother paced before me moments ago.

"You need to leave. We need to pretend this never happened," Enzo mutters, like a madman, nervously glancing at the path on the other side of the clearing. "Do you remember where you fell?"

I blink, my brain too slow to catch that he was directing his words at me. "What?"

"I don't know where a portal is to send you back, but maybe if we get you to where you fell before she—"

"Enz, baby, you can't run away," a darkly feminine voice calls out. It's teasing, in all the wrong ways.

"Shit, shit, shit, shit, shit," Enzo mutters. "You need to hide."

"I'm sorry I hurt you, but we've only started training for the day." A tall, muscular redhead steps out from the path I had hoped to escape through. She swings a long sword as she saunters, as if it weighs nothing. Enzo clams up, body trembling. "Oh? What do we have here?"

Maven.

I glance at Enzo, whose back is to his Champion; he subtly shakes his head.

Why is he scared of her?

Enzo's shoulders rise with a single deep breath, as if to collect himself before he turns towards the woman.

"It's okay," he says, forced chipper notes in his tone. He angles his body in front of me, doing what he can to obscure my visage from Maven's line of sight. "My dragon went a little crazy after that last spar. You know how we get when our wings get nicked." Enzo laughs, but it's a tight, controlled sound. Fake. "I landed here to heal but I stumbled upon a nymph. I told her to leave so we can have it to ourselves."

Why is he covering for me?

My brain can't reconcile his actions with the image of him in my head; the others had made me believe Enzo was evil. Corrupt. He murdered his parents, for fuck's sake.

"Is that so?" Maven says, stewing on his made-up story.

Maven approaches him languidly, like she has all the time in the world. I can't see exactly what she does, but I think she kisses him, because her free hand curls around his nape. Pointed nails scratch along his flesh, and her fingers weave into his dark waves.

I should use this moment to flee, but they're still blocking my way out, and I don't have a weapon. I could launch myself into the brush and hope for the best—which is probably better than whatever will happen if I stay here any longer.

"*Ach*," Maven tuts, as if she can read my mind.

In the three seconds I looked away from the pair to assess my options, she's turned Enzo around. One arm is slung over his shoulder and the other holds her blade against his gut. The flat of it slides up his navel, shining metal scraping against the trail of dark hair there.

"Where do you think you're going?" she tuts.

Enzo subtly shakes his head again, so I don't speak, only pointing at the woods.

Do nymphs know how to talk? I glance down at my jean shorts and hold back my grimace. I definitely don't think nymphs wear jean.

Maven's searing gaze trails over me, seeing too much. "Golden curls. Freckled complexion. An expression that screams *save me*." She points her blade at me, a smirk shining over the metal. "It's been a long while, Alice."

"Would rather it be longer."

"You're still mouthy," Maven says, dropping her smirk.

"And you're still a bitch."

Maven barks a laugh. Then tilts her head to whisper something in Enzo's ear, her terrifying eyes never leaving me.

Enzo shudders as she steps away, as if he's fighting the shift that's overtaking him. Red sparks of magic fizzle over his body as he grows into his beast.

"You're coming home with us," Maven says, casually. "Enzo will carry you."

The dragon swings its head between both of us, wary. His eyes soften on me, begging me to heed her commands. But just as his wings spread to launch into the sky and presumably snatch me up, a roar cracks the air.

The opalescent dragon I've grown used to sparring with

soars into the clearing, blowing fire across the foliage. I dive out of the way, but so does Maven. Enzo accepts the brunt of the attack, his scales unblemished by the flames. He shakes them off, the embers fizzling out in the scorched earth.

Ori's dragon banks along the passing clouds, hurtling towards us. He shifts before he lands, rolling to brace the impact, then breaks into a sprint to me.

"Are you hurt?" Ori asks, hands fitting under my arms to lift me to standing.

I shake my head.

"I'm getting you out of here," he vows. Magic glitters on his skin as he starts to shift.

However, the moment Ori took to check if I was okay was enough for the others to recover. Maven yells for Enzo, and the red dragon dives for us at her command.

Red and white collide; the dragons tangle, crashing into the trees and clawing at each other violently. In the frenzy, Enzo's sharp tail whips out, with farther reach than I realize, and catches me across my middle. Luckily, it's the flat side of the pointed barb that hits my gut, and I'm spared being turned into a human shish kebab, though I am flung into the air from the force of his swing.

I careen across the field, green and burnt yellow blurring underneath me, and slam into a tree. My head flings back, cracking against bark.

I crumble, branches scraping cuts over my skin as I fall, and the grass welcomes me into a forced nap.

There's commotion; flares of red and orange burn my closed lids.

I can't make out the garbled shouts, but I'm able to hear the roars. They're painful cries. Worried howls. Guttural screams.

At some point, I'm lifted in the air, cradled not by cool, dewy grass, but by hot, smooth scales. And then I'm wrapped in a set of muscular arms, just as balmy. I curl into the overwhelming scent of leather and campfire, burrowing my nose against the chest it emanates from.

"You're going to be fine," a deep, hushed voice says against my crown.

I groan.

My head hurts.

"You're going to be fine," the voice repeats, as if the speaker is consoling himself, not me. "You're going to be fine."

"I'm totally fine," I slur. "Four Advil and a Coca-Cola. Mom's secret remedy."

"What?" the voice says, and I think we're climbing carpeted stairs, because his steps *thunk* repeatedly, muted and hollow.

"Head hurts," I mumble.

The arms wrapped around me grip me tighter. "I know."

I fade in and out from there.

∼

SOFT SHEETS AND PLUSH PILLOWS. Sleep.

∼

I TURN. Fresh cold pillow on my cheek. Warm body at my back, rumbling, like a storm.

∼

"WHAT ARE YOU DOING? *Get out of our bed.*"

"Please, can I stay? My beast is riding me hard to make sure she's okay."

"Fine, but if she wakes up and murders you, I'll say I told you so."

∼

WARMTH AT MY FRONT. This one smells like cinnamon and home. I curl up tighter; more arms wrap around me. Four turns to six? Six is too many.

I turn again. My nose nuzzles into a broad chest, sucks in smoke and leather.

I sigh. I sleep. And then, I dream.

40

I REMEMBER

ALICE

We're walking through the woods, like we always do when we want to adventure. Today we don't have any destination, we're letting the Wandering Woods decide where to take us.

Jessa and Harley whisper to each other up front, leading the way, meanwhile Ori walks beside me. He doesn't whisper in my ear.

I kind of wish he would.

A blur of motion smears my periphery. My head whips to the side, brows furrowing at the empty spaces between the trees.

"Huh," I sigh.

"What?" Ori asks.

I shake my head. "Nothing."

A little later, it happens again. My feet stop short, and I squint into the trees. I swear, a boy was—there!

"Hey!" I shout, but he dashes behind a tree trunk.

"Alice?" Ori calls my name, stopped a few paces ahead of me. "Are you coming?"

Again, the boy darts in the distance. I catch a glimpse of a peacock blue T-shirt, warm, earthy brown hair, and tan skin.

"Hey!" I yell again, this time stepping off the marked path.

"Alice, what are you doing?" Harley calls out. But my friend's concern is lost to the breeze as I weave through the thick brush.

"You shouldn't stray from the path!" Ori yells. "Do you remember the last time—ugh!"

My tights catch on a thorny rosebush. I pull the fabric free—it rips—but I don't care. I sprint after the boy, shouting, "Hey! Stop!"

If there's another human here, that means a portal might be nearby.

"I'll go after her. You guys stay here."

I run, jumping over rocks and roots and fallen trees like they're hurdles. The boy is fast, though. He laughs as if to tease me. It's a joyous sound.

"Alice! Slow down!" *Ori shouts.*

But there's something drawing me to the mystery boy. I have to know why he's here. Why he's running. Why he won't turn around and look at me.

Branches scrape over my arms as I push through the thicket; I'm on the boy's Converse-clad heels, and Ori is on mine. I can hear him huffing his frustration as he tries to keep up. Ori's strong but he's a slow runner.

We break through a slit in the trees and stumble into the Meadow—the one with the mean flowers. I haven't been back since the day I landed in Arcadia; we've tried, but the Woods never lets us wander here.

"Will you stop running!" *I shout at the boy, panting, with my hands on my knees.* "Who are you?"

"Wanna play tag?" *He giggles, hopping in place.*

"Alice! You can't run off!" *Ori calls, stomping into the field.*

The boy glances over my shoulder, lips popping over a muttered 'ope'. "He looks scary."

I wave a hand in the air. "That's just his face."

A squinty smile spreads the boy's cheeks wide, and his oddly familiar brown eyes glitter beneath thick lashes. He dashes to me, one finger outstretched to poke my arm. "You're it. Give me a ten-second head start."

The boy turns and breaks into a sprint towards the big tree. But he doesn't run around it, he races straight through it.

"What the heck?" I whisper. I catch my breath enough to start after him, but Ori grabs my hand.

"Alice, stop," he pants. "Do you know how unsafe that is? You could have gotten hurt!"

I wave him off, tugging my hand from his, making for the big tree. "You always save me, it's fine."

"It's not fine!"

I reach the large trunk and stick my hand out. My fingers pass through the bark.

I yank them to my chest and examine them. Completely normal.

I flex them. Completely functional.

"Is that a portal?" Ori asks, voice small, lacking all its usual confidence.

I press forward, following the directions of my beating heart. "I'll be right back."

"What? No, you can't—"

I step through the tree and into the sunset laden Meadowbrook Park. It's deserted, the lonely swings creaking in the jungle gym.

The wind howls, and I wrap my arms around my middle to brace against the breeze. Something hits my shin, wrapping around it, and I glance down to find a torn paper from the community bulletin board they have by the parking lot.

It's a flyer for a back-to-school sale at the local bookstore.

I blink, confused.

There's no way.

It can't be August again; it's the end of November...

"Alice, my mom is going to flip out if we—" Ori stops short, barreling into my back as he runs through the tree. His voice is full of terrified awe when he speaks. "Where are we?"

"Home," I whisper.

"Your home?" he squeaks.

"Yeah."

My feet are stuck in place as the world tilts.

I'm home. I didn't think I'd get to come home, based on what Memaw and the Queen had told me... Tears well in my eyes. I wipe them away with my sleeve.

"Let's go back. We have to tell my parents. We have to—"

"Ori," I say, turning to him. "I have to go get my parents."

He looks stricken. "What?"

"Now that I'm home, I... I need to go make sure they're okay."

"But... I don't want you to leave Arcadia," he says.

"I don't want to leave Arcadia," I whisper, almost afraid to admit it. "I like it more than the city. School is annoying. And not everyone gets me. You guys get me." My lips pinch. "But what if I never get to see them again, and I don't get to say goodbye?"

"Oh." Ori blinks. Once. Twice. "Yeah. Okay. We can go say bye to your parents. I just don't know how long the portal will stay open for and—"

"Ori, I can't show up to my Nana's after being gone for months with some random boy," I say. Then softer, "They'll be worried and think you were lost with me. They'll call the police. I've seen it on my mom's TV shows. That'll take forever."

"I didn't know about that," he says, softly. He gazes out at the moonlit field. "Do you promise to be fast?"

"So fast. Like lightning."

"Are you sure I shouldn't come with you?" Ori asks. "You get lost so easily."

"How about this." I shove my pinky in his face. "We'll make it a pinky promise."

"A pinky promise?"

"They can't be broken, duh," I say. "Plus, best friends don't leave each other hanging. I'll run to my Nana's, call them, say goodbye, and come right back. You should stay here and make sure the portal stays open. Or, if you're scared, wait for me on the other side."

"I'm not scared," he huffs. "But if that's what you want... then fine. My mom says Heirs and their Champions need to compromise if they want to be good partners in the tourney. So, I'll go get Harley and Jessa and all three of us will wait for you in the Meadow. They're probably super worried right now."

Ori stares down at my little finger, hesitating.

I roll my eyes, grabbing his hand and linking our pinkies.

"I promise I'll come back to you, Ori," I say.

A spark shocks our hands, as if magic was able to reach through the portal and zap us with a confirmation of my vow.

"See? Unbreakable," I say, turning away with a wink. "Be right back."

THE FARTHER I get from the park, the stranger I feel. By the time I stomp up Nana's porch, demanding she give me the landline so I can call my parents, I can't quite remember what I'm supposed to be telling them in the first place.

They ask me how my day was, and when I think about it, all I can recount is a tale of new friends found at the park, how we played realm-hopper all day, and how a boy started a game of tag and then disappeared.

"Also, I need to learn how to sword fight," I say, at the end of our conversation.

My dad's chuckles fill the line. "Okay. We can enroll you in a fencing class."

"No. I mean like fighting dragons with swords. So that when I'm older I can win a duel," I say. I don't fully understand why it's important, but it is.

My parents laugh. They think I'm joking. I'm not.

"You've got such an imaginative mind, Ali," my mom titters. "Why don't we get you into an art class too?"

"Fine," I mutter. "As long as I get to fight."

My parents laugh again before hanging up.

I stare out the glass panes of my Nana's sunroom, watching the day end. It's pretty, streaks of yellow, pink, and orange blurred together, with navy blues of night waiting at the horizon for their moment to run across the sky.

It's a normal sunset, but for some reason it all feels backwards.

THE MEMORY IS mundane in comparison to what I had conjured in my mind to fill the blanks.

No epic battles. No threats.

Just one girl and one boy.

A pinky promise.

A meddlesome Wood that knew she had more to learn before she could stay.

And a great love waiting for her in the distance.

41

GIVING UP OR GIVING IN

ORAZIO

"We're not doing the tourney."

"Ori..." Jessa sighs from her perch against the doorframe.

Alice is tucked protectively in my arms, her rhythmic breath puffing over my skin. Harley is spooned to her back, also asleep, face nuzzled into her crown of curls. She hasn't woken in over twenty-four hours, only stirring enough to turn over in her slumber, and so I haven't left her side.

I can't. Can't move. Can't do anything else but stare at her to ensure she's still breathing.

I trace over one of the red scratches that mar her skin from tumbling through the brush. This one is on her cheek; it slices through her freckles, and while it isn't deep enough to scar, I'm overcome with rage that she's been marked like this.

It can never happen again.

"It's not happening, Jessa," I rumble with finality. "I was wrong to allow you all to think the tourney was possible. She's not ready. And now that Maven and Enzo know she's back…" I swallow around the lump in my throat. "Fuck Arcadia. They can have it. I care about our people but not as much as I care about you all. Let's just be happy here. Together."

A quiet beat passes before Jessa pushes off the molding and approaches the bed; the action is a mirror to what I've done so many times over the past two months, waking up Alice in this very room to go train. The bed sinks with her weight.

"Okay," Jessa says, quietly, reaching out to toy with a strand of Harley's white hair. "She said something similar on the Fourth of July, you know." She sighs, tonguing her cheek. "Has Alice told you that she was married?"

"Jessa, I've known since we were twenty-two," I admit. "I saw them. In the city."

Jessa's shocked expression melts away as realization clicks. My drunken night with Harley. My subsequent distance. My visceral reaction to Alice coming back.

"You thought she rejected you."

"She did reject me," I whisper, the hurt pinging in my chest. "And she all but did again, right before Enzo found her." I chew on my bottom lip, rip into the skin until I taste blood. "But I don't care about that anymore."

"You're giving up?"

I shake my head, curling closer to the woman I've finally admitted to wanting and the man I've been holding myself back from. "Giving in."

"About damn time," Jessa huffs, though its full of affection as she stands and rounds the bed. She ruffles my hair, patting my crown. "Tell them that when they wake up, will you?"

I swat her hand away, but she just chuckles, leaving me to watch over our pack.

That's what we are, even if I've been too stupid to admit it.

"Did you mean that?" Harley's red-brown eyes peer at me over Alice's head, burning bright.

My throat tightens as I whisper, "I didn't know you were awake."

"I can be sneaky when I want to," he says. "Did you mean what you said?"

"Yeah," I sigh. My fingers twitch to brush over his cheek, so I let them, rather than holding them back. His white lashes flutter at the first touch of our skin. He's soft, with the same freckles as Alice dotting over his cheeks and nose. "I'm sorry for being a dick. I've always had feelings for you, but that doesn't excuse the—"

"I forgive you."

"I didn't finish my apology yet."

"I once told Alice that I'm not a hard person to convince when it comes to pleasing the women in my life," Harley says, glancing down at the woman slumbering between us. "I'm also not someone who withholds forgiveness from the man in my life who clearly needs it."

"Harley—"

"Just promise me you won't hold back your feelings going forward," he says. My thumb swipes over his cheek and down his jaw, which is stubbly from two days' worth of growth. His lithe hand reaches up, gripping my wrist, squeezing all his hope and love into my pulse point. "It's okay if it's slow. And it's okay if it's messy at first." He pulls our hands from his face and plants them on Alice's waist, fingers laced together. She doesn't stir, but with her warmth added to ours, I almost feel complete. "You can trust us with your heart, Ori. We won't let it break again."

42

100

ALICE

When I wake, my head pounds worse than it did when it initially cracked against the tree. I tenderly poke at my scalp, wincing when my fingers graze over a large bump.

At least it's *only* a bump, and my fingers don't come away bloody.

I rub the crust from the corner of my eyes and blink away my daze, focusing on the chest I'm curled against. A plush chest. Not hard. Soft.

Jessa.

"You're living up to your nickname," she teases. "Good morning, Trouble."

"Not my fault." I yawn, snuggling closer. She accepts me, tucking my head tighter to her chest. "Ori's fault. He made me upset. He also saved me."

He always saves me.

"Yeah, I heard."

"Where's Harley?" I ask.

"Work."

"And Ori?"

"Sleeping. In the other room. I finally forced him out because the only thing worse than regular grouchy Ori is sleep-deprived grouchy Ori."

I pull back, staring into Jessa's concerned expression. She seems tired—her hair is piled into a bun on the top of her head, her bangs are messy, and she's missing her fierce makeup.

My lips part to ask a question. Then close. Then open again. Then close and twist. I don't think they actually want to ask the question, and I don't think I actually want the answer.

"You've been asleep for thirty-six hours," Jessa says. "Ori stayed with you for the first thirty-two."

I nod, knowing that already. I remember his overwhelming heat and scent. It's more of the *why* that's bothering me.

"Want to tell me what happened?" Jessa asks softly. Her hand brushes against my cheek, and I lean into the touch.

I hum, thinking. "It's complicated."

"I'm smart."

"It's messy."

"I've got a bin of Clorox wipes under the sink."

I laugh, then wince as the pounding in my head increases. "I don't know where to start."

"Pick a place and go from there," she eases.

Jessa traces over my freckles as if they're a connect-the-dots coloring page. My cheek feels taught where her finger brushes, puckered from the scabbed over cut.

My tongue runs over my teeth, they're fuzzy and taste like two-day-old mouth. I'm sure my breath stinks, but Jessa doesn't seem perturbed.

"I'll figure out the rest with context clues," she adds.

I glance away, torn apart by the sharp emotions that strike me something fierce.

"I'm terrified of not being able to love again," I whisper my confession, the heart of the argument Ori and I got into in Arcadia. "And I'm terrified of losing someone I love again."

Jessa hums. "You know the great thing about loving more than one person is that if one of us is gone, there's someone else there to comfort you."

"But what if I'm still the last one?"

"That's the risk we take." Jessa sighs, hand sliding down my neck to cradle my nape. "You're the only one who can decide if it's worth it."

I remember too much. Of them. Of him. The memories are razor blades hidden in candy that I swallow down. There's one in particular I'm choking on, and I need to gather the courage to pull it out or force it down.

"Can you take me to my studio?" I rasp. "I have one last painting to finish for the gallery."

THE CANVAS IS heavy as I pull it from its drawer.

Heavy physically. Heavy emotionally.

I heave it onto my easel and stare at the half-finished painting. I had started on Ryan first, so he's mostly done. Meanwhile, I'm a specter of paint taking up half the canvas.

"Is that your hubby?" Jessa asks, arms wrapping around my waist. Her chin finds my shoulder. "He's cute."

One corner of my mouth lifts. "He was."

"Is this one old?" Jessa asks.

I hum. "From... before."

"Ah."

"I was going to do a whole series of us as a gift for when he got home," I say, digging my phone out of my pocket to find the picture of us that I once referenced. I hold it up for Jessa. "It's from when we got engaged."

"You look happy."

"We were."

I place my phone on the stand next to my easel. My gaze flits between the picture and the canvas, already calculating the changes I'm going to make to the painted version of us.

Poetic it will be, that's for certain. Ryan will remain the same. I'll change.

"Sometimes I question the exact shade of his eyes." My fingertips graze the canvas. "What people don't realize is that when you're apart for someone for months at a time, you go through a kind of grieving."

Jessa's hands spread across my belly in quiet encouragement, and I anchor my hands on her forearms, leaning into her strength.

"You mourn the life before the separation. The exact way you slept next to each other. The jokes you'd toss back and forth. The small habits you'd formed are broken in the effort to survive the interim. Then, they come back different. Everyone says it, warns you about it. But you change too—they don't warn you about that, though."

My face scrunches, and I shake my head.

"That sounds ominous," I say. "It's not a bad thing. Not necessarily. Only a truth. If he had come back I'm sure he'd be different, and *I'd* be different, and *we'd* be different."

But not *this* different, my mind whispers.

"I'm sad I didn't get to meet that version of him," I finish, breaking Jessa's hold. "You can pull the beanbag over if you want to watch from this side. I need to get started if I want to get this done tonight."

Jessa watches as I paint. I speak to her with my brush strokes, bristles narrating my story; she hears every pass over the canvas and hums her understanding.

It's an intimate thing, to share your act of creation with someone.

Harley joins a bit later, when the sun dips low enough to

shine golden beams between the slats of my blinds. No one talks, and yet everything is said between our contented sighs.

The painting takes shape. Ryan stares at me, love in his eyes. I stare at the viewer, tears in mine. One rolls down my cheek. Our rings dangle down my chest, set on their chain, just as they do now, cold against my skin.

He is the past, and I am the future.

Ryan and I lay in a meadow of flowers—funny how similar the location of our engagement shoot was to the Meadow in Arcadia. Now that I remember, I understand why I keep going back to it.

I saw him there.

How, I don't know. But I know it was him.

Maybe Arcadia knew I needed him.

Or maybe I'm crazy, drawing meaning from magic I can't explain.

I set my brush down. Either way, it's done. My vulnerability laid bare for everyone. The final painting in the series. The last canvas for the gallery.

The boy in the painting is closure—or, at least, the start of it.

43

PRE-BIRTHDAY PARTY

ORAZIO

I've been avoiding Alice. We haven't talked about what happened in the Woods, but there isn't much to say. She has a concussion; she needs rest and comfort, not me hovering over her like a caveman. Since she's woken up, Harley and Jessa have made sure she isn't alone. They've taken care of her.

I also haven't figured out what I would say. And so, I've said nothing.

My entire world tilted on its axis when she hit that tree and crumpled to the grass; I've heard Jessa affectionately call her Trouble, and Alice certainly has proven the accuracy of the nickname.

Trouble is what she gives me—a searing pain between my ribs whenever I take too large a breath. Troubled is the organ in my chest skipping beats when she's near. Trouble is what I'm in, having continuously fucked up every interaction I've had with her since she came to Meadowbrook.

I shift my stance, oxfords scraping against the rough

wooden slats of Alice's front porch as I pull my phone from my pocket and open my messages. The texts came through three days ago, while I squinted at my needle stabbing through fabric. Staccato vibrations had buzzed the phone off my worktable, and I'd shucked off my readers just in time to catch it before it fell.

> **Hey. It's Alice.**
> UNKNOWN NUMBER
>
> **Harley and Jessa are helping me pack up my paintings on Thursday.**
> UNKNOWN NUMBER
>
> **Do you want to help?**
> UNKNOWN NUMBER
>
> **We're also ordering food. It'll be a pre-birthday party of sorts.**
> UNKNOWN NUMBER
>
> **No pressure though. Figured I'd extend an invite since it's your birthday too. Do you like sushi?**
> UNKNOWN NUMBER
>
> I'll check my calendar.
>
> And yes. I do.

I haven't saved her number, that felt like too big a commitment—a part of me is still scared she'll leave.

But I came anyway.

I knock on the door, and I hear Alice's muffled shout from deep within the house. A few moments later, she fills the threshold.

I'd never let myself look at her too long before. It hurt too much. But as I take her in now, I can push the pain down and appreciate that she's here. Breathing. Alive. And staring back at me with something other than confusion. Excitement, maybe?

Her blonde curls are woven in a French braid, stray pieces framing her pixie-like face; they brush the healed cut on her cheek, which is now a faint pink line. And on the tip of her freckled nose is a smear of green paint, as if she'd swiped her hand over it and unknowingly deposited the pigment.

"I thought we were packing paintings, not making them," I say.

"What?"

I point to my nose. Her eyes cross.

"Oh." Alice picks the dried speck away with her nail. "This is from last night. Just a fun piece." The flakes fall like colored snow, drifting onto the welcome mat. "Thanks for telling me. The two upstairs didn't say anything. Assholes."

"Sure," I grunt.

Alice's lips pucker and twist to the side as she leans against the threshold, one hand curled around the door and the other braced against the molding, blocking my way in. She stares me down, lashes dipping with the slow glide of her gaze along my body. Assessing. Concerned.

The air shifts, the tension palpable. A chill crawls up my spine.

"You came," she states.

I shrug. "You asked."

Alice hums, continuing to stare, as if I'm art hanging on the wall of the gallery we're about to pack up her paintings for. I don't know what she's looking for, but I hope she finds whatever it is—and is pleased rather than disappointed.

She steps back, throwing the door open wide so I can enter. "Take your shoes off."

Alice bounds up the stairs as I close and lock the door before slipping off my shoes. I add them to the line of her tossed aside Chucks, Jessa's dirtied Vans, and Harley's shining brown boat shoes. The sight tightens my throat.

The four pairs look like they were meant to be next to each other.

THINGS HAVE DEVOLVED since I arrived. Not between the four of us—the others chatter as they complete their tasks, wrapping up the paintings in protective layers of packaging and taping the boxes shut—but in my head. It's a jumble of thoughts that I'm unable to sort through.

All the paintings are of them.

Alice... painted *them*.

Each is beautiful and haunting, full of emotion; she has real talent with a brush.

"Alright, last one!" Alice calls, pulling a large canvas from the rack.

I rip a strip of packing paper and place it on the ground. Alice and I teamed up while Jessa and Harley mirrored on the other side of the studio. It's a two-person job, with how big the paintings are, and I'm glad Alice didn't have to carry them all down the stairs herself. I've handled most of the carting up and down; the last thing we need is her tripping and cracking her head on the hardwood.

When Alice straightens, stepping back from the canvas with her hands braced on her waist, I freeze.

The painting is of her, in her leathers, and me... shirtless. My arm is bleeding, and she's tying a strip of my shirt around the wound.

The scar heats beneath my T-shirt as my head shakes in disbelief. My fingers instinctively reach for the wound, dipping under my sleeve and tracing over the raised flesh. Wounds from others never scar, it's only those from Champions that do.

I'm so fucking *confused*.

"You painted me?" I whisper.

"Yeah..."

My head whips to catch Alice scratching the back of her neck. Her face is pinched with embarrassment, and she looks up at me through squinted blonde lashes.

"Is that okay?" she asks. "I know I should have asked earlier but..."

"*Why*?" I ask, voice cracking on the word.

Jessa barks a laugh, and I quickly shoot her a glare.

"Sorry! Ignore me," she says, covering her mouth.

"Kind of hard to when you're so loud," I say, my skin itching all over with nerves.

"Harley, why don't we go downstairs and place the dinner order while these two finish up," Jessa says.

"Oh, yeah, that'd be great. My card is in the purse on the counter," Alice says.

Jessa waves a hand in the air while pushing Harley out the studio with the over. "Ori's paying. I already have his card hooked up to my account."

"But it's his birthday too—" Alice says at the same time I speak.

"Is *that* why I keep getting random charges from that stupid delivery app?"

"Don't know what you're talking about," Jessa drawls as she disappears into the hall. "Okay, leaving now, bye! Don't murder each other!"

Alice sighs. The sound of it brushes up against me like a tired and warm wind.

A beat passes where we both study the painting. The brushstrokes are raw; the colors are dark and vibrant. Emotion is palpable in the pigment.

These versions of us cradle each other so tenderly.

Is that how we looked that day?

"Why?" I repeat, quiet. *Why me?*

Alice shrugs with one shoulder. "'Cause I wanted to."

Something in her response heals a part of me that's long been broken; one of those tiny fissures in my heart seals up, the flesh fusing together again.

I don't know what to say in response, so I crouch down and start to wrap the packing paper around the canvas. Alice kneels to help, and we finish packaging the piece together.

"Thank you," I say, hushed, as I press tape onto cardboard.

It's only two words, but as our eyes meet—our two shades of blue blending together—it's so much more than that. There's understanding reflecting back at me.

"You're welcome," Alice says. "I made cake, by the way."

"Why?" I ask again.

"It's part of the job," she says, like I'm dumb. "They told me you don't like celebrating your birthday on the actual day. So, I figured we could have cake tonight." Alice shrugs. "And even ex-best friends deserve a birthday present."

Her eyes, they *remember*. Much more than I realized. Or maybe that knowing glint that shines in them is new.

Or maybe I'm the idiot who didn't take enough time to look and *see*.

44

PINKY PROMISE

ALICE

I jolt awake at the feel of metal on my jugular. It's a disarming, disorienting sensation. Violent, as it's meant to be, and utterly blood chilling. I have just enough sense to not jerk against it when my eyes open, vision blocked by a sneering face framed in blood-red hair.

"Ah-uh," Maven tuts, looming above me. "Don't make a fuss if you want that pretty little neck to stay that way. I don't think the rabbit in the shower upstairs would enjoy seeing it all cut up."

I don't move—don't breathe, not until the blade eases from my skin. I check my periphery, noting I'm still on the couch where I fell asleep for an afternoon nap. At least I'm in Meadowbrook and hadn't accidentally fallen into Arcadia.

Maven looks around the room, curious, but mostly calculating.

"I haven't been in this realm since I was a child," she says, lips curling into a sneer. "It's so dull." She lifts her knee from the couch and holds out her hand. "Come on. We're having tea."

"What?" I croak.

"*We're having tea*," Maven repeats, snapping her fingers. "Let's get a move on. We don't have all day, and we need to have a chat."

MAVEN TAKES me back to Arcadia. We walk through the portal in the park, beyond the red oak and into the Meadow. The place that started it all.

This time, I hear the flowers chattering.

The queen's back.

Shhhh. She might hear us.

Oh, she's brought Alice.

I can't believe the girl's still alive.

Me too.

Me three.

Maven cuts a withering glare across the field, squinting, as if she can pick out which blooms are the ones gossiping. The voices hush, and Maven adopts a small, lopsided smirk.

There's a table in the center of the field, set with all the fixings. A red organza runner snakes across the cherrywood and gold candlesticks flicker with dainty flames. Trays of sweets fill the space between white and red rose-patterned teacups. A large teapot steams at the head of the table, where Maven goes to sit.

I pause, taking in the armored guards that line the edge of the Meadow, stationed on either side of the oak tree.

"How did you find me?" I ask, finally grasping my courage.

"Ori did a good job of burning your scents from the trail—if it were anyone else we wouldn't have found the portal—but Enzo's a remarkable tracker." She takes her seat. "And you must have made the Woods mad. They practically let us waltz right over here—and after how many years of hiding the Meadow from us?" She snorts. A beastly shadow passes over us, and both our heads tilt to the sky. "Ah, there he is."

Enzo's red dragon soars into the Meadow, shifting before he lands. His knees bend deep to break the fall, his hand splaying into the grass in front of him.

"Sit, Alice, I don't want to kill you," Maven says, nodding to the seat to her left. "I mean, I used to. It would make all this easier. But I'm petty, and I have a better use for you now."

"And what is that?" I ask, pulling out my chair.

"Torture."

The blood rushes from my face as my ass hits the cushioned seat; Maven rolls her eyes.

"Don't be so dramatic. I'm not torturing *you*. Your Heir however..." she says, bobbing her head back and forth as if the decision is up in the air. She pops a tart in her mouth. "I have a few ideas." She points to the steaming pot, glancing at the butler. "Is this done steeping?"

"Yes, ma'am."

"Excellent," Maven says, pouring herself a cup, then Enzo, who's taken his seat to her right. Then she serves me and sets the pot down on its trivet. The liquid has a pleasant enough smell and a rich maroon tint. "Now, this is what's going to happen. Orazio and his two lemmings are going to run through that portal, searching for you. When they do so, you're going to tell them to sit. They will listen. Then, you will tell them to drink this tea. They will do so. Then, you're going to walk through that portal and never come back. And then we're going to burn down the tree to ensure you can't."

I glance at Enzo, whose long black waves hang around his face like a curtain. He stares at his cup of tea. Untouched.

"If this is about the tourney," I start, swallowing around the lump in my throat. "We're not participating."

"Oh?"

"No. Ori said he doesn't want to." I wasn't shocked when Jessa told me that, Ori had made his priorities clear from the beginning of summer, though I was surprised that Jessa and Harley didn't argue. Despite our altercation, I would have participated. If only to wipe the satisfied smirk off Maven's face.

I'm not the same timid girl I was when I was a child.

"I don't believe you," Maven says, simply. "And what he does or doesn't want doesn't matter." Maven takes a sip of her tea, smacking the flavor between her lips. "Drink, Alice."

"Do it," Enzo urges on a whisper, though he looks pained doing so. Maven pets his head at his paltry support, nails raking through the strands with rough affection.

I lift the teacup to my lips and sip; warmth sluices down my throat, sweet but with a sour aftertaste. "What if I don't do what you want me to when they get here?"

"Then they die."

I shake my head. "They're better fighters than me."

"They won't fight, because you just drank poison. And I'm the only one with the antidote," Maven says, tugging a chain from her neck. A small bottle dangles on the end. "Don't worry, it's slow acting. Once you do as I ask, you'll get this bottle. And once you're through the portal, the others will get theirs. Then we'll all live happily ever after. Jessa and Harley can go do whatever the fuck they want to in the villages, as long as they behave. And Orazio can accept his rightful place in this kingdom."

"Which is..."

"As a subordinate." Her face is impassive. Unmoving. Cold.

My gaze slides across the table, stopping at the teacup Maven's nails tap against. She's practically drained the tea she poured for herself...

"You poisoned yourself?" I ask.

"Of course. I have to commit to the deception, don't I?"

Maven laughs. "Though I am partial to the taste of bitterberry leaves. They're quite unique, aren't they?"

I blink at her with disbelief. "What is *wrong* with you?"

"You ask a godawful amount of questions," Maven drawls. "And none of them are the right ones." She busies herself with picking through the petit fours. One bright pink macaron piques her interest, and she pops it in her mouth. "Nothing is wrong with me, Alice. I simply am what I want to be. And that makes me correct. If you don't like the answer, go take a different test."

Maven pulls my phone out from her pocket.

"Gods, they are insufferably clingy," Maven mutters, flashing the screen at me to unlock it and poking through my messages. "How do you deal with *three*? One is more than enough." She clicks her tongue. "Ah, they should be here momentarily." Maven sticks out her arm, pinky finger sticking out from her closed fist. "Let's get on with it. Pinky promise you'll do what I want."

I stare at the offending appendage.

"A pinky promise," I deadpan.

"It's the strongest of promises between friends. Arcadia's magic loves them, makes them binding."

I chew on the inside of my cheek.

If I *didn't* do this, the bitch will kill me. And then she'll kill the others too.

If I *did*, I would break their hearts. But at least they'd live.

Maven quirks a brow, impatient, and I know I have to decide quickly.

My throat tightens.

At least if I followed her plans, I could say goodbye...

"*Tik-tok*," Maven tuts.

"Fine. If that's what it will take." I link my pinky with hers. I meet Maven's dark eyes with a challenge. "You first."

A slow, evil smile grows on her cheeks. "I promise not to kill them."

"And?"

She clicks her tongue. "And I promise to give you all the antidote as long as your promises are fulfilled."

I expel a breath of relief. "Then I promise to tell them to drink."

"And?" Maven drawls.

"I promise to leave and never come back..." I swallow around the lump in my throat. "I promise to never come back to this place."

Magic shocks our pinkies; I jerk my hand from hers and sit on it, as if tucking it out of sight can hide the devastation the promise causes me.

This isn't a choice—it's a forced end.

A commotion at the red oak pulls our attention.

Ori storms through the portal first, followed by Jessa and Harley. They're immediately swarmed by guards.

Harley evades more than fights back but is eventually tackled to the grass by one of the more agile assailants. Jessa puts up a good effort, falling a slew of the guards with her swordsmanship, but she's at a number disadvantage, and ends up being restrained.

Then, there's Ori.

He's a monster, barreling through the forces that flock to him in droves. He bats them aside, as if they weigh nothing. Magic sparks over his skin with his impending shift and Enzo stands abruptly, his own magic doing the same.

Maven stands with him, pulling a sword from beside her chair and pointing it at my neck.

"Do not shift or she dies!" Maven calls out, her voice somehow cutting through the commotion. She waves a lazy hand at Enzo. "Stand down, darling. I've got this handled."

Enzo stiffens, then sits, obediently resuming his stare-off with his untouched tea.

Ori has stiffened in a similar fashion, entire body rigid as his gaze roves over me. I glance away, unable to face the righteous passion carved into the line of his jaw.

I don't know what Maven texted to get them here. But I can't imagine it was good.

"What's going on?" Ori demands as the guards shove them forward.

"We're having a tea party," Maven chirps. She motions for the three of them to join us at the table as her butler starts filling their cups with tea. "Take a seat. I have plenty of snacks to go around."

"Alice..." Harley murmurs.

I swallow my nerves to speak, though I refuse to meet any of their eyes. "I'm okay. Come sit with us?"

Maven lowers into her seat, and her hand smacks my knee, patting me, like a pup who's performed a trick.

I think I'm going to be sick.

I grab my tea and chug. If I'm already poisoned, I might as well make use of the tea. It staves the cottony sensation of my tongue on the roof of my mouth.

The trio are quiet as they pull out their chairs, Ori taking the head seat at the other end of the table. Jessa and Harley take up the two empty seats on either side of him. Harley leans into my space, immediately grabbing my free hand.

I'm still sitting on the other one.

His lips find my cheek, pressing his love into my freckles, and his fingers weave through mine, squeezing his worry between our palms.

"Are you okay?" Harley asks, low, so only I can hear. "When I got out of the shower and couldn't find you, I freaked. And then your text came through. We were so confused, but then Ori—"

"Whispering at the table isn't polite," Maven tuts.

"What is this about, Maven?" Ori slams a hand on the table, rattling the dishes. "You've already attacked and threatened my Champion, which is against the rules of the tourney."

"I make the rules," Maven says. "And I'm adjusting them to an anything-goes policy. Right, Enz?" Enzo nods. "Now everyone, drink up."

"What did she do to you?" Harley whispers, eyes shining at me from behind his glasses. He pays no attention to Maven and Ori's glare-off.

"Just play along, okay?" I say, between clenched teeth. "Drink the tea."

Harley glances at his cup, nose twitching. He tentatively reaches out. Jessa follows suit.

I'm surprised at how quiet she is right now, but there's a calculated tilt to her head, and her predatory eyes scan over the remaining guards as if she's running scenarios on how to incapacitate all of them.

Then I glance at Ori, whose stubborn nature needs a push, and nod. He frowns, but sips at my insistence.

They all smack their lips in confusion.

"Bitterberry?" Harley questions suddenly, panic rising in his tone. He looks at my drained cup. "Did you drink this too?"

"Yes—"

"Alice—"

"—but we made a deal. She has a remedy and—"

Ori smashes his glass onto the table, standing. Ceramic shatters. Liquid splashes. It knocks a candlestick over, and the flame catches on the runner. Enzo quickly jumps up, blotting out the flame with his bare hand.

"If you want to kill me, do it with pride in battle. Not with tricks and poison," Ori spits.

"I don't want to kill you," Maven drawls. "I want to watch you watch your precious Champion walk out of here, and then realize, as we're burning down the portal, that you lost her. Again." She sighs dreamily, with her chin perched on her palm. "And then I want to boss you around until you break. Just for fun."

Ori's mouth opens to protest, but his face contorts in pain. He falls into his seat, clutching at his chest. Jessa and Harley convulse in pain too, necks straining as if they're holding back screams of agony. Harley's hand crushes mine with his grip.

"What's happening to them?" I ask, frantic. "I thought you said this was slow acting!"

"For humans. Shifters react differently to the tea than we do," Maven says, casually. "Something about their beast. It paralyzes them at first. They'll be able to speak, but they won't be able to follow you. If we wait an hour or so, then they'll stop breathing, but we should be done by then."

I jolt from my seat, letting go of Harley as my chair falls to the grass. "You're a real cunt, you know that?"

"So vulgar," Maven scolds.

"Alice?" Harley asks, far too quiet. "What deal did you make?"

I kneel next to Harley; the man who was a kind stranger only a few months ago now one of the most important people in my life. One of the *only* people in my life.

"You'll still have *them*, okay?" I say softly.

I've never seen heartbreak in someone's eyes other than my own before.

His fingers twitch next to mine on the arm rest, and I lace our hands together one final time. It's a bruising grip, and I hope he leaves his fingerprints in black and blue. I want something of him to take home.

"I'm sorry," I whisper. I stand, pressing a gentle kiss to Harley's forehead. "I have to go now. I—I don't want you hurting more, okay?"

As painful as it is, I release him and cross to the other side of the table. I squeeze Jessa's shoulder and plant a kiss to her crown. "Thank you, for everything," I murmur against it.

"Trouble…" she chokes out as I back away.

I sidle up to Maven and hold out my hand for the antidote. She smirks, pulling the chain from her neck.

"Nice doing business with you," Maven says, dropping it into my open palm. "See you never."

I scoff, grabbing my phone from the table, and make towards the red oak, ignoring the heated pinpricks my lovers' gazes.

I stop by Ori last.

Leaning in close to his ear, I whisper, "Take care of them, okay?"

"Alice—"

I press a kiss to his stubbled cheek, and shudders rack his body as I add, "And take care of yourself. Do not let that bitch break you."

Closing my eyes, I straighten to my full height, and walk away.

A guard pours a thick, black liquid around the base of the tree as I approach. Another holds a lit torch, ready to set the foliage ablaze the second I'm gone.

"Alice!" Ori's call of agony rocks through me, falters my stride. "Do not step through that portal!"

I glance back. I shouldn't have.

Devastation. On all three faces.

I try to smile. I try to give them something not so teary-eyed and snot-faced to remember, I really do. But I don't think I succeed.

"I made a pinky promise," I choke out. And I hope Ori understands. I hope he explains it to the others. I hope they forgive me. "Goodbye."

∽

THE SECOND TIME I leave Ori, it's a lot like the first.

My choice. My promises. My feet running back to an old blue Victorian. My figurative blade running over our throats.

The difference? I'm leaving the potential of a great love behind, not chasing after it. And I said goodbye. Not *see you later*. Not *be right back*.

Goodbye.

At least I got to say it this time.

Maybe that's a good thing.

45

WHEN HOME BECOMES
A PERSON... OR PERSONS

ALICE

I was wrong. It's not a good thing, and I don't think I can gaslight myself into thinking otherwise.
 I'm so alone.
I'd almost forgotten how that felt.
Strangely, the world keeps moving without them.
Everyone walks past, chattering about what they're going to do for Labor Day weekend and how excited they are for fall weather. Always looking forward. Always planning for a future they're so sure will come.
My blank sketchbook mocks me from its place on the café table.
I lean back in my chair and close my eyes.
A sweet voice speaks gentle words behind me. She's someone's mom, or maybe a grandma, whispering wisdom on a phone call to someone she loves. A group of teenage girls laugh a few tables over. Someone has a crush. They're going on a date, and they need to figure out what to wear. I tune out after that. The rev of an engine floats through the open window,

created by the hard-pressed foot of a man who's probably having a mid-life crisis. A bird titters at my feet for crumbs. The milk steamer whooshes. Dishes clank together when one of the baristas swings by, plucking empty mugs from deserted tables.

The soundscape of a café in summer makes a comforting blanket for the restless mind. Gives me lots of things to focus on all at once, so there's no room for bad thoughts except one.

It's weird being in Mad Mug without Jessa behind the counter.

I shove the rest of my chocolate croissant into my mouth and wash it down with cold cappuccino. My tongue barely tastes them—they're just sustenance now.

I'VE ALREADY CHECKED the tree in the park three times. But as I pass by it on the way home I figure, *what's a fourth time gonna do?*

Have me slamming my fist into the bark and pulling my knuckles away bloodied, apparently.

"Fuck!" I grit out, cradling my hand to my chest.

The kids playing kickball in the field pause and curl their lips at me in confusion.

"Sorry! Nothing to see here!" I say, forcing a grimaced smile.

I know I look insane, muttering curses and bloodying my hand on a tree in a children's park. I mean, who *does* that? Insane people. That's who.

But that's where I'm at.

I glare at the living wood and all the dead loves carved into its trunk. Initialed scars spread over the bark, big and small, old and fresh. How many of these romances does this tree serve as a headstone for?

A and C.

J and N.

B and... I can't make out the other letter. Is it an R or another B?

Whatever.

I pull my utility knife from my bag—glad I tossed it in there for the gallery set up yesterday—and carve five letters into the bark.

"Hey!" a high-pitched voice calls. I glance down to find a kid with a missing front tooth stomping over. "You're not supposed to vanda-ma-lize things."

"And you're not supposed to talk to strangers," I volley back.

The kid's eyes widen, and he scurries away, realizing I'm right.

My phone buzzes. I sigh, knowing what I'll find on the screen before I pull it from my pocket.

Today: **BIRTHDAY!!!**

I was fourteen when I added the alert to my calendar. All caps. Three exclamation points. I enjoyed how I could gift myself some excitement.

But it's not only my birthday anymore.

I sigh, tossing the phone into my bag along with my utility knife, and admire my shoddy woodworking skills.

R A H J O

At home, I stare at a blank canvas for an hour before giving up.

For dinner I eat lemon cake; it feels doubly sentimental as I lick the sweet icing from my fork. For dessert, I treat myself by donning my Arcadian leathers. They're the only piece of them I have, since Harley's final grip on my hand didn't leave any marks.

I grab the sword Jessa gave me and pretend to look fierce in the full-length mirror of my bedroom. I snarl and growl, swing the blade through the air in the patterns she taught me.

It doesn't make me feel better.

My shoulders sag as I stare at myself.

I wish I could have lived up to what they expected, wish I could have put up more of a fight against Maven. But I made my choice, terrified of the thought of losing them, and took the deal she offered me.

I run my hand over the rough leather, trace the stitching with my nail. I'm still impressed that Ori made this for me. It must have taken him days to complete.

God, it's so stupid how much he's in my head after everything. Almost as much as Harley and Jessa. Almost as much as Ryan.

Things between Ori and I feel... unfinished.

I sigh, tilting my head to the side. My unruly curls hang loose down my back. Would a true Champion tie their hair up? Braid it?

"This is silly," I mutter at my reflection. "Playing dress up like a child."

But I don't move, mesmerized by my mirror image. I lose myself in it—and all the *what ifs* of competing crash over me.

I don't think I realized how much I wanted it. Not just them, but a future to look forward to again.

Somewhere between imagining the third trial and ten years down the line, a shimmer catches my eye.

No.

Wait. There, in the corner.

What is that?

I blink. Shake my head. But it's still shimmering.

"Are you serious right now?" I ask, in awe.

The ghosts of my grandma's house quiet, as if they too are shocked by the image of Arcadia forming in the ripples that spread over the mirror.

I promise never to come back to this place...

My promise to Maven blares like an alarm in my ears. I wasn't specific, was I? Did I do that on purpose? Did my subconscious gift me a loophole as a birthday present?

"Holy shit," I whisper, panicking as I dart around the bedroom looking for my phone. "Holy fuck. Holy shit."

I quickly text Steph that I'm taking an impromptu trip to Montauk with Harley and Jessa for my birthday, and that I'll be without service for a while.

I toss the phone on the bed, slap two hair ties on my wrist, and grab my sword before facing the mirror again. My jaw drops at the image beyond my transparent reflection, because it's not the Meadow I see within the shimmering pane, but the center of an *arena*.

Arcadia's calling me.

More than that, it's offering me a chance to fulfill a broken promise.

Gooseflesh spreads over my skin.

It's only been a few days since they've been gone, but if those few days have been any indication of my new forever, I'm going to wither away by November. Turn to mulch like the fallen leaves.

Tears well in my eyes.

I'm not ready to return to the ground, and I'm tired of not living anymore.

I step through the looking glass.

ALSO BY G.B. BANCROFT

MEADOWBROOK DUET

A MFFM why-choose portal fantasy romance...

The Boy in the Painting

The Girl in the Mirror (August 2026)

SINS & VIRTUES DUET

A 1920's fae mafia revenge story inspired by the seven deadly sins...

A Sin so Pure

A Love so Brutal

To stay up to date with new releases, bonus content, and ARC opportunities, join G.B. Bancroft's newsletter: https://authorgbbancroft.beehiiv.com/subscribe

ACKNOWLEDGMENTS

We meet again, dear reader. Or maybe this is the first time we're meeting—in which case, hello! This is the part where I thank you for making my dreams possible. It's an honor to be able to write the stories of my heart and to have you read them.

Alice's story was born from the fury of July heat and the turmoil of a depressed mind. I like to joke that TBITP is my deployment breakdown book, but it's not really a joke. This story is a direct result of me struggling with fear after learning that my husband's deployment was extended (and essentially doubled) as their boat changed mission sets. There's so much of me in Alice, but I imagine many of you also see yourselves in her struggles, so thank you for joining us on this wild journey of healing.

As always, there are a million others who need to be thanked for bringing this story to life:

My editors, Maddi and Kay, who never fail in polishing all the smudged bits of my manuscripts until they are sparkling.

My beta readers, Jenna, Charity, Nicole, Amber, Brandy, and Hana, whose feedback was instrumental in refining the emotional arcs of this book.

My family & my bestie, Erin, who had to deal with my depressed ass all year. Thank you for being there for me when I needed you.

My San Diego author friends—Sienna, Nicolette, Corina, Rachel, & crew—who gave me something to look forward to every week and are the best folks to do this whole authoring thing with.

My ride-or-die during deployment: Chelsea. I literally wouldn't have survived those nine months without you, our K-drama nights, or our bookstore adventures. Here's to (hopefully) never doing that shit again.

And of course, last, but not least: my husband. Thank you for supporting my dreams, and for not making my irrational fears a nightmarish reality. Next time, let's skip the scary parts, 'kay?

ABOUT THE AUTHOR

G.B. Bancroft, *aka Gabs*, is an event producer by day and author by night. She loves all things magical, gritty, and romantic, and is a voracious mood reader. Originally from New York, she's currently enjoying a few-year stint in sunny California with her husband and her grumpy orange tabby, Miso.

You can find her @authorgbbancroft on Instagram, Threads, and TikTok. You can also add her on Goodreads and Amazon.

www.ingramcontent.com/pod-product-compliance
Lightning Source LLC
LaVergne TN
LVHW091659070526
838199LV00050B/2215